Luke Bitmead studied at Reading University before disappearing for three years. It should have been a gap year, but not being able to find an airport home, Luke ended up travelling the world. *The Body is a Temple* is inspired by Luke's time in South-East Asia.

Tragically, shortly after the launch of Luke's debut novel *White Summer* in 2006, Luke died, aged just 34. The Luke Bitmead Bursary, set up in his memory, supports struggling authors and has led to the successful publication of debut novels by Andrew Blackman, Ruth Dugdall, Sophie Duffy and J.R. Crook. Luke is also the author of *Heading South*, co-written by Catherine Richards.

Further information about Luke can be found at:

www.lukebitmead.com

The Body is a Temple

Luke Bitmead

Legend Press
Independent Book Publisher

Legend Press Ltd, 2 London Wall Buildings,
London EC2M 5UU
info@legend-paperbooks.co.uk
www.legendpress.co.uk

Contents © Luke Bitmead 2012

The right of the above author to be identified as the author of this work has been asserted in accordance with the Copyright, Designs and Patent Act 1988.

British Library Cataloguing in Publication Data available.

ISBN 978-1-9082482-6-8

Set in Times
Printed by CPI Books, United Kingdom

Cover design by Gudrun Jobst
www.yotedesign.com

All rights reserved. No part of this publication may be reproduced, stored in or introduced into a retrieval system, or transmitted, in any form, or by any means electronic, mechanical, photocopying, recording or otherwise, without the prior permission of the publisher. Any person who commits any unauthorised act in relation to this publication may be liable to criminal prosecution and civil claims for damages.

Independent Book Publisher

Praise for Luke Bitmead

'I hope Luke's book takes off into the Heavens.' **Jilly Cooper**

'With a deceptively light touch Luke Bitmead takes us into a world of gigolos and drug pushers, where love is at a price and pain is never far away. Sensitive and compelling, Bitmead's swansong novel is a triumph.' **Ruth Dugdall**

'A fast-paced, exciting, adrenaline-fuelled and yet deeply philosophical look at youth, disillusionment and the search for true happiness.' **Andrew Blackman**

'Luke Bitmead's narrative races along at break-neck speed, crackling with energy. Its emotional depth reveals not only the darker side of what it is to be human but also the hopes and dreams each of us have to be a better person.' **Sophie Duffy**

'A well written, beautifully paced romantic thriller - my favourite of all Bitmead's novels.' **Deborah Wright**

*"In the end these things matter most:
How well did you love? How fully did you live?
How deeply did you learn to let go?"*

Jack Kornfield,
Author of *Buddha's Little Instruction Book*

Chapter One - Bangkok. The Present.

Standing in the kitchen, lost in my own world, I prepare breakfast. I fry the eggs, slice the meat and chop some chillies.

As usual, I'm thinking about getting out. I'm always trying, like a salmon swimming upstream: Thrusting forward. Falling back. Jumping up. Crashing back down.

Never quite making it.

The portable radio plays a Thai pop station. The sun's yellow fingers reach out to the balustrade bordering the balcony. Steam rises from the cooking noodles. Sukhumvhit Road slowly comes alive. My beautiful girlfriend, sprawled in our double bed, continues to sleep. Her skin is dark against the white sheets. Her breath light against the heavy pillow.

The loud crash against the door makes her stir. I drop the tongs in the boiling water.

"Shit," I say, turning.

Another thud. "*Sawat-di krab,*" followed by a splintering sound. The door bursts open and Ratty, urged on by his momentum, crashes into the bathroom wall.

"Lek," I shout. "Wake up!"

Ratty pushes himself off the wall and spins round, his dreads dancing with the speed, his eyes wild. He lunges at me, grabbing at my shoulder. I manage to shake him off, ready to reason with him, but his eyes are glazed with madness. He throws himself at me again. I grab the keys and skid over the kitchen counter. The sweat on my hands leaving marks on the marble surface.

"Lek!" I shout again and race towards the balcony.

Ratty gains his equilibrium and follows. He leaps over the cheap bamboo sofa, stumbling low as he moves forward. I sprint through the open doors and, grabbing the base of the black iron railings, vault over. My legs swing high, like the pistons on a nodding donkey, blocking the sun for a moment.

By the time Ratty reaches the edge, I've swung myself over and am dropping down to the balcony below. Ratty attempts to grab my wrist and misses.

"Shit," he hisses and throws himself back through the apartment to the staircase, clipping Lek on the way.

"Ratty," she says bleary eyed, rocking back, "what happen this time. Where you going?"

Ratty ignores her, crunching over the broken door on his way out.

On the floor below I catch sight of him rounding the corner.

"Josh!" he shouts. "You mollerfucker!" The words sound muffled with the Thai accent.

I don't look back. I increase my speed, jumping down whole sets of stairs, sweat already running through my cropped hair.

At the exit to the apartment block I swing left and charge up the road. My bare feet kicking up dust. My khaki combat trousers hidden in plumes of parched dirt. Grabbing the handlebars to my 1000cc Kawasaki, I pull it off its stand and fling myself on to the leather saddle in one clean move. I bang the key into the ignition and hit the red starter button. The revs go high, and I release the clutch. The bike surges forward, the front wheel lifting off the ground, spinning through the air. The back squirms for grip on the gravel surface. I put my chin on the speedo to allow the air to rush over me, and I'm away.

Twenty metres in front, and now twenty metres behind, Ratty skids his black Honda round in the middle of the road, leaving behind a black horseshoe of rubber. Struggling to control the power, wrestling to balance the bike, he lunges forward. Every sinew strains to handle the rapid acceleration. The force of the wind like a glass wall against his face. He is on the red tail light of my Kawasaki by the time I hit the expressway.

Rush hour traffic, Bangkok: a seething mass of green and yellow cabs. Growling tuk tuks. Glinting Mercedes. Pop popping Honda Dreams. Exhaust fumes. Distorting heat waves and horns.

And this morning, two bikes bucking through it like wild Mustang.

I weave through the traffic, gunning the bike into every space I can find. Accelerating, braking, thrusting, hanging back. I work the front suspension hard. I check the rear view mirrors constantly. Ratty gains, massive in the mirrors, then falls back. He comes almost parallel, separated only by a single vehicle, then gets snarled up. I dance my bike through the crush, using all my skill to keep out of reach. Little by little, I pull away.

After several blocks, Ratty is nowhere. I ease off the gas, reducing the engine's roar to a purr. Two miles south I turn east towards Klong Toey market, follow the expressway for several hundred metres, then pull off into a busy, but narrower street.

I look back.

Ratty is straining to see what is happening in front of him. With the traffic and the dust and the confusion, it's hard for him to keep track. Just as I think I've lost him, he spots me at the turn off. He yanks the throttle. The Honda pulls forward.

Ratty rounds the bend. The Kawasaki idles between my legs as I assess my options. I wipe the sweat from my brow. The sound of the roaring engine makes me react. My eyes widen. I select first and turn.

In front of me is a city bus.

Twisting the throttle I push off from the kerb and swerve

out, beeping as I go.

Two yards ahead: three mopeds. To the left a battered, dusty Honda Civic. To the right, the pavement. Hitting the back brake, then revving hard, I dump the clutch and lift the front tyre onto the slabs a foot above the road. The back wheel skids, then follows.

Pedestrians: kids in navy school uniform, men in suits, young girls in flared trousers, rush to plaster themselves thinly against the glittering shop fronts. All I can see is camera stills: legs, open mouths, wide eyes, a hand, a lamppost.

I drop down off the pavement at an intersection. Off the grey and onto the black, then, lifting the wheel, back on to the grey. All I can see is people. All I can hear: the buzz of his engine.

And then at the next interchange a black bolt charges out at me, making me swerve. Ratty is right next to me, like a shadow. His dark, bloodshot eyes a metre from my nose. His dreads fanning out at his neck like black ropes. I glance over and see a fist sailing in towards the side of my head. I flick the handlebars. Ratty's punch lands on my ear.

"What the fuck are you doing?" I scream as we tear down a side street back towards the market.

"Fuck you!"

"What is your problem, man?"

"The money. I tell you what can happen if you no gib me."

Ratty gives the brakes a quick jolt and steers his front wheel into my back, jerking the bike off to the left. I fight to control the swerve.

"Are you mad?" I yell as Ratty pulls parallel, his left leg brushing against a wicker rubbish basket.

"I just want the money," Ratty yells, sticking his boot out and thrusting against the Kawasaki's fuel tank. "Like I tell you."

I fight the handlebars to correct my direction but with a stall selling satays fast expanding in my vision, I brake and go into a skid. There's a high shriek of rubber being ripped from the tyres. The sound of scuffling feet as pedestrians scatter, and finally the incongruously innocent thud and scrape of the bike coming to rest in a shop porch. My leg is trapped beneath it.

Ratty's skinny figure casts a stick wide shadow over me, blocking out a narrow segment of bright yellow sun. He looks round at the tan Thai faces staring at us, before re-focusing his attention. "I know," he says.

"What?"

"That *falang* don't pay."

"You're kidding. I've been ill. I'm a bit late… "

I try to free my leg. My combats are jagged on the brake pedal and there's blood oozing through. Ratty raises his foot and kicks me in the chest. I shield my face.

"No, I no joking," Ratty snaps. "I want it. I want what you owe me. Okay?"

He strides away on skinny legs and jumps back on the bike. It roars into life and he disappears.

"Thanks, Marcus," I whisper. "Thanks a million."

Chapter Two

I sip a second vodka and tonic and light another Kron Thip. The smoke spirals up and out into the atmosphere. It's early evening and I'm back at home. Above me a sparse collection of stars pierce the heavy darkness. Below the smell of hot spiced food being cooked at street stalls wafts up to the fifth floor apartment.

I lie back on the lounger. Quiet music filters out onto the balcony.

"Lek," I call in through the open French windows. "Have you finished in the bathroom?"

The sound of my voice echoes round the open plan space of the apartment, eventually finding its way through the master bedroom and into the en suite bathroom.

"What?" Lek replies, still getting dressed. Her inexpert English sounding soft and lisping with her Thai accent.

"Are you finished?"

"I finish already," she says after a pause, putting the last touches to her make-up in the large, well lit mirror.

"Good. I need to leave at eight."

I run a hand down my stomach, which is still hot from the afternoon sun at Lumphini Park.

We spent several hours there after Ratty's early morning call. I drank bottles of Singha while Lek wove me a reggae coloured friendship band in the shade of a green brown palm. Young children laughed and splashed in the glittering blue lake. Teenagers flew kites, their arms straining against the wind. Old Chinese women did the floating movements of T'ai Chi, perhaps having woken too late for the more traditional morning session.

The park seemed a million miles from our problems. I felt relaxed. On my CD player, I listened to beach music. I watched Lek take food to the monks sitting near the lake, their orange robes lit like summer bonfires next to the blue of the water, reflecting the green, ochre tinged grass.

Lek helped the monks whenever she could. She prayed at any temple she passed. Three or four joss ticks clasped in her little hands, her eyes closed, an earnest expression on her usually cheeky face. Lek believed in the Buddha. She believed she had to be good in this life to reach nirvana in the next. It was a constant source of sadness for her she wasn't a better person. As much as she tried, she never lost the guilt of being human.

The sun eventually dropped to the earth as if on a parachute, turning the leaves golden and then steely grey. We relaxed in each other's arms, feeling calm with nature's cycle.

The park began to clear, revealing a lost child, three or four years old. A little girl, her hair in bunches, tears rolling down her cheeks. Not even a dot in the eyes of the universe.

She came staggering towards us with uncoordinated speed. Her limbs were not yet practiced enough to transport her smoothly. Her greying shadow ambled in front of her like a jaunty minstrel.

Lek scooped her up in her arms and comforted her. Jigging her up and down, making her feel safe.

'Where's your mummy?' she had asked. 'Where is she?'

The child was too distraught to speak. Her tiny brow was covered in pinheads of perspiration. Her little heart hammered beneath her light blue dress. Ba boom, ba boom. Ba boom.

'Come on. She will be here soon. There is no need to worry.'

She clung to Lek, wrapping her arms round her neck.
Ba boom.
'I think she likes you,' I said.
'All baby like me.'
Ba boom.
'And the scared cling to the strong.'
'I not strong,' said Lek.
I laughed. 'What you've been through, you've no idea.'
We had looked after the child for quarter of an hour. Then her distraught mother came rushing over for her. Her face clicking from horror to relief.
By the time she arrived the child seemed happy enough to stay but Lek handed her back with a smile.
'I think she miss her mummy very much,' she told the lady. 'She is a beautiful child. I think one day she can be Miss Thailand.'
The mother nodded, her eyes brimming with gratitude. Relieved to have the child back in her care. 'Thank you so much,' she said. 'I was shopping and she wandered off. I was so worried she may have been taken by someone.'
'I have my own baby,' said Lek. 'It can be very hard. They move like a cockroach sometimes. Very fast. But don't worry. She is okay.'
The woman left with a polite bow, her hands clasped.
'I think if I lose my baby like that, I die with scare,' said Lek. 'There many bad people in Bangkok.'
'I think your baby's safe with Nong.'
'I think so. But I worry all the time.'
'Don't. She has a good life. She's not in any danger.'
A pensive look crossed Lek's delicate features.
'Come here. I want to kiss you.'
'Why?'
Lek grinned down at me, her white teeth gleaming in the sun. She liked to tease. She did it so she could hear me say it.
'Because my lips are cold.'

'Your lips cold? I don't think so. It very hot today. Look you have water on your head,' she said, touching it, inspecting it. 'Very hot. Why you want to kiss me really?'

'I just want to.'

'What if I say no?'

'You'll make me sad.'

'Why?' she laughed again, her eyes sparkling.

'Why?' I said. 'Because I love you.'

'One hundred percent?'

'One thousand.'

I put a hand round the back of her head and pull her towards me, kissing her.

'I like it when you do like that,' said Lek.

'I like it too. Come on. We have to go. Otherwise you'll be late for work.'

I get up off the lounger, smiling at the memory. Lying in the park on the coarse grass with the sun beating down on me had reminded me of my childhood, those implausibly hot summers in the late seventies. I was an innocent boy back then, drinking orange squash in huge gulps, learning to ride a bike, climbing trees with my brother, running up and down a street in North London, playing tag with the other kids. Life seemed so simple. So pure and uncomplicated, like the clear blue sky. When did the clouds start rolling in, I often wonder. When did the light around me start to dim…

My predominant memory of my childhood is of me on my navy blue Chopper with the reflectors on the wheels, racing my brother down the street. Not a day goes by when I don't think of this. I don't know why.

I walk into the tiled living room and kitchen area, then through to the bedroom, my hands brushing the cool walls as I go.

"Can I have a shower then?" I smile.

Lek turns to look at me. Her slanted eyes accentuated by

a line of black charcoal. Her full lips crimson and shining. She's wearing tight silk trousers flattering to her slim hips, and a yellow shirt that sets off her soft brown skin.

She grins a cheeky grin. "Do what you want."

I give her a light kiss and pinch her arse. "Aren't you late?"

She shrugs. "I always late. They know that. They want some people early, they can have another."

I smile at her, running a hand over her shining hair. "What time will you be home?" I ask, slipping out of my tracksuit bottoms and into the shower.

"I don't know. Late. You?"

"Probably after midnight. I'll wait up for you."

Before I have a chance to turn on the shower, Lek lunges in and gives me a kiss, putting herself firmly against my naked body.

"You love me?"

I wink at her.

"I love you too," she replies, turning on the shower and walking out of the bathroom. "Newer forget me, babe."

I turn the shower on, stand under the water, and rub my skin with shower gel. The water suddenly goes cold.

"Lek!" There is silence. I turn off the water. I strain to hear. "Lek if you're still here, you're going to die."

I hear a stifled laugh. I open the shower door and run into the living space. Lek is standing giggling by the hot water switch.

"What happen with you, naked man?" she asks.

"What do you mean, what happened? Some little minx turned the hot water off."

I grab her and hug her close making her wet. She squeals and tries to escape. "You want to die young?" I ask.

"I no young. I nineteen already. But I no want to see the Buddha right now."

I let her go and she scoots out the door, sticking her tongue out at me.

Grinning to myself, I get back in the shower and twist the tap. It's hot again, but just before I hear the door slam it turns cold. I race out of the shower and flick it back on, laughing.

"I'm going to murder you when you get back," I yell from the balcony.

Lek waves at me as she gets in a taxi. "I love you too, babe," she says and is gone.

After a long time under the water, I turn the tap to off, wipe the condensation from the mirror and shave, standing there naked. I gel my hair, apply moisturiser and finally aftershave. I stare at myself. The minutes tick by.

To my left, blu-tacked to the mirror, is a photo taken two, three years ago. It's misty and out of focus with steam, but I can still make out the image. Me, a tall guy with long blonde hair, another guy my height, his hair grey. I'm in the middle, arms over their shoulders. I look very young. We're all smiling.

The photo was taken in Hong Kong. The guy with grey hair is Adrian. He was my boss. I worked for him, studying stocks. Shortly after the photo was taken he came to Thailand. In his mid-forties, having lived in Hong Kong for ten years, he'd decided he wanted to spend more time with his wife and kids. He bought himself a busy restaurant in West Bangkok and settled. Some time later, with only two years in the money markets, I followed. I'd had enough too.

I see quite a bit of Adrian. I like hanging out with his family. I sometimes go round his place for lunch and end up staying for dinner. Lisa, his wife, is like a mother to me, always making sure I'm eating properly, not staying up too late. She doesn't know what I do. It would be too awkward for her. She simply knows me as the guy who gives her flowers when I visit and plays with her kids. Sometimes we have to keep secrets.

The other guy in the photo is Conrad, my best mate. He always gets me in trouble, but I love him. The last time I saw him was back in Hong Kong, a few months ago. I look at my face. I still have the scars to remind me of that trip. For a moment the memories start to rush back, but I shove them away. Tonight I need to keep my mind on business. I'm out of practice. I need to restore some focus.

Wandering through to the bedroom I open the closet and select a beige single breasted suit, a white shirt, tan loafers.

Using my mobile I phone for a cab.

"Five minutes," the operator says.

I dress quickly then smoke another Kron Thip. The cab arrives. The driver calls me on the intercom.

I take the lift down and stride out on to Sukhumvhit Road. I'm at the east end where the hustle of the city is starting to die out. I take a breath. The air is a little fresher out here and the street a little quieter. We agreed it was the right move, me and Lek, even though the money was going to be hard.

I get in the back of the cab, running a hand round my neck.

"Mind if I smoke?" I ask, pulling out a cigarette. The cab driver, an old guy, looks confused. I repeat the question in my badly pronounced Thai.

He nods. I light up, giving him one. The flash from the lighter illuminates my face. I catch sight of it in the rear view mirror. I look serious. The lighter clicks off and I inhale. I tap my left hand on my knee to calm myself. I exhale. I blow smoke out of the window. I let my mind drift.

After two cigarettes the car pulls up at the grand entrance to the Oriental. I see a porch supported by Corinthian columns, large yellow windows and the open doorway. I pay the driver, exit the car and make my way through the dimly lit reception, nodding to the doorman. Soothing Thai music plays out from hidden speakers. Elegant couples wander through the restaurant. The sound of shoes clipping on tiles, padding on carpets. I feel a sense of transition. My heart beats a little quicker, like an athlete before a race.

Sitting at the half empty bar, I order a double V&T and sip it slowly while chain smoking. I catch myself looking nervous in the large mirror, between the bottles. I'm too early. I fiddle with my watch strap, glancing at couples and friends talking and laughing.

I close my eyes and try to clear my mind of guilt. When I open them, my client is walking towards me. She's wearing a lightweight red dress with a string of pearls.

"Hello," I say, in English. They like me to speak English.

"Hello," the girl replies, sitting down.

She seems nervous. Her hand shakes as she drinks quickly from a brandy and Coke.

The girl is attractive, if a little heavy. She has long hair and immaculately filed nails, red polish. She is five four, five five. Her face is open and smiling. Her eyes jumpy, but eager.

"I heard you work for a bank," I say.

The girl nods. I ask her if she enjoys it. She says she does. The conversation drifts on. We have two drinks in the bar before taking the lift to the room. I booked it earlier in the day using a false surname, not that I need to. It's just habit. Paranoia.

"Have you ever done this before?" I ask.

"No," the girl says with a demure smile. The lift glides up to the tenth floor. I wink at her reassuringly.

In the room I set the scene. One bedside light on dimmed so it's almost black, a portable stereo I've specially requested playing a popular Thai pop band so quietly it's barely audible.

The girl waits patiently for my full attention. I know I shall give it, though every cell of my being would rather go home. My feelings about this job have changed drastically over time. Time, the great healer, the great destroyer.

"Come here," I say when I'm ready.

The girl comes close, as if in a trance. I wonder what bad circumstance at home or dark depression has brought her here. An hour or two of fun for months of guilt. This is not an equation for the sane, the level headed.

"I shy," she says as I touch her.

"You don't have to be. You're very beautiful."

Her dress falls to the floor. I touch my lips on her neck.

"What do you want?"

"I want you... love," she says and collapses on the bed. I follow, closing my eyes, slipping her out of her panties in one movement, lowering my mouth to her already naked breasts. She gasps and responds by clawing at my muscular back. I give her what she wants, expertly, but my eyes, when open, are never far from the luminous dials of the alarm clock on the bedside table, just like they were on the profit margins of the financial advice I used to give out in Hong Kong.

After two full hours her time is up.

"I have to go now," I say. "You can stay here until morning if you want."

I slip out of the bed and head for the bathroom. When I return I'm already dressed and ready to leave.

"You sleep well," I say. "If you need to see me again, just call."

There's an envelope on the bedside table, swollen with a wad of American dollars. I take it and put it in my pocket.

The woman looks up at me, slight embarrassment in her eyes. "*Kap kun ka.*"

I lean down and squeeze her hand. "You take care."

I put the envelope in my jacket pocket and head for the door. I take the lift down to reception, checking my reflection in its mirrors. As I'm walking out a guy I know glides in.

"New suit?" I say. He looks good.

He nods.

"Regular or first timer?" I ask.

"I've seen her a few times," he sighs. "I can see why her husband doesn't bother."

"That's what we're here for. To provide a service others

can't be bothered to."

"Yeah, right," he says. "Just keep thinking money, hey."

The lift doors groan as they start to move.

"See you," he says.

The doors close and he begins his ascent.

This is our life. We are Bangkok's unsung heroes, its worker bees. Less visible than the girls, but just as important. And there are more of us out here than you'd imagine.

Even Marcus was one.

Chapter Three

When I arrive home, I stride through the apartment and slide open the double doors to the balcony. Lek has not yet returned. I stick on a trance CD and fix myself a drink. Moving outside, I lean against the black railings, staring back into the apartment. It's not what it was. The leather sofas have gone, replaced with bamboo. The space where the powerful Nakamichi stood is now inhabited by Lek's portable pink beat box. The well stocked bar lies almost empty and the expensive rugs have been sold, leaving the white tiles bare.

The couple of weeks I spent in Hong Kong screwed up my savings. When I made it back I got sick with dengue fever and couldn't work. I was behind with the mortgage, so I borrowed a thousand quid from Ratty to keep things cool.

It was a bad move. The fever hung around so long I lost my client base. The interest Ratty was charging increased, causing the lines on the profit and loss chart to go in all the wrong directions. I desperately wanted to get on with the repayments, but all I had the energy for was lying in bed, worrying, reading fitness magazines.

This lasted six weeks, until I owed Ratty double what I borrowed, and rising. I've started working again, but it's slow and I get tired. I don't want to do it any more. The guilt engulfed me slowly, over a period of months, like rising water. Now I'm drowning in it. I never used to feel bad about sleeping with women for money, but I do now. I've crossed a line I can't re-cross and this depresses me. It's time to change. It's time to move on, but I'll never be the sweet young boy I was.

To keep my spirits up I drink too much. I know I shouldn't but it helps take the edge off the situation. Selling the furniture means we can still go out, too, and drown out the problem with whisky and loud music. I just hope Ratty isn't going to crash through my door again. I have to talk to Marcus about him. I pick up the cordless and dial his number. It rings to answer phone. I leave a brief message, asking him to call back.

On my third beer I turn to face the city. I gaze out at its concrete horrors and joys, its twists and turns, its ups and downs, its foul, fetid smells and sweet, stagnant dreams. The pleasure. The guilt. I love this place, and hate it. I cannot resolve the two.

I'm lost in thought when Lek returns. Because of the music and the mental static, I don't hear her come in. The first time I'm aware of her presence is when she pinches my bum. It gives me such a shock I almost spill my drink over the balcony.

"God, Lek. What are you, the silent mover?"

Lek is keen on sneaking up on me, thinking it's hysterical to raise my blood pressure.

"Sorry, I little bit drunk," she says, squinting her eyes and rubbing her brow. "I not working too much. Just have some customer buy me drink and dancing just short time."

"Easy life, hey?" I say, knowing it isn't.

She giggles, suggesting we go out dancing at a bar we like called The Peppermint.

I swig the rest of my beer. "Why? Are you feeling bad?"

"I want have some fun. We no go out long time now. You want? Say you want, please."

"I want," I say. The girl tonight gave me a big tip. A little spent on a few drinks wouldn't hurt. "Let me just put my shirt on."

"Thank you babe," Lek sing songs. "Thank you."

The club is packed when we get there, full of sweaty drinkers but I don't see too much evidence of E or coke abuse. Thai, English, French, German, Israeli. They're all wasted. The music is house, the vibe happy. Young singles flit about like little birds, chatting, and being chatted up. Lek takes me straight to the low podiums at the back wall where she gyrates in a strangely arrhythmic fashion. Her sense of time is unique, but her moves are still sexy. We dance together, standing close. Tonight she seems keen on running her hands up and down my thighs. I flatter myself it's my sex appeal, but experience tells me it's the pure silk trousers I changed into before coming out.

After a while I have to take a break. There's too many beers fighting to escape my bladder. I make my way to the loos at the back. In the tiny cubicle, with only a crouch hole / hose / wastepaper basket combo to use for anything you may want to do, I find a pair of white cotton knickers hanging on the peg. I smile. Looking closer, I find a note written on them in black marker. It reads: LOVE IS ALL

I laugh out loud. This brings back memories.

A while back Lek and I had some all American meal at the Hard Rock Café, followed by a couple of cocktails. In a silly mood, I went to the loos and left my boxer shorts in there with a note. It read TO HR WITH LOVE. I don't know why I did it, just to be cheeky, I suppose. Getting back to the table, I persuaded Lek to do it too. She left her knickers in the ladies with LOVE LEK written on them. I didn't really think much of it at the time, but this little stunt started something. Everywhere we went in Bangkok after we'd find underwear left hanging in loos with little messages written on them. It felt like it had some meaning. What it was I was wasn't sure, but I guessed it was about alienation. In a city where sex was so easily available, people actually wanted love, a deeper human connection, even though they couldn't vocalise it. The best they could do was hint at it, using anonymous notes.

That night we went home and cuddled up in bed. I think we both realised at the same time we had to change our lives. We'd had fun, but now we were together the immaturity had to stop. Lek had a daughter, and we couldn't sell our bodies forever. It was time to grow up.

I head out of the loo, get a couple of beers from the bar and join Lek on the podium. I give her a hug. Lek and I are really together. I can't stop smiling. I kiss her, putting my tongue lazily in her mouth. The nightclub envelops us. It's hard to make out where we stop and it begins. We've been dancing for a while when a guy cuts in on us, getting up on the podium where we are. He's been eyeing Lek for some time from the other side of the club. He's got gingery-blonde hair and an evil smirk and his eyes, I notice, are too close together. He wraps his arms round Lek's stomach, and sticks his groin firmly in her back. I hang on for a minute before tapping him on the shoulder and telling him to get lost.

The guy turns to look at me, his close-set eyes widening. He has a thin pink scar which curls down from his eyebrow round the corner of his eye, shaped like a hook.

"We're only dancing," he says with a heavy European accent.

"And this is your last dance," I say pushing him firmly away. He loses his balance on the podium and has to jump down. His eyes burn with anger. He looks menacing, before regaining his composure.

"She likes me," he says. "She told me. She doesn't want to go out with you."

"Who are you, man?"

"Eric," he says.

"Do I know you?" I'm sure I've seen him before.

He smiles. "No. But I know you. Josh." This rocks me a bit, going through me like the bass from the club speakers.

"I want to go out with your girlfriend," he says, eyes

glinting, back on the podium now, standing over me. "Or stay in with her, if you know what I mean…"

I know he's trying to wind me up, but I've had a few drinks and can't help getting sucked in. "Most of Bangkok wants to go out with my girlfriend," I shout over the music.

"Most of Bangkok can if they go to Queen's Castle," he sneers.

This is enough. I won't have anyone speaking about Lek like this. I punch him straight in the chest, knocking him back off the podium against a burly guy who shakes him to the floor like a leaf. Jumping down, I stand over him and hit him twice in the jaw. "You don't dance with Lek again. Understand?"

He wriggles away from me, kicking out, scrambling between the legs of other dancers, his hands on their calves making their mouths fall open as if there's some mechanism, or puppet string attached. I catch up with him, getting a knee on his chest, winding him.

"I just want to make sure you got the message. I don't want to see you near my girlfriend again, okay?"

Eric's expression flicks from shock, to rage, then back to that knowing smirk. He doesn't say a thing. I take my knee off his chest and walk away. I scan the room for Lek. As my head swivels I feel a boot connect with my hamstring. My leg buckles and I sprawl on the floor. When I get up Eric is sneering, but too far away to lunge at.

"Fuck you," I can just hear him say over the music. "I'll get you. We'll nick you."

"Nick me? What are you, the police?" I say moving towards him, but he's turning and hurrying away. I lose track of him quickly, there are so many people. I scan the pulsing, churning, undulating crowd anxiously for a few seconds, fingers and hands waving like anemone in a swirling current, but Eric has truly vanished. I take a breath to regain my composure and look round for Lek.

"Hey Josh," a girl shouts, flinging her arms in the air.

"Good to see you, mate! Nice move on that guy!"

She's grooving towards me with Lek, shaking her shoulders. Pim is a friend of mine from my single days. She's a little ball of energy, instantly recognisable by a set of phrases she's picked up from various international boyfriends. She gives me a kiss full on the lips. "You want a drink, my man?" she asks, putting an arm round me, leading me to the bar. I grab Lek's hand and squeeze it, pleased she wasn't caught up in the argument.

"You want to stay away from that loser, man," says Pim, tossing her corkscrew hair. "He hang out with some crazy guy, you know. Some crazy *falang*. I see him many time. He always make problem."

I pay for three beers and we move into some space. Pim starts dirty dancing with some guy and I wink at Lek, but she ignores me, the good humour of earlier gone. After another ten minutes, we've had enough, and even though Pim tries to persuade us to stay, we climb the steps out of the club.

When we get home, Lek tells me off for making a scene. I apologise and we go to bed. I'm too tired to argue.

Chapter Four

The next night all the friction has gone and Lek and I cuddle up on the balcony, gazing at the clouds crossing the moon. I'm lost in thought again, wondering what strange wind has blown me all the way to Bangkok, and when, if ever, I'm going to find my way back.

The phone rings.

I wander inside, slump on the sofa, and answer it. It's Marcus wanting to know if I can meet him for breakfast.

"We haven't done this for a long time," he says. "We should catch up."

His voice, usually American sounding, is more German through the electronics of the phone line.

"Breakfast is cool, the usual place?"

Marcus agrees. The Monkey Bar around eight.

I hang up the phone.

Marcus and I have been friends since I arrived in Bangkok. I used to see a lot more of him when we were both single. We used to work and hang out together, chat about clients. I'm not sure what he's been up to since quitting the gigolo life. I just know he's recruiting lot of girls for some venture, but he's pretty secretive about the details.

I go outside and sit back on the lounger, stretching out. I hold out my arms, and Lek comes and sits on my lap. She's so tiny, she's no heavier than a large teddy. She buries her head in my chest and tells me she thought it was Ratty on the phone.

She's sorry to have caused me a financial problem.

Lek is convinced my life was better before I met her. I had more money, I was out every night, I had lots of different girl friends. She thinks our being in debt to Ratty is her fault, because she wanted to move to a bigger apartment and for me to work less. I try to convince her she's improved my life beyond belief, but she doesn't really believe me. Tonight she insists on giving me a massage to relax away the worries. I don't argue with that.

She takes my hand and leads me through to the bedroom. I lie on my stomach while she kneads my shoulders, then inches down my back, making me shudder.

"So I no trouble for you?" she says, her voice a low burble. "Just Ratty give you problem?"

"Mmm."

Lek's hands are easing the tension out of me. I could lie here all night with her fingers massaging my muscles.

"I'll talk to Marcus about him tomorrow. Don't worry."

Lek massages me for a few minutes before her hands suddenly stop and she turns to look at the alarm clock. She has to go to work. Before she heads out she leaves a drink by the bed.

"Be good," she says, but I don't hear her. I'm already asleep.

Chapter Five

I meet Marcus the next day, as arranged. I find him leaning against the bar, looking louche, his eyes hooded, baggy. His pallor the colour of dead trout. Grey and insipid. Thai rock plays on the stereo.

"Hey," I say giving him a firm handshake.

He looks at me with dark eyes and shrugs. Marcus doesn't sleep well. He suffers from a particularly virulent form of insomnia that keeps him awake no matter how much Valium, Xanax or Temazepam he takes. This deprivation has got worse in recent months.

I pull up a stool. He moves a shot glass of tequila towards me with his fingertips.

"For you," he says.

I down it.

Some nights we used to hang out here till dawn and keep going through the day before racing our bikes round The Expressway. Him on his Fireblade and me on the Kawasaki. We don't anymore. His life is all business and money so we can only make time for breakfast. Our friendship is more sporadic now, like all friendships are as you get older. You have to snatch time together. Catch it while you can.

These days Marcus is preoccupied much of the time. I think it's girl trouble. He and Wow are having problems. He doesn't tell me this, she does. Wow and I meet for drinks regularly. Neither of us tells Marcus about these times we spend together. We've never agreed not to, or discussed why we don't, we just don't.

Today he's pretending everything is okay, but I can tell he's depressed. When he's down he talks with forced enthusiasm about Bangkok to convince himself he still likes it here. Marcus has lived all over the world, in so many exotic locations, I sometimes wonder why he doesn't leave and start again somewhere new. Maybe he really does care about Wow.

"We had a big fight," he says looking down, long dark hair falling across pale skin.

I look at him. He's dressed entirely in black, as if in mourning: a lightweight suit, a silk shirt open at the neck and black biker boots hidden beneath the slight flare of his trousers.

He runs his fingers through his hair, looking hurt. I look away, not wanting to meet his gaze. I scan The Monkey Bar. It stays open twenty-four hours, this place. The building's road frontage is small, but inside the bar is deep. It's lit by a single bulb on each table. From above it looks like a police street map, incident areas shining. Hour by hour the mood of the place changes. To start: quiet and serene. Then rowdy. A lull. Then hectic again as drinking parties crash and stagger through the blur of the Bangkok night, hurtling towards the painful sunlight of morning.

At nine a.m. the place has a split personality. Men in suits sit munching rice with fried egg for breakfast. Young partiers who've been up all night shout for another round of beers. Marcus likes this diversity, this meeting of disparate groups. People who would not normally mix, but find themselves together, like pools of petrol and water.

We sit at the bar for a while longer, waiting for more drinks. The barman is chatting to some girls at a table. Marcus calls him over with a "*Sawat-di krab!*"

I close my eyes and let them rotate, searching the darkness in my head.

He orders two more tequilas and a tall glass of iced water.
I open my eyes, my pupils momentarily dilating.

The barman, who is tall with cropped hair, and a jangle of bangles on his left arm, chats as he serves the drinks. Marcus is a regular, he knows him as well as any barman knows any drinker.

"Chok-di," Marcus says as he downs the drink. He places it on the bar, sucking air in through his small white teeth, he scans the room. I down mine too, chasing it up with water. Still it cracks the roof of my mouth. It's too early in the day for more than a couple of these, but for Marcus, who may not have slept, this is still night, the drinking hour. I used to enjoy the unorthodoxy this brings, the blurring of night and day, but recently I've been recognising the appeal of convention. It's safe. Kicking routine is not always good. I dodged it for too long. Now I get why night is night and day is day. Routine keeps the brain from spinning out of control. It keeps those marbles from popping out of the bag and clattering towards chaos.

It isn't long before Marcus spots what he came for. He becomes more animated. Flicking the barman on the arm, he says, "My friend. What is this girl's name? The young one."

The barman follows his gaze and shrugs. The girl is five seven, beautifully lean, her long hair tied back in a high ponytail.

"She's new I think. I don't know her."

"Can you get someone to tell her I want to see her?"

He recedes out of sight, returning several minutes later. "She will join you in a minute," he says with a half smile. He knows Marcus well: he knows his business. Or some of it.

Marcus hands him a couple of hundred baht notes, and orders another two Tequilas and a Coke, indicating the table where we'll sit. It's five minutes before the girl joins us.

"There's no need to be so nervous," he tells her as she eases into the chair. Her delicate hand shakes as she sips the Coke. Her face really is exquisite, though, so young and clear and full of hope and life and innocence.

He asks her how long she's worked here. She seems to relax once she realises he speaks Thai. Marcus likes to think his Thai is better than mine. He knows more words, but he mispronounces them. If he didn't carry himself with so much pride he'd get laughed at.

The girl's only been here a week, having arrived from Nakkhon Sawan. It'll take her some time to adjust to the cauldron of craziness that is Bangkok. Marcus asks the girl how much she earns. She looks uneasy.

"No, don't answer that. I bet it's not more than a hundred." He slugs back the tequila. "How would you like to earn two thousand a day?"

The girl's eyes widen, then she looks suspicious. "What would I have to do?"

"Just be pretty," Marcus says, giving her a business card.

She looks at it briefly before putting it in her top pocket.

"Do you have a sister?" he asks.

The girl nods.

Marcus gives her another card. "Give this to her would you? If I'm not in, or my mobile's not on, leave a message. Do you want another drink?"

The girl refuses, saying she has to get back to work.

She's eager to get away from Marcus. Something about his confidence makes her nervous. She begins to turn before he reaches in his wallet again, pulling out five hundred baht.

"Thank you for talking to me," he says, catching her arm. "I will see you soon."

She accepts it with a small smile and walks back towards the kitchen. Marcus lights a cigarette and asks me what I think. I tell him she's very attractive.

"I think she'll do well," he says, but he still won't tell me what it is she'll do well at. "It's a new project," is all he'll say.

I don't see the need for this kind of secrecy but this is the way Marcus likes to play things.

I sip my glass of water and ask him what's going on with him and Wow.

"I think I stayed out late a few times," he says. "Then she stayed out, and... "

"You're going to have to learn to control that jealousy of yours. She loves you. She's not doing anything with anyone else."

"Have you seen her recently? For one of your little chats?"

"No," I shake my head, knowing Marcus doesn't approve of the time we spend together.

Marcus draws on his cigarette. He asks me to tell him if I see her, and to find out what's wrong. I say I will. Now that I've promised to do him a favour I feel free to tell him about Ratty.

He taps his knuckles together pensively, advising me not to worry, that he'll talk to him, but he still won't lend me the money, for all his usual reasons. He asks me if I understand and I tell him I do, though I don't.

"That's why I sent you to Ratty when you came back from Hong Kong broke," he says.

"I know. I know. But the interest. I borrow a grand, okay. He tells me I pay him back 1,200 in a month. No problem. Now I'm late, I owe him over two and he's charging me two hundred quid a week on that. I can just about pay the two hundred and live okay, but now he wants the whole lot. And soon."

Marcus breathes in. "What is this in baht? I don't understand pounds."

"Twelve and a half thousand baht. That's what he's asking for. A week. And I owe him a hundred and thirty thousand."

"I will tell Ratty you don't have the money right now, because of all that bullshit with Conrad, but you will get it to him soon. And I'll ask him to lower the interest, and back off a little."

"Thanks."

"Yes," Marcus says. "And at the next time you will know not to give money to your friends."

After our business chat, Marcus and I have a light breakfast. I have pineapple and mango, cut in slices, fanned in semi-circles on the plate. He has steaming pancakes, which he eats with meticulous care, cutting the light discs into even squares before popping them in his mouth.

Before parting company we hug and say we should get together more often. I'm pleased we met up. I feel more relaxed about my financial situation now and can chill out for the rest of the day, recovering my strength. On the way back to Sukhumvhit I pull the bike over and buy a copy of *The Bangkok Post* from a little newsstand. I get some ice lollies too.

At home I sit out on the balcony with my shirt off, sucking on an ice stick whilst flicking through the paper. I skim read the first few pages, but on page five an article on a recent crime wave catches my attention. There have been a rash of burglaries in West Bangkok. The police think a group of *falang* are responsible. More police will be fed into the area. I feel mildly irritated that I might be under suspicion from locals because of the colour of my skin. I don't need this guilt by proxy, I have enough trouble in this department already, with the various mistakes I've made.

Confused and kind of resigned, I throw the paper inside and pick up a book some backpacker gave me. It's about a Chinese girl struggling to come to terms with her sexuality and rebellious, artistic existence in a puritanical society. I identify with her feelings. Bangkok may be more liberal, but we all struggle with our sexual urges through our lives. It's strange. The act that keeps the race alive can give us terrible guilt. Anything that gives us pleasure will give us pain. It's the way the human mind orders the world to prevent us from

The Body is a Temple

getting out of control.

After a few chapters I feel tired. I put the book down, stretch out on the lounger and in the hot afternoon sun, I fall asleep. When I wake it's dark. Lek has already returned from seeing her daughter, changed and gone to work. Restless after my lazy day, I decide to take the bike for a spin, to pick up some fish cakes from the street stalls west of my place. Maybe some satays too.

Hunched on the Kawasaki, the night air feels cool and soothing against my face. I accelerate hard, following the headlight's yellow path. I love riding at night with the darkness insulating me from the rest of the world. It's like you're on your own, but not lonely.

The little market is unusually quiet when I arrive. The Thai women, with their bubbling pots and smoky grills, are pleased to see me. I like these ladies, so I buy more than I want, taking time to chose exactly the right satay, the tastiest looking chicken wing or dumpling, whilst chatting to them. I like to have them smile and talk to me like an old friend, so I also pay them more than they ask. When I'm finished, they wave as I drive off. I have paid for this courtesy, but I like it. The women I see tip me too. We're all happy to pay a little extra for some good will.

When I get home the answer phone light is on. I play back the message to hear Ratty demanding his money. Jesus, I think. Can't this guy get off my case for five minutes?

I go back out on the balcony without putting the light on. I sit in the half-light munching satays dipped in peanut sauce. Ratty's tough. He may not be a heavyweight boxer, but he's hard. Sometime after he lent me the money he took me out west in his battered pick-up to a deserted suburb and gave me a little demo. He showed me what happens to guys who don't pay up.

'You come,' he had said when we pulled up outside this guy's house. 'See. Okay?' These were the first words he'd spoken on the journey. I too had said nothing. Ratty's English wasn't good enough for a chat, and I knew it'd be best if he thought I didn't speak Thai.

We walked up to the building, Ratty itching the back of his neck under his dreadlocks. The black singlet he wore hung loose on his skinny shoulders. His combat trousers were covered in dust and grime. His All Star trainers were scuffed, the white toe caps grey. The laces were broken and undone.

He knocked on the battered door. I stood next to him, but further back from the house. The cheap digital watch on his thin, olive skinned wrist beeped twice: 2 a.m. The street fell silent.

Not for the first time, I wondered what I'd got myself into.

While we waited for the door to be answered, he leant up against the wall and rolled himself a cigarette, his bony fingers creating a tapered cylinder. He didn't offer me one.

At last the door opened. A dim interior light revealed a short, slim man in his forties. His lined, peasant face hazy with sleep.

As his eyes focused the grogginess left him. His expression turned to fear.

Ratty said nothing. He lit the roll up, pulling on it hard. While the smoke escaped his lips, he stared the man down, then he raised his eyebrows.

'So... '

'I... I wasn't expecting you until next week.'

Ratty looked left up the street before checking slowly right. He nodded, a sudden movement, which briefly animated the tendrils of his hair. Then he flew at the man. The area of his skull just below the hairline connecting with the man's nose.

There was a dull crack, like a heavy china bowl breaking on a wooden floor, followed by some blood. The man staggered back, turning away. An angry red stream cascaded down his forehead, parted at his eyebrows like curtains and ran quickly down his temples. Ratty followed him into the small house, kicking him hard in the kidneys. I stayed by the door, fighting the instinct to intervene.

The man wailed and pitched on to the tiles, his blood amber against the bright white. In a panic now, he attempted to crawl to the little kitchen, but Ratty stopped him short, grabbed his hair by the handful and tugged hard, snapping his head back.

In a voice empty of emotion, he had said, 'I want the money. My boss is a more impatient man than I am. If I don't get it by the end of the week, he will slaughter me like a new born calf.'

The man nodded.

'But I will slit your throat first.'

Colour drained from his face.

'You will have it by Wednesday.'

The man nodded hurriedly.

'And you can promise me this.'

'Yes.' He was almost crying now. A middle-aged man trying to do the best for his family. Not used to violence. Weak. Vulnerable.

Ratty drew on his cigarette and exhaled. Saying nothing he turned and walked from the room. I followed, tempted, but unable, to help this poor man. He put his hands over his injured face and sobbed. The door to the street remained open. His tears ran into the blood, diluting it.

A lean mosquito made its arrival known with a high pitched whine. It landed on the man's neck and pricked his skin, taking from him, the way we all take from each other. The man slapped at his skin, but was too late. The damage had been done. A red welt appeared under his ear. A tear rolled across it.

I felt numb. The violence was so real and gratuitous.

Ratty climbed into the pick-up and gunned the engine. I pulled open the passenger door, took one last look at the house and we moved off with a jolt. Ratty didn't say a word because he didn't need to. If I didn't keep up the repayments and the interest he'd be on to me too. That was the deal.

And now, as I wander in from the balcony to get myself another beer, the knowledge that Ratty is after me seems closer, more frightening, and I think again: if only it had all worked out in Hong Kong, my life would be so much easier.

Chapter Six
Hong Kong. The Recent Past. Part I

A phone call was all it had taken. Conrad saying come back for a break, it'll be great, come on. We haven't seen each other for months, man. We'll have some laughs, we'll party.

I'd resisted, but not too hard. I needed a holiday, everything was cool in Bangkok at this point, so I thought, why not? Even Lek thought I should go.

'Your friend is very important for you, I know,' she'd said. She also explained she could spend some time with her family while I was gone. Visit Samsook more often.

Two days later I boarded an early flight to Hong Kong, arriving at Kai Tak at ten past nine. The landing was dramatic with the bright morning sunshine glinting on the skyscrapers, the buildings' glass fascias looking like kitchen knives slicing into the skyline. Half an hour later I'd cleared customs and was in a red and white cab transporting me to bustling Central. I had to sprint across the square to the harbour to catch the 10 a.m. ferry to Lantau.

On the boat I sat at the bow, sucking in the fresh sea air, enjoying the rumble of the engines beneath me, and the anticipation of seeing an old friend. Above me the sky remained cloudless, the sun gaining in intensity.

I felt free, excited and alive. My life in Thailand hadn't nosedived yet. I was enjoying my new apartment, being with

Lek, and cruising round Bangkok on my new bike. I was on the up, and I was in the mood to have some fun.

The ferry eventually docked, the motors groaning in full reverse to restrain its forward inertia. The ramp came down and I disembarked, pushed on by the jostling throng.

In front of me was a dilapidated square with a bus depot, surrounded by rickety shops and stalls selling useless nik naks. Behind them were several shabby hotels set at the foot of the hills. They badly needed a fresh coat of paint. There were the golden arches of a McDonalds to the left, the only concession I could see to modernity. This didn't feel anything like the Hong Kong I'd lived in. It felt fifty years behind, the way I imagined China to be.

I came down the plank in a middle group, straining to spot Conrad. I heard his whisky and tobacco coarsened bellow call my name, but because there were so many bodies, I couldn't see him. I turned, attempting to locate the sound.

'Conrad,' I said, disorientated.

'Josh,' the voice that'd tried to seduce a hundred girls in a hundred night clubs round the world shouted, 'over here, you blind sod.'

Eventually my directional hearing worked and I turned to face his tall frame lolloping towards me.

'Fantastic to see you,' he said, bounding the last few steps towards me and lifting me off the ground with a bear hug. He set me down, smiled and shook my hand, pumping it like he'd get water out of me. He was wearing a black singlet, Adidas track suit bottoms and a pair of flip-flops. His dirty blonde hair was tied back, but wisps of it fell over his face. He looked a complete mess.

Before I had time to punch him in the shoulder, he'd gone off to rescue my discarded rucksack from the crowds. I glanced round, trying to get my bearings. I took in the rolling hills, the palms, the narrow beaches.

'This place is... hippyville, man,' I said when he reappeared next to me. 'I can't believe you live here. Where's your flat?'

Conrad pointed to the east, past the curved beach, to a small village.

'There,' he said. 'And before you ask, no we can't get a taxi, we have to walk. Mad, hey?'

We strode across the busy square in the direction of the beach, me following Conrad's blonde ponytail and trudging gait.

'I hope we're going for breakfast,' I said. 'I'm starving.'

Conrad led the way past the busy bus depot, along the road, then down some steps on to a herringbone grey and white stone patio set back from the beach. I looked out at the twinkling ocean, at the Chinese in their rickety old sampans, heading out for a day's fishing.

'I can't believe I never came out here,' I said. 'Two years in Hong Kong and I never once got on the ferry.'

'What do you think of it? I mean really.'

'It's cool. Peaceful. I can see why you like it.'

'It's a break from the madness. We can eat just here,' Conrad said, pointing to a hotel with a large veranda, 'they do a great English breakfast.'

We sat out on the plastic chairs, looking out to sea. An attractive Chinese girl with a boyish haircut took our order, then brought coffee. Conrad flirted with her, asking her out three times. After she'd knocked him back each time he said, 'I must be losing my touch.'

'Or maybe your reputation just goes before you?'

'It's time to relocate, isn't it?' he laughed. 'And that's what I'm going to do. That's why you're here.'

The breakfast wasn't bad, but it weighed heavy in my stomach. I just wasn't used to it. Conrad had to eat half of mine, demolishing it in no time.

'You're turning into such a girl, all that healthy Thai eating's having a bad effect on you.'

When we'd finished I lit a cigarette and asked Conrad why

he'd asked me out here. He tried to be coy with me, like what are you talking about, does there have to be a reason to see you? But eventually he breathed a long sigh, held up his big hands, and looked out to sea. He ran them through his hair, searching for a way to begin.

'I'm listening,' I said after a minute, looking at his craggy face with all his wild history etched in it. There were more flecks of grey in his blonde hair than I remembered, the skin on his face was sallow and puffy beneath the tan. His eyes were clouded and baggy. He was tired but trying to hide it. The guy I shared a flat with in Causeway Bay had so much energy he couldn't sit still; today Conrad slouched in his chair, almost inanimate.

Eventually he said, 'To put it simply, brother: I'm screwed.'

'More than just financially, you mean?'

'Oh yeah,' he said, nodding. 'Money's only half the problem.'

'And what's the other half?'

'The other half I don't even want to go in to. Not now anyway, but like you've probably guessed, I need a loan.'

I took a long drag on my cigarette and exhaled slowly, the smoke coming out in a fine stream, as sharp as an aircraft's vapour trail on a cloudless sky.

This wasn't a complete shock. It was pretty much what I'd expected.

'And you've got some crack pot scheme, yeah?' I said, smiling. I knew Conrad and his penchant for mad ideas.

'Too right. And this one's a real chestnut. You'll love it.'

I was sceptical. Of all Conrad's get rich quick schemes, I couldn't remember any of them being safe or legal.

Conrad looked at his watch. It was approaching twelve.

'Come on,' he said. 'The pub's open. I'll tell you about it over a beer.'

'Something tells me I'm going to need it.'

Sitting outside a bar called Papa Docs under a red and white sunshade, Conrad told me his plan. Occasionally he looked over his shoulder, checking no-one was listening. As he talked, I watched the ferries to-ing and fro-ing at the jetty. I sipped my pint and slowly smoked a cigarette. Sometimes I switched my attention to the tattoo that ran the length of Conrad's left arm. A large octopus on the ball of his shoulder, sharks, dolphin and mermaids beneath, a chain of starfish round his wrist. A nod to his love of diving.

When he was finished I said, 'This is the same idea you had before, isn't it? Didn't we talk about this ages ago, the last time you were on your arse. When we were living in Causeway Bay.'

'It is similar.'

'Tell me one way it's different.'

He smiled. 'It's been done. I know a guy who's pulled it off.'

'You're telling me he posted the stuff? It came all the way from Amsterdam, through customs at both ends, and he didn't get caught?'

'That's exactly what I'm saying. If you know a few tricks, it's possible.'

I lit another cigarette and leant back in my chair. Conrad looked different, but his way of thinking hadn't changed. He hadn't grown up, and I liked him for it.

When we lived in Causeway Bay it was the same. I tried to be sensible while Conrad always wanted to push the boundaries. If I managed to stay out with him all night one night, he'd want to stay out all night the next. There was no way I could win. He always pushed me that little bit further than I wanted to go. I was older now, and could stand up for myself, but this excited me, this little plan, even though I didn't want to show it.

'Why is it,' I asked after a long pause, 'that you still think this is a good idea?'

'The buying and selling of drugs is a very lucrative business.'

'And a very risky one.'

Conrad nodded. 'You can't have the one without the other. If it isn't risky, it isn't lucrative. If it isn't dangerous, it isn't fun. You don't see trapeze artists hanging a foot off the ground, do you?'

'How much profit can you make on, say, a thousand quid's worth of what? Cocaine? Ecstasy?'

'E's,' Conrad said. 'I can buy them from Amsterdam at two quid a pop and I can sell them here for twenty, twenty five.'

Hong Kong was an island sinking under the weight of foreign money. Two hundred Hong Kong dollars was nothing to anyone. I couldn't see Conrad having trouble getting that price for them, but it would mean selling the drugs on an individual basis, pill by pill. In bulk he could sell them at around the eight quid mark, still a big profit.

I puffed on my cigarette. There was money to be made here, and profit margins were something I could relate to. I liked that line on the graph that went up and up.

'Still not a good idea though, is it?' I said with a twinkle in my eye.

Conrad looked at me dead straight, smiling. 'For the people who died during the early heart transplants,' he said. 'For those men who were killed testing aircraft and those guys who froze to death trying to climb Everest then, yeah, maybe the risk was too great. But for what I want to do, what's the worst that could happen?'

'Ten years, Lei Chi Kok.'

'Of which I'd only serve a few. And it ain't going to happen.'

I rolled the tip of my cigarette round the ashtray.

'I need your help,' Conrad said. 'Are you in?'

I wandered into the bar and ordered two pints, thinking about Conrad's proposal. I wasn't into being illegal, but I liked making money. I wanted to help my friend and Lek and I could benefit. Besides which, I had to admit, it'd be a rush.

Paying the barman, I walked back outside, setting the beers down on the plastic table. Conrad had a couple of pills on the table he was chasing round with his fingers, waiting for the pint to wash them down.

'What are they?' I asked.

'My oral agents. My pills for diabetes. Helps keep my blood sugar down.'

'How is it these days?'

Conrad shrugged. He'd been diagnosed when I was in Hong Kong. The doctors thought he'd probably had it for a while. It was difficult to tell. Most of the symptoms were just like a hangover: thirst, irritability, blurry vision, numbness in hands and feet and extreme fatigue. This had been Conrad's normal state of being for years. It was Sophie who'd finally persuaded him to go for a check up. She was worried about the numb hands symptom.

'Same as ever,' he said. 'Just got to live with it. I don't let it affect my lifestyle, obviously. Anyway,' he continued, having washed them down. 'Let's not change the subject. What do you think of my little scam?'

'What if I said no?'

Conrad tried to look composed but ended up looking desperate. He didn't need to tell me I was his only hope. We sat in silence for a while, Conrad, I guessed, thinking of how this might turn out.

'So will you do it? Will you lend me the money?'

'How much do you want?'

'Five grand if you can spare it.'

I stubbed out my cigarette, crushing it with my thumb. 'I'll tell you what,' I said. 'I'll give you four. You can have three and I want one. This is all the money I can spare. I've got a mortgage on this new apartment with Lek and it's pricey. So this has got to work, okay? Seriously. I can't afford to lose four thousand quid.'

'We'll make over twelve grand on this,' Conrad smiled. 'You'll clear three for doing nothing.'

I sat back, only half believing I'd got involved in this plan. It was hardly Howard Marks, but it was still a hell of a risk. I hoped I wasn't going to regret it. I told Conrad I didn't want to get any further involved than I already was. I would supply him with the money and lend him a hand if he needed it, but as far as possible I wanted to stay in the background. Not even in the shadows, but behind them. Conrad seemed happy enough with that. How could he not be in his situation? We shook hands, then high fived.

'You will stick around though, won't you?'

'I can stay for a week, maybe two. That's all.'

Conrad's eyes sparkled. 'You're my best friend by a mile, man. But hey, you look tired, flying is exhausting. We should get you home.'

The walk back to Conrad's flat took us along a series of narrow paths that stretched through the coarse grass. On the way we crossed and re-crossed a shallow river before coming to an area of flat land in the valley where water buffalo grazed. In the place before the ground began to rise up again into the hills, there was a cluster of white three story apartments.

'Here we are,' he said, opening the door to one of them. 'Home sweet home.'

I grimaced as I walked in. It was hotter inside than it was out. The air conditioning had broken some time ago and Conrad hadn't got round to having it fixed.

'Make yourself comfortable,' he said, disappearing into his bedroom, returning a few seconds later with a towel wrapped round his waist. 'There's plenty of beer in the fridge, if you want one. I'm going to have a quick shower.'

'You've put on a bit of weight haven't you?' I said, eyeing the bulge over the towel.

'It's to give the girls something to hang on to,' he laughed, shutting himself in the bathroom, the sound of running water filtering out into the living space seconds later.

I looked round the flat. The place was like a squat. Empty beer cans and cigarette papers littered every available surface. Half drunk bottles of milk sat on the fridge. The floor was littered with CDs and clothes. The walls all had vast canvases leant against them, six feet, by four feet high, Conrad's surreal paintings of sunsets. Purple slashes of fading light, pink, grey and brown clouds. And black suns disappearing beneath the horizon. Always black suns. And always sunsets. Never sunrises.

It reminded me of the flat we shared, that darkness. We never saw the floor tiles – they were permanently hidden beneath a carpet of clothes and rubbish. We never opened the blinds because we were too hung over and smoking drugs, so the sun never got in. And although we were desperate for our heads to be full of light, they were full of darkness.

I sat on the sofa and turned the TV on. Knowing there'd be nothing but Chinese soaps, I pressed play on the remote.

The screen was a grey storm for a second before resolving itself into a live band playing at a huge outdoor gig. I looked at the video box next to me on the sofa. Aerosmith Live at the Texas Jam. I watched it while Conrad showered. He'd always been a fan of heavy rock, particularly the old stuff. Deep Purple, Led Zeppelin, Free. They say rockers never grow up, they just grow old. I think Conrad had lived his life by this epithet.

He came out of the shower as Steven Tyler started in on Sweet Emotion.

'Classic band. They partied hard, spent the millions they earned on fast living, then lost the lot and came back clean and better than ever.'

'That's what you're going to do, is it?' I joked.

'I've got to make the money first, bro,' Conrad replied.

'First, I've got to make the money, then we'll see.'

I asked him if he was still painting. Maybe he could sell some.

'No-one'd buy this depressing shit. This is my therapy.'

Chapter Seven

During the afternoon Conrad and I chatted and watched TV. He told me stuff I never knew about him. Like he went on the wagon for a year when he was living in Berkshire and got really into bee keeping. I laughed my head off at this, imagining him with the big gloves and the hat with the netting round it. Conrad seemed quite hurt. It went some way to confirm what I'd always suspected about the guy. That underneath the wild exterior and laid on bravado was a very quiet and gentle man trying to get out. I'd always known he had a secret longing to start a family, but hadn't met the right girl yet. All the excess in his crazy life was just filling time until the big moment came when he'd go teetotal, become a born again Christian, marry the sweetest, gentlest, squarest girl he'd ever meet and have fifteen kids. I could see it in him, lurking deep inside with the pipe and slippers, even though he did his best to hide it.

His desire to paint was also a clue to his real personality. He showed me his portfolio from an art college in Dubai he'd dropped out of. It was impressive stuff. Surreal like William Blake, but with a dramatic talent for light and shade, like Carravaggio. I only know this because he told me those were his influences, and on a bored Sunday afternoon I'd gone over to the library in Jordan and checked out their paintings. I thought his stuff was better, but I didn't tell him. It was like he'd combined their drama with his own contemporary feel.

He used to paint light. Now he specialised in darkness. It worried me.

I thought he had a real talent and could pursue his painting as a career, but for now he was determined to remain Conrad the party animal. He liked to be overbearing and act like he was in control, but I took this charade for what it was. A joke aimed squarely at the ludicrousness of life. He knew it was all crazy, so why didn't we just go with it for a while?

At five he tried to convince me to go out for a few drinks. I really wanted to have some fun with him, but I was shattered.

'I'm like a human sloth,' I said. 'Why don't we stay in?'

'I'm meeting people. You might want to say hi, but if you're tired, old, partially disabled...'

He waited for a reaction.

'I am,' I said being stubborn. 'All those things. I'll see you later.'

He hovered for a bit, before eventually leaving.

'Don't be shy about popping down to Papa's if you get bored,' was the last thing he said to me.

After he'd gone I crashed straight out. I'd had two clients the night before and hadn't got to bed until four. I stretched out, my mind formed a big zero, and I slept. No thoughts passed through my brain. It was like a lake without a single ripple.

Then I was woken. The doorbell buzzed me back to life, like an unwelcome bluebottle. And the big 'o' became a super highway. The lake had a thousand stones thrown in.

It was dark. I sat up, rubbing my eyes. Feeling disorientated, I wandered through the kitchen and opened the door. I expected Conrad: Conrad drunk and demanding me to get drunk with him.

I stared in disbelief at the girl in front of me. She looked stunning. I hadn't seen her in over a year, not since I left.

There were a few seconds of lost time. A glitch. A pause. A freeze frame. I wondered what to say. Sophie broke the spell.

Her luminous green eyes held my look. Then she focused beyond me into the room and said, 'Are you going to invite me in then?'

And we moved back into real time.

I walked backwards away from the door, so I could still keep looking at her. I was surprised to feel my heart blip at seeing her.

'Let's sit on the patio,' I said. 'It's cooler out there.'

Sophie shrugged. I offered her a beer, which she refused, preferring a glass of water.

I got one from the kitchen, and a beer from the fridge before joining her outside.

'God,' I said, bringing the can to my lips, 'I can't believe it's you. Give me a hug.'

We embraced before sitting down. It felt awkward, like two pieces of a jigsaw, which had been warped by damp and didn't quite fit any more. I asked her why she'd come over. She said Conrad had told her I was here. They'd been having a few drinks in Papa Docs with her friend Claire.

'He said you'd flown in so I thought I'd come and see you. I was *intrigued* to see you after a year of nothing.'

'Yeah… it's good to see you.'

'So how are things with Lord Lucan?' Sophie asked, her voice clipped. She sounded pretty bored, like she always did when she was nervous. This was her defense mechanism: a hedgehog curling itself into a ball, the spikes protecting its vulnerable belly and heart.

I smiled at her joke. 'You?'

'On the brink of something good, I hope. My portfolio looks pretty impressive now and the last year's been okay. Fairly steady.'

Sophie was a photographer, but as with anything in this life that was fun to do, she had struggled to get her talent recognised. Sophie hadn't been much good at sport at school, so she'd turned to the arts. When she discovered she wasn't much good at painting or sculpting she became despondent. It wasn't until her teacher suggested she get behind a camera that she found a way to express herself which gave her the satisfaction she was seeking. I admired her for sticking with it, even through all the rejections. I knew I'd have given up and moved on to something else, if I'd been treated the way she had.

I drank my beer, wondering what to say next. Sophie beat me to it.

'So why are you here?' she asked.

I told her Conrad had called me. It was the truth, but it wasn't a good start.

'What for?'

'Oh you know,' I said lighting two cigarettes and handing Sophie one. She declined it, lighting one of her own.

'That old thing called friendship, I suppose.'

This was worse.

'And what about that old thing called love?' Sophie asked. 'I'm sorry, I shouldn't have said that.'

I smiled, though it was forced. 'You're still as direct as ever.'

'I know, it gets me into trouble.'

'Anything else you want to say while you're in direct mood?'

'Yes. Dinner, tonight, and you're paying.'

We went to a restaurant a ten minute trip round the island, down by the beach. We got a cab from the bay. It wound us up into the lush, densely wooded hills through a small village, then down again to the coastline. We didn't speak much on the journey. The noise of the cab's blown exhaust was so loud it made conversation impossible unless you wanted to shout. I didn't, and neither did Sophie, so we spent the time gazing out the large windows, wincing every time the bus bumped over a severe pot hole, or rolled alarmingly round a corner.

The Body is a Temple

'Well, this is it,' Sophie said after we'd walked down some steps into the restaurant.

I looked round at the rustic tables, the low wall which hemmed them in, the fierce, spitting barbeque. Beyond the flickering candles was the beach, illuminated by the moon. A cool breeze wafted over us.

'The food's great,' Sophie said. 'The South Africans who run it are big on pommes dauphinoise. Delicious potato dish.'

We sat near the large sizzling grills, the sound of the sea lapping the shoreline not far off. I tried to relax. I looked down at the beach where a gang of young Chinese children played in the sand. I glanced at the other diners, a mix of families and couples. The place was full and alive.

I wished I'd been bothered to come out here before, but it always seemed such an effort after a long, tedious day in the office. There was a lot I regretted about my time in Hong Kong. Not visiting more places was just one of them.

I poured Sophie some wine.

'Were you ever tempted to move out here?' I asked, easily imagining her living a Bohemian artists life up in the hills, photographing everything in sight.

'Kind of. There are some stunning landscapes. And little fishing villages and lovely countryside, interesting people, but... I don't know. It's remote on a daily basis. And I like living with my parents right now. They give me security and support. And you. What are your living arrangements?'

'I've got an apartment,' I said. 'I'm paying for it, but it's... I don't know. I like it.'

'And who are you sharing this apartment with?'

'A girl,' I said, not meeting her eye.

'Nationality?'

'Thai.'

'Oh Christ. I knew it. I got dumped for a Thai girl.'

I sipped the wine. Sophie scowled. I asked her if she had anyone new. She said once you'd had your heart broken it was difficult to get up the enthusiasm to go through it all again.

'Hey that's not fair,' I said. 'When I went to Thailand, you said you weren't coming. So that was it.'

'You make it sound so clinical. Like the time we spent together meant nothing.'

'I'd had it here. My job was like a roller coaster. Lots of highs and lows, but not really going anywhere. I needed to get away. I wanted you to come with me.'

'You could have changed jobs. You didn't like being a financial adviser. You could have quit and started something else.'

'I needed to get away,' I repeated. 'Me and Conrad weren't doing each other any good.'

'No-one forced you to jump into a swimming pool of booze every night.'

'Yeah, but we did. I'm sorry for what happened Soph, but it was better for everyone.'

Our food arrived before the conversation veered out of control. Rare steaks and the potatoes of the house. Nice timing, I thought. A sombre silence descended as we ate. Sophie eventually lifted it, asking in a forced casual way that didn't quite come off, how long I was planning on staying.

I told her about a week. She asked if I'd thought about calling her. Of course I had. Sophie had been an extremely important part of my life. I told her this, but she didn't seem convinced.

The conversation bogged down severely after this exchange. Sophie picked at her food, and though I tried chatting, she preferred to conduct most of the rest of the meal in silence. When we'd finished I asked for the pudding menu. Sophie flipped it like a playing card or a fan.

'Do you want anything?'
'No.'
'Coffee?'
'No.'

'Anything?'

'Actually I want to go home,' she said tightly.

I reached out for her hand but she withdrew it.

'I'm tired, Josh. Can we go?'

'Sure,' I said quietly, waving my hand for the bill.

It took ages to arrive. Sophie managed to smoke three cigarettes before we left, followed by another two in the cab on the way back to Silvermine Bay. As we approached the ferry pier, she apologised for being so moody.

'This is hard for me,' she said. It had been tough for me too. Seeing her again had brought back all sorts of memories.

She joined her friend Claire in the queue for the ferry once we were out of the cab and I walked back past the bus station and on to the beach.

When I got back to Conrad's flat, I found the place empty. He was still in the pub. I had a quick shower and crashed out in the spare room, feeling depressed.

Chapter Eight

Three days on, late in the morning, I heard banging on Conrad's front door. I felt terrible. We'd stayed up till four, drinking whisky from a bottle he'd pinched from the Seven Eleven. It wasn't what I wanted to be doing, and for the hundredth time I wondered why, no matter how hard I tried, I continually fell into the same trap. I guessed Conrad and I both suffered from the same fear. We were scared of growing up too soon, then looking back with regret at what fun we could have had.

I rubbed my dry, sore eyes. I couldn't remember much of what we'd talked about, though I did recall Conrad saying he felt BAD. I wasn't sure if he was being serious or not. BAD was an acronym we used for ex-pats going off the rails in South East Asia. Bitter, Alienated, Desperate. We used to sit in bars, looking round, going, yeah, he's BAD. Michael Jackson would have been proud.

I heard Conrad get up, the sound like a mini earthquake in his bedroom, pulling me out of my thoughts.

'Ken!' he said as he opened the door. A flood of light poured in, in the middle of which stood his Chinese friend.

Ken slapped Conrad on the shoulder and walked into the apartment.

Conrad gave him a big bear hug, then went into the kitchen, put the kettle on and set about making coffee.

I came out of the spare room wearing just boxer shorts. We exchanged hellos. I hadn't seen Ken in months.

Conrad came out of the kitchen and handed round the coffee.

'Mate, you look like shit,' he said to me. 'Go and have a shower.'

My head was pounding. I walked like a robot into the bathroom and closed the door. I didn't dare look at my reflection. I think the mirror would have cracked.

'He got hammered last night,' I heard Conrad say. 'He can't handle his booze anymore. I reckon he lives on water in Thailand.'

I turned the shower on.

Conrad had got to know Ken through one of his friends who used to buy gear off him. Their relationship started out on a business level – Conrad the dealer, Ken the casual student pot smoker. Now they were pretty good buddies. Ken a kind of replacement for me, I guessed.

They were on their second joint when I joined them outside. I felt fresher but still jaded. Conrad smiled at me as I sat down. He looked like a dead man. Super pale, gaunt and grey. But he placed a can of San Miguel in front of me, chinking his against it. Conrad was never a man to wave the white flag.

'That'll sort you out,' he said.

While Ken intently rolled another joint, Conrad explained he needed Ken to sign for a parcel his mother had sent over for him.

Ken looked confused. 'Hey, if it's your parcel,' he said. 'Why do I have to sign for it?'

Conrad had had it addressed to the previous tenant of the apartment – a Mr Ho, done as a precaution against receiving illegal goods. If the police made an appearance, Conrad figured he couldn't be implicated if his name wasn't on the package. The trouble was, the postman wouldn't sign over a package addressed to a Chinese guy to an English ex-pat.

'My mother did it,' he said, 'so I wouldn't have to pay tax.

Funnily enough I don't look Chinese.'

Ken finally got the drift. He knew anything that surrounded Conrad was bound to be dodgy. He seemed to weigh up the risk before saying. 'That's cool, man. I can do that for you. What time's it arriving?'

I got up and wandered round the patio, getting some air. I gazed out at the burnt, parched hillside, the ragged, browning, swaying palms. I heard Conrad tell Ken the parcel might not arrive till four. Ken looked pained. He was hungry. He wanted to go for lunch. I was hungry too. I walked back inside and offered to make us some toast.

In the kitchen there wasn't a single clean knife or plate. The sink was full of cold brown water and saucepans. There was a bowl on the floor containing congealed dog food. The bread was lying on the hob, left unwrapped so it was stale. I groaned, rubbed my eyes again and put two slices of bread in the toaster. I thought of the luxurious apartment I'd left in Bangkok, momentarily wishing I was back there. To keep my spirits up I reminded myself of all the money I was about to make. The surroundings suddenly became easier to handle.

The toast popped. Burnt. You play with fire, I thought.

As I was buttering it the phone rang. I wandered through to the living room and answered it.

'Conrad's hell hole,' I said into the receiver. 'Josh speaking.'

I heard Sophie's laugh at the other end of the line, and a vague tenseness appeared in the pit of my stomach.

'Your sense of humour gets you into as much trouble as my directness,' she said. 'Listen. I... I was tired the other night. I think we need to talk. Do you want to meet later?'

She suggested another, friendlier (I promise!) dinner at a Thai restaurant we used to hang out in, on the edge of Wan Chai. I agreed to meet her there at eight. After I'd hung up, I relaxed. I was pleased Sophie'd phoned. I never liked the feeling of her being mad at me. Tonight would be a good opportunity to clear the bad vibes between us.

'Who was that?' Conrad asked when I got outside. 'Not the police I hope.'

'No. Customs and Excise.'

'No way!' Conrad paled.

'No dipshit. Not unless Sophie's working undercover for them. We're meeting up later.'

Conrad raised an eyebrow. 'That wise? What about the lovely Lek?'

'I want us to be friends,' I said. 'That's all. You shouldn't sleep with someone for that long, get to know them that well, and then just piss it all away.'

'I thought that's exactly what you did do.'

'Oh ha, bloody, ha.'

'And what does she want?'

'The same, I reckon. You ready for your toast, Ken?' I didn't want to discuss this any further.

We sat in the sun chatting for several hours, killing time with funny stories and shared memories, until the conversation got snagged on Ken's girlfriend. He was having trouble with her. She was from New York and very uptight, her harsh accent reflecting her uncompromising personality.

Ken had been sharing a flat with her in Mongkok for a couple of months. The honeymoon period was over and the little differences in their personalities were starting to clash. Conrad suggested he ease himself out of the relationship.

'American girls are all the same,' he said. 'They look great, but you can't trust them.'

Ken drew on the joint, holding the smoke in before exhaling and coughing. 'Yeah, you can,' he said.

'And how would you know?'

'I'm American,' he pointed out.

'You're Chinese American. That's a big difference.'

'I still grew up in Boston.'

'Okay and how many girls were you dating at the time?' Conrad asked.

'None,' said Ken. 'I left when I was twelve. I didn't get started till I was sixteen.'

'So you don't know American women – they're trouble.'

Conrad had been married to a Texan for eight months. A beautiful, long limbed, sultry girl whose faults were far outweighed by the heart pumping passion Conrad felt for her. He was obsessed by her, and was delighted when she agreed to marry him, shortly after his twenty-second birthday.

They moved to Vancouver where Conrad got a job building roads. The hours were long and the work hard, but it was worth it. He was with the woman he loved, and he was making a comfortable life for them both.

They'd been married three months when he decided to take the afternoon off work and slip home to be with her. He arrived back at their luxury bungalow with flowers, champagne and a desire to go straight to bed with her. What could be more romantic or thoughtful? Trouble was when he walked into the marital bedroom with his arms held aloft and a big smile on his face, like an upturned banana, he found his wife was not alone. He found his wife in bed with a friend of theirs.

After a tearful apology and several months of humble repentance, Conrad forgave her this little indiscretion, but when he returned home one night at the usual time to find her in bed with their next door neighbour, he knew she was taking advantage. He stared at the scene, felt his head about to explode, and left the house. He never even went back for so much as a clean pair of underwear, and he'd never got divorced. Technically, he'd now been married fourteen years. On paper, it looked good. In reality, I don't think Conrad had ever quite recovered from the heartache.

'Take it from me,' he said, still looking anguished by the memory. 'They are not to be trusted.'

Ken looked like he ought to say something but was saved by a knock at the door.

'Shit, that could be it,' I said.

Conrad's face lit up, the past receding from it. He looked at Ken and pointed at the door.

Ken put the joint in the ashtray and headed for the door, clearing his throat as he did so.

'Fingers crossed,' Conrad said.

We watched the door intently, trying to see what was happening.

'Is it?' I said.

'I think so. All I can see is Ken's back but it looks like he's signing something.'

I grinned at him. 'This could be your big moment, buddy. How do you want to play it from here?'

'Leave the package here while we go for lunch. Open it when we get back this evening. That way we've given anyone who wants to turn up and ask questions time to do that. Sound sensible?'

Ken was walking towards us, a box about a foot and a half square clamped to his chest. He handed it to Conrad who accepted it with a deep reverence, like a religious man accepting the communion wafer.

Resting it on his knees, Conrad examined the parcel. It was covered in Federal Express stickers. It was taped up securely. There was no sign that it had been tampered with.

'What is it?' Ken asked.

Conrad shrugged innocently. 'It's a surprise.'

'Are you going to open it?'

'My mother said I've got to phone her before I open it,' he said, 'she wants to tell me something.'

Ken sipped his drink. He looked disappointed. 'Shall we go for lunch then?'

Before we left the flat, Conrad did something unusual. He locked all the windows and doors: the apartment that was famous for having nothing worth nicking had suddenly gone upmarket.

From coal mine to goldmine.
Pass Go. Collect two hundred pounds.

Chapter Nine

The restaurant we went to was The Old China Hand, regarded by us as the best in the world.

It was run by Filipinos, and didn't, as its name suggested, serve Chinese food. It served English grub and cheap booze. It didn't really look like a pub either, it looked like a road side cafe. If you were English, it didn't matter if you were a construction worker or a broker or a property developer or a barman, you knew one thing about the China Hand. You knew it served the best steak and kidney pie anywhere in the world.

When we arrived Conrad ordered three pies and three pints.

The drinks arrived first. He proposed a toast, standing on his chair, and with a pint in his hand held high he said,

'To The Hand. The best pub in the world.'

Then he downed it in one, to muted applause, and a single call of 'Get in there, son!'

'Cheers,' I said, raising my glass. 'Here's to good mates and to good luck. Get this man another pint.'

The pub applauded louder. Some guys Conrad knew clapped him on the back. A fresh couple of pints arrived.

'Neck yours then,' he said.

I threw it back.

'Ken?'

'Cheers,' said Ken. And sipped his.

Conrad glared, then laughed.

'Don't force him,' I said. 'You know they've got an enzyme missing. He can't handle it like us.'

'Like me, you mean,' Conrad said, sitting back down. 'You're a poof. I'll let you off this once Ken as I'm in such a good mood.'

The food arrived after our second pint.

'I'd almost forgotten how good this tasted,' I said, tucking in, the steam from the pie rising up to my face. 'It's even better than the stuff back home.'

'How come?' Ken asked. 'Why wouldn't English food be better in England?'

I gave him a look.

Ken could be a bit naive. At twenty-two he was fresh faced and innocent. His eyes were clear and uncomplicated; he could pass for sixteen. He was gullible but he absorbed information like a sponge and could see his way through complicated problems.

His naturally inquiring mind was occupied by a masters degree in sociology he was taking at Hong Kong university. Any information he could get on how other societies worked fascinated him.

I told him the world wasn't as clear-cut as it should be.

'There's always the exception that proves the rule, my friend,' I said. 'I mean look at Conrad.'

Ken looked confused. 'What rule does he prove?'

'Loads. I mean... men have short hair. Conrad doesn't. People over thirty stay in all the time. Conrad doesn't.'

'You have to go to the gym to stay in shape,' said Conrad sucking in his stomach.

'The evidence is there for all to see,' I said pinching a roll of flab.

Conrad flicked my hand away. 'It's all muscle,' he said getting up. 'Anyhow, I'll have to leave you girls to discuss this. I've got to make a call.'

Me and Ken continued to chat while Conrad made his way

to the back of the pub. Ken thought the English ex-pats the craziest people he'd ever met, and he couldn't understand why, given England was such a civilised place. I told him that was the problem. The pressure to behave correctly all the time got to people. When they landed in a different country and had a bit more freedom, they went mental, like boarding school boys on a weekend out of school.

'So that's why Conrad's like he is, is it?' he asked.

'That and a few other things.'

'What other things?' Conrad asked, having returned from the phone and caught the end of our conversation.

'Being mental and thinking you're a woman trapped in a man's body,' I said. 'How did you get on?'

'Sorted,' said Conrad, stuffing a scrap of paper in his pocket. He was so preoccupied he hadn't heard what I'd said. He was also pretty keen to leave, and by the look of him, he clearly didn't want Ken coming with us.

He needn't have worried. Ken had a pressing essay to do and was heading for the library in Jordan.

'Give me a call next week,' Conrad said as we parted company. 'We'll go for a beer or something.'

Ken walked down the steps to the MTR station. 'I hope your mother got you a decent present,' he said before disappearing.

'So do I,' Conrad murmured, turning to follow me up Lockhart Road. 'If only she got me this kind of thing when I was a teenager.'

The sun was high in the sky when we came out of the pub. The humidity was intensifying. After only a few metres, I could feel the sweat begin to run down my back. Little beads of it collecting at the waistband of my trousers. The street was crowded with Chinese, and sweltering *gweilo* businessmen suffering in suits. A bent old Chinese woman in a wicker hat held up the traffic, pushing a large waste disposal cart laden with bulging baskets. Car horns blared until she finally managed to haul it round a corner where she stopped to catch her breath. As I watched her, trying to imagine how a small woman could push such a large cart in this weather, I felt Conrad tense up next to me.

I followed his gaze. He was looking at a couple of Chinese guys. Two wiry, mean looking men dressed in baggy trousers and grubby white tshirts. They were standing smoking at a busy interchange. Grabbing my shoulder and hissing for me to keep moving Conrad ducked down behind me as inconspicuously as he could, pivoting me slightly to shield himself from searching eyes. We walked for several metres, some of the lunchtime crowd giving us inquiring looks.

'What's up with you?' I asked as he relaxed his grip. 'I know I'm good looking but... '

'I thought I saw a couple of people I didn't want to see.'

'Ex girlfriends?'

'No. Ex-colleagues.'

'Trouble?'

Conrad pulled a face like he was being strangled.

Something told me there was a complicated story behind this. I wasn't wrong.

On the ferry back to Lantau, standing at the back of the boat where we could get away with smoking, Conrad told me about the situation with the Chinese guys. It half surprised me and half didn't. I knew everything had its role in life. Fly paper attracted flies, pollen attracted bees, and Conrad attracted trouble. That's the way it was.

The trouble started the same time the enormous, curved roof Convention Centre in Wan Chai was completed. Some of the locals thought it looked like a giant bird, its wings open, placed atop the lines of blue tinted windows.

Conrad had been in charge of building the huge four and five metre wide gutters on the slopping roof. It was grueling work, but because of the pressure of the Handover Ceremony,

The Body is a Temple

there could be no excuses. In normal circumstances it was standard practice to drag the job out. It made sense for everyone, and everyone made more money, but this time it had to get done. On completion, Conrad was knackered and out of a job.

He'd hoped to be put on a snagging detail after its completion, a real cushy number, but it hadn't happened.

So having lost his job in Wan Chai, he relocated to Lantau, and the apartment in Luk Tei Tong he was in now. Every day he took the bus to the new airport site, being built on reclaimed land on the northwest tip of the island, hoping to get work. It took a week of trudging round rows of dusty prefab site offices before he landed himself a position.

The job entailed re-cladding the binnacles in the terminal buildings. Conrad found the work dull. He didn't like his colleagues, and the rat and mosquito infested corridors were getting him down, as was the heat that clung to him like a heavy towelling robe, even when stripped to the waist. There was another problem. The projects manager, an officious guy from Berlin, told him at the interview that they were well behind time, and they needed to press on.

Conrad put on a fake German accent. 'Therefore anyvone seen to have poor time keeping will be sacked on ze spot. No excuses will be considered.'

Conrad's time keeping had always been terrible, but with a Herculean effort he managed to get it right. His job seemed secure until Siggi said he wanted the guys to work Sunday for normal pay. Conrad said no way, they were all exhausted. Siggi wouldn't listen, so Conrad set up a strike. No-one went in on Sunday. Everyone sat in the pub and Conrad paid for them to get drunk. He thought it was the best thing for the boys. Come Monday, he and a few other 'trouble makers' got the sack.

Conrad and the other guys sued for unfair dismissal and won twenty grand each. Unfortunately Siggi didn't want to pay up. So Conrad told him, unless he got the cash, he'd report the company to immigration. He knew they had people working for the company illegally. Cheap labour from China. Shanghai. It would cost them a hundred thousand dollars a bloke if they get busted. The company paid up. The bad news was, they sacked the Chinese guys, who then blamed Conrad.

'Youch,' I said.

'Yeah. I wasn't going to report the company either. It was a threat, not a promise.'

'They're not Triads are they?' I said.

'No. They've got Triad connections. Least that's what they told me. Don't they all? Gives them protection from this kind of thing. First thing they do when they come over on the boat is get connected. They're bully boys. Not people you want to be in debt to.'

'So we need to avoid them at all costs?'

'Absolutely. If we see them, we run. Fast.'

When we got back to the apartment I went out on the patio for a cigarette. Conrad was nervous and needed some space. I crouched down on the concrete and watched lines of ants marching over its dusty surface. I considered what he'd told me on the ferry. He'd done the right thing, I thought, and it had backfired on him. His situation was dangerous, but not imminently so. If the Chinese guys did ever get hold of him, at least now he might have some cash. Then the whole incident wouldn't matter. The contents of this parcel were suddenly more important than I'd realised.

I peered in through the window to see how Conrad was getting on. He was facing away from me, gazing down at the box. Stalling. Not doing a thing. I drew on my cigarette. I wished he'd get on with it.

Eventually he took a breath, rubbed his head, mumbled and cracked his knuckles.

He strode into the kitchen, emerging with a sharp knife.

The Body is a Temple

The box was well taped up. Covered in Federal Express stickers and bound with nylon bands for extra security. There was some Dutch writing on it I didn't understand and a white sticker containing customs information.

'Come to papa,' Conrad said, sliding the knife under the first binding and snapping it off, then doing the same with the second.

Now he'd started, I wandered in and slid down on the sofa. I watched him cut through the brown tape down the centre line of the box and unfold the flaps.

'You look like a schoolboy at Christmas,' I said. 'Apart from the tshirt, obviously.'

On the front it read, in large black letters: REALITY IS FOR THOSE WHO CAN'T HANDLE DRUGS. On the back: REHAB IS FOR QUITTERS.

'I'm shaking, man,' said Conrad.

'Deep breaths. Take deep breaths.'

Conrad scooped out handfuls of polystyrene packing, the sort that looks like pasta tubes. A sea of it gathered round his knees before he finally pulled out another box, this one smaller and constructed from thinner cardboard. On its glossy side was a picture of a rice steamer.

Conrad smiled, 'That's what he said it would be. A rice cooker.'

I smiled down at him. 'Is it pass the parcel? Do I get a turn?'

He guarded the package with his arms. 'This is my baby.'

Taking the knife again he slit the smaller box open and lifted out a large stainless steal steamer. He held it briefly like some religious artefact before placing it on the coffee table. With great reverence, he lifted the lid.

I almost expected to see a shaft of light appear as he did this but none came. Conrad's smile was dazzling enough.

'And the result is?'

Conrad didn't say anything. He stuck his hand inside and

pulled out the inner sheath of the cooker. Then he peered inside. I watched his expression, which was slightly puzzled. The left eye twitched.

'What is it?'

Conrad put his hand inside and appeared to feel round its outer edges. 'All I can see is black,' he said. 'But it feels weird.'

'Like what?'

'Just weird. I don't know. There's a torch in my room. Can you get it? I want to see what's going on here.'

I got the torch and handed it to him, looking inside the pot myself as he shone the light over my shoulder. Conrad was right. It looked black, just black. While I dug round Conrad explained how the pot would be lined with lead to prevent it being X-rayed at customs, together with any other measure they saw fit to foil the authorities.

'Can you see anything?' he asked.

There was some kind of paint covering the bottom. I could see brush strokes. I put my hand in, moving my fingers along the base.

I took the torch and looked deeper inside. 'I can see what they've done here. They've welded a plate a few inches from the base. You'll need a cutter or something to get it open.' I stood up and shone the torch in Conrad's face making him squint. I turned it off. 'It's very impressive work. Very safe.'

Conrad nodded, looking slightly pissed off. 'It means we need to get hold of the tool though.' He rubbed his brow. 'There's a shop down the road I've bought stuff from before, I reckon they'd lend me one.'

'Then I suggest you get down there.'

'Will you keep your eye on this?'

'I think so,' I said sarcastically, not seeing what else I was going to do. 'I'll give you half an hour. If you're not back, I'm flying home.'

Conrad grabbed his wallet and left, leaving me sitting

back on the sofa massaging the back of my neck. I felt tired from the lunchtime drinking, even with all the excitement. I stretched and yawned a few times as if to confirm my need for sleep, then lay back on the sofa and closed my eyes. The next thing I knew I was being woken by a dig in the ribs.

'Great fucking guard you are!' said Conrad loudly, his face not far from mine.

I squinted back up at him. 'It hasn't gone anywhere has it? The place hasn't been ransacked. We haven't lost anything.'

'No thanks to you.'

Blackie the dog was back in the flat, his friendly mutt face forcing its way through Conrad's legs to give me a lick. I fended him off with the flat of my hand.

'That's your replacement,' said Conrad. 'He's better looking and more intelligent.'

'He's got a better tan as well.'

Conrad nodded, taking the small electric grinder he'd managed to borrow and plugging it into the wall socket. He flicked the mains switch to 'on' and squeezed the trigger. A screeching sound filled the room. Blackie whimpered at the noise, perhaps paranoid he was about to have his coat sheared.

'Don't worry,' said Conrad, roughly rubbing his back, making the hairs stand on end, 'this isn't for you.'

'I'll take him out to the patio,' I said, getting up and grabbing the dog's collar. 'We don't want a stray spark setting him on fire.'

Conrad lifted the pot and placed it on the sofa. To keep the whole thing steady he wedged it sideways between the cushions where the vibrations would be absorbed. 'Josh,' he called before he started, 'can I borrow your sunglasses?'

I came back inside and handed them to him. 'You know what you're doing, do you?' I asked.

'Sure,' he said and flicked the grinder on, while I retreated several paces.

As the grinder blade connected with the metal cylinder a

searing sound broke the calm. An orange Katherine Wheel of sparks shot up towards the ceiling.

Conrad hunched over his work intently. For thirty seconds he carved into the pot before stopping to check his work.

'Is it doing it?' I asked.

He rested the sunglasses on his head and had a closer look.

'Yeah, it's going through. It's getting hot though. Can you get me a towel from my room? I'm going to end up burning my hand otherwise.'

I retrieved the towel and handed it to him. 'I'm going to leave you to it,' I said, going back outside. 'It's too loud in here.'

Outside I took a breath and stared up at the bright sky. Blackie crouched at my feet, taking comfort in the warmth from my legs. It wasn't long before Conrad called out again.

'Josh. The moment of truth has arrived.'

I walked in bringing Blackie with me.

Conrad placed the pot on the table. He used the towel to protect his hands from the latent heat before lifting the lid. It opened as easily as a can of beans.

All three of us hunched over it, Blackie's nose twitching inquisitively.

'Get me a beer,' said Conrad putting his hand in and pulling out one of the many clear plastic bags that contained a hundred or two white pills. 'The eagle has landed.'

'Or the doves,' I said, unable to keep a broad smile from my face. 'I don't believe you actually did this.'

Conrad opened the bag and examined one of the pills. It was embossed with a flying dove. Touching it on his tongue he tasted the bitterness of the pill. Then he kissed it.

'Ecstasy,' he said quietly. 'It's what everybody wants.'

'It's what we're feeling right now.'

Then everything went crazy for a few minutes. It was a special moment. The vibe in the room was unbeatable. Conrad and I hugged each other, the hi-fi went on, blaring hard rock and Blackie went mad, chasing his tail in celebration.

During the mayhem an old Chinese woman appeared at the patio door, grinning at us blankly, chattering in Cantonese. Conrad threw a cushion over the drugs and went outside and danced with her, waltzing her down the path before returning.

'Who's she?' I asked, laughing but confused.

Conrad pointed at the ceiling. 'She lives upstairs, she's great. She never complains about the noise. Not even when I come home boxed at six in the morning and put the stereo on. She comes in here and has a smoke with me sometimes.'

'No way.'

'Yeah. She's cool. She's one of us. One of the party people. I couldn't have a better neighbour.'

Chapter Ten

Soon after we'd opened the parcel, and given the contents of each bag a cursory check, Conrad gathered them up and hid them in an old suitcase in his room. We didn't want Blackie getting his chops round them, or uninvited guests eyeing up the stash and asking awkward questions. We wanted to be as carefree about this as possible.

Satisfied the drugs were now reasonably safe, we relaxed on the patio playing Jenga, the bricks slowly building up, falling, then building up again. Such a simple game held our attention surprisingly well, but just as I was really beginning to unwind there was a knock at the door. I tensed up. I had visions of men in uniform asking tricky questions.

'Don't worry,' Conrad said, walking back through into the apartment. 'I know who this is. And don't piss him off, right, because he's got a bit of a temper.' He opened the door, pulling it only half way. 'You made it then,' Conrad said as the guy pushed his way in. He flicked his head back in acknowledgement.

'Man of my word I am,' he said. 'Not like some cunts out here.'

He was dressed in an old Sex Pistols tshirt with the sleeves ripped off, a pair of combat trousers which had been cut off below the knee, and a pair of Doc Marten boots. I wondered if he realised punk finished in the seventies.

'Hot innit?' he said, pulling at the neck of his tshirt. 'I'm sweating like a fucking rapist here.'

He dropped a knapsack on the tiles and rubbed his hands on his trousers. He was short, his face as ugly as his attitude, scarred from acne and fighting, and he smelt.

'Air con's broken,' said Conrad. 'It's better if we sit outside.'

'Probably, innit,' the guy said, following Conrad through the living room.

As he came through the sliding glass doors, he fixed his gaze on me.

'And who the fuck are you?'

'Nick this is Josh. Josh, this is Nick,' Conrad said.

I put a hand out. Nick eyed me warily. 'He's cool is he?' he said to Conrad.

'He's the reason I got the pills here in the first place.'

Nick nodded, dumping himself on one of the plastic chairs. As he rearranged his buttocks, he farted. 'Fucking Chinese food, innit,' he said.

I stuck my tongue out at him when he wasn't looking. Conrad smiled.

'So have you got the money?' he said, getting straight down to business.

Nick pointed at the grubby sack he'd brought with him. 'All in there.'

'Let's see it,' said Conrad.

'The gear first, mate. Let's see the goods.'

Routine I thought: you couldn't get away from it. We were into the routine of drug dealing here. Lack of trust mixed with paranoia. The clash of wills. Almost as bad as the 9 to 5.

Conrad went to his room, eventually bringing back a sample bag. He dropped it on Nick's lap, telling him there were a hundred in each one like it. Nick lifted it up and stared at the white pills inside. 'They look alright,' he said. 'Doves, yeah?'

Conrad nodded.

'Mind if I open it?'

'Go ahead.'

Nick split open the top of the bag like it was a packet of Jelly Babies and removed a single pill. Smirking, he put it in his mouth, rolled it round his tongue for a second before swallowing.

Conrad shook his head. I rubbed my hand over my forehead. I didn't like this guy straight. I couldn't imagine what he was going to be like high.

Nick grinned at us. 'We'll give it half an hour, yeah? Forty minutes. If they ain't kicked in by then, I'll fuck off home.'

I wished he'd go right now, but Conrad agreed. He had to.

'I'd better have one as well,' he said. I guessed he was thinking the only way to tolerate Nick high would be to be high also. Putting one in his mouth and swallowing he offered the bag to me. 'I think you better as well, mate,' he said.

'It's four thirty in the afternoon. Hardly the time is it?'

'Says who? You've got an etiquette guide to drug taking have you? Go on,' said Conrad. 'We need a third opinion.'

'It'll blow my head off. I haven't touched this stuff in months.'

'It fucking better,' said Nick. 'I ain't paying for shit.'

Conrad took a pill from the bag and put it in my mouth. 'Go on brother,' he said. 'Give it a whirl.'

I took a pill. The worse thing that could happen was that I wouldn't get high. Or perhaps it would be worse if I did. I wasn't sure. I swallowed, the bitterness catching the back of my tongue as the pill went down. I was pleased to clock they tasted the part. Time would tell.

Half an hour passed in idle chit chat. Nick did most of the talking. He blithered on about nothing but football and how the previous season had gone. Whether I'd ever seen Millwall play, if I supported Millwall, if I thought they were the best team in the division, had the best striker, could win the cup...

I tried to ignore him, but his voice was insistent. I watched a couple of cats play fighting in the coarse grass. The sunlight making their coats gleam. I looked up and saw sea gulls circling, their wings quivering in the thermals. I ran my hand up and down my forearm, smoothing the hairs down, then spiking them up. But whatever I did, I couldn't get his cockney rasp out of my head.

My dislike for the guy grew as he got on to football violence. He talked about it with such enthusiasm, his eyes gleaming.

'I don't see,' I said, 'that there's anything clever about stabbing someone in the back with a screwdriver. Is there?'

'The buzz, innit,' said Nick. 'The fucking buzz.'

I was confused. The concept was completely alien to me. 'In what way? How?'

'The blood and that. The fear. The buzz.'

I looked at Conrad. 'Do you get it?'

Conrad said he didn't but Nick wasn't put off. Like any fanatic, anyone else's opinion didn't count. The whites who hated the blacks because they were black. The blacks who hated the whites because they thought they were hated.

'You never tried it?' he demanded. 'You never been there. In the thick of it. With the crowd behind you. The shouting and screaming. It's the buzz, mate. The fucking buzz. The fucking buzz. There ain't nothing like it. There ain't. I'll do anything that gives me a buzz.'

Conrad looked panicked. He signalled me to keep cool.

Nick's speech was starting to quicken. His arm gestures were becoming more animated. The pupils of his eyes dilating. He was getting high.

'What do you reckon?' said Conrad, indicating the bag of pills on the white plastic table, clearly wanting to get Nick out of his flat. 'They're alright aren't they?'

'Not bad,' Nick nodded starting to gnaw his lip. 'They might be alright, yeah.'

'They're good,' I said. Not because I wanted to agree with Nick but because I couldn't help myself. 'They're strong.'

'Mm.' Conrad agreed, his knees jiggling up and down as the drug began to affect him. He was relieved he hadn't received a shipment of aspirin. 'Pretty tasty… '

He turned to Nick. Triumph in his eyes. He asked him how many he wanted.

'How many you got?'

'More than you can handle.'

'Since when did you become Mr. Big?'

'Since today. How many do you want?'

'At the price you said on the phone?'

Conrad nodded.

'I want seven hundred and fifty. Sixty thousand Hong Kong dollars worth. Four thousand eight hundred quid.'

'Done.'

'Fucking hell,' said Nick. 'You don't fuck about, do you?'

Conrad shook his head. He didn't fuck about. And I could see he didn't want Nick to outstay his welcome.

'I'll get the rest of the pills,' he said rocking his chair back off the wall and walking back into the apartment.

Several minutes later he reappeared. Nick looked like he was on a roller coaster ride. His little grey eyes were surprised, his jaw was clenching and unclenching, his limbs were starting to judder. I wasn't far behind.

'Ready for take off?' Conrad laughed.

I exhaled slowly. 'Man, these are something else,' I said. 'I feel like my chest is going to split open.'

'They're the bollocks, mate,' said Nick. 'I've got to say. They're the fucking bollocks.'

Conrad put the rest of the pills on the table. 'That's seven hundred,' he said, laying out the bags, before splitting another open and counting out: 'That's fifty.'

Nick leaned under the table, pulled out his knapsack and started piling money on the table. 'There's the cash,' he said. There was a small mountain of it. Conrad couldn't help smiling.

'It's all there is it?'

Nick nodded. 'They're grand bundles. An' if it ain't you know where I am don't you? I'm not a fucking idiot.'

I could see Conrad didn't agree with this, but acknowledged Nick had a point. He shrugged.

Nick packed the pills into his bag. 'Same goes for you and all. If I'm short, I'll be back. With a sledgehammer. Or,' he said pulling a revolver out of his bag. 'This.' He pointed it at Conrad's head.

'Where the fuck did you get that?' Conrad asked.

'Nice, innit?'

'Put it down.'

'It's all right. It ain't loaded.'

Nick pulled the trigger. The gun clicked making Conrad wince. Nick laughed a sadist's laugh.

'Yeah. Got to get some bullets. Protection, innit. Need it with all this gear. Until I offload it to Boris.'

'Boris?' said Conrad.

'German tennis player, wasn't he?' said Nick. 'It's a nickname.'

I wasn't sure if he was joking or not but I laughed anyway. I was confused from the drugs.

'They're all there,' Conrad said slapping him on the back. 'You won't need to use that.'

Nick's bag was full now and over his meaty shoulder. 'Innit,' he said. 'You guys going to be out tonight then?'

'Could be,' said Conrad.

'Might see you then,' said Nick heading for the door. 'I'm going to get these home then I'm hitting the clubs. Wan Chai, innit. The hookers. Fuck, I'm going to get off my tits.'

I thought he was off them already. At the door Conrad shook Nick's hand but the cockney almost brushed him out of the way, his eyes unfocused, his mind overcome by the drug. He looked at me and threw a dummy punch. I jumped while he laughed. God I hated this guy.

'Fucking... innit?' he said as he left, slamming the door behind him. 'Fuck, I'm going to be loaded.'

I looked at Conrad, relieved Nick had left the flat without destroying it.

Conrad gave a little smile of recognition. 'Don't need to worry about him now,' he said. 'Look at all this money.'

We wandered back to the table and picked up handfuls of it, letting it run through our fingers, the coloured notes twirling down like leaves. It felt amazing to have made so much money so quickly. I asked Conrad if he thought it was all here.

He lit a cigarette and nodded. 'Nick might be an arsehole,' he said. 'But he's rich. He's got money.'

Nick had been in Hong Kong for years, taking advantage of various ex-pat deals, free accommodation and a tax free income. He'd worked on the Convention Centre with Conrad, Nick putting up some of the original steel work, then he'd done a few tower blocks in Central, before also moving out to Lantau to work on the airport terminal buildings.

Virtually all the money he earned, he saved. The clubs were free, he used to steal beers from the Seven Elevens and he'd deal drugs, which would pay for any other entertainment he might need. He was sitting on a mountain of cash which he was intending to use to retire to a village in the north of Thailand. As far as Conrad knew he'd met a girl out there, a real sweetheart. He was going to build a house, settle down with her, and have kids. A whole football team of them. He'd spend his days teaching them the off side rule, and his nights getting as drunk as he liked. Whenever he got bored, he could take a bus down to Bangkok or Pattaya and have a bit of fun.

'Can't blame him for wanting the good life,' I said.

'No. But he doesn't deserve it. He'll probably end up treating the girl like shit, then he'll get dumped and blame her. And move on to someone new.'

'Again and again.'

It'd be the same old story. South East Asian dream turned nightmare. I ran a hand over my hair and suggested we count the money. Conrad sat down, mumbling something about me being right, flicking his cigarette into the shrubbery.

It wasn't the best time to count all that money, with the drugs renting our nervous systems as a race track, but common sense told me if there was a mistake to be corrected, it was better handled sooner than later. We kept quiet as we worked. Counting and talking, like British politicians and hookers, didn't achieve a good result when mixed. After ten minutes all sixty bundles had been checked. Conrad looked pleased but I was worried.

'I've got twenty five grand here,' he said. 'How about you?'

I was busy recounting. Once I'd finished I said, 'We've got a problem.'

A dark look crossed his face. He asked how much of a problem. It was a twenty thousand dollar one. A lot of my bundles were short.

Conrad pulled at his ponytail. He didn't bother to ask me to check it again. He knew I could count. I used to be a financial adviser for God's sake.

'I didn't like the way he legged it,' I said. 'Once he'd given you the money he was keen to get out of here. Call him, call him right now.'

Conrad went inside, made the call, and returned seconds later. 'I got his answer phone.'

'Did you leave a message?'

'No.'

'Why not?'

Conrad lit himself another cigarette. 'I'm thinking Nick is not the kind of guy to admit he stiffed me for twenty thousand Hong Kong. We've got three thousand two hundred quid. We should have four thousand eight hundred. That's a big difference. Fuck. I hate being ripped off. And I fucking hate Nick.'

Conrad had to work out what to do. My heart sank. This was just the kind of worst case scenario I'd dreaded. A simple scam going pear shaped. Thankfully Conrad had other buyers lined up and was determined to sell the lot on that night. But before that, we had to straighten ourselves out and come up with a plan for Nick.

'Let's go for a walk,' Conrad said. 'Get some air in our heads.'

'So we can become airheads?' I joked. Conrad winked at me.

We wandered along the beach, past the ice cream stalls and picnic areas, past the black scars round the barbecue areas, until we were far from anyone. After twenty minutes or so I asked Conrad what he wanted to do.

'Well, we're not going to call the cops,' he laughed. 'No. I've got a few ideas. We've got some options.'

'Anything I'm likely to support?' I was starting to get worried. If you've ever seen a wheel come off a car travelling at high speed, you'll know it travels straight for some distance before kicking up, bouncing and going completely out of control. I feared this was what would happen to our deal. The wheel was off the car now. How wildly was it going to bounce?

Conrad ran his hands through his lank blonde hair and smiled. 'You'll support anything with a little persuasion,' he said.

'You mean a Full Nelson?'

'Something like that. Come on. Let's sit on that bench over there and I'll tell you what I think.'

'I can't wait.'

And it was then, even though I was having kind of a good time, like getting drunk at the races but losing money on every horse you bet on, I should have flown back to Bangkok. I should have gone home and left Conrad to handle the remains of the skittering automobile on his own.

But this little voice from the past said *no*. It was only a whisper. Something I could barely hear, but it was there, buzzing with the mental static. *You can't leave him on his own. He never left you.*

Chapter Eleven - Bangkok. The Present.

Dr Miller's office is on the second floor of the Saint Sebastian Hospital. Its sole window looks out over the brown swathes of the Chao Phraya River. When I arrive I find him sitting on a low leather chair, his legs casually crossed.

Dr Miller is in his fifties. His hair is swept back and receding with flecks of grey round the ears. He has an angular face, the edges of which are only just starting to blur with age. His eyes are alert. His expression concerned, but not overly so. He's been my therapist for several months.

I sit in the chair, set at an angle to the other.

"Hi," I say. We never get anywhere unless I speak first. I pay. I speak. I do the work. Johnny gets a good deal.

"Hello," he replies in a mellow baritone. The kind of voice you'd expect to hear rounding up the news headlines.

I look up at the big clock. The second hand glides round smoothly. As usual I wonder what I'm doing here, and as usual the answer comes to me immediately. Lek was worried about my drinking. She wanted me to get some help, so I did. I wasn't worried. Drinking stopped me from worrying.

We sit in silence for a long time before we start discussing my life. We talk about how I find it in Bangkok as opposed to Hong Kong, and how I see the future, where my relationships are at, and how my job is. Towards the end of the session a recurring theme arises.

"Can you remember a time in your life when you were

truly happy?" he asks.

"I'm happy now," I say. It's true. There's much to be happy about, despite the problems.

"At this moment. Or generally?"

"Both."

"And do you believe you chose to be happy, or it just happened to you? I'm going back to our free will versus determinism argument again."

"I'd like to think I could control when I'm happy and when I'm sad," I say. "I'd like to think I had free will to chose what mood I was in. But I don't. You don't. It's like the loss of innocence. Nobody wants to lose that but we all do. We can't help it."

"But we can control the degree to which we lose it, can't we?"

"Not all of us," I mumble. "Some of us just fall over the edge. Some of us just keep skidding down that slippery slope."

The world doesn't change as we get older, we do. The loss of innocence doesn't take place in the physical world, it's mental. Once we leave childhood something happens. The projector on which we focus the film of our lives swings ever more crazily toward real danger and recklessness, as opposed to imagined, fantastical fictions. The clear eyed belief the world is a good, fun place is replaced by fear, paranoia, irrational bouts of self loathing. And once we've had a thought, we can't take it back. It leaves its mark.

"And much of the time you're... depressed?" Dr Miller says.

"Yeah."

"Do you want to tell me how you deal with these times, these periods of depression?"

"I drink," I say.

Dr Miller sighs. He maintains we need to tackle the deep set 'core issues'. They shouldn't be drowned in a lake of booze. We need to get my mind to jump the tracks from negative thinking to positive. Dr Miller is the points where this transition can be made.

"What makes you drink?" he asks.

"Because I sometimes feel alone. Kind of left out. I'm surrounded by people but I don't connect with hardly any of them. It's like there's all this noise, but nothing I can understand. Nothing I can relate to."

"Your girlfriend is Thai isn't she? Do you have problems relating to her?"

"No more than anyone else." This is true too. Lek and I connect at a deep level. We have trouble with the everyday cultural differences, our line of work, but we're very close.

"What about other friends?"

"I have some."

"Good ones?"

"Not bad."

He nods. "So where does the loneliness come from?"

I suddenly feel very small. Receding. Like I'm rushing backwards. Running from stuff I don't want to discuss. "From loss… and from the inside. From a dissatisfaction with who I am. It's been the same wherever I go. Here. Hong Kong. London. Anywhere."

"But you're overcoming this feeling of emptiness. Something is growing inside you?"

"I think so. I feel better. More… complete. Human? I have more humanity, I think."

Dr Miller looks up at the clock. It's nearly five. "We'll have to leave it there for today," he says. "I'll be here at the same time next week."

After the session I wander around, soaking up the solitude, watching the sun come down. I think about what I was like as a teenager. I guess I was like everyone else. Angry, rebellious, trying to be cool. The teenage years are the ones where we're desperate to be different. The clothes, the hair, the music, we all strive for an individuality that's never quite achieved. When

The Body is a Temple

we slip into adulthood that sense of individuality is finally granted us, but suddenly we don't want it. We all want to be normal, the same. Where we wanted to be older, we now want to be younger. It has to do with wanting what we can't have.

When I eventually get on the bike, it's already dark and I feel ready to go home. I drive slowly, enjoying the relative cool of the night air.

By the time I pull up at my apartment I feel tired. I switch off the engine and rock the bike back on its stand. As I get off and head towards the doors I see a familiar head of blonde hair on the other side of the street. A sudden buzz runs through me.

"Hey," Eric says with that strange European accent. "So this is where you're living, hey?"

"I guess so," I say as calm as possible, but my heart is starting to surge. "What are you doing out here?"

"I like exploring. Looking round."

He's still standing on the other side of the road, shoulders back, looking straight at me. He looks taller than in the club, and broader. My anxious buzz increases to full paranoia. I don't need any more enemies.

"Hey. About the other night," I say. "I, I over reacted, I guess and…"

"This can happen," he says before I finish. His voice cold and sinister. "Some drinks and you feel tough, yes?"

"Yeah, I guess."

"But you are not as tough as you think. Are you, Josh? You have a weak punch."

This hurts. And I hate the way he emphasises my name. It gives me the creeps.

I don't reply. Eric laughs. A low, barely audible sound, almost like a gentle clearing of the throat.

"So. I'll see you," he says.

"Yeah. See you," I say as cheerfully as possible. "Bye."

I walk into the block. Getting in the lift and turning to press the button I see he's still staring at me, arms crossed, head level. Eric appearing from nowhere isn't helping my paranoia. First Ratty, now him. This stuff is shredding my nerves.

And… a weak punch? I think as the lift takes me up.

Lek gives me a big hug as I walk in the door. She knows I'm often edgy after seeing the doctor and I won't want to talk. She doesn't know I've just had another worry put in my mind. I give her a kiss and a hug and walk outside. She fixes me a weak vodka and tonic and sits with me on the balcony. A scented candle burns on the table. By our feet a mosquito coil smoulders. The stereo plays a quiet Thai love song. After a while she asks me if I'm coming to bed. I tell her I'm going to stay up a while longer. Once I've heard her settle down, I fix myself another drink, a strong one this time, and sit staring out at the night.

A weak punch, hey? Fuck.

The next morning I sit at my desk in the living room doodling on gym training programs. Lek interrupts me, arriving back with the shopping. Her slender arms are straining to carry the bags. Mid morning sun streams in from the balcony window, creating swirling patterns on the floor.

I get up to help her.

"Thanks, babe," she says as we store the bundles of noodles, the pak choi, papaya, chillies, packets of prawn crackers which Lek seems to munch on constantly. "I think when I walk very far my arm go like this," she bends down and lets her fingers hang near the floor. "Like a monkey."

"You look like a monkey anyway. You don't need long arms."

"Why I look like monkey? Because I have black skin?"

"No. Because you have no nose."

"I have nose. Just no big like you," she grabs hold of mine and squeezes it. "You have big nose, misser *falang*."

Her hand is hot and sweaty from carrying the food from the market. I pull her fingers off my face and rub it on her top, making her squeal. We play fight for a bit, tussling on the sofa, before I realise I'm running late for the gym.

I push Lek off and tell her I have to hurry. She laughs and kisses my cheek, "Mr Busy!" she says. Then getting up and straightening her clothes, she asks me if I want to see her baby later.

"Sure, I'll be back at one thirty."

I take the Kawasaki to the gym. Silom Road is only a short drive west. I arrive five minutes early for my appointment.

The gym is newly renovated. The weight machines are state of the art, black leather and chrome pulley operated systems. The gym is divided in two sections. On one side there are the aerobic machines: jogger, ski machine, stepper, shoulder roller and stationary bikes. On the other are the weights: bench press, bicep curl, lat pull down, tricep extension and exercises for the muscles in the legs. The air conditioning is icy.

I nod to a couple of guys I see regularly and warm up with shoulder rolls and some leg stretches. I do a hundred press-ups, then have a drink from the water fountain.

My eleven o'clock shows up late, apologising. I tell her not to worry, getting her straight into a warm up on the jogger.

I like being a personal trainer. I feel almost proud doing it. After a few weeks of helping friends work out, I decided I wanted to pursue it more seriously. I put an ad in *The Bangkok Post*, got myself a forged P.E. qualification from Oxford University and a One Year Diploma Course in Nutritional Science. Then I sat back and waited for the phone to ring.

Before Hong Kong it seemed I could become a personal trainer full time, even though it paid less than a gigolo. Right now, with what I owe Ratty, it isn't viable. I have to do as much of both as possible. One day I'll bin the condoms. I'll have to work a lot more hours in the gym to bring in less money, but that's cool. I'll take a drop in salary and a quantum leap in self esteem.

"Do another five," I say encouragingly as she begins to

struggle with the lat pull down. "Do it nice and slowly down and slowly up. Don't rest in between. Always keep the muscles working."

I speak in Thai. In this business there's no need to hide anything.

"Well done," I say when she's finished. "Now it's time for your favourite. Sit ups. I know they're hard," I say, helping her into the correct position on the mat. "But if you have a firm stomach, everything else will fall into place. You'll look fantastic."

She looks unsure but begins a set of twenty crunches, with me holding her legs bent. She performs them with grim determination.

At the end of the session the diaries come out and she books another session.

"You realise," I say, "that you have to come to the gym two or three times on your own to get the maximum out of your program. Coming here once a week is not enough." I ask her how many times she came last week. She says only once. I tell her mock sternly she must make it three times, or she'll never see any results. She reluctantly agrees.

"Good," I smile. "You can go now. The battle is over."

When she leaves I don't have to wait long for my next client. In the ten minutes I have, I put on the gloves and give the punch bag some grief, concentrating on power.

I head back to the apartment some hours later, after I've done some strokes on the rowing machine and another round with the punch bag. On the journey home, I see a discarded bicycle with a bent front wheel, lying in an area of scrub near the road, like a spoked tomb stone. I stop and inspect it. The damage isn't too bad. It's repairable.

Lek likes to help the TCC, the Thai Cycling Club. They're an organisation run by a friendly old doctor. His idea is to renovate any old bike he can find, then give it to kids in the countryside who have too far to walk to school. In bare feet, their legs start to hurt, and in torrential rainstorms, they won't go to school at all. Some drop out altogether because of the hardship.

I hail a tuk tuk and ask the driver to deliver it to the TCC headquarters north of Sukhumvhit. I pay him a tip for the service and continue my journey home. I feel good helping the cause. I know what pleasure the freedom of a bike can bring.

Lek is looking smart in a yellow summer dress and open toed sandals when I arrive home. Her face touched with eye make-up and a dab of lipstick. I give her a kiss before getting in the shower. Lek settles herself on the balcony. The water stays hot today whilst I'm under the jets. Lek won't want to slow me down this time. I quickly wash my hair, massage myself with shower gel, get out and dry off.

"I'm ready," I call from inside after a few minutes. I've rushed because I know she's keen to get going. "Do you want to take the bike or get a taxi?"

"Taxi please, babe, I wearing dress remember?"

"Oh yeah. Sorry. We don't want you showing your knickers to the whole of Bangkok."

Lek comes in from the balcony frowning.

"Not joke like that please," she says. "Not polite."

"I was only kidding," I grin, knowing how sensitive Lek can be. I give her a hug.

"Good," she smiles. "We can go now. No wait! I nearly forget this," she collects a bulging plastic carrier off the coffee table.

"What's in there?"

Lek puts her hand inside and pulls out a large soft teddy bear with big googly eyes and huge paws.

"Present for Samsook," she says with a giggle. "You think she like, or what?"

"I think she'll love it."

Lek's aunt lives east of Ekamai bus station in Phra

Khanong. She's married to an older guy who works in construction, who is, I think, chronically depressed. He has the kind of expression that looks like he's viewing a never ending road accident. I think I looked like that once, like Brett Easton Ellis on the back cover of *American Psycho*, but now I'm okay, mollified somehow, anaesthetised. At least for the time being.

Nong's apartment is always clean and tidy, if small and noisy. It's on the second floor of the building, close to the busy street. Even so, I enjoy our visits there.

"You looking forward to seeing Samsook?" I ask Lek as we cab out there.

She smiles. Her eyes twinkle. "Wa you think?"

I take her hand, smile and nod.

Little Samsook is the centre of Lek's world. She is desperate for her to live with us, but as we both work nights it's impossible. We're edging towards the day. I look forward to it as much as Lek, even though Samsook is not my child. I like the idea of being a daddy. I think I'd be okay at it. Perhaps it'd give my life some focus.

The cab pulls up at the apartment block. I pay the driver. We go straight in the building and climb the stairs.

As we go in the front door, the buzz of the traffic follows us into the room, like a swarm of bees. A strong smell of chillies fills the thick, humid air. There is no air conditioning. The lazy ceiling fan licks hot air round the room.

Nong greets us with excited chattering, putting Lek's daughter straight in her arms.

Nong has an open, friendly face, with bright eyes. She always makes us feel welcome. Once we've been kissed and told how well we're looking, she gives out glasses of water and carries on cooking. The vegetables sound like stray cats spitting as they cook in the wok. As usual, we're staying for a meal.

We sit on the bamboo sofa for a while, tickling the baby's

chin. Nong and Lek discuss how much she's grown. She's almost a year old now. Every time I see her she seems to have doubled in size.

But I don't watch the baby. Instead I watch Lek. The joy on her face as she bounces the child on her lap, gurgling to it softly. There's something special about the real closeness of the mother-child relationship and its evolving history. I feel a twinge of jealousy. I'll never feel as strongly about anything as Lek feels about Samsook.

I go out on to the small balcony and smoke a Kron Thip. I guess I have most history with Conrad, of all people. He should be here by now. I helped him out in Hong Kong so he could start a new life. I wanted him to come here. I thought it would help me feel less lost, but now I'm not sure if he's ever going to show up.

"Babe," Lek calls. "We eat now, okay?"

I go inside. Samsook has a big smile on her face. Her eyes are smiling too, scrunched up small. Her chubby little arms wrapped round the teddy, which is three times her size.

"I told you she'd like it," I say.

Lek laughs. "My baby like everything I do for her. I her mother."

We sit cross-legged on the floor and eat rice with dried fish and papaya salad, washed down with iced water.

Nong tells Lek everything Samsook has done. Every gurgle is described, every crawl across the floor, every spilt cup of water recounted. Lek is enthralled. Her eyes shine at the stories. She hugs her baby like a koala hugs a tree – relaxed, content. She feeds her fingerfuls of rice, arranges her dark, wispy hair and burbles to her constantly in reassuring tones.

Some time in the early evening, I get up to go. I have to work and I need to shower and change at home before heading out again. Nong's apartment is so stuffy, I've been sweating heavily. Seeing the disappointment in Lek's eyes, I ask her if she wants to stay.

"You can come home later," I say. "I'll be out late anyway. You'll only be sitting at home on your own."

"Is okay," says Lek. "I have some job I need to do in the home. I can come now, with you."

She hands Samsook carefully back to Nong, kissing her on both cheeks twice, sucking air in through her nose in the Thai manner, before letting her go.

"Don't forget who your mummy is," she says in Thai, before kissing Nong and thanking her for taking care of her daughter.

Nong smiles, pleased she can be of help. She and her husband never had children. They wanted them but none came. Samsook is like a gift, a kind of compensation for what they were denied themselves. She's happy to look after her for as long as it's necessary. I know she fears the day Lek will come to take her back for good.

Chapter Twelve

On Friday I feel so tired, I lie in till midday. The echoes of dengue fever still reverberate round my body. The illness has long fingers. They reach up constantly to drag me down. I stare up at the ceiling, thinking about Lek. There was a time, early in our relationship, when I wondered if it'd all work out. A lot of guys told me it was a bad idea. A young Thai girl with a child was only after one thing: money. Or if not, a passport. I'd worried about it for a while, but it never bothered me much. If she wanted money, she could have it. If she was looking for a passport, why wasn't she hassling me to get married?

Lek had never pushed me to delve too deeply into my bank account. If anything, I owed her more than she owed me. While I was ill, she took care of both of us, financially and emotionally. If she was after money, she'd picked the wrong guy, or assumed I'd one day be a tycoon and was playing a subtle waiting game.

I always had one thought in my head, though. If anyone wanted my money badly enough to try and scam me out of it, they were welcome. It obviously meant more to them than to me. And that included Lek, more than anyone else I knew.

When I eventually rise I put the radio on, have a long shower, then make myself lunch. Noodles, spiced with chillies and bulked out with boiled fish. Nothing too expensive, but still full of protein. I look at the note Lek has left me: I go swim. I smile at her handwriting. Spidery and inexpert. It makes me smile, not because it's childlike but because I taught her. I did a good thing, which might help to cancel out some of the bad, some of that exhausting, insidious guilt.

Before we met, Lek was going out with an American. A young guy in the army. A strong man with blonde hair she thought would take care of her. She'd been through a bad time. After the nightmare of living with her Thai husband, she thought a *falang*, a Westerner, would be a good call.

Jim was good to her in the beginning. He bought her flowers. He took her to expensive hotels. He said he wanted to take her back to the States with him.

Lek liked that. But she was scared of going to America. She had two kids she didn't want to leave. She was torn for months, until she found Jim drunk in Pat Pong, 'weaving like a snake' with another girl. That ended it. She didn't want to repeat the same mistakes she had with her husband.

I didn't want her to either. We try every day to avoid it.

After lunch I get in the shower again. As the water falls over my body, I meticulously wash, especially my face. I need time with my body alone. I share so much, I need to keep some moments for myself. I enjoy being alone in the shower. I think of it as a mental release. It gives me strength. It cheers me up after life and the doctor have brought me down. A good long shower suits me better than therapy, I sometimes think. It helps me forget, just like the drink.

I remember Dr Miller and I talking about motivation. How when you're depressed it all goes. Drifts out of you like fine sand through a sieve. You don't even want any physicality, not even a gentle touch. You don't feel like you deserve it. That made work hard, but I'm over it. The sand in my sieve is coarser now. It no longer falls through. I can function, even if reluctantly.

When I'm done there's a knock at the door. I get my trousers on and wander through to the hall, towelling my hair dry.

"Wow," I say as I open up. "Great to see you. Come in."

The Body is a Temple

"Hello," she smiles. "What you doing?"

I blush slightly; showering is such a personal thing for me now, it's like a guilty pleasure I don't want to admit to.

"Just, you know, washing. Felt a bit sweaty."

"I know," says Wow. "Very hot today, yes?"

"I felt like I was melting before."

She leans forward and gives me a kiss. The smell of her tangy perfume makes me blush even more.

Wow is beautiful. Possibly more so than any girl I've met. She has curves in all the right places and is also kind and funny. She's so attractive I feel guilty having her in my house. To disguise my awkwardness, I get a tshirt from the bedroom, suggesting on the way we go for a drink. If Lek came home and found us chatting here, she'd get jealous, even though she knows nothing would ever happen between me and Wow. Sometimes being good looking is hard for a girl. Other girls don't like it and men find it intimidating. It creates barriers.

Fully dressed I return to the living room.

"Let's go," I say.

"Okay, Mr Fish man."

She calls me this because of the drinking, though I've never understood that expression. Do fish drink a lot? And if they do, isn't it mostly water, not beer and whisky?

"I like the new flowers you have here." She's been checking out the plants and the red and white flowers on the balcony. I don't know their names.

"They're Lek's hobby," I explain. She likes looking after things. I'm terrible. If they were mine, they'd die.

"I think she look after the flowers, you look after her," Wow says.

"I try," I smile. "I try. I give her water every now and again."

We head out of the apartment and walk to a nearby bar where we sit at a table next to the door. Fans revolve lazily above us. The walls are off white and cracked, the tables unsteady on their legs. Wow drinks mineral water (would this not make her Miss Fish Woman?), while I drink Singha. We chat for a good half an hour as if she doesn't have a care in the world. She laughs about some good nights out she's had and about various guys who've chatted her up. She mocks her lack of co-ordination in her aerobics class, and tells me about some new Thai friends she's made. Her three other sisters and two brothers are well. Only two children are left at home in the country now. The family is becoming upwardly mobile. Wow even confesses she's planning to start a jewellery shop with her eldest sister who's come up with some interesting designs and knows people up north who can produce them cheaply. Currently they're looking for a suitable property in West Bangkok.

I enjoy listening to her plans. When she laughs, she puts her hand over her mouth as if she's doing something naughty, and her eyes widen. Wow's grown up a lot, but there are still elements of the shy country girl about her. So it comes as a complete shock when she turns to me with a serious expression and says, "But you know, Marcus. Thing no good wit him. Last week he hit me."

I feel a shockwave detonate somewhere at the back of my head. I knew Marcus' inability to sleep sometimes gave him a temper, but I didn't think he was a hitter. I take a pull on my cigarette and ask her why. She says he was angry, always angry.

"Because?"

"He jealous, like you know. He thinking I like someone."

"This Belgian guy?"

'We just friends, that all. Men like me, like you like me. But Marcus my boyfriend, he know that. I love him."

I look in her eyes. They seem calm.

"But can you still love a man that does this to you?" I ask.

Wow sips her mineral water. A drop is left on her plump, creamy upper lip. She wipes it away with a slender finger. "He do so many thing for me."

I hold her hand across the table and give her a look. Her left shoulder rises imperceptibly and she looks at the table.

"Actually, I lie. This guy from Belgium," she says. "He say he want to marry with me, take me to he country. I no have sex with him."

Wow has told me about this guy several times before. I think she's considering him more seriously now. I ask her if she wants to go. It's clear she's not sure.

"Have you thought about it?"

"Yes."

"Is he kind? Does he love you?"

"I think so."

I sit back and light a Kron Thip, the bamboo chair digging in my back. "So?"

Wow raises a perfectly plucked brow. "Marcus do so much for me," she says again. "He save me."

I can see she's confused and frightened even though she's trying to hide it. She knows Marcus is my friend, so I can't make any decision for her, but I offer to talk to him, perhaps straighten out his attitude a little. She looks shocked. She doesn't think this is a good idea.

"It's up to you," I say.

To ease the tension we chat again about mutual friends. She knows Pim. Apparently they've been getting drunk together.

"She very naughty," Wow laughs. "She tell me many thing about you."

"Yeah. She is wild," I say, hoping Pim hasn't given away too much of our past. "You take it steady with her."

Wow finishes her drink and looks at her watch. She has to go to her English class. After she's meeting her cousin who's recently arrived from the country. She hasn't seen her in three years.

I say goodbye and watch her swing her hips up the street.

After she's gone I sit in another bar and have a few more Singha, wondering if Marcus does hit her. Somehow I can't picture it. I'm not sure if this is because Marcus is my friend, or because I don't trust Wow's motives. If she wanted to get away from Marcus whilst still keeping me as a friend, this would be the only way she could do it. If she left Marcus for someone else on a whim, I'd probably never speak to her again. Infidelity doesn't work. You're either in, or you're out. You can't be in and out with a whole range of people. Sounds mad coming from a gigolo, but I'm a pretty loyal person. At least I try to be.

By early afternoon I've convinced myself that they may be going through a tough time, but Wow has blown their arguments out of proportion. A natural reaction for a young woman in her first real relationship.

I feel much better having reached this conclusion. Both my friends are still my friends. Everything is right with the world.

I love kidding myself.

After I get home and shower, the night rolls round with surprising speed. The Ferris wheel of life just keeps on turning. Before I know it I'm in bed with another girl. She's about thirty-five, fun and speaks good English. She's also highly sexual. We've had a few drinks, as is normal, and now we're doing what I'm paid for.

"Is this what you like?" I ask her, putting two fingers inside, my thumb on top, on her clitoris. My cock half inside her, next to the fingers.

She moans as I push in further. "*Chai.*" She closes her eyes.

I move in out of her. My fingers reach up for the G spot. Not with passion, but precision. I feel nothing, or try to. My mind is not here.

After several minutes she asks me if I can go quicker. I say sure and up the tempo.

"I like that," she says. "Can you give me more?"

I keep pounding away, wondering if I'm going to come or

if I'm going to have to fake it.

She writhes and screams, her fingers pressing into my arms. It takes another ten minutes, but I finally get there. When I'm done the girl looks like she's been drugged. When she doesn't move for several minutes I ask her if she's okay.

She doesn't answer.

"Are you okay?" I say again.

Still no answer.

I start to panic. This is my worst nightmare. A client having a heart attack whilst in bed with me. I've often wondered what I'd do in this situation. I guess my first instinct would be to run. Quickly go round the room wiping off any finger prints, removing any sign I was there. Putting the woman in a bathroom robe, laying her back in bed, smoothing the sheets, and then leaving. Just calmly taking the elevator down to reception, saying goodbye to the receptionist without looking at her, walking swiftly for several blocks before hailing a taxi to a bar on the edge of town and getting so drunk I'd forget all about it and pretend it never happened.

Or.

Perhaps I'd realise she's dead, tidy up a little, then phone reception, telling them my friend's just had a heart attack, and then leave.

Or.

Staying to face it.

I don't like the idea of that. That's not my style. The story would probably go international. My whole family would get to hear about it and my lifestyle would catch up with me. The embarrassment would be too great.

But.

I'd like to think I'd do this. Stay and handle it like a man. Admit my faults and move on. I don't know...

Heart kicking, I touch the woman to feel if she's cold. She smiles. Relief floods my whole being. I was just being paranoid.

"I don understand why my husband no do like that," she says.

I smile, so happy she hasn't died. "You probably don't pay him as well."

She laughs, though there is a sadness to it. "You're probly right," she says.

I leave her to her thoughts while I shower, then dress in the bathroom. When I come out she is ready to go. I almost have to run out of the room so I don't have to go down with her in the lift. For me, when it's over, it's over. It has to be.

When I get home later, Lek is already in bed. The apartment is very still. I have another shower before joining her. Getting in I feel exhausted, though I enjoy Lek cuddling up to me as I lie on my back. As I'm closing my eyes, she says, "You okay?"

"I'm tired, it's been a long day."

"Do you love me?"

I say of course. There's a long pause where I almost fall asleep.

"I have something I need tell you," she says. "I think you no like."

"Go on," I say. I'm so tired I feel calm.

"I solly, babe," she says. "Toni I sleep wit some man. I need money for the baby."

I don't say anything. I let it sink in, but somehow it doesn't. The information pours over my brain like water over an upturned plate.

"I feel bad," she says. "But I have to tell you."

"Why?" I feel a sudden burst of anger coming on me like a flower blooming fast in time lapse photography. There's a hole in the plate, the liquid pain is starting to seep in.

"I… " she says. "I no want, but… "

"But?"

Her hand comes up to hold my shoulder. "Don hate me," she says, her eyes looking watery.

I stay quiet. I don't have the energy for this now.

Her hand moves over my forehead. It feels loving. The warmth of her soft palm seems to calm me.

"Don't worry," is all I have the energy to say. "It's okay. Did you use a condom?"

Lek nods.

"Good," I say. "Go to sleep."

"You still love me?" she asks, kissing my chest.

"Yes."

She cuddles up. I stare at the ceiling, searching for sleep. How could she? I think. But I do it too. It's the life we've both chosen. I take a breath. Sleep comes, not through peace of mind, but from total exhaustion. Eventually, I get there.

In the morning, having woken late, and with Lek gone, I phone Marcus. He doesn't answer. I leave a message on his answer phone asking him if he phoned Ratty and requesting that he call me. I give his mobile a try too and leave the same message. Lek has left a note saying she's gone to visit Samsook.

I go back to sleep after this and have wild dreams. What Lek said to me last night has sunk in. She screwed someone for money. She said she couldn't do it anymore, not for anything. I try to work out what has changed, but I can't. I try to control my jealousy, but it comes bubbling up through my subconscious, like heated treacle. I wake again in a foul mood, staring up at the whitewashed ceiling. I realise this is total hypocrisy but I can't help it. If we weren't broke, I keep thinking, this would never have happened.

When I eventually go through to the kitchen I find a slim brown envelope pushed under the door. I reach down and pick it up in a state of confusion. No-one hand delivers me notes. No-one sends me letters. Hardly anyone knows I'm here. I keep a very low profile. If I was a tyre, I'd be only a millimetre thick.

I brush a hand over my almost hairless chest, itch the back of my neck and open it.

Inside the envelope is a photo. The picture is of a man lying on a white tiled floor, a miniature oasis of red blood surrounding his head. Through squinted vision it looks like chocolate sponge cake ringed with raspberry sauce. The accompanying note reads: You next.

I go out to the balcony and stare at the image. I don't recognise the man. I can't place the location. I go back inside and pour myself a vodka and tonic and think.

Panic rises slowly in my chest, like mercury in a thermometer.

I do know the man. He's the one Ratty threatened. This is serious. I phone Marcus again. Still there's no reply. Hands shaking, I phone Adrian. We arrange to meet for lunch.

Chapter Thirteen

I arrive a good ten minutes or three cigarettes before him, but it feels like longer. I take deep breaths to slow my heart rate down, and stretch my hands over my head to ease the built up tension. By the time Adrian arrives I've calmed down. I'm not in any imminent danger, after all, it's simply approaching, like middle age.

"Sorry I'm a bit late," he says when he arrives, shaking my hand. I'm sitting at a small table outside a restaurant in West Bangkok, under the sun, under the white hot sky where there are no clouds. "Christ, I used to see more of you in Hong Kong."

"We worked together," I say, turning my palms up in mock irony.

Adrian smiles. He has a wide mouth set in a heavy five o'clock shadow. "Bet you miss the cut and thrust of the financial markets, don't you?"

"Give me a gun and put a hole in my head. That's how much I miss it. Same as you."

Adrian laughs. He was getting pretty stressed out by the end of his time on the island. Hunched over his desk in the skyscraper overlooking Central ferry pier, his shirt collar always looking too tight, he had a permanent wrinkle on his forehead from staring at figures. That line had gone now, erased by the hand of an easier life.

"Been up to anything exciting?" he asks in his deep rasping tone.

"Nothing I'd tell a respectable family man about," I tell him.

Adrian's forehead creases. For a second he looks like the old Adrian again. The one with worries.

"I've been meaning to call you, actually," he says. "Lisa's gone back to Hong Kong."

"No way. There's nothing wrong is there?"

"No, nothing," he laughs, though he looks awkward. "Well, not much. The kids didn't like it here. And... we've been having a few problems, that's all. It's nothing."

"Wait. She's really gone back? What does this mean? Are you separated?"

"No. We just needed some time apart. Shit. I'll explain it to you another time."

Before moving to Hong Kong, Adrian had been a Lieutenant in the Green Berets, stationed for a year in Cyprus. Lisa was there on holiday before starting her nursing course back in London. They'd met one afternoon, whilst lazing round the tranquil pool at one of the many local hotels. Adrian's best buddy had got chatting to her friend and they'd all ended up having a few Keos together. Adrian and Lisa hit it off straight away.

He asked her out, and the next day they took his rented Wrangler Jeep out and explored the island. They went to Polis, a rugged, sun drenched hillside village, dotted with farm cattle and terracotta roofed outbuildings. Hardy trees gathered in groups, their leaves rustling in the breeze that came in off the ocean. Lisa said the trees looked like schoolboys gathered round puddles; hunched over, conspiratorial. Adrian liked that. Not that his focus of attention could stay on the geography of the place for long. As hard as he tried, he couldn't take his eyes off Lisa.

It wasn't the way she looked that struck him most that afternoon, though her gorgeous curves were accentuated in yellow shorts and pale blue tshirt. It was her laugh, her easy

The Body is a Temple

sense of humour, the way she dug him in the ribs and grinned when he said something funny. And Adrian, he would freely admit, wasn't that funny.

They ate a traditional Cypriot meze at a family run taverna, which was so hospitable, after several glasses of wine they felt like they were lunching with old friends. After they'd finished, they were serenaded by a young band of musicians playing Greek music. When the wind blew through Lisa's hair, covering her face, Adrian felt bold enough to tuck it behind her ear. It was a natural gesture, one that felt right, though it was more intimate than he'd intended. Lisa gave him a look and they kissed, and Adrian knew she was the one for him.

A year later, back in England, they got married. They honeymooned in Bali before heading to Hong Kong where Adrian had already accepted a job for the broking house I ended up working for eight years later.

They were the kind of couple who always held hands and kissed each other hello and goodbye. I couldn't believe they were having problems.

Though I try to talk about it some more, Adrian's more interested in hearing about my strife. This is typical of him. He's always happier helping someone else than moaning about his own stuff. I take a breath to clear my head and tell him about the loan, that Ratty is becoming extremely threatening and I'm worried someone may get hurt.

"I wish you'd told me when you got back from Hong Kong," Adrian says. "You know I would have helped you out."

"I didn't want to bother you," I say. "A man should handle his own problems."

"But now it's getting out of control. Come round to the restaurant tomorrow, I'll have the money for you."

I thank him, truly grateful, and he smiles. He's gone greyer since that photo in my bathroom, the wrinkles round his eyes have deepened and he's thickened round the middle. The result of ageing speeded up by emotional stress. I wish I could help him as easily as he's helping me.

We order food and eat slowly, not talking much. After, we both have a cigarette and I tell Adrian again how sorry I am Lisa's gone back to Hong Kong, though I think I'm as sorry for myself as for him. My idea of the perfect family has been crushed.

He shrugs, trying to look cool about it, but I can tell he's emotional. Before we leave the restaurant I tell him to call me any time he likes if he needs to talk. He says he will, but I know he won't. Talking about his feelings is not Adrian's idea of fun.

On the Kawasaki, on the way home, I think how tough life is. I thought Adrian had everything, but now he's having problems. You never know when your situation is going to change. In the time it takes for a goldfish to open and close its mouth, your whole world can be turned upside down.

I wonder idly how much goldfish drink.

When I arrive home, still deep in thought, I find we have a little guest.

Lek puts her hands under Samsook's arms and lifts her on to the sofa. She kisses her on both cheeks, breathing in through her nose, before tickling her under her chubby little chin.

"You don mind she stay here tonight?" she says as I walk into the living room.

"We talked about this before," I say gently, but with slight irritation. This is a complication we don't need right now. I really need some peace and quiet.

"So you angry wit me?" says Lek, being over sensitive.

"Not angry," I say, starting to feel my temperature rising. "But we said we didn't think it was a good idea. Not until we got our lives organised. It might confuse Samsook if she's constantly moving from one place to another."

"But it just one night, I won't try for this every week."

"Is this why you need more money?" I ask, the memory of last night's confession springing to the front of my mind. "Is this what sleeping with that guy was all about? Because, in case you hadn't forgotten, we need to pay Ratty. So if you do have any spare cash it should go to him, not to buying Samsook presents."

Lek looks up at me, tears in her eyes. "I hate it when you talk angry wit me."

"Then you shouldn't piss me off," I whisper.

Lek puts Samsook carefully on the sofa and follows me to the bathroom. "So it okay for you to sleep wit other women, but not for me, right?"

"We've talked about this before, you said you wanted to stop."

"You too."

"I know, but someone has to bring in the money."

I'm taking my shirt off, getting ready to shave. I've got to be at The Royal Palm Hotel in an hour to meet a client and I can't skip it. She pays too well. Lek starts pleading her case but I interrupt her.

"We'll talk about this later," I say, massaging the soft white shaving foam into my dark stubble; it looks virgin white against my tan.

Lek comes to stand outside the bathroom door, Samsook cradled and gurgling in the crook of her left arm. She gives me a pained look.

I pull the razor across my face in long gentle strokes. Still looking in the mirror, concentrating on what I'm doing. "Just make sure you don't make a habit of this. You might regret it when she keeps you awake half the night."

I really don't want to upset her. Her life has been tough enough and having Samsook round isn't a problem. If ever a baby had good karma it's this one. She hardly cries at all. But my comment has come out sounding all wrong.

Lek smiles thinly before going back to the living room. I

suddenly feel bad for saying what I did. For Lek, the chance to have Samsook to stay is like a dream come true, she doesn't see her daughter much and she sees her son even less.

Pao was taken away after her divorce. He would be four now, walking and talking, full of life and eager to learn its mysteries. Lek said she couldn't understand why her husband's family took him away and forbade her to see him. A child needs its mother. A mother needs her child. She'd tried many times to make contact but recently they'd moved and she now had no idea where Pao lived.

I wipe my face.

"You can always stay with me," Lek whispers next door. "I won't let anyone take you away."

Lek never had the money to go through the courts, or the time. Besides, with the nature of her job, no judge would see her as a fit mother. It would be a waste of time. Lek's only hope was that one day Pao would find her and she'd be able to explain everything: how his father beat her up, how he lost his job and forced her into working at Queens Castle. How he took all the money she made and spent it on Singh Thip and whores.

"I love you with all my heart," she says to Samsook. The little child's eyes shining happily. "I try to be a good mummy."

I go next door and put my hand on her shoulder.

"Sorry," I say.

Lek had said many times, without humour: one mistake had done all this. Falling in love at school, dropping out and having a baby. It had seemed such fun at the time. But it didn't last. Only now could she smile again with any conviction from her heart. I have to remember this when I get angry. She hasn't had an easy time. And she always forgives me, even though I'm far from a great boyfriend. Forgiveness, I often think, is what it's all about for both of us.

"What time you be home?" she asks me.

"No idea. I have to go round to Adrian's after. He's helping out with the money."

"We wait for you, okay. It don matter how late you are, babe, we wait for you okay?"

I half smile to myself as I slip on my jacket. What a crazy life. Then I laugh. I know Lek's only looking for an excuse to keep Samsook awake, but it doesn't worry me. I'm pleased she's happy and the baby needs to know she's loved. Even if she does end up tired at the end of it all.

Coming out of the bathroom from checking my reflection, I stand behind Lek and stroke my hand down her back as she plays with the baby. I want her to know I'm happy with her decision. She turns to look up at me, her face filling with joy.

"I'll leave you two to play," I say.

Lek twists her neck and gives me a kiss. "You not jealous?"

I laugh, the rest of the tension leaving me, "I'm happy for you, babe. I'll see you when I get home."

"I hope so," she says.

I straighten my suit jacket and as I turn to make my way to the door, I hear the lift bell go. Perfect timing.

"See you, girls," I say over my shoulder.

Chapter Fourteen

I bet Ratty had trouble rounding up a couple of guys. Friday night was not a night to stay sober, nor was it a night to work. Especially for the kind of peanuts he paid.

Ratty's famous for being tight with cash. As a debt collector he has to be. Money's his business. And business, whatever anyone says, is not pleasure.

Ratty also has a temper. No-one wants to handle that before the weekend, unless he spits the dummy at you and forces you into a situation you can't avoid.

So I'm surprised when I open the door to find not only him standing in front of me, but also two other Thai guys. My heart rate kicks up.

"Joshua," Ratty says as friendly as possible, which only serves to make him sound more sinister. "Joshua, you are looking good, no? Going out?"

He has his hand on my chest and is pushing me back into the apartment.

"These are my friends," he says as they follow, towering over him. Almost as tall, but wider than I am.

"Ratty," I say. Trying to crack a smile. "Did Marcus talk to you? I will have the money soon. A month. Two at the most. I can get some of it for you tonight."

"I want today," says Ratty through gritted teeth. The speed he took in the lift rushing to his brain. He pushes me firmly back into the apartment, past the kitchen on my right and into the living area where Lek is kneeling in front of Samsook, bouncing her on the sofa.

"I'm going out to work now," I say. "Let me go to work and I can keep paying you back every month. A bit more, maybe."

"That's not good enough. You've had enough warnings."

Ratty flicks his head at one of the guys, his dreadlocks moving round his neck like long streams of viscous paint.

He advances quickly. His right fist draws level with his chin before punching forward and striking me in the jaw, hard enough to knock me back, but not to break it. I reel from the blow. My eyes roll into my head. My legs crumple like wet bamboo and I tilt back, falling heavily on Lek. She pitches sideways, knocking Samsook off the sofa. They both crash to the floor. The baby rolls on the hard tiles. Lek's mouth falls open, but makes no sound.

The big man bends down and pulls me upright. He hits me twice in the stomach, then in the kidneys, finally elbowing me in the sternum. I'm so dazed I can do nothing to defend myself. Lek cowers on the floor, cradling Samsook in her arms. The baby seems calm, but Lek is scared. Something's not right.

Ratty puts his hand in the air to prevent the man from going further. The apartment, once agitated, becomes still, almost serene. "He's got the message," he says.

Lek watches them blankly. She's in shock. I've stopped groaning. I'm half passed out on the floor.

"One more week," says Ratty, and leaves with his men. They don't wait for the lift. They head straight for the stairs. Their shoes and trainers clattering and squeaking on the tiles.

Minutes later I'm coming to. My vision is blurred but I'm aware Lek is distraught. Without even looking at her, I can feel it.

"What's wrong?" I ask groggily, putting my hand on her leg, the nearest part of her body I can reach. The light on the ceiling seems particularly bright in my eyes.

As I focus I see Lek hunched over a motionless body. I prop myself up on my arm so I can look at her face and find her crying.

"What is it, *tilak*?" I ask. "*Alai?*"

"Look Samsook," she says. "She look strange. Her eyes stay open long time."

I look at the baby. She is breathing normally, but is clearly in shock. Like a china doll. Pretty, but expressionless and vaguely sinister.

"I'll call the doctor," I say, staggering to my feet and rolling like I'm drunk. There is something definitely not right. As I get up a searing pain flashes at my temple. I flinch and rub my hand across it to ease the discomfort. Already the side of my head is swelling.

I phone for an ambulance. Once I've hung up I crouch next to Lek and stroke the baby's head.

"She'll be fine," I whisper to her in Thai. "She had a knock on the head like me. Soon she will be laughing again. You'll see. There is no need to worry."

Silent tears roll down Lek's soft cheeks. Her lip trembles as she tries to speak, but welled up with emotion she gulps and stays silent. Eventually she says,

"She only stay one night... how can this happen? I think Buddha think I very bad girl make do this with me. My baby."

The tears come more quickly. She shakes as she holds her baby, trying to comprehend what happened. Hoping there is no lasting damage.

"I'm so sorry," I say, realising now that if I'd never got us into debt, none of this would have taken place.

Lek sniffs. "We cannot stop what is meant to be," she says quietly. "Sometime good happen, sometime bad. You come to me was good," the tears come stronger again. "This make bad time. It's fair I think."

I put my hand round her stomach, needing to be close to her.

"Don't cry," I say. "She'll be fine. I know she will."

The ambulance arrives ten minutes after my phone call. The two men who call at the door are friendly and efficient. They give Samsook a quick check over; heart, breathing, reflexes, then carry her carefully to the waiting vehicle. Lek and I are allowed to ride in the back with her. I'm also scrutinised for any serious damage, but there is none. I'm bruised and in shock, but nothing worse.

Lek gazes at her baby as the ambulance makes its way west to the Saint Sebastian Hospital. The expression on her face is one of intense concentration, as if she's willing the baby to be undamaged.

Samsook, who has been placed in a cot on the stabilised stretcher, vacantly eyes the roof surface of the vehicle. She doesn't gurgle. She doesn't fidget babyishly. She simply watches, serene and impassive. An impartial participator in life's complex dance.

I watch too, but am far from impartial. A deep panic is setting in, low in my stomach. For every second, every minute Samsook does not blink or move, the dread increases.

I've had this sensation before. The perception that something very bad is happening. I had it when my brother and I were pulled from a car wreck. We were on holiday in Bali. I don't remember much. I recall the Wrangler Jeep coming off the road and that's it. Next thing I was in hospital. After some terrible nightmares, from which I always awoke bathed in sweat, heart hammering, I got up and approached Zack's bed. There were tubes coming out of every part of his body. I knew it was bad. I stared at his face for a long time. It had a ruminative expression, like he was deep in thought. I knelt on the floor and prayed. A while later a nurse came and guided me back to my ward where I relapsed into a coma. A week further on I'd woken up and flew back to London. Zack came too, in the cargo bay, in a black bag.

London was never the same after that. Everywhere I went I was reminded of him. I couldn't walk down streets we'd hung out on. I felt sick in pubs we used to drink in. I avoided our favourite restaurants in Soho and Islington. I was a mess.

When I got a job offer in Hong Kong I went without hesitation. I escaped all the bad thoughts by drowning myself in a new existence that contained booze, drugs, short memory spans and Conrad. I began to accept life was deeply unfair. Events could take a nasty turn, but they could be got through. They could be squared. And, somehow, they made sense.

Zack was a lot like Conrad. He was so hungry for life, he ate it up too fast. By the age of thirty he'd gorged on it so much, he couldn't handle any more. I guess this is why Conrad and I became such good friends. He was a replacement for my dead brother. The same age. The same attitude. The same edge. And I worried like hell about him.

I look again at Samsook, an innocent child who hasn't had time to develop an appetite, let alone get greedy. She's been knocked to the ground by a series of events that don't even concern her... It isn't right. It isn't fair, and I pray that Lek and I will be spared another loss.

Chapter Fifteen

The casualty ward in the Saint Sebastian Hospital is animated with many people in various states of distress. Head wounds, gashed legs and broken fingers are complemented with sounds of muffled moans and groans. Sobbing is soothed by the sympathy of loved ones. Everyone is scared and desperate for attention in this white, hollow space.

Lek and I wait in one corner on a plastic bench while Samsook is taken away to be examined. We sit in silence, both in shock, surveying the spectrum of illness that surrounds us. To take pleasure from life, it is thought, one must first experience pain. But in the Saint Sebastian Hospital, in the casualty ward, there is no pleasure. There are only varying degrees of distress. It slips down the walls like poisonous goo. It drips from the ceiling like thick, contaminated dew.

I stare at the murky tiled floor with dead eyes. The minutes drag out like increasingly faint cries for help.

Finally, after however many hours or minutes I cannot tell, we are called to reception. A white coated and sympathetic doctor, his skin very brown against it, takes us briskly along a wide corridor to a small antiseptic smelling ward.

Inside we walk past several sleeping patients before coming to a cheap plastic cot. Samsook lies inside, a tiny tube snaking from her arm, up to a drip suspended above her. Her eyes remain open and glazed. The steady rhythm of a heart monitor pulses next to her.

"Her condition is at present stable," the doctor says. "She has suffered a blow to the cranium which has caused a fracture and some swelling of the brain. Until the swelling reduces we have no way of knowing what damage has been done. She will have to stay with us, under observation, until we have a clearer picture."

"Will she be okay?" Lek asks.

The doctor is polite but blunt. "She will have some brain damage from a trauma of this kind. It could be very minor. We hope it is very minor. But at this stage, I hope you understand I would not wish to guess. Time will tell."

Lek looks at him intently, "How much time?"

"That is also impossible to say. From my experience it can take days or weeks. It simply depends on the severity of the damage. I'm sorry I can't be more specific."

"Can we sit with her?" I ask.

"You can, yes. For a short time. We recommend that you go home and rest, however. She is in safe hands. You may come back tomorrow."

"Just ten minutes," says Lek. "Is it good to speak to her?"

The doctor nods. "Reassure her everything will be fine. It can help for a baby to hear her mother's voice."

The doctor half smiles and leaves us. Lek moves her head down and kisses Samsook warmly on the forehead. She whispers soothingly to her, reassuring her she will wake up from this dream and everything will be fine.

An hour after the doctor first left us, we retire from the ward and make our way out of the hospital. On the taxi ride home we hold hands but gaze out of opposite sides of the cab.

At home we go to bed in silence, both too shocked to speak.

The next morning I wake early. I lie in bed for some time, thinking of Samsook in her hospital cot, staring, snow blind, at the world. Having sent her good karma, I shower, dress, and busy myself tidying the apartment. Keeping occupied seems to help the worry dissipate. I try to sympathise with how Lek feels. When she gets up at eleven we have a brief chat where I try to reassure her, but she's still in a state of deep shock.

"I can believe what happen," she says.

The irony of her poor English is not funny today.

I give her a hug and tell her the doctors know what they're doing. After a comforting half hour, I tell her I have to go and see Adrian. Getting our financial situation under control is even more important now. She nods, though I'm not sure she's been listening to anything I'm saying.

"Everything will be okay," I say. It sounds pathetic, but it's all I can manage. "I'll be as quick as I can."

Lek says nothing. She simply sits on the sofa and stares at the white tiles.

"See you soon," I say. I take the lift down to the ground floor and walk out into the light. I throw my leg over the bike's saddle and hit the starter, revving the engine before pulling away. Quarter of an hour later, I pull the Kawasaki to a stop outside Adrian's restaurant. A couple of police bikes are parked further up the street.

Nice to see the establishment attracting a good grade of customer.

I wander into the dining area and walk down the central aisle. On either side are two rows of tables made from bamboo. In the corner on the right is a large bar with ten or fifteen stools round it.

"Adrian?" I call out, guessing he's in the kitchen.

I walk down and sit myself at the bar. I seem to spend much of my life hanging around in bars like this, for clients, friends or just inspiration. I light a cigarette and look back up the restaurant. On a sofa in the lounge area a couple are kissing. A Thai guy and a white girl. No matter how many times I see this I'm still shocked. Somehow the equation seems wrong.

The time of day seems wrong. Apart from them, the restaurant is empty. The place feels tense.

Just as I'm finishing my cigarette, Adrian appears through the large, gold-rimmed ogee archway which leads to the kitchen. Two Thai policemen, immaculate in their dark brown uniforms, walk behind him.

"Hey," I say, unable to make my voice sound as light-hearted as I'd like.

Adrian looks at me with a mixture of concern and compassion.

"Josh," he says, his heavily lined brow furrowing. "I wish I had good news for you, but... "

"What?" I say a little too quickly.

The policemen stride past Adrian and through the restaurant.

"We were burgled last night," he says. "They broke into the safe and got away with the cash. We've had the police here all morning. I've had to close the restaurant. We're just doing drinks."

"Christ, I'm sorry," I say. "What is wrong with people? Did anyone see anything?"

"One of the girls who lives upstairs. She heard something early this morning, but no, no-one saw anything. The police think it could be these *falang* again."

"Convenient for them."

"Sure. I'm more worried about you, though. As the situation is now, I don't have any cash."

"Not even in the bank?" I ask.

"All that's gone back for Lisa and the kids this month."

"Adrian," I say, in a strangely calm voice. "I'm in a big situation here, everything's spinning out of control. If I don't come up with something soon, my whole life could be flipped upside down. It's already on its side."

Adrian goes behind the bar, its rows of bottles glinting in the sunlight. He rubs his brow with one of his big, straw veined hands, strengthened from being in the army.

"I'll be able to help you in a week, Josh, ten days maybe, but right now... "

I feel a tightening in my stomach. The slow creep of anxiety up my back.

Sensing my unease Adrian bends down and gets a couple of beers from the stainless steel fridge. Resting them on the bar he clicks the lids off with his opener and pushes one towards me. I clink my bottle against his and take a sip.

"Cheers," he says, giving me a consoling look.

A girl comes out of the kitchen. She's tall, tanned, and has an athletic body. She collects some bottles from behind the bar and disappears again.

"Let's go over your situation again," says Adrian, coming round the bar to sit next to me. "I want all the details this time. Don't leave anything out."

It takes a while to explain everything that's happened in the last few weeks, but when I've finished I already feel more relaxed. Adrian reassures me the hospital won't want any money up front and Ratty can be kept out with a dead bolt that he'll help me fix. He's already put them on his doors.

"He probably won't bother you again for a week anyway. By that time we'll be able to pay him enough to calm him down."

The girl reappears from the kitchen and Adrian calls her over, introducing us. There's nothing left to discuss. We need to move on.

Jane is from New Zealand. Close up she is very good looking with full lips, wide blue eyes and straw blonde hair. She has little freckles on her nose. Her voice is delicate, the accent clear and precise and quietly endearing. I'm instantly drawn to her. She's shy and fragile and looks like she needs a hug. When she speaks she looks at me from under gorgeous long eyelashes. She twiddles a cocktail stick in her fingers.

I ask her how long she's thinking of staying in Bangkok.

"I'm not totally sure," she says. "I've been here a month

and I felt like I was only just getting to know the place. I really like the temples and I'm interested in Buddhism. It's a very calm, beautiful religion, isn't it? I like looking round the temples."

She says temples like 'tinpulls'.

"Wat Po is really good," I say. "Have you seen that one? It's being re-built."

Jane hasn't, so I suggest we go some time.

She seems grateful and keen. She only recently arrived in Bangkok, and doesn't know too many people.

"Where were you before?" I ask.

"Island hopping in the Philippines. I loved it there," she says. "It was so beautiful and unspoilt. But I guess the people were very poor. I liked Sulawesi as well, but the people there had even less."

I tell her about my time in Hong Kong, where everyone had more, but it never seemed enough, while Adrian goes out to the kitchen and fixes us some basic sandwiches.

After we've eaten I feel like Jane's a friend. Her initial reticence has given way to a warm and friendly attitude. I'd like to stay chatting to her for longer, but Adrian is keen to get on. He runs his life like an army schedule.

"That dead bolt won't fix itself," he says, so we say our goodbyes before we take his Jeep back to my apartment, stopping at a hardware store on the way where we buy the lock. It takes half an hour to fit. Once it's done I feel more secure, confident no-one can break the door down. Adrian takes me back to his place to pick up my bike and I head back out on to the hot, black tarmac feeling almost euphoric. Security is a wonderful feeling.

I drive home at speed, beeping my horn in a rare moment of happiness.

When I get in I find Lek sitting in the living room listening to some Thai rock band. She looks isolated and alone, her legs curled up underneath her, her eyes downcast. Even her pretty red summer dress doesn't make the scene any happier. I ask her how Samsook is.

"She the same. Still at hospital." She gets up, her whole body seems very heavy under the strain of the grief. "I get ready to go out," she says. "I have working tonight."

"When do you have to leave?" I ask, sitting on the sofa, pulling her down to join me, anxious to be with her, if only for a while. Sometimes the disappointment of her leaving in the evening makes me melancholy. Chilling on the balcony is dull without her.

She looks at the clock on the wall, staring at it for longer than necessary, as if considering her options. "Half an hour," she says.

"Why don't you skip it tonight? We can stay in, cuddle up."

"We need money," she says. "I have save money for hospital. For help Samsook, you know that."

This comment immediately pricks my male pride. Like a needle in a jellyfish, I flinch, closing up. "You're not going to sleep with anyone are you?" I blurt, before immediately apologising.

Lek shakes her head sulkily.

I hate to think of her working at Queens Castle, but she's right. We need the money. But getting paid for sex is only okay if you're doing it. Not your girlfriend. We kiss and hug on the sofa for a few minutes before she goes to the bedroom to dress for work. I lie back, my arms folded over my chest, an empty feeling creeping up on me.

When she's dressed Lek looks and smells beautiful and I want her to stay home even more. I can see in her eyes she is thinking the same, but there's also a determination there, a mother's powerful need to help her child. I kiss her again and hug her tightly before she heads out the door. I switch on the TV after she's gone and stare blankly at the moving pictures, trying to block out the bad thoughts. After half an hour I begin to feel restless. I start thinking about the financial trouble we're in and Samsook lying in hospital and Lek getting felt up by sweaty Germans.

Eventually the weight of the problems becomes too much. My resolution to remain calm and in control folds. I have to go out.

I get in a tuk tuk and pop pop my way to Koa San Road. I swore I wouldn't go back now that I'd started my new life, but tonight I cannot stay away. I need to see my old drinking partners, to get so drunk with them that I'll forget everything that's going wrong.

The Bangkok street lights blur past. The clambering sound of the city is right up against me but seems far off. When I arrive I smile at the sight of so many old drinking haunts. The open air bars that spill out on to the street. The buzz of travellers getting to know each other. The market stalls selling bootlegged goods. The wandering bar girls, looking to have a good time, and to give one, for cash. Westerners with a bulge of baht in their pockets. It all seems comfortingly familiar.

I pay the tuk tuk driver and head straight for the Buddy Beer, its yellow sign welcoming and warm. This is where I used to drink with Marcus, where we got to know each other. He was different then. He smiled more and slept better.

"Namkeng, song Coke, Singh Thip," I say to the girl working behind the bar. It's been so long since I've been here, I don't recognise her. I used to know all the girls, but now they've moved on, some to better lives, some to worse.

I sit next to the aviator sized fan and pour myself a whisky, adding plenty of ice, but not too much Coke. I look round at the faces. The tanned and the pale. The long stayers and the new arrivals. Bangkok has a lot to offer. Some will get lost here and not make their flights. Some will get a bad habit and sell their passports. Some will laugh at its pull and move on. Whatever, it will change us, the way it's changing me. The experience of Thailand is one that's hard to forget. No matter how easy you take it abnormal becomes normal here and normal will never be the same. The stereo plays a Mariah Carey album. I've heard it so often I almost like it, kind of illustrating my point. I drink through this.

I watch the people come and go. Halfway through the first bottle I suddenly think: coming out here again was a mistake. I don't belong any longer, but it's like there's nowhere else for me to go and I feel safe here at the bar, if alone.

When I can hold my bladder no longer I go to the loo. In the urinal there's a scattering of white balls to keep it fresh. They look like Mint Imperials. I'm tempted to reach in and put one in my mouth to freshen myself up. As I piss I look down at them and laugh. I know my mind is becoming distorted.

When I'm done, I zip up and grab the door handle to leave. The guy standing at the urinal next to me says,

"En France, nous lavons les mains après."

"In England," I tell him, "we don't piss on them in the first place."

He has the good grace to laugh.

I walk back to the bar and order another bottle of Singh Thip. The girl puts the pink slip in the green plastic holder.

"Thanks," I say.

I pour myself another full glass with a dash of Coke. As I drink it down I wonder why I feel happiest when I've drunk myself into a state of helplessness, like a six-month-old baby, or a pensioner with Alzheimer's. When I look most depressed to the outside world: a drunk with hooded eyes, slurred speech, unable to do anything except drink, I am happiest. Are babies happy, are old people? They're not. That's why they moan and scream. But as an adult we're not allowed to cry and wet ourselves to command attention, so we do the next best thing. We get drunk and pray for something good to happen…

When I'm on my third bottle of self-delusion, Cho arrives. He's as integral to Koa San as any of its bars. Cho has one great attribute. He looks like Elvis before he got into the pep pills and fried cheese sandwiches. He dresses in Hawaiian shirts (when he's not bare chested, sweating from the booze) and has an American accent, courtesy of seven years in a Californian jail. Manslaughter. He wasn't guilty, he was set up, a patsy.

"Man," he says falling against my shoulder, grinning down at me, the air from the aviator fan ruffling his short dark hair, cut with a razor. "Man. Where you been?"

"Just living," I say, ordering another bottle of Singh Thip, slapping him on the back. "Sit, man. Have a drink."

If there's a guy in Bangkok who'll never refuse a drink, it's Cho. Right up to the point he falls flat on his face and passes out, he'll have one. I've seen him, perfectly cool on a high bar stool, minding his own business, drinking away. Then suddenly he'll go, like an invisible explosive has been detonated and sent him tumbling. Seconds before he can appear lucid, doing controlled karate moves with his hands, talking them through, and then... he's gone. Lost in the drinks cabinet in his head. To look at him some days, you'd think he was a bar room brawler. Nothing could be further from the truth. Cho wouldn't hit anyone. He's placid, like the panda his eyes sometimes recall. I once saw him drink eight days straight. His insides must be a mess. I'm concerned for the severity of his hangovers.

"How've you been?" I ask.

"Drunk, man," he laughs. "Why not?"

I once asked why he drank so much. It was a difficult question to answer. He was happier talking about the fret work of Steve Vai, or the three cars he had at home in his garage. But this one night he said to me in a low tone, "I have a lot family problems, man. That's it. A lot family problems. My dad. He hates me, man."

He spent plenty of time asking English girls if they'd like to live with him in his house in West Bangkok. There were never too many takers. Cho is a great guy, but he's an alcoholic, which doesn't feature too heavily on most girls' wish list. But what they didn't know, was that he's rich. Quite how nobody knew, but he had cash.

After some back chat about fellow drinkers, Cho starts telling me about this beautiful Swedish girl he met. He's in love again, I can tell. His alcohol frosted eyes go milky with booze and lust. A good combination, I always think, the mixture of the pain of love and the pain of booze. That's a difficult one to beat. That's masochism, and Cho, I know, is a masochist. You couldn't drink for eight days straight if you weren't.

"She stay at my house this week," he says, slurring his words. "She stay at my house, but today she's gone, man. I don't know where."

"That's bad," I say.

"Yeah, man," he nods. "Yeah."

I tell him about Samsook. He says that's bad too. "Can you help with the money?" I say. I'm drunk and bold enough to ask. "I hate to ask, man, but..."

"For sure, man," he says straight away. He's drunk enough to say it. "For sure."

I think he means it, though. I've bought Cho a million drinks when we've been out. He may be rich, but he always runs out of baht mid session.

We arrange to meet the next day then we carry on drinking. I like being with Cho. His light-hearted banter takes me to a world of bright lights and sunshine. Not many people can do that for me these days. Despite this, in the early hours my sense of responsibility returns and I drag myself away.

When I arrive home the sun is already coming up. Its red and yellow and silver rays finger the balcony. I get an orange juice from the fridge and walk outside. I take my shirt off and sit, sipping from the glass. Lek is asleep in our bed. I smoke endless cigarettes while I think of her soft brown flesh against those white sheets, soon to be joined by my paler skin. I hope my flesh is more comforting to her than the cotton. I hope it is. I need it to be.

As I sober up, guilt and regret begin to set in, like dry rot in the brain. It starts off patchy, but then spreads through my whole consciousness. I shouldn't have gone out. I should have been with my girlfriend all along, comforting her. Earlier the booze drowned this feeling out; now it's insistent, constant. I think again how our minds level life out. For every up, we create a down. Manic depressives feel this most keenly. They get their portions of ups and downs in six month helpings. Large ones too. Insane joy, followed by wretched depression and self loathing. The rest of us receive the daily half measures of both. What goes up... Newton's law of gravity, also the quantity theory of pleasure and pain.

I've had my fun. Now it's time to pay.

I flick my cigarette end over the balcony railing and head inside to bed.

Chapter Sixteen

When I wake the next morning Lek is pissed off, just like I expected. When I reach out for her in bed she rolls away. I try to talk to her but she ignores me, burying her head in the soft white pillow. I shouldn't have gone out when her daughter is lying in hospital. I apologise, but she shrugs it off. Hoping to placate her, I say I think I've solved our money problems. She's not impressed, telling me it shouldn't have taken all night to sort that out.

"And you don have to drink to find money," she says. "I worry when you come home late."

I try again to convey my remorse, wincing at how terribly empty my words sound.

"I have enough worry already," she says.

I try to give her a hug, but she brushes me off, getting out of bed and locking herself in the bathroom. She has the longest shower I remember her having, possibly in an attempt to use up all the hot water. Wisely, I decide to skip my morning wash and instead fix some papaya salad and egg fried noodles. Lek reprimands me for making the salad with too few chillies. I agree with her, offering to add more, but she refuses.

After breakfast, we go to the hospital. She puts her arms round my waist as I accelerate away from our apartment on the Kawasaki. She does this not with fondness, but for security. The hot wind fans her hair out. From above it would look like a black scarf, swirling round her face. Though her silky hair is something I love, today its blackness is indicative of her mood, and the tendrils that sometimes hit my cheeks remind me of it.

I feel the heat of the exhaust moving up round my legs, under my shorts. Lek has had many moped accidents and has circular dark scars on her calves where the exhaust has landed on her. When I first met her I thought she had some rare skin complaint but I didn't love her any less. If you love someone, you handle their quirks and possibly come to love them too.

You also handle their moods.

When we arrive at the Saint Sebastian we go straight to Samsook's ward, on the third floor, and stare down at her tiny form in the plastic cot. She's still as a sculpture, her skin paler than before. She looks lost.

When we find the doctor he tells us there's been no change. Lek talks to Samsook in encouraging tones. I speak to her also in English, wondering if something different to what she's used to will bring her out of Ratty's spell.

It's several hours before I can convince Lek to take a breather. We go on the bike to a cafe near the murky brown roaring river where we eat noodles.

I have several beers to calm my raging hangover. Lek cries and I put my arm round her. To take her mind off things we go down to the water and feed bread to the fish. We throw white chunks into the brown water. The bread looks like croutons floating in onion soup. In seconds there is a torrent of activity and the water is alive with silvery, seething scales and thrashing tails, the fish coming up to feed.

Lek smiles for the first time since the trauma. I kiss her and hug her again but it isn't long before her expression clouds over and her stare becomes glazed. I don't know what to say. We return to the hospital. Time moves slowly.

Hours later, when we're back at home we both take our own space. Lek goes to bed while I sit on the balcony with an orange juice. We found another broken bike on the way home and sent it to the TCC by tuk tuk, but it only lifted our mood for a brief moment.

Smoking as I look at the stars, I think back to happier times, to when we first met.

I'd woken late in the day and decided to go to Lumphini Park to relax and lie in the sun. I needed to escape the hectic city. Lying on the grass, staring up at the bright blue sky, I could block out the hustle and feel calm. The sound of the motorbikes roaring past on the Expressway didn't annoy me. It was good to know the rest of Bangkok carried on while I stopped.

On the way to the park, I called in at a street stall to buy noodles with beef and fried egg. Two girls approached the counter at the same time. They giggled and nudged each other. I smiled and waited for my food while the girls carried on giggling.

Eventually one said, in broken English, 'Our friend, she see you many time.'

I looked at the girl. She was young and skinny and her hair was long and shiny, like she had too much time to spend on it. I thought she might be beautiful when she reached her twenties.

'Who is your friend?' I had asked back in Thai, creating more excitement.

The girl pointed in the direction of the park. 'She sits over there and eats her lunch every day. She sometimes sees you. She thinks you're very handsome.'

I strained my neck to see, but the row of benches was blocked by a hedge and some palms. 'Is she pretty?' I asked.

'She is beautiful. Why don't you go and talk to her?'

I thought for a minute. I didn't have any plans for the day. Meeting a girl who fancied me could be cool. 'Okay,' I said. 'How will I know which one is her?'

'You will know,' the friends laughed.

'How?'

'I think she will be smiling.'

The girls waved me off, their brown hands blocking the sunlight. A couple of steps away from them, I turned and said, 'What's her name?'

'Her name is Lek,' came the reply in unison. 'In Thai mean small.'

I turned and carried on walking.

When I rounded the corner and entered the lush green of Lumphini Park, my heartbeat increased. I was used to meeting new women every night, but this was different. Here, I would not be expected to behave like a gigolo. I'd have to be myself, something I was finding increasingly hard to do.

As I walked towards the row of wooden benches, I scanned those seated there. Amongst the ten or so people, one girl stood out.

It wasn't anything she was wearing, or how she looked. It was a feeling I got when I looked at her. Sitting very upright, she looked directly at me and smiled a radiant and warm smile that was so uninhibited it took me completely by surprise. It was as if we'd been great friends for years.

Feeling my legs go weak, I walked over and sat down next to her.

Before I could say anything, she said in Thai, 'I've seen you many times in this park. Every day I see you, I feel happy. Any day I do not, I feel sad. I think you look like a friendly man. But shy. I wanted to talk with you before, but you never see me.'

'I've never seen you before,' I said, touched at her openness and suddenly realising how attractive she was.

'So I know you a little bit,' she smiled, 'and you don't know me at all.'

I smiled back at her. Since I'd sat down, the girl had kept unwavering eye contact. It was sucking me in. I felt like my mind was entering a safe place. 'What do you know about me?' I asked.

'I know you like noodles,' she said, taking my hand tenderly in hers, making my heartbeat faster. 'I know you speak Thai. I know sometimes you like to drink beer. Sometimes you look sad. You don't have a girlfriend.'

I felt overcome. I'd never been spoken to like this before. This girl cared for me deeply without ever having spoken to me. Purely on sight, she had found some connection.

'Three months ago I first see you and my heart,' she rolled her eyes and shook her head, 'it goes crazy. I don't know why. You are handsome. But it was more than that.'

'Why didn't you say hello?'

'I'm shy,' she said. 'I was hoping you would speak to me.'

'I'm sorry.'

'It's no problem now,' Lek smiled. 'We are talking already.' Her fingers intertwined with mine. She put her hand on my leg and kissed my cheek. 'I had to speak to you today otherwise I think I might die!'

I smiled. 'This is incredible,' I whispered. 'It feels like a dream.'

'For me too.'

We sat there holding hands until it got dark. Neither of us spoke about our jobs. Instead we talked about Bangkok, about Lek's family and how she'd been married before, when she was very young. I told how I'd left London for the Far East, very confused and alone.

We'd both made mistakes, but we were decent people, struggling to get by.

When we left Lumphini Park, we took a tuk tuk to Lek's apartment in Ekamai. It seemed a natural thing to do. We drank several bottles of Singha and talked more. Lek said she had dreamt many months before ever seeing me that she would meet and fall in love with an Englishman.

We kissed after that. The dim table lamp cast shadows over our faces and the smell of joss sticks wafted over us. Lek felt impossibly soft and giving in my arms. There was a relief when I kissed her, like she was an antidote to all my pain. She felt the same, she said. Kissing me was like returning home after a long day. It was familiar and comforting. She wondered how she'd made it through life this far without me.

I smile at the memory, feeling an overpowering need to be with Lek. I take my clothes off and wander into the bedroom. Lek is lying on her back under the white sheet, her little nose peeping over the top. I walk over, pulling the sheet back to reveal the smooth curves and exciting undulations of her naked body. I lie on the bed next to her and pull her towards me. She rolls over, still asleep, her arm falling carelessly over my side. Her mouth is very close to mine now. I can feel her breath on my cheek.

"Lek," I whisper very quietly. "What are you dreaming about?"

Her eyelids flutter like a butterfly's wings but she doesn't stir.

"Lek," I whisper again. "Come here."

I pull her closer. We're both on our sides. Our knees touching, our thighs touching, our hips, our stomachs, our chests. I feel myself becoming rapidly hard.

I look at her sweet face in the half light and touch my lips against hers. I kiss her gently, running my fingers through her hair, tracing a hand over her cheek.

I put my hand on her shoulder and gently roll her on to her back. Lek is a good sleeper. I need to wake her gently. I look down at her. My hand moves slowly from her neck, over the swelling of her breast, lingering on the tightening nipple and down her soft stomach, before reaching between her legs. I part the folds of flesh with my first two fingers and gently massage with my third. Some of the moves are the same as with a client, but the feeling is totally different.

So much more arousing. Loving, after all, is ninety-nine percent in the mind.

Lek sleeps on, though her breathing becomes more rapid.

I say in an almost inaudible whisper, full of irony, "You are about to make love to the stud of the century. The best lover in the whole world. I can do things to you that will make you think you're in heaven."

I laugh to myself, enjoying my own joke.

My hand keeps working away for several minutes. Very, very gently.

As it moves, I change position. Extending my left arm I raise myself off the mattress and position myself above my girlfriend, between her legs. I let my hand stop what it's doing (do I fully control it?) and simply hold myself above her. My legs between hers, my arms either side of her head.

I look down at her and wait. I wonder how long it will be before she admits she's awake.

I slowly lower myself down and kiss her on either cheek.

"If you want me to carry on," I say, "you should do something so I know you want me to."

Nothing happens for maybe thirty seconds. I wait, poised above her. As my arms begin to tire I feel a soft, delicate hand move up my thigh to my buttocks.

I smile to myself. She's such a tease.

"Okay," I whisper. "You asked for the full treatment."

Her hand goes back down to her side on the mattress and I lower my mouth to her neck, kissing it very gently for several minutes. Lek is trying hard to be cool, but I know she's loving it. Her neck is her weak spot.

My mouth traces over her skin to her right breast, biting the distended nipple. Lek doesn't react. I bite a little harder. I see a faint smile come to her lips.

We often play like this. It's a game of patience.

I linger on her breasts for some time, occasionally returning to her neck, licking both sides. Then I begin to kiss down her stomach. Just as I'm about to go further, my tongue flicking the start of her pubic hair, I deny her the pleasure and roll her on to her front.

"I have to kiss your beautiful back," I say, to tease, "before anything else can happen."

I'm trying to coax her into saying something, but she's a stubborn girl. She can wait, if she has to. She can wait if it shows she has the upper hand.

I kiss her neck again, from behind, then lie my body on her back and do nothing. Again I'm trying to get her to talk to me, but I know I'll lose. Like this, Lek will be quite happy to go back to sleep. So I lie like this for three, maybe four minutes, doing nothing before my libido gets the better of me.

"So you're playing hard to get?" I say, grabbing myself.

"Hard?" she whispers.

"You're awake!" I say, flipping her over.

"Yes, I just wake up," she says.

I laugh out loud. "You are such a tease." I put my hand between her legs and find an oasis of warmth. "Shall I put it in now?" I ask.

"If you want."

"Do you want?"

"Maybe."

"Or do you want to sleep?"

"Maybe."

"Or do you want me to drive you wild?"

"I don understand this. You want drive me like a motorbike?"

I push myself inside. "Like this," I say.

Lek gasps and smiles, her pupils dilating. "Like this I like," she says. "But no quick quick, okay?"

"This could take all night," I say and I sink it slowly, very slowly, into her until my pelvis rests on hers.

Lek groans. It takes some time – forever – before we

come. I have controlled the whole show like always. I'm good at this. I'm a pro. But with Lek it's not for show. It's for her. It's for love.

Chapter Seventeen

The next morning Lek goes to the hospital and I try to get hold of Cho on his never answered phone. I pace round the apartment constantly hitting redial and becoming increasingly frustrated as the ring tone jeers at me. To fill time and block out bad thoughts, I play loud rock music and shadow box, sparring my way from the living room to the balcony, then to the bedroom. Coming up to midday, someone knocks at the door. My heart rate, already high from the exercise, immediately jumps into my mouth.

I move into the apartment from the balcony clutching a bottle of Singha, ready to swing if it's Ratty. Reaching the door I look through the fish eye lens. With a fish eye the world expands and distorts, exactly what I feel is happening to my own life. It takes me a couple of seconds to focus.

As my eye becomes accustomed to the new perspective, I'm relieved to see it's not Ratty standing there, but my sense of gratitude soon swerves to a different emotion when the figure at the door moves forward an inch and becomes more clear. The person at the barrier to my private life is someone else I don't want to see from my past.

"I know you're there, Josh," I hear the lisping voice say. "Come on," it continues seductively, "open the door."

I think about ignoring the voice but I know it won't go away. The incessant phone calls. The badgering in the clubs. The harassment in the streets of Pat Pong. When this girl

The Body is a Temple

wanted to be with someone, she really went for it.

I pull the dead bolt on the door, then flick the catch and let the girl in.

"My God," I say as she brushes past. "You're fat as a whale."

"I pregnant," she says.

She goes straight to the fridge and gets a Coke, before slumping on the sofa.

I stand in the kitchen, pulling hard on my cigarette. "So," I say. "What can I do for you?"

Jiab smiles. She's an attractive girl with a rinky dinky nose and a fun mouth, but she's evil. It's why I never returned her calls. She moves closer, taking my hand.

"Josh, I need you help," she says.

She smiles again, the corners of her mouth curling at the edges. She looks like Jack Nicholson's Joker from *Batman*. I don't want to help her. All she'd ever done was flirt outrageously with me in front of Lek and tried to convince her we'd slept together.

She explains I wouldn't be helping her, but the baby, and the three children she had before this one.

"Don't you think it's time you considered some form of birth control?" I say. "Like the pill?"

"I don't like. Make me fat," she says.

I look at her swollen stomach and can't help laughing. "Okay," I say. "That's up to you."

"Yes. I think so. I like have baby. I love my children."

"You never see them as far as I can remember."

"I love them." Her expression is one of hurt. She fiddles round in her leather handbag and extracts a Polaroid, grasped between scarlet nails, perfectly painted. She holds it up for inspection.

"See? Me. And three lovely children."

I look at the photo. Jiab holds a baby with huge brown eyes and a mop of jet black curls. There's a little boy, hugging her leg and an older girl, maybe five, holding her hand. Their skin is like milky coffee. They all have a narrow nose. They all have a Western father, but not the same one. They're beautiful children, born into a very uncertain world.

"You still haven't told me why you're here," I say.

"Yes. I here because I need find Marcus. I need he number telephone. He address. The baby. The baby is Marcus."

I'm incredulous. I guess she's joking but for the sake of brevity I simply ask her if she believes Marcus will give her a cash hand out.

Jiab's expression darkens. Like a mounting storm. "You what?" she asks. "You think he can fuck me for free when he want and no pay for the baby?"

"You're a bar girl," I say. "You sleep with hundreds of guys a year."

"Yes, wit condom. But wit Marcus, no. You asshole."

She's standing up now, jabbing me in the chest. I pretend I don't know where Marcus lives and she goes crazy, lashing out and screaming. It takes considerable strength to hold her back. She tries to bite my arm and kicks out at my legs.

She shouts until her tan face is purple with rage. Finally she gives me a good punch in the stomach and struts for the door. "You wait," she says turning on me. "You wait. When I find him, I kill him. An I kill you too. You fucking *falang*. Asshole! Asshole! Fucking shit!"

And then she's gone and I'm left in a state of shock. I pick up my phone to call Marcus and then decide it's not worth it. She's just a crazy girl trying to get some fast cash. There's no need to worry him. If she ever did find him, he'd be more than able to handle it. I don't believe he slept with her and even if he did, she'd never make the story stick. I take a final drag on my cigarette, stub it out and, while I've got the phone, give Cho another try. He's still not answering. I get on my bike to find him.

I go to his house first, just outside Banglampoo, a large

unkempt dwelling with a roof in need of repair, a broken window on the first floor and a lawn that is overgrown like a scrappy meadow. Cho's money does not get spent on DIY.

I wander past the garage and look round the property. Of course he's not there. I peek in to see his three cars. There are none. Sold for booze, I guess. I bang on both doors for some time and peer in all the downstairs windows, crunching round the broken pieces of bamboo and palm, lying around like outsize salad spoons, but there's no sign of him. I even call his name once or twice, but I know he's not in residence. If he was, I would feel it. I would sense his slumbering presence.

Getting back on the Kawasaki, I tour slowly round the Banglampoo area, glancing in the bars, scanning the pavements dotted with food stalls, and even making sure to check the passengers in tuk tuks. One guy I see I think is Cho, but as I draw level with him I realise it's not even a Thai guy, but a tourist with an identical short haircut and deep tan.

After half an hour I park up and investigate Koa San on foot. The jerkiness of walking feels strange after the smooth glide of the Kawasaki. As I walk I nod to acquaintances but refuse the offers of drinks. I don't have time today.

This padding around reminds me of my teenage years in London. My parents were often still at work when I got home, so I'd head out on the tube, just pick a stop on the map, ride the train out there and explore the unfamiliar streets. I liked the unknown even then. I liked the freedom of it, the possibility that just round the next corner there'd be someone or something that'd change my life forever. Usually, of course, there wasn't. But you never knew. There was always hope.

I'm convinced Cho is not in Koa San so I head to Nana Plaza and the bars round Pat Pong. Here the market place is littered with scaffold poles not unlike fallen branches. People mill about, browsing shop windows and restaurant menus, but still Cho is nowhere to be seen. I move on to the outer areas of Sukhumvhit, spending an hour touring round, asking people in bars if they've seen him, before admitting it's not my day and heading home.

As I scream back to my apartment I yell with all my strength, "Cho, where the fuck are you?"

I get some startled looks from some Thai pedestrians, their faces question marks and exclamation marks simultaneously, but feel better having vented my frustrations. At home I phone him twice more, but without success. Feeling desperate, I go to the hospital, praying on the way for good news.

"She the same," Lek says after a long pause. My heart sinks. I put my arm round her but she draws away and scowls at me. I wonder what I've done to upset her now.

"I know what you thinking," she says. "I know you thinking I no bring her aparment, better. You say many time no bring her."

I tell her I wasn't thinking that at all but it doesn't do any good.

"I know I bad mummy," she says, tears springing to her dark eyes, making them look bigger. I don't know what to do. Her grief is turning to guilt. Her mind is beginning to torture her with 'what ifs'. I hug her again, hoping I can absorb some of her pain. She buries her head in my chest this time. I feel my tshirt slowly become damp from her tears. After a while her body gives in to heaving sobs. She doesn't say anything more, her throat choked with emotion. I don't speak, either. I simply stare at the white tiles, and the little hairline cracks beginning to appear in them.

Chapter Eighteen

Sometime later, it's hard to say how long, I take her home on the bike, driving slowly so as not to alarm her. I make us some pad thai with chicken and we eat in silence. Lek takes very small deliberate mouthfuls, her jaw on autopilot. It's an effort for her to eat. I think the stress has tightened and shrunk her stomach.

Eventually she says, "I lose one baby already. I think my heart die if I lose again. I always lose."

She's on the brink of tears again. I don't know what to do.

"Why don't you have a shower?" I suggest after a pause that is so long I wonder if I've blacked out at some point. "I always feel better after a shower."

Lek gets up without speaking and soon I hear the angel tap dancing of water hitting the tiles in the bathroom, then the heavier slosh as it falls off her body in more sustained amounts. I pick up the phone and call Cho's house. To my amazement he answers the phone.

"Come on over, man," he says. "We can get the money in the morning, when the bank's open, okay?"

I'm torn. I should really stay with Lek but we need the money. If I leave Cho at home on his own, he'll completely forget our conversation, get bored and go out, not to be seen again for several days.

When Lek comes out of the shower I explain I have to go out. She looks at me with resignation, but not anger. "You get drunk again," she says in a tone as flat and cold as an ice rink.

"No, I'm going to get us the money."

"From Cho?" she laughs, or rather scoffs. "You think we can get from that coconut head?"

I tell her it's our only choice. Reluctantly, she tells me to go.

"In the morning I at hospital," she says, hardly accepting my kiss. "I meet you there."

When I arrive at Cho's house, I find a party in progress with the usual continuous bombarding of the senses that such events provide. There are some dodgy looking Thai characters covered in tattoos in his living room with their shirts off, smoking a drain pipe size bong. A few tanned European girls are sprawled on the sofa, their bare legs intertwined, like pretzels, clearly stoned. In the basic kitchen (just two gas hobs run off a rusty tank and a table with four chairs, cupboards with broken doors) I find Cho. His right hand combs through a girl's Bardot blonde hair. I can't see her face because it's buried in his chest, laughing. "Cho," I say, making his glazed eyes swivel towards me. I hold out my hands but say no more.

He puts his arms up and yells, "We're having a party man. Everybody welcome! Here have a drink!"

I take the bottle of Singh Thip and pour myself a glass. It's going to be a long night. The amphetamines in the whisky will help me stay awake.

Cho turns up the stereo. Pumping, hardcore reggae. "Come and give me a kiss, man! Forget all your troubles! Hey, meet my girlfriend. Isn't she beautiful?" He spins the girl on his knees, so I can see her face. She has a good tan to go with her blonde hair, but she isn't what I'd call pretty. Her face is too long and her nose too wide, but she has nice blue eyes with flecks of sunflower.

"Hi," she says with that peculiar Northern European accent, all the words sounding too short, even 'hi'. She extends a slim hand attached to a gangly arm. I shake it, and swig my drink. I suddenly realise how smoky the room is.

The Body is a Temple

"Cho, can I talk to you for a second?" I ask and help his girlfriend off his lap.

"Sure man," he says, tipping forward slightly after the sudden release of weight. "Sure."

I remind him of why I've come and say we definitely need to get to the bank first thing in the morning. He reassures me this is no problem. "So we'll stay here?" I say. "We won't go anywhere tonight?"

"We don need to go anywhere," he says, pointing to the beer and whisky that litter the table and dirty floor. "We have enough here." The night drags on. I used to relish this kind of party. Now I find it hard work. I'd rather be in the park with Lek, or on the balcony at home. To take the edge off the boredom – all the travellers' stories – I drink more Singh Thip. The seconds go by like millimetres and the minutes like miles. For a while I doze on one of the bare mattresses upstairs before a French girl comes up and starts yabbering on to me about how great 'E's are. I nod and agree and say, yes, *oui*, and it's the best thing and think (despite my cynicism and with some sadness) she's probably right. We do have the best times of our lives on drugs, and when we get married and have kids and get all serious about our lives all we'll do is lie to other people about how great we feel, but inside we'll be crying and secretly wishing we could get hold of another kind of pill, one that wouldn't make us feel like shit in the morning but would give us the necessary enthusiasm to make it through talking to our families who we love but also secretly hate sometimes, whilst wishing we were still twenty, even though we hated being that age too, despite getting laid more often with better looking girls, but we didn't really like them, either, did we, and we start to wonder, when, in fact, we did have a good time and then… and then the sad realisation that perhaps life is not a river of tears, as is popular thought, but a waterfall, and then…

"Have another beer," says Cho who's appeared out of

nowhere. I rub my eyes and look up at him. "What you thinking about man?" he yells at me over the music which has now reached club level. And I yank myself out of this abseiling thought.

"Money," I yell back, knowing he'll understand.

He smiles back at me, his white teeth cracking open the brown Elvis face. "We'll get it tomorrow, man," he says, his face very close to me. "We'll get it tomorrow." Cho doesn't allow us to stay in. The litres of beer and whisky soon get drunk and we're out in Pat Pong, in the all night bars, drinking more. I'm powerless to stop it.

"Cho," I say as I slump at one of the open air bars, head just about up.

"No." The girl next to me smiles, having misheard me say 'Cho'. "No, what?" she asks.

"Just no," I say. I can't see straight now. I'm looking for Cho, but I can't see him. All I can see is hazy lights, blurred bodies.

"You want another beer?" the girl asks. Through the glaze she looks alluring. Bucked teeth and large breasts.

I nod. "Why not?" I say.

The girl laughs and attracts the bar man's attention with a yell of "*Sawat-di Kah!*" I stare at the bar. "Why the fu no?" the girl says and pushes a beer in my direction. I drink and drink. We go from bar to bar, all I notice are wood bar tops and bottles backlit behind the staff. I don't see Cho for a long time. The sun begins to come up. Its bright rays hurt my eyes. Eventually I find Cho at the Beer Garden, a quad of open air bars, and the flow of the night stops.

"Let's go," I say. "The banks will open soon."

He gives me the panda eyed look and carries on drinking.

At ten I slap him round the face. A hard whap, which seems to bring him round. "Let's go," I say.

We leave the bar and take a tuk tuk back to his house. The Swedish girl is not with us. It's just me and Cho. I find his cash card and take him to the bank at the end of Koa San, on the main road with the monument. It looks bright at night when it's all lit up but during the day it's nothing. It looks like a fallen angel with crumpled wings.

I get Cho to put his card in the ATM. It rejects it. I take him into the bank with a fear so intense it sobers me up. The cashier is all smiles. The inverse, exactly, of what I'm feeling. I'm finding it hard to tolerate the hot sun, the bright light, the chance stuff will turn out okay, then the disappointment when it doesn't.

"Good morning, Sir," she says to Cho.

He tells her he needs to withdraw some money. She looks at his panda eyes with amusement as if to say, 'You have got to be kidding me.' But he hands over his card, and after a computer check, during which I feel my buttocks tighten, my eyes narrow and my brain boil, the money is counted and handed over.

Cho puts it in my hand. It should be enough to keep Ratty off my back for another month.

"Thanks, man."

"No problem," he says. "Let's go for a beer, yeah?"

I shake my head. "I need to get home."

There are large beads of sweat on Cho's forehead. I consider how his liver's doing. I wonder, briefly, if I can hear it screaming. The thought is trippy and it lingers in my mind. Cho's liver crying for help, help, help.

"I'll call you later," I say, laughing. "Go find your girlfriend."

"Yeah," he says, looking over his shoulder as we exit the bank, back on to the glowing street. "Where is she? Where she go?"

I hail a brightly coloured tuk tuk, its silver metal work looking like harps, and before it buzzes me away to a world far worse even than the one I've just been in, with more troubles and heartache, I ask, "Looking for love?" And we pull away, me and the driver, and I see, before he's out of sight, that Cho doesn't register the irony in my question, and I laugh hollowly, but with sympathy. "Love, Cho," I mutter. "Keep looking."

Chapter Nineteen
Hong Kong. The Recent Past. Part II

On the fourth evening of my trip back to Hong Kong, I showered and dressed for dinner with Sophie. I wasn't so obsessed about showering back then. I liked to be clean and fresh, but being under the water didn't satisfy some deep psychological need. I wasn't screwed up yet.

I was looking forward to our date. After three hours of listening to Conrad babbling on the beach I felt I needed to get away from him. I'd nearly threatened to fly back to Thailand, but decided I couldn't. He would have only begged me to stay, and that would have been embarrassing. As I was preparing to leave I told him not to do anything stupid. He promised me he wouldn't, but that's what everybody says isn't it? When a mother leaves her teenage son alone in the house for the first time and says, 'do your homework, don't play on the computer,' the kid always says, 'of course, mum, see you later.' Then he does five minutes of homework, till she's well up the road in her Audi, and turns the computer on and selects Tomb Raider, or logs on for porn.

I double-checked with him.

'I'm not doing a thing,' he said. 'I may be jumpy as a fish that's just been pulled from a river, but no, I'm not doing anything tonight. Mind you, twenty thousand dollars can go a long way, you know. Anywhere in South East Asia apart from here, I could live for months on that. I need that money.'

I said we'd get it to him somehow, closed the door and headed off down the concrete path, the sound of cicadas filling my ears.

When I arrived at The Blue Elephant, Sophie was already seated, sipping a glass of white wine.

'You look shattered,' she said. 'But I can guess why.' She knew hanging out with Conrad could be exhausting. She and I had done it many times when we were together and it always took her a few days to recover.

'I've decided what we're having,' she said as I sat down, so you don't need to bother looking at the menu.'

This made me smile. Sophie always liked to be in control.

I sipped the beer which arrived seconds after me, leaning back on the padded bench. We were in a very private little booth. The light above our table was surrounded by a stained glass shade and didn't give out much light. Scanning the dining room, I realised we were one of only three other couples. It felt almost like being at a private dinner party. Perhaps the trend for Thai food had abated.

I sat back and rubbed the back of my neck, relaxing now it was obvious we could have a quiet meal.

Sophie did most of the talking before our starters arrived, getting very animated. She was definitely on better form. Her piercing green eyes were constantly wide and she laughed easily, sometimes running a hand through her hair as she put her head back to let the giggles bubble out of her. I listened, quietly sipping my beer, enjoying her stories, trying to remember some of the times she was talking about. Sophie, unlike me, had a great memory.

'Do you remember when we went up The Peak and we missed the last tram down?' she giggled.

'Oh, yeah. We tried to walk it, didn't we?'

'Not a good idea,' she laughed. 'Those shoes I ruined were

expensive too.'

'It was your idea,' I said.

'But I was drunk. You should have stopped me.'

Having spent the day wandering around the roads of The Peak checking out the sprawling houses, we'd left it too late to get the tram back down to Central. We decided to have a meal at one of the restaurants near the look out area, and worry about it after. On the way we got distracted first by the bustling aerial view of Hong Kong Island fully lit in the darkness and then by an intricate water fountain. At first glance, it was simply spot lit holes bored in a raised concrete slab, but when it was switched on, the water would jump from one hole to another in a dizzying array of patterns that soon became hypnotic. Soph and I watched it until our stomachs started to rumble and we had to eat.

In the busy restaurant we had an English style pub meal, washed down with several bottles of wine. After, we attempted to follow the line down. It was way too steep and we eventually had to give up, taking a taxi instead. But not before Sophie had broken the heels on both her shoes.

'You're very difficult to dissuade when you get an idea in your head,' I said. 'Not unlike Conrad come to think of it.'

'Christ, don't lump me in with him!' she laughed.

As she took a sip of her wine our food arrived, Sophie squealing with delight at the sight of it. The Thai waitress smiled with her, pleased to have received a positive response.

'Anybody'd think you hadn't eaten in a week,' I said.

'Haven't had Thai in ages,' she winked, loading our plates, stacking them with fish cakes, satays, sticky rice, and fish curry. 'Mm, that's so good,' she said, biting in to a plump prawn she'd rolled in the Thai dipping sauce. 'Mm. Try it. Try it.'

She waved one in front of my mouth. I took it with my fingers and placed it on my tongue. It had beautifully layered flavours, and was very hot.

As we ate, Sophie hit me with question after question about Thailand. I didn't say too much. I talked mostly about the culture and the people, avoiding touching on my private life. I told her I was a full time personal trainer that I didn't go out much, and pretty much kept myself to myself. She stifled a fake yawn as I droned on.

'You can be so exasperating sometimes,' she said when she got a chance. 'So closed and secretive.'

'Maybe there's just not much to tell,' I said. 'Honest to God I lead a really boring life. Even the monks look at me with pity.'

'That,' said Sophie. 'I find very hard to believe.'

When we finished eating, I asked her if she'd like to go on to a bar or a club and have another drink. We used to go clubbing loads when we first started seeing each other. Besides, the hot food had perked me up and I wasn't ready to go back to Conrad.

She smiled at me, fiddling with a short strand of hair at the nape of her neck. 'I think that would be very... cool,' she said after a pause, clearly a little tipsy.

We went to a large club called Neptunes on Lockhart Road, famous for featuring DJ's from overseas. It usually drew a large ex-pat crowd.

We walked down the steps, past the bouncers into an area of sporadic light, constant sound and energetic, sweaty bodies. The music was so loud it went right through my chest, the bass echoing somewhere inside my sternum. This was far better than the Thai clubs, most of which played tinny dance pop that was three years out of date. It felt good to be back.

Because it was impossible to talk or get a drink at the packed bar, we danced, just managing to get a place on the crowded dance floor. Sophie put her whole body into it. Her legs spaced wide, her hips swinging, her shoulders dipping low with the rhythm. I loved watching her dance. It brought back all the memories of the fantastic nights we'd shared. The ones where we started to get to know each other, to realise we had something that most boys and girls don't: a real physical attraction. And things in common.

As we danced, I looked round the club at the other people, all lost in the pounding music, the alcohol and the drugs. We like to lose ourselves from time to time. We like to get near the edge, to experience the thrill of looking down. Perhaps that's why I ran from Sophie. I needed to lose myself a bit more before settling down.

'Do you want to come back to my place?' I heard her voice say through the confusion. 'It's too late to get a ferry.'

I took her hand and started walking towards the exit. As we made our way round the dance floor I saw a fight break out. Four tall guys and several shorter men were throwing punches at a group of Chinese. I paused to watch, but Sophie dragged me on. Reaching the steps, I turned and looked again, just in time to see Nick emerge from the gloom. His face was full of rage, his fists swinging wildly in all directions. I saw him for a split second before he was pulled back into the brawl.

Sophie's hand squeezed mine a little tighter and we hurried up the steps on to the street.

'Those guys are maniacs,' said Sophie as we got into a cab. 'They're always causing trouble. Not even Conrad'd get involved with them. And that's saying something.'

I smiled to myself and sat back in the car. Nick was certainly proving to be more of a handful than I'd reckoned on.

At her place she took photos of us, posing like we were a couple in love.

Chapter Twenty

The next day, after a late and civilised breakfast, I kissed Sophie goodbye and set off back to Conrad's. It was already mid morning and the sun was high in the sky. At the ferry pier with the sparkling ocean laid out in front of me, I found a quiet spot to sit and wait for the next boat. I smoked a cigarette, the wind blowing over my hair.

I didn't sleep with Sophie. We stayed up late chatting and drinking. She said she still loved me in some ways. There were times when she wanted her life to be like it was when we were together, even though she knew it could never be the same. I had similar emotions. Sophie was the first girl I slept with after Zack's death. After a year's sabbatical my ability to have sex, which had totally vanished, returned, and my life, which had been like a clock that's wound down, seemed to tick again. It's not easy to walk away from the woman that's restored your male pride. I'd found it difficult, too.

After a heavy sigh, she asked me why I left in the first place. I didn't want to tell her. I didn't think it would do any good, so I lied. I wanted to see Thailand, I said. Come on. You knew that. I wanted to go, and you didn't.

As excuses went it was terrible and she didn't believe me. Soon after we went to bed, in separate rooms. I was relieved. It would have been so easy to end up next to her, and comforting for both of us, in a short lived way. But Lek was never far from my mind, and I knew if I did anything with Sophie the guilt would grind me down, until I'd have to admit it to Lek and she'd hate me, and probably never forgive me. Guilt, like they say, outlasts the pleasure of forbidden sex.

Back on Lantau, after a soothing ferry journey, I found Conrad on the floor in the living room, stretched out like a corpse. I went to the fridge and got a beer, putting it on his bare stomach.

The cold metal woke him up before rolling off him.

'What the fuck was that?' he said, keeping his eyes closed.

'Stick out your right hand and you'll get it,' I said, stopping it with my foot.

Conrad moved his hand and fumbled like an OAP for a second before locating the beer and snapping back the ring pull.

'Breakfast is served,' I said. 'Enjoy.'

'Where are my sunglasses?' he asked, sitting up and taking a long swig.

I leaned forward on to the table and handed them to him as he put the beer down. With his glasses safely on, he opened his eyes.

'Christ, it's bright even with these on.'

I nodded gently. 'It's going to be a hot day. A good day for hanging out at the beach. Chilling out. Considering our options.'

'I don't think so,' Conrad replied. 'We have another problem.'

He told me he'd managed to sell all the drugs, but not at the price he wanted, not by a long way. We'd ended up with eight grand where we'd expected to make sixteen. I groaned inwardly.

'So what now?'

'We call Darren.'

Conrad picked up the phone and dialled his number. They had a brief conversation, and then he hung up.

'He wants in,' Conrad smiled.

He'd spoken to Darren the previous night, offering him a good deal. Darren had said he'd think about it. He'd thought about it now, and he wanted to go for it.

Darren was an old friend of ours. A Scotsman who ran a pub in Kowloon. He was fat as a new born baby, liked junk food and Chinese girls, horse racing and darts. He had no morals.

Conrad took a sip of his beer. 'Darren'll pay us four grand,' he said. 'That'll give us twelve altogether.'

I asked him what for. We no longer had anything to sell.

'We're going to rob the gear back off Nick and sell it on to Darren. Think of it as a Robin Hood kind of deal.'

I pointed out Robin Hood robbed from the rich and gave to the poor.

'We're robbing from the nasty and selling to the nice, brother. Remember Nick left us twenty thousand Hong Kong short. I sort of like it.'

I looked at Conrad. He slid his shades on top of his head and squinted at me.

'Nick'll never pay up. He's a bad, bad dude. Besides, we get more money this way.'

'And what if we get caught?' I asked.

'Oh come on,' said Conrad. 'It'll be fun. It'll be like old times... all the mad shit we used to get up to... '

'We never robbed anyone,' I said. 'And it was you who called last orders in bars, set off fire alarms and let taxis' tyres down.'

'All the more reason for us to try it then,' said Conrad. 'Unless you're happy to turn into a boring bastard before you're thirty. Come on. Experience. That's all we get before we die. Think it over.' Conrad lit a cigarette and smoked in silence.

I took his advice. I thought about Nick and his crappy attitude. He'd played outside the rules, so why shouldn't we? It wouldn't be like robbing an innocent man.

'Think of the money,' Conrad pushed.

I thought about Lek and the vast amount more I could earn here than in Bangkok. It was tempting. I could help those I loved simply by robbing someone I despised. I was getting good at convincing myself wrong was right. Yet again, I was sold. I asked Conrad when.

'Now,' he said. 'He'll be at work. Let's shower up and go.'

'What about tomorrow?'

'We shouldn't put this off. He may have sold half of it by then. Come on.'

'Yes, sir,' I said.

Conrad laughed. 'Good man. How did it go with Soph, by the way?'

'Interesting,' I said, pulling my shirt off. Things were moving fast. 'I'll shower first. I don't want to go robbing while I'm dirty.'

We took a shabby green bus to Pui O. It was packed, hot and humid, but we couldn't get a taxi. All the drivers were betting on the races, like they always did on a Wednesday.

It took about fifteen minutes to get up the winding road. The sun flooded in through the smeared windows, making us squint. By the time we got to our stop sweat was coming through our clothes. We got off the bus and made our way down a narrow concrete path, the rye grass brushing our legs as we went. The lower we descended into the valley, the less air there was. By the time we hit the bottom there was no breeze at all. I could hardly breathe.

As we walked a thought occurred to me. If we robbed Nick, he'd know it was us, and come looking. Conrad had this covered.

'We're staying with Ken,' he said.

'What about his girlfriend?'

Conrad told me not to worry. He had everything organised. I let it go. I wasn't in the mood for an argument.

We carried on walking until we got to a whitewashed

apartment block. Conrad surveyed it for some time, hands on hips.

'Shit,' he said finally, scratching his shoulder. 'I can't remember which is Nick's flat.'

I stared at him. 'You – have – got – to – be – kidding.'

Conrad looked at the row of flats, squinting against the morning sun. I followed his gaze to the high end of Pui O, up the hillside. There all the flats were old, different. But down in the valley the buildings were modern. They had the same slanted terracotta roofs. Balconies ringed by black iron railings bulged in the middle, as if blown out by an explosion. They had sliding doors. And there was another problem.

'I've only come here once before,' said Conrad, 'and I was leathered.'

'Do you at least know what floor he lives on?'

'First.'

'You're sure?'

'Fuck off,' Conrad replied, moving slowly, wiping sweat from his face. It felt like the humidity was intensifying, the hot air clinging to every living thing, drawing the energy out, making already frayed nerves crack and splinter like burning wood. My patience was evaporating.

'This is it here,' Conrad said at last, triumphant. 'That's his AC-DC tshirt hanging on the balcony. '*For those about to rock...* ' he said, looking up. 'Now the only way in, is through the sliding door on the balcony, so one of us is going to have to climb up. The other one can wait here and keep a check on things.' He glanced around, checking for lazy Chinese peasants who may be wandering around. 'Okay, there's no-one around. Up you go.'

'You're sense of humour is getting way out of hand, Conrad,' I said. 'This is your idea, you get up there.'

'I'm way older than you,' he complained. 'It'd take me hours. Go on.'

'If you're too old, you'll have to leave it. Let's go,' I replied and started to walk away. I wasn't carrying the responsibility of actually doing the robbery.

'Josh,' Conrad called in a stage whisper, looking anxious. 'Everything we want is in there. Everything. Two minutes work for that.'

'Everything you want, you mean.'

'Two minutes!'

'If it's only two minutes, you do it!'

'Josh!'

'Knowing my luck, I'll get caught.'

'You're not going to get caught. I'll keep a look out down here.'

I looked round. I wasn't keen, but judging it, it wouldn't take a second to get up there. We were more likely to get caught arguing, and arouse suspicion. Perhaps I should just get on with it.

'Go on,' Conrad urged.

The balcony was so low I could jump up and grab hold of it, pull myself up.

I looked up again. A large spider with yellow markings clung to a web between the bars, hoping for a mosquito or a fly, delirious from the heat, to stray into its web. I rubbed the back of my neck, weighing up the risk. I looked at the hope in Conrad's expression, which thinly disguised his desperation. I thought again of Lek and the cash. 'You'll really owe me for this,' I said.

'Yes, I know!'

'One day something will need doing, Conrad, and I won't want to do it... '

Conrad inhaled deeply.

'... and when that day comes. I'll be calling on you, my friend.'

'I get the picture. Go on, before anyone sees us.'

'I'm going,' I jumped up, grabbing the concrete floor of the balcony with both hands. With my upward momentum I got my shoulders level with the floor. I grabbed the railing with my left hand, hauling myself up and then vaulting over, landing catlike in front of the doors. Pushing hard against the glass panelling I eased the screwdriver Conrad gave me in the gap and, with some jiggling, flicked the latch. The door opened smoothly. Sliding it across I made my way in. A second later I was going through Nick's flat like a regular burglar. It took me under a minute to find the package. Neatly bagged and taped up, floating in the cistern.

I returned to the balcony. Outside I paused. An old Chinese woman, bent and haggard, was trying to sell Conrad vegetables, shaking his sleeve, trying to get him to part with some money. I ducked back inside, taking the time to scan Nick's apartment. Everything was whitewashed. Standard tiled floor, small kitchen, small bathroom, bamboo furniture. Decent brand of air conditioner, though. A photo on the TV looked as if it might be his family. They all looked mean and ugly. The sort of family that scared school children as they came off the bus onto the housing estate. On the coffee table was another picture. Nick with an attractive Thai girl. Next to the photo was an open guide book. He'd circled one of the most expensive hotels in Bangkok.

You might not be able to afford it after this, I thought.

I went back to the window. The old woman had shuffled away. I eased myself over the railing and jumped down.

'Should have bought the carrots,' I said, putting the parcel in Conrad's day pack.

He looked impressed. 'We could make a criminal of you yet.'

'It was in the cistern,' I said, rolling my eyes.

'What an idiot. If you do that you deserve to get done.'

'Mm. I feel better about robbing him now. It feels almost natural.'

And as I handed Conrad the rucksack I looked over my

shoulder at the spider, its yellow spotted legs glinting in the sunshine, a dragonfly caught in its web.

Chapter Twenty One

We got back to Conrad's an hour later, so sweaty we looked like we'd been swimming and neglected to towel ourselves dry. On the way back down from Pui O, we'd decided to get over to Ken's apartment straight away, to avoid any possible run in with Nick. This meant we had to pack up Conrad's stuff and cart it over to the ferry pier. It was the last thing we wanted to do in the terrible heat, but we had to play it safe. We had two hours before Nick was due back from work. Any time after that he could discover his stash was gone and come looking for us. We didn't want to be anywhere near when his temper, always on a short fuse, detonated.

'I've never seen so much shit,' I said as I emptied drawer upon drawer of nightclub flyers, telephone numbers, match boxes, Bic biros and photos, in an attempt to clear Conrad's belongings.

'Just bin it,' said Conrad. 'I'm taking that rucksack and that suitcase and that's it.'

I opened up a shiny yellow envelope of photos. They were of Conrad's birthday a few years back. I flipped through them, smiling at the memory. They were the usual birthday snaps. People arm in arm, sticking their tongues out, rubbing each other on the head. The kind of shots no-one wants to see unless they were actually there. I found them fascinating. Again, I thought how young we looked.

'What did you do this birthday?' I asked Conrad.

'Nothing. I sat where you're sitting now and I drank a six pack watching *The Day of the Jackal*.'

'Why didn't you go out?'

'I was skint. But the way we're going, I won't be again for a while.'

I got off the sofa, walked round the room, and started collecting Conrad's stuff. His flat really was a dive. There was dust and bits of dried food and dog hair all over the floor. I wouldn't have come back here if I'd known it was going to be like this. I'd started to enjoy a good standard of living. I didn't want to regress. I hoped Ken's place would at least be clean.

After half an hour we were finished. Conrad zipped up his rucksack and announced he was going to Silvermine Bay to get a trolley, then we'd wheel all his stuff out of the apartment and down to the pier.

'Don't be long,' I said. 'And try and stay out of trouble.'

'Yes, mum,' Conrad agreed as he closed the door behind him.

I stretched out on the sofa and flicked the TV on. After about quarter of an hour the phone rang. I picked up, expecting it to be Sophie.

'Josh... I've had a bit of an accident,' Conrad said, trying to speak without his voice quavering too much. I held the phone tighter. He'd only been gone fifteen minutes. Nothing too bad could have happened.

'Doesn't surprise me,' I tried to be cool.

'I think I need to go to hospital.'

'What?' I was suddenly sharp. 'How bad is it? I mean are we talking serious like failing a GCSE? Or... '

'More like failing a four year degree course. I'll show you when I see you. I'll meet you at Ken's. Bring as much stuff as you can manage – the money and the gear.'

'Okay. Give me the address.'

Conrad gave me the address. I double-checked it with him before hanging up. Straight after I raced round the apartment, gathering the stuff up. All the time wondering what the hell had happened to Conrad, hoping it was nothing permanent. Praying I'd be able to get on the same ferry as him. But the more I hurried and panicked the more I couldn't find what I was looking for and fell over stuff, getting myself in a mess.

'Fuck,' I breathed, trying to slow myself down. 'Fuck.'

Eventually I stopped and took some deep breaths. I remembered something I'd read about being able to function more effectively if there was more oxygen in the brain. Now a lot calmer, I got Conrad's green Karrimor rucksack on my back, so heavy it almost tipped me over backwards, then I slung his holdall over my shoulder and across my chest. This counterbalanced me enough so I could walk, though I looked like I was on the moon, anchored down with gravity boots.

'Okay,' I said, putting one foot in front of the other. 'So this is what it feels like to weigh twenty stone. No wonder guys that heavy sweat.'

I trudged out of the flat, not bothering to lock the door. There was once again nothing of value in this dump. I walked round the shaded area of the building and on to the crumbling concrete path. Coming into the sun, the heat immediately opened up the pores in my skin and the glands re-doubled their efforts at drowning me. I paced along, keeping my eyes fixed on the path ahead, my mind full of cool thoughts. In my peripheral vision I could see the green palms, flecked with brown and yellow, the water buffalo swishing their tails, the various dried up streams, strewn across the ground like giant dead worms. I kept my head down and my feet going one in front of the other. I'd never been a marathon runner or long distance walker as a kid, I couldn't stand the pain and monotony. I wasn't enjoying the experience any more as an adult.

The odd Chinese person passed me on the route, going at twice my speed. I think they were secretly laughing at me. The English weren't popular in Hong Kong anymore, not that they ever were.

Half an hour after leaving the apartment I arrived at Silvermine Bay. Crossing the square I made it to the ferry pier. The next ferry was just docking, its huge engines rumbling like a giant's stomach, the propeller turning in reverse for... how many times must it have turned in its life? As many as my heart beat? More?

I watched the mass of people jostle down the ramp like cattle and proceeded to the turnstile to buy a ticket. I smiled at the grumpy looking guy in the kiosk and reached in my pocket. Finding nothing I reached in the other pocket. Still nothing. I started to panic. I checked all the pockets in my combats, letting people through, sweat pouring off me. I pulled Conrad's holdall open and checked in that, then his rucksack.

'Fucking hell,' I said, loud enough for some of the waiting passengers to give me an alarmed look. 'Sorry,' I said, half joking.

In my hurry to leave, I'd left my wallet in Conrad's flat. I could picture it on his shitty little coffee table. Like the propeller on the boat, I wondered how many times I'd done this before. Once I'd left my house, gone all the way into central London and suddenly remembered I hadn't locked the back door after I'd hung the washing out. Cursing, I'd taken the tube all the way back, only to find the door locked after all. But this time I was right. I definitely didn't have my wallet.

Wanting to scream I strutted over to the side of the concrete bus station in the centre of the square and dumped Conrad's stuff on to a rusty trolley, one of the ones he'd set out to find. I pushed the damn thing all the way back to the flat, praying no-one had been in there and nicked my wallet.

When I arrived I found it sitting on the table. At least I had some luck. I kissed it, put it in my pocket and made my way back to the ferry pier. As I arrived I saw the next ferry sailing out into the South China Sea.

This time I saw the funny side, went to Papa Doc's, and had a beer.

Chapter Twenty Two

It took two hours to get to Mongkok.

The ferry journey seemed slow, particularly as I'd missed the first available and had to wait an hour. The taxi ride was even slower. By the time I arrived at the flat with all the gear I was exhausted.

Ken let me in, a worried look on his face.

'What's up, man?' I asked.

He pointed at Conrad. He was lying on the sofa in Ken's disappointingly pokey apartment, a near empty bottle of Jack Daniels next to him and a big joint in his hand. His eyes were half closed. Ken gave me an anxious look and started saying something. I wasn't really listening. I was staring at Conrad's hand, which lay strangely inanimate on the side of the grubby sofa.

'What happened to you?' I said looking at the bloody bandage. 'Did you go to hospital? Shouldn't you be there?'

'Oh yeah,' Conrad said, his voice drowsy. 'I ran into the Chinese guys. They wanted money. I didn't have any on me.'

He unwrapped the bandage to reveal a severed finger.

'Oh, no way!'

'Yeah. They knocked me off my bike and did it. And if I don't get to Wan Chai tonight, they're going to do it again,' he said, doing the cutting motion.

'So we're going yeah?' I said.

'Just getting my nerve up,' Conrad replied. 'Just getting

ready.'

'And what about the hospital?'

'The hospital can wait. They were too busy when I got there, so I walked out. Wrong colour skin, I guess. I'll go another time. Tomorrow.'

We had to take four grand to pay off the Chinese. I wanted to get to Wan Chai as soon as possible to prepare but Conrad wasn't in the mood for advice. Before we left, twenty minutes later, he finished the rest of the whisky and had a beer. He was getting out of control.

In the cab on the way to Wan Chai, Conrad sunk drunkenly into the back seats. I asked him if we had to meet the Chinese guys in or outside the club. He didn't know. I asked him what he wanted us to do. He didn't know. I asked him what the Chinese guys had said to him. He said he couldn't remember exactly. They didn't speak great English. I was getting more and more worried. Conrad was so out of it, he didn't care anymore. And that was dangerous. I asked him if he'd taken his oral agents. He hadn't so I rummaged through his pockets and forced a few down his throat. If his blood sugar went too high, it'd probably send him over the edge. I often wondered if his diabetes didn't affect his brain more than he thought. Like he got drunk and high all the time to block out some depression it was giving him.

Eventually I got him to agree that he'd go in the club while me and Ken waited right outside. If he wasn't out in three minutes we'd come in looking for him. If we saw a couple of likely looking Chinese guys hanging round outside, we'd also come get him.

We sat in silence for a while. The cab drove us through the darkness. I told myself this transaction would go smoothly, but I couldn't believe how our little stunt was starting to go awry. I was getting panicked. I asked Conrad if he had the cash.

He tapped the day pack on his lap and nodded.

I tried to breathe slowly.

Ken didn't say a word. He looked nervous, like he was about to be cross-examined by the police or something. I worried about him, too. I didn't think he'd be good under pressure.

The car moved haltingly through the traffic. As we came into Wan Chai, Conrad sat forward in his chair, looking for a good place to stop. He didn't want to end up right outside the club.

Fifty yards from the neon sign of Hot Lips he told the driver to pull over. He'd suddenly focused and was back in charge.

'Right,' he said to me. 'You pay the driver. Ken and I'll get out.'

I paid the fare while Conrad and Ken got out and waited by the curb. Once I'd got the change, I joined them.

'Keep your eyes open,' Conrad said as we began to walk down the road, crowds of tourists going the other way. 'Any sign of trouble, we'll all just split up, okay? Meet in Strawberry. Or if not there, La Bamba.'

I nodded. Ken whispered, 'Okay.'

We moved forward, the tangy, heavy, peat and meths smell of street food filling our nostrils, the pulsing sound of dance music sometimes faint, sometimes louder in our ears as people entered or exited the clubs. The volume of human traffic on the pavement and crossing the roads was intense. I didn't think I'd ever seen this part of Hong Kong empty, not even at five in the morning.

As we headed towards the club I saw a stocky figure thrust his way through the crowds like a snowplough cutting through the morning drift. People staggered back, creating a narrow path. The man came rushing out towards us. It was Nick, his eyes lit with an insane, vengeful lust, his face contorted the way I'd seen it in the club. I felt adrenalin surge through my veins, like thick amphetamine. My heart rate surged.

'Oh fuck,' Conrad said.

I turned to see Ken sprinting away. He went round the corner like a four hundred metre runner off the first bend.

'You fucking... ' Nick screamed, flying forward, moving so quickly he was a blur.

I watched as his head connected with Conrad's cheekbone rocking him back. Nick had aimed for Conrad's nose, but he'd swiveled his head at the last minute. It was still a brutal blow. Staggering, he clutched at his face, dropping the money.

As he recoiled, Nick saw me lunging towards him, hands outstretched. He jinked to his left, thrusting a pint glass in my face. He'd had it in his hand as he came sprinting out of the little bar he was in. I felt the itching sensation of cut glass digging into my skin. I groaned and sank to my knees, crouching over the tarmac, instinctively covering my face.

Conrad then hit Nick with a glancing upper cut. He staggered, tripped and fell back.

Things happened quickly after that. Once Nick was on the floor, he didn't have a chance. Conrad wasn't a fighter, but he was a very angry and aggressive man, fuelled with whisky. He swung his heavy boot back and cracked it into Nick's temple. Injured, he began to crawl away across the pavement, blood coming from the side of his head. So Conrad, walking next to him, shouting at him to dare, just fucking dare to walk away, lifted his boot in the air and this time went to stamp on his head. But Nick was too quick. He rolled and got himself into a crouching position. As he pushed his knuckles against the pavement to get upright Conrad kicked him once again, this time in the knee. I heard something crack and saw Nick's leg bend awkwardly. His face contorted, but he stifled his scream.

Having recovered from the shock of being glassed, I moved forward and pulled Conrad away.

'That's enough,' I said, grabbing him and bundling him towards a taxi. 'Let's go.'

Conrad didn't hear me. He kept straining to get at Nick,

the adrenalin in his system numbing his mind and his ability to think.

It took all my strength to get him in the cab and still Conrad was trying to stop the car from moving, trying to get out the other door.

Several minutes into the ride, he came out of his violent trance and began to panic.

'The money,' he said. 'Where's the money?'

'It's gone. Disappeared.'

'I had it... '

'And then you dropped it. I saw it on the ground. The next time I looked it had gone.'

'Fuck! What are we going to do?'

'We're going back to get some more.'

'Shit, I can't believe it's gone.'

After calming Conrad I looked at my watch. It was ten to seven. The entire fight had only taken two minutes, though it felt like hours.

'We'll never get back there by seven,' Conrad said looking at the traffic. It was pretty bad. People making their way home from work late or heading out for dinner.

'They'll wait. We'll give them twenty five thousand dollars as a sweetener. Two grand.'

Conrad shook his head. 'I can't believe this has fucked up.'

'It'll work out, we'll give them the money. We'll apologise. Everything will be cool.'

We both lapsed into silence as our minds reviewed what had happened. I sensed Conrad staring at me, pulling me out of my thoughts. 'What?' I asked as he returned my gaze.

'Fuck!' he said, grimacing. He'd noticed my face for the first time. It was starting to throb. I raised my hand to touch it.

'Don't,' said Conrad, grabbing my wrist. 'It needs washing.'

I'd forgotten all about it. The adrenalin had iced it. But as soon as Conrad mentioned it, my whole face killed. 'Is it bad?'

'It's bloody. There's a few deep cuts.'

'Shit. Why couldn't he have glassed you? I mean, you deserve it,' I joked.

Conrad shrugged. There wasn't time to answer. The cab had already arrived at Mongkok.

When we walked into the apartment, we were met by Ken. He looked awkward, like his zip had burst. I told him not to worry about running away. He'd done the right thing.

I left him with Conrad while I went to the bathroom. I felt tired and groggy.

I heard Conrad tell Ken we were going back.

'Why?' he asked, sounding anxious.

Conrad explained the situation, Ken occasionally protesting.

I closed the door and flicked the light on in the bathroom. I looked in the mirror. I saw red, I felt queasy and then everything went black.

Chapter Twenty Three

It was morning before I came to. I know because I sensed the light, even with my eyes closed. I felt pain, and then worry. Slowly I worked out where I was. Ken's apartment. I could tell by the smell. The musky, thick odour that lined the hair in my nostrils. I could tell by the uncomfortable silence, the unfamiliar bed. I didn't want to move. My head was pulsing. I needed a Nurofen, or better, a Valium or two. And some Xanax. Lots of Xanax.

I lay on the bed, flat on my back, keeping my eyes closed. I searched my mind for information about the previous night. I remembered Nick. I remembered getting into a taxi and talking to Conrad and then... I was back in Mongkok, I was looking in the mirror. My face was a mess and...

Carefully I opened my eyes, squinting at the ceiling. It was grey from the damp. Small droplets of water dotted the paintwork like blisters. Sunlight shone onto the narrow bed. I propped myself up on my elbows and looked at my shirt, my trousers. Blood was splattered down my torso like a red bib. Splashes of blood covered my trousers. I was tempted to touch my face but decided to look first.

In the bathroom I washed my hands in the small basin, then bent at the knees so I could look in the low mirror. As my head came level with the reflection I winced. Hollow eyes peered out from a livid screen of scarlet, claret, black. As I looked, a deep cut over my right eye opened, trickling thin bright blood down my cheek. With a towel, I wiped round the maze of cuts until some areas of normal skin became visible. I had a shower, letting the water wash over my face for as long as I could bear the sting. With a towel round my waist I walked into the kitchen. Ken was sitting at the table looking strangely sheepish.

'Morning,' he said nervously. 'Are you okay?'

I nodded. 'I think I need to see a doctor, though. Some of these cuts look like they need stitches.'

I windmilled my hand round my face.

'Could you phone Sophie for me? Get her to come over?'

'Sure. I mean you can phone her yourself if you like.'

'I don't like,' I said. 'I was supposed to meet her last night. She won't be happy with me. Phone her and tell her I need to see her doctor.'

'What if she wants to talk to you?'

'Tell her I'm asleep or in the shower or something.'

'Okay.' Ken picked up the phone. I dialled the number.

I listened to him deliver the message. As expected Sophie asked to speak to me. Ken delivered the excuse. Sophie asked him a whole stack of questions.

'He had a slight accident,' he said.

He was hazy on the details. Sophie probed deeper. Ken, who was now looking harassed, suggested again that she come over. Sophie asked for the address. Ken gave it and hung up.

'She's coming straight over,' he said.

I made us both coffee and we sat at the table. I asked Ken where Conrad was and if they'd delivered the money.

Ken stirred his coffee with a shaking hand.

'No. He... he, ah... '

It took a while for Ken to vocalise what happened. As he picked his way through the story I got a very bad feeling. It started at my feet and rose up my body like ink up litmus paper.

'Why do you think they didn't show up?' I asked when he'd finished.

'Those sort of people don't hang around. If they waited there all night they would have looked like idiots. They would have lost face. To the Chinese that's the worst embarrassment. They would rather not have the money and exact revenge.'

'Would they have done it last night?'

'No. They'd want more men to make a really good job of it. They'd probably concentrate on catching him at home now. They know he lives on Lantau, obviously. With their network it wouldn't be hard to find his flat. They'd probably go round there today, so it's lucky you've left. But they don't give up easy. Money is one thing. Face another. They'll be even more determined to get him now.'

'Fuck,' I breathed. 'Would you mind staying here? So when Conrad shows up you can keep him here safe. Explain the situation.'

Ken didn't have a problem with that.

We both fell into silence. I stared vacantly at the rucksack under the table. Ken seemed to tense up.

'You want another coffee?' he asked.

'Thanks.' I rubbed my hand over the smooth surface of the foldable Formica table. Conrad had done some dumb stuff in his life, but this was the first time he'd really put himself in serious danger. I tried not to think of the worst possible outcome.

'Oh Jesus,' Sophie said when she arrived. She stood in the doorway staring at my face. 'How the hell did this happen?'

I looked at her. Her hair had been cut shorter, accentuating her cheekbones. Her eyes were bright, the body firm. She looked more gorgeous than ever.

'Glass,' I said, miming the incident with my right hand, 'smack in the face.'

'It looks awful,' she said, grabbing my shoulders and scrutinising me. 'Let's get you to the doctor.' She pulled her mobile out of her bag and dialled a number. 'I think you're going to need to be stitched up.'

'Thanks,' I said, sitting back down at the table. 'I feel like I have been already.'

Sophie spoke on the phone for several minutes in Cantonese before hanging up. Having lived in Hong Kong her entire life she was fluent. Still an impressive achievement considering the languages' tonal demands. Mispronounce a single syllable and you wouldn't be understood.

'We can go right now,' she said putting the phone back in her bag and re-shouldering it. I gave Ken Sophie's number so he could call us if Conrad showed up and said goodbye.

Sophie had kept a cab waiting outside. We got straight in. As soon as we were settled on the back seat she said in her rapid business like tone, 'I want to know what's going on, Josh. I want the absolute truth as to why you're here, and if you lie to me this time, I'll never speak to you again.'

I stared at my hands. I told her she wouldn't like it.

'I don't like it now.'

'I know. It's just... Things have got out of control. I didn't think it was all going to turn out this way... '

'Just tell it, Josh. From the beginning.'

I looked at her fierce green eyes. I told the whole story.

Sophie listened to the revelations about the drug smuggling. The difficulties with the Chinese. Conrad losing a finger. The cock up in Wan Chai.

'And what about you?' she asked when I'd finished.

'They're not after me, Soph. They don't even know me.'

'Well that's something, I suppose. What are you going to do now?'

'My role in the whole deal is financial. It's up to Conrad to sort out the rest of it.'

'You really mean that?'

'Well. If Conrad asks for my help, I'll help him. I can't leave him in the shit.'

'That figures.'

The Body is a Temple

'I can't let him down.'

'Why not?' Sophie scoffed. 'What has he ever done for you?'

And it was then, completely naturally, that I told Sophie about the night Conrad pulled me out of a coma. He'd come back to Causeway Bay and found me collapsed in the living room. My heart stopped soon after, and he got it started again. Then I stopped breathing and he breathed for me. That night he had to pack ice cubes around me and put me in the bath to keep my body temperature down.

I'd been depressed and had spent a week drinking solidly. When that hadn't removed the pain of Zack's death, I'd done enough speed balls to floor a horse. I hadn't been immediately grateful to Conrad for saving me, but he'd been a true friend, and I wasn't going to forget it. I was happy to be alive now.

'I do owe him,' I said.

Sophie nodded. 'It still haunts you, doesn't it? Zack… '

'Yeah. So I don't want anything similar happening to Conrad.'

She said she understood.

'Don't mention this again, okay?'

She squeezed my hand and gave me a thin smile.

Pretty soon we reached the doctor's surgery. It was a grubby building that badly needed a whitewash. It was nicer inside though, and I didn't have to wait long to be seen.

'I'll wait for you here,' Sophie said when they called my name. 'You can put the bill on my account, okay?'

I disappeared down the stairs. I was with the doctor under half an hour.

'That looks better,' she said as I walked back up the steps. The doctor was good with my face, stitching it up as gently and accurately as a seamstress.

'Yeah. I have three in this one and four in the other,' I said pointing. 'I got some antibiotics too.'

'Okay. Then I'm taking you home. You can have a bath

and change your clothes, you stink.'

'I always do in Hong Kong,' I said. 'Must be the air.'

Back at her house in the mid levels, Sophie ran me a bath and made soup. It was some kind of Chinese herbal medicine and it smelt disgusting. It tasted even worse. I complained to Sophie, but she was adamant I should eat it all.

'Believe me Josh, you'll thank me tomorrow.'

'That's if I make it through the night. This stuff is poison.'

'I'm going to find you a tshirt you can wear. By the time I get back, I want you to have eaten all that.'

When she returned I'd eaten the soup but I didn't feel a whole lot better.

'Bath time,' she said, leading me down the stairs. In the bathroom she undressed me and helped me in, then washed my hair. Her hands on me felt good, though I did wish they were Lek's.

'I think you should rest after this,' she said. 'I'll tell you if Conrad calls.'

'Okay.'

She massaged my shoulders briefly, dragged me out of the bath, dried me and put me in bed.

She kissed me again. It seemed a shy, nervous kiss.

I fell asleep, dreaming of unending dark corridors, ignored stop signs, and fast running water.

I was woken later by a mobile ringing next to my ear. It took a while to work out where I was. For a moment I presumed I was still at Ken's, but then the smell of Sophie's fragrant sheets hit me. Fumbling round the bedside table, my eyes still closed, I located the phone and put it to my ear. Answering it I got Conrad's croaky voice. I was relieved to hear from him, but the news wasn't good. He'd lost the second lot of money in Wan Chai. He was in The Kiss Bar waiting for Darren. He needed a favour.

'I need you to get your arse over here… '

I swung my legs out of bed, my head throbbing. I groaned.

'… and drop by Ken's place on the way and pick up the E's.'

'What? Are you out of your mind? Mongkok's miles away. I'm in the mid levels. Didn't you do that?'

Conrad told me he'd had a tricky morning.

I pulled my jeans on. There wasn't any point in arguing, not at this stage. I told him I'd see him in an hour.

'Cool. I'll buy you a drink.'

'You'll buy me a pub,' I hung up.

'Who was that?' Sophie asked. She'd been standing in the room for half the conversation.

'Conrad. I'm meeting him in Tsim Tsa Tsui,' I said, slipping my arms through my tshirt.

Sophie stood silent, looking at her shoes. 'I understand you and Conrad better after what you told me earlier. I'm sorry for being down on him. I know he's a genuine guy really.'

I was beginning to wonder if he was, but I agreed.

'You're right to help him. But be careful, won't you?' she said looking at me.

'I'll be back soon,' I said.

'That's what you said a year ago.'

I gave her a wry smile. 'Don't wait up then,' I grinned.

Chapter Twenty Four

Half an hour later I was knocking on Ken's door in Mongkok. I used my left hand. For some reason my right arm hurt. I figured I must have landed awkwardly when Nick decked me.

I waited for a minute before a girl answered the door. She had short blonde hair and an aggravated look, as if she'd recently been told some bad news. Simone, I guessed.

'You must be Ken's girlfriend,' I offered, trying to be charming.

'Was Ken's girlfriend,' she said scrutinising my face.

This sounded like a story. I prepared myself for an angry soliloquy. She didn't talk for long, but she made it clear she wasn't happy. She was concerned Ken hadn't been in the previous night, and that he was now nowhere to be found.

I explained we were out last night, but he'd been in this morning. I was confused as to where he'd gone. He said he'd stick around in case Conrad came back. Still, Ken wasn't my problem. All I wanted was the rucksack. I cast my eye round for the bag.

'I have a bad feeling,' said Simone. Her mood shifting rapidly from aggressive to vulnerable.

I told her not to worry.

Simone looked unsure, on the verge of an emotional moment. 'We've never been apart for two days before... ' Her eyes started to fill with tears. 'We had an argument and I think he doesn't want to be with me anymore.'

The Body is a Temple

'I'm sure that's not true.'

'It is,' Simone murmured, starting to cry, throwing herself into my arms. Fuck, I thought. I don't need this.

I was surprised. Appearances and reality and all that... This was no tough girl. But I didn't have time to play agony uncle. I looked at my watch. The minutes were ticking on. Simone sobbed on my shoulder. I patted her back, feeling like a bad soap actor.

'He'll be back any minute, I'm sure.' I wanted to get the hell out of there. 'Look, I've got to meet a friend of mine. Do you mind if I go? I just came over to collect my stuff.'

Simone shook her head.

'I'll come back as soon as I can.'

Simone nodded.

'You better give me your number. If I run into Ken I'll call you.'

Simone wrote her number down as I scrabbled under the bed for Conrad's bag. I found mine and some of Ken's sweaty socks, but Conrad's bag... It wasn't there. I checked in the bathroom, the living room, everywhere. It was nowhere to be seen. Fear tore at my stomach. That icy caterpillar started going up my back again. Where the fuck was it?

As my head swivelled, scanning the room, the phone rang. I snatched at the receiver.

'Yes?' I barked into it, hoping it was Ken.

It was Conrad. He wanted me to get a move on. I told him I couldn't find the bag. He told me to ask Simone.

'Simone,' I said, holding the receiver. 'Have you seen a medium sized black rucksack anywhere?'

'Ahh, I don't think so... no... I haven't.'

'You're sure?'

'Err, yeah... I guess.'

I scanned her expression to see if she was lying. No noticeable twitches. Talking into the phone again I said, 'She hasn't seen it.'

Conrad said 'fuck', three or four times. 'Ken must have it then.'

'Why would he?'

'I don't know. I'm not psychic.'

This was starting to wind me up. 'Any ideas where he might be?'

'In the pub? High as a kite somewhere if he's got that load of drugs with him.'

'So you have no idea where he might have fucked off to?'

'No.'

There was a long pause before Conrad let rip a stream of expletives. Followed by a whole lot of self-pity.

'I'm not having a picnic myself,' I said, feeling tired. I wasn't sure if I had the energy to do this anymore. 'Why don't we leave it and you can do what you want to do and I'll do what I want to do? Just split what cash we've got.'

'Because,' Conrad said tersely, 'we lost nearly four grand in Wan Chai, we still haven't paid the Chinese... and we need this money to get the fuck out of here. Come over anyway. Fill a bag full of aspirins or any shit. I don't care. We'll have to blag him.'

'I'm not doing that.'

'You've got to.'

'Conrad, I said I wasn't going to get involved in all this. I was going to give you the money and that was it. Now I'm up to my eyeballs in it. Come on, man.'

There was an icy silence.

'Just… okay. We're almost there. If we can pull this off we're made. But if we can't, I'm fucking dead, my friend. These guys I've got after me aren't going to fuck about. We are so close to making this happen. Don't piss it away.'

I thought fast. Conrad was right. There was no point running a marathon to give up a hundred metres from the finish line.

'Okay. I'll do it,' I said. 'I'll bring the bag.'

'Are you in some kind of trouble?' Simone asked when I put the phone down.

I laughed, kind of. 'I've got to go out,' I said. 'When Ken gets back, can you get him to phone me immediately on this number?' I indicated the number of The Kiss Bar, which I'd left on the kitchen table.

Simone nodded reluctantly.

'Is there a pharmacy round here?' I asked.

'On the main road. Fifty metres down or so, I guess. Why? You got a headache?'

'Getting one,' I said and left without smiling. I wondered how many aspirins the pharmacy would sell me without thinking I was trying to top myself. Hopefully enough to have a chance of making the dummy look halfway convincing. I assumed Conrad had some E's on him that Darren could try if he wanted, so he'd only need to glance in the bag before paying up. With a few drinks inside him, some dim lighting, it might just work.

I made my way down the grubby staircase, deep in thought, again contemplating how far reaching the consequences of Conrad's scheme had become.

This whole thing was getting way out of control.

I stepped out of the stairwell and into the light. I stopped, my mouth falling open in horror. Ten yards to my right I saw Nick. He had his head down, a baseball bat flung carelessly, like a tie, over one shoulder. I looked left. Further off, I saw Ken hurrying towards me, weighed down by the precious rucksack.

'Fuck,' I breathed. I stood right where I was. I gazed at the sharp end of the ever diminishing triangle. The catalyst.

I looked first at Ken, then at Nick. Closer now.

Nick looked back at me.

Time stopped.

Chapter Twenty Five

A heavy cloud moved over the sun, dimming its rays. Time started again. Nick reacted first, not because he was quick witted but because he had no options to consider. While Ken and I were wondering whether to talk or run or reason, Nick's mental processes led him straight to violence.

He raised the baseball bat and swung it at my head, a sneer on his face so wide it looked like he could swallow me. So much anger in his eyes that they looked like they might burn right through me. I ducked, the wind from the force of the swing ruffling my hair. As Nick's body pivoted from the effort, I punched him hard in the kidneys and knocked his legs from under him, sending him to the floor.

'You cunt!' Nick screamed, falling awkwardly. He tried to get up but with his leg in plaster it was useless. I wrestled the bat from him and brought it crashing down on his good leg, around the point of his kneecap. Nick screamed in agony, clasping it in his hands.

Again the violence was swift and uncomplicated, and Ken was nowhere near it. True to form, he was charging down the street, out of trouble.

I watched him. He flew down the street even quicker than before. Like a two hundred metre runner this time.

I assumed he'd soon stop to see if he was out of danger.

He wasn't stopping. He was getting away. And for a little guy, he was extremely quick.

The Body is a Temple

'Ken!' I called after him, 'Ken! Ken! Look... oh fuck,' and I put my head down and chased after him, leaving Nick writhing and cursing on the floor, like one of those yappie toy dogs that does back flips.

'Ken, wait! Give me the bag!' But Ken was in the thick of the Mongkok market now and he wasn't slowing down. He was getting further away. I pumped my arms hard, wishing I didn't smoke as I felt the sting in the lungs and the ache in the legs.

'Ken!'

It was difficult to keep track of where he was going. I bumped into shoppers as I sprinted down the street, looking more for Ken and the bobbing bag than at the people in front of me. Ten metres ahead Ken suddenly jinked down a side road. Two seconds later I was round the bend and staring at something my mind chose to play in slow motion. I didn't want it in slow motion. But there it was. Like a car crash, this played slow:

Ken, both arms raised, the bag sailing into the thick air, came crashing down on a man in a khaki green uniform, his hat flying into a bamboo basket full of vegetable waste.

'Fuck,' I breathed as I slowed to a walk, wondering how this situation was going to pan out.

The police officer wasn't impressed.

Lying on his back in the road he babbled away in Cantonese so fast it sounded like a tape fast forwarding. Ken, realising he'd rammed a police officer whilst in possession of thousands of dollars worth of drugs, looked like he was going to have a nervous breakdown. I stood a couple of metres from the incident, my eyes flicking from bag to policeman to Ken. My mind clicking from the safety of my Bangkok apartment to courtrooms to crowded cells in Lei Chi Kok. I fought my first instinct: to turn and run. For every second I stood there, the urge increased. Slowly Ken stood up, helping the officer off the road, his entire being radiating remorse. The policeman had stopped babbling now and was striding towards the bag. He hadn't seen me. I was still considering bolting down the road in the opposite direction. The officer was speaking again now, but more calmly. Ken was speaking too and nodding vigorously, almost bowing, laughing nervously. As the policeman went to hand the bag back, he caught sight of me. Speaking to Ken, he kept hold of the sack and called me over, looking concerned.

'This your bag?' he said.

Ken laughed nervously.

I didn't say a word. He looked at Ken. A wrong word here could be costly.

Ken kept laughing. Then he spoke in rapid Cantonese, his hands whirling like a mime artist.

The policeman looked at me. 'This your friend?' he said indicating Ken.

'We were only fooling around.'

The policeman nodded jerkily. 'You want to play you can go to Hong Kong Park. In street danger, okay?'

'Okay.'

'What your problem. You play like chilren. Big danger here.'

'We're sorry.'

'You not do again.'

'No.'

The policeman offered me the bag.

'What inside?' he asked, suddenly suspicious.

I shrugged, my eyes widening. 'Just clothes. My laundry.'

The policeman raised and lowered the bag, as if weighing it.

'Okay,' he said, giving it to me. 'Please don't run in the street next time.'

'We won't.'

'Okay,' said the police officer again. 'Fankyou.' And with that he left us standing together in the street.

The Body is a Temple

I looked at Ken. 'Please God tell me the gear's in here.'
Ken nodded.
'What were you doing with it?'
'I don't know. I'm real sorry, man. I got scared. I didn't want to get busted with this at home so I hid it in a skip out here last night. Then I thought it might get nicked and... '
'We nearly were,' I said. I knew Ken wasn't the type of guy to deliberately cause trouble. I told him to go home and be nice to Simone. I had to get going.

In the Kiss Bar, its sign done in Rolling Stones style lips, flashing red, I arrived to find Conrad drinking heavily with a fat guy with a big laugh. They were surrounded by glasses, most of which were empty.
'Josh!' Conrad said with enthusiasm, his eyes lighting up. He grabbed me by the shoulders and dragged me down onto the chair next to him. 'My best mate. Where have you been?'
'Getting here.'
Conrad laughed. 'He's got such a sense of humour this guy. Josh, you remember Darren.'
'How ye doen,' Darren said sounding even more Scottish than usual, his eyes glazed from the Carlsberg. 'Good to see ye.'
'You too.' I hardly recognised him, he'd put on so much weight. He had more chins than before, no neck now, and swollen and puffy hands.
'So you've got the gear for me?' he asked, stretching out a meaty arm.
I handed him the bag. Conrad looked startled. I put my hand on his shoulder and winked.
Darren had a good rummage about inside saying, 'Looks good to me,' before re-zipping it.
'Cool,' said Conrad punching me in the shoulder, smiling broadly. 'You've done well, my friend.'
'You don't know the half of it.'

'That's fifty thousand dollars then,' Conrad said to Darren triumphantly.

'That's right,' Darren agreed, burping loudly. 'Do you want a drink?' he looked at me. 'You look thirsty.'

'I'll have a Carlsberg.'

'Cool. Sally!' he roared. 'Two more pints and another double JD and Coke for the wild man.'

Sally gave a thumbs up. She had swollen, thrusting breasts and a wide smile. Conrad's type. Not mine. I sat down. Over a couple of beers we chatted over the pros and cons of living in South East Asia. We all agreed Hong Kong was the worst option, but the only option if you wanted to make money rather than just spend it. Darren admitted he could only see himself staying in Kowloon for another two years max. The Chinese were turning against the ex-pats and it was only going to get worse.

'I'm looking forward to getting back to Thailand,' I said. 'And it should be even more fun with Conrad.'

Conrad looked awkward. 'I've got to make a quick detour to the Philippines first, mate.'

This was news to me, and I didn't like the sound of it. But I knew Conrad. He'd have his reasons and he wouldn't be talked out of a plan once he'd set his mind to it. Rather than pull him on it, I just nodded.

'You will come out to Bangkok though, won't you?'

'I'll be in the Philippines two weeks at the most,' Conrad nodded. 'Don't worry, mate, Thailand is where I want to be. But right now, I need to go for a piss, so I want to be in the loos. Shift would you Josh, so I can get out before my bladder bursts?'

I got up, leaving a path clear for my friend to get by.

'He may be able to drink,' Darren observed, 'but he's still got a weak bladder.'

He laughed to himself, before he got out of breath and downed another half pint to dull the pain of living.

I didn't know what Conrad did in the loo but when he came out he seemed to have a different attitude. He seemed much more on edge. Like he needed to go for a piss even more.

When he got back to the table he suggested to Darren that he pay up before he got too drunk. Darren agreed, lumbering to his feet unsteadily. He managed to squeeze his bulk out between the table and the bench and headed slowly for the stairs breathing hard. Conrad and I followed. My heartbeat began to pick up.

'Christ,' I said as we reached the top of the stairs which opened out into Darren's office. 'I haven't seen a lava lamp in years.'

'Aye. Great aren't they. I love 'em. Great way to get you thinking. I can waste hours in front of those... '

The office was cosy. The windows were blacked out and drapes covered the walls and ceiling. The floor was covered in brightly patterned rugs. Darren's desk was piled high with papers. Behind it, there was a poster of Farrah Fawcett in her *Charlie's Angels* days. All American hair, spread legs and owl eyes.

There was a small safe in the corner, which Darren crouched next to, turning the dial. Conrad was standing behind him, about a step away. I was on the other side of the room, leaning against the desk, staring at the carpet, thinking the day from hell was almost over and that I'd soon be in bed, head cradled in a soft pillow. As I came out of my thoughts, dragging my attention away from the textured flooring, I was aware of Conrad waving his hands at me, mouthing some words.

I squinted at him. 'What?' I mouthed back.

Conrad put his finger to his lips, hunched his shoulders and indicated Darren's neck.

I frowned, wondering what he was on about.

Conrad mimed Darren opening the safe, then pointed at his neck again.

I bared my teeth at him, shaking my head.

'Aye that's it,' said Darren swinging the safe door open, reaching his hands inside.

Conrad hovered, like a moth, next to him. He put both his hands together as if he was praying, raised them above his head and brought them crashing down on the back of Darren's head, sending him forward into the safe. Darren grunted as his hands scraped at the metal before passing out on the floor.

My mouth fell open. 'What... what the fuck are you doing?'

He let out a long breath. 'Well,' he said, scraping his hair behind his ears, 'he was going to find out sooner or later that he's got a bag full of nothing. And I've got enough people after me.'

I put my hands over my eyes and rubbed my forehead. 'Oh fuck.'

'What?'

'I wish you wouldn't get pissed all the time.'

Conrad looked confused. 'I haven't had a drink in hours. I was acting it down there to get Darren drunk.'

'Well, I wish you'd think then.'

'What?'

'Oh shit,' I said rubbing the top of my head. 'Listen Conrad, I ran into Ken on the way here. Look in the bag.'

'Oh...' he said, looking inside and pulling out the contents, the plastic bags full of Ecstasy. '... shit. Oops.'

I scratched at my temple. 'Nice one, Skippy.'

'How was I to know?'

'Try opening your eyes.'

'Fuck it. We'll take the money and leave the gear.'

I paused. 'Sounds fair.'

Conrad put his hands in the safe and pulled out a stack of money. 'Christ he's loaded,' he said looking at all the cash.

'Take the fifty grand and let's go. Don't take the lot.'

'Of course, mate. Who do you think I am?'

'I'm starting to think I don't know. Can we see if we can stay out of trouble until we both get out of the country?'

'Hey I'm not going looking for it you know. I want a quiet life as much as anyone.'

I shook my head. 'I'm not convinced, my friend.'

Conrad put the cash in the bag and zipped it up. 'There's one more thing I want to do quickly. I'm feeling lucky.'

I followed him out of the bar.

Chapter Twenty Six

In the bookies, so full of smoke I could hardly breathe, Conrad grabbed a paper and flicked back to the racing pages. I looked round at the punters. Earnest faces, eyes more narrowed than normal, fags stuck to lower lips, scrawny bodies. Gambling was as bad as any addiction, coming up on the outside there with sex addiction to take on the more usual photo finish of alcohol and drug problems.

As I stared blankly at the screens, Conrad suddenly tensed up, just like he had when he saw the Chinese guys in Wan Chai.

'What's happened, missed the hot tip?'

'No,' he hung his head. Colour draining from his face. 'Look at this.'

I read the article: *Woman stabbed in Luk Tei Tong. The peace of Lantau Island is disturbed in the afternoon when....* I looked down the page... *police are investigating... possible racial attack.*

'So?'

'Look closely at the photo,' Conrad said, looking behind him.

The picture above the article was of Conrad's flat, the patio window shattered, blood on the concrete.

I re-read the article, trying to work out what it meant. 'What do you reckon?'

'I reckon,' Conrad said in a hushed tone. 'I reckon, that

little cockney went round to my flat to break my legs and killed the old lady.'

'The woman who lived upstairs?'

'Yeah, it's her.'

'Nick killed her? Why would he have killed her?'

'For getting in the way. Standing between him and the money. And he hates the Chinese. If she heard someone break in, she'd have checked it out. Let's get the fuck out of here.'

Walking along the crowded streets we sweated freely, our bodies trying to rid themselves of toxic build up. We headed straight for the Body Shop nestled in amongst a row of fast food joints off Hennessy Road. Above the store was a tattooists run by an old Chinese guy and a haggard Cambodian. Besides doing tattoos, they also did a little side-line in forged passports.

Conrad figured he needed one. If he tried to fly out on his own passport, he was likely to get arrested for stabbing the old woman. His landlord had a photocopy of his ID card with his photo on. The police would have that by now and would have circulated it. If he had a false passport, he reckoned he had half a chance of getting out of the country safely.

'I don't need this,' he said as we climbed the stairs.

I don't need it either, I thought, but I kept my mouth shut. No point in starting an argument.

On the second floor, I followed Conrad left down the corridor, arriving at a cast iron grill, behind which was a metal door with a postcard of a Buddha on. The sign said closed. Conrad rang the bell. He knocked on the door. Nothing. He rang the bell again. There was some shuffling, and the sound of a Chinese voice. Slowly the voice approached the door. The sound of bolts being drawn back echo-ed down the dim corridor, then the door opened a crack. A wrinkled face peeped out, looked Conrad up and down.

'What you want?'

'Passport.'

'We close. Open two.' The man went to close the door. Conrad put his hand through the bars to stop it. His injured hand awkwardly waved some money under the man's nose.

'Passport,' he said. 'Lido,' then shook the money.

The man eyed the money through his half moon spectacles. 'You want today?'

'Yup.'

'Ten thousand.'

Conrad glared at the man. 'Eight.'

'Oh no,' the man smiled and receded from the doorway again.

Conrad settled on nine.

The man smiled slowly, staring at Conrad's open wallet. He opened the outer door and gestured for us to come in.

Inside the man's apartment were clusters of Chinese Lanterns and burning joss sticks. He had an altar where he prayed. There was fruit placed carefully either side of the Buddha, pyramids of oranges and apples. The Buddha ate well. It looked serene and at peace with the universe. The room smelt of rose petals and cigarette smoke.

'You want English passport?' the man said, guiding us to his desk.

'Yes. Old style. Black, bigger. Not red.'

The man sat down in a creaky office swivel chair. The type made out of tubular aluminium. He adjusted his glasses on his broad nose. He unlocked the top drawer of his desk and pulled out a bundle of passports held together with a rubber band. Carefully he removed it and fanned out the documents like a pack of cards.

'You want Australia visa? America?'

Conrad thought about this. 'Why not?' he said, leafing through the options. He looked at the faces of the photos. People half smiling at the camera, perhaps looking forward to their first trip abroad. They wouldn't be smiling now. They'd be frantically phoning embassies and consulates trying to renew their passports. They should have been more careful. The Triad operations involved crews of young men scouring the airport terminals for useful documents. Any that weren't in button down or zip up pockets were in danger of being pinched.

'I'll take this one,' he said, holding up Daniel Peterson's passport. He was thirty, this poor kid, born in Ipswich. He had a year's work visa for Australia. 'You take the photo now?'

The old man nodded.

'You have scissors?' Conrad made a cutting motion with his hand.

'Ah yes.'

Conrad took them from him and with one snip, cut off his ponytail. Standing in front of the mirror he cut in a fringe. For a two minute job it didn't look bad. He looked like a fashionable, grungy backpacker, or a raggedy Kurt Cobain.

The Chinese man smiled at him, clasping his hands together.

'Very good. I fink you have good job if you want.'

Conrad smiled. He looked ten years younger. The man positioned him against the back wall and took his photo. Afterwards, he gave him five thousand and told him he'd get the rest when it was ready. The old man nodded, shuffling in his desk drawer for the equipment he needed to replace the photo, re-stamp it and laminate it. Conrad asked him what time it'd be ready.

The man pointed at his watch.

'Six?'

He nodded.

'Okay,' said Conrad, 'I'll come back at six. You'll be open?'

The man nodded again.

'It's very important,' Conrad said. 'I fly tomorrow night.' He put his arms out to his sides, level with his shoulders like wings.

The man smiled. 'No probrem, no probrem.'
'That's what you all say,' Conrad muttered, and we left.

On the street we went straight to the nearest telephone box. Conrad called Kai Tak airport. The booth smelt of urine. It wafted over us as he lifted the receiver. The hand piece was covered in greasy sweat. I stood outside watching the Chinese girls walk past in flares. Conrad held the receiver through his shirt cuff, keeping it away from his ear. He dialled the number for Emirates and cancelled his eleven forty flight to Manila.

'Part one done,' he said to me and hung up the phone. He dug his hand in his pocket to get more change to ring them back. He didn't have any.

'Fuck,' he whispered. 'You got any change Josh?'

I shook my head.

We ducked into the Seven Eleven. It took five minutes before we were back on the phone. Queuing: the same nightmare in any country.

In his best north of England accent he asked the girl to book him on the 23.40, Kai Tak to Manila. She asked him to hold.

'Don't tell me its gone already,' Conrad said to me.

'It can't be. She's just checking. It's normal.'

There was a wait on the line. He held his breath. The girl eventually came back on. There were no available seats on the flight. Would he like to try another day?

Conrad glared at me. 'Yes,' he said tightly.

There was another pause. Then the girl spoke again. The next available seat was on the 14:20 the next day. Did he want to reserve a seat?

Conrad made a face and booked it, spelling out the name Peterson, Daniel.

'You want to pay now?' I heard the girl ask.

Conrad covered the phone. 'Give us your credit card, mate.'

'What? What about yours?'

'I can't use mine can I?'

This was a fair point. I gave him my Mastercard. It was already nearly on the limit.

'Cheers man.'

He read the number out to the girl. It took her a few minutes to complete the transaction. He could collect his ticket from the Emirates desk no less than two hours before departure. Conrad thanked her and hung up the phone.

'There are no guarantees,' he said, raising an eyebrow, 'as we know only too well by now, but I think I might actually get out of here, you know.'

'There is nothing,' I said, 'nothing worth having, without risk.'

We looked at each other.

'But to play it safe,' I said. 'Let's go to Sophie's. We should be okay there.'

We had dinner at Sophie's that night. Spaghetti bolognaise we all helped to cook. Her parents were celebrating a friend's birthday at The Mandarin Hotel in Central, so we didn't have to make polite conversation. Her father, a retired Major, could be overbearing, and had a nasty habit of asking pertinent questions with an unwavering gaze. I didn't think I could handle that stare with the weight of bad stuff we'd been up to, so I was relieved he was otherwise employed.

After supper we packed our things. The money we put in two black day bags. We had only eight grand to split. Conrad insisted I take five and he took three. I didn't put up much resistance. It was only a thousand more than my original stake. Besides, Conrad had something lined up in the Philippines. I decided not to ask what it was.

As we were about to go out, Ken showed up. He looked freaked out. His door was off its hinges, he said, and Simone had vanished to a friend's. He couldn't understand it, though Conrad and I could.

After we'd calmed him down, we went out to the Bit Point Bar in Lan Kwai Fong to get some perspective. Conrad promised Ken he'd get his door sorted and also agreed he needed to apologise to a few people before he left the country. Seemingly proud of these decisions, he then proceeded to get very drunk. After a long period of rowdiness, he sat at the bar looking like he was going to lose his balance at any minute, meekly sipping his JD and Coke.

Me and Sophie stood gallantly next to him, drinking a bottle of white wine. Ken was on Diet Coke, and very quiet. He had too much on his mind to make polite conversation.

'Are you and Conrad going to come and see me in Bangkok?' I asked Sophie. I was pretty drunk too, trying to finish our little reunion on a high.

She looked deep in my eyes, trying to convey some heavy meaning. 'What are you doing out there?'

'This and that.'

Sophie took another sip of her wine and looked round the busy bar. 'This is where I live,' she said. 'This is where my life is. This is where your life was as well, and you chose to leave. You didn't tell me why. You just went. You skipped like a stone across the water.'

'I was… confused,' I said.

'You'll always be confused. Won't you? It's that confusion that bounces you along. It's like your motivation. We all have something that keeps us going. Fear, ambition, love. Your thing is confusion. You'd be lost without it.'

I looked down at my trainers, at the untied laces and the scuffs. 'I wasn't very good at being a boyfriend,' I said. 'I tried. But I wasn't good at it. I'm sorry.'

'I hope you're better to the girl you're with at the moment.'

'I think I'm getting better.'

'Does she love you?'

'Yeah.'

'Does she love you more than I did?'

She put one of the photos of us grinning for the camera after we'd got back from Neptunes on the bar. It looked so real. So romantic.

I nodded and didn't say anything. I continued to look at the photo. But it was like a forgery. I wasn't sure if Lek loved me more or less than Sophie. You can't rate the love two very different people give you. But this much I knew. Lek was much easier to live with. The reason Sophie and I split up was simple. Those green eyes, those slinky limbs, that sassy attitude, they all disguised one element of her being I couldn't handle. Her temper. When she flew off the handle at me, it reminded of all the bad things. It gave me the same tight feeling I had when Zack died. I couldn't live with that. I had to get out.

But I didn't want to remind myself of that now, after we'd had such a good time. And I certainly didn't want to mention it, for fear of it triggering that anger.

'I had to move on,' I said. 'That's all. You'll always be a part of me.'

'I won't be coming to Bangkok,' she said. 'It'll be too awkward. But good luck.'

'You too.'

I put the photo in my pocket. And then. Nothing. No drama, no pain. Just a statement.

I didn't know what else to say, so I said something mundane to Ken and he just nodded and looked blank and then I looked over at Conrad slumped on the bar, and felt jealous he was sleeping through a difficult emotional moment that he should, somehow, have been involved in. So I tried to involve him. Using him as a scapegoat, I said:'I think we better take him home,' in a fatherly way.

'Yes,' Sophie said, and looked fondly at him. 'He's partied out.'

And so that was the last drink I had in Hong Kong. We went home, to sleep at Sophie's. I wept for the past, and I think she did too, but we both knew there was no going back.

And that was it. There was nothing more. The continuity stopped.

Chapter Twenty Seven

The next morning I woke early as planned. I'd slept well, except for the disturbing kind of dreams you get when you're under pressure. Stuff like being pushed out of aircraft, giant spiders crawling over your face, witches digging about in your ribs. I always had bad dreams as a kid, so these didn't really worry me. I got up, showered and dressed and then went to Conrad's room. It smelt like a boarding school dormitory, the air thick and musky.

'Get up fat boy,' I said as I walked in the bedroom. 'You have to make good before you leave the country, remember?'

Conrad groaned. 'Vaguely, what's my schedule?'

I repeated what I'd said the previous night. We should see Simone and Darren first, then head to the tattooists in Kowloon to get his passport before legging it to the airport. Conrad mumbled some kind of agreement through a long yawn.

'Get in the shower. Sophie and I'll get breakfast on.'

Ken sat up in the other bed. Sophie had invited him to stay. She didn't like the idea of him sleeping in an apartment with a missing door.

'You too, Ken. But not at the same time.'

He nodded, rubbing sleep out of his eyes.

'You've both got quarter of an hour,' I said and left them to get up.

After a couple of rounds of chunky bacon sandwiches followed by vodka and orange chasers, we headed out. On the steps of her house, I gave Sophie a hug and said goodbye. I think we both wanted to keep it as short as possible. We didn't want to hear the imaginary violins playing in the background. I was on such an emotional knife-edge, I couldn't even look her in the eye.

'I'm sorry for being a shit,' I said, giving her one last hug after the others had got in the taxi.

'You can't help it. That's just you.'

'Oh thanks.' I kissed her on both cheeks.

'You take care,' she replied. 'Don't forget me.'

'I won't. Thanks for everything.'

I walked to the road without looking back. In a way, I still loved her, but I knew I was never going to see her again. It was time for life to move forward. I had too many problems in the present to have time to try sorting out the ones from the past.

I got in the back of the taxi and asked the driver to take us to Mongkok.

'I'm really fucking sorry about what's happened over the last few days, Ken,' said Conrad as we rode through the Kowloon tunnel, a mirror image of the route we took several days earlier. 'I can't remember exactly what happened that night, but I think I owe you a big apology.'

'That's okay,' said Ken. 'Forget it. You were under a lot of stress.'

'Too right. Too fucking right. Still I feel okay now and... well, I'm sorry. That's all.'

'Forget it. Shit happens.'

The cab pulled up outside Ken's apartment in Mongkok. Conrad paid the driver. The stocky little carpenter we phoned on the way was already there when we arrived, hanging a new door. Conrad asked him how much he owed and paid him.

Nick had battered the door down after me and Ken ran off. He'd hobbled, or dragged himself up the stairs with his broken legs. You had to admire his willpower. Simone managed to get away to a friend's. She was refusing to speak to Ken, knowing he was mixed up in it.

She was nowhere to be seen. We persuaded Ken to phone her at the friend's house. She answered sounding tense, as usual. Ken passed the phone to Conrad, who did his best to explain the situation without giving away too much information that would get Ken in more trouble.

Conrad handled it pretty well, I think, considering he couldn't stand the girl.

'All I want you to do,' he said soothingly into the receiver, 'is to stop blaming Ken for any of this. It isn't his fault. I got him mixed up in something he didn't want to be involved in and that's it. I apologise. He's blame free. That's all I can say. Why don't you come over, smoke a... no forget that. Just come and make up, yeah.'

Simone resisted for some time, but eventually he persuaded her.

Hanging up the phone, he turned to Ken. 'She's coming over,' he said. 'Sounds like everything should work out. Just remember rule one of relationships. When in doubt: deny, deny, deny.'

Ken smiled. 'Thanks, I guess this is goodbye then?'

'You said it brother,' said Conrad, giving him a hug. 'But we'll meet again. I don't doubt that.'

Ken and I shook hands.

'Will you say goodbye to the others for me?'

'Sure.'

'Do you reckon we'll all get together again?'

'I think we might,' said Conrad, 'but it might not be advisable.' He walked towards the newly hung door. 'And forget what I said about Simone, okay? I was out of it then. She wouldn't be right for me, but she might just be right for you. You have to make up your own mind, brother. Go your own way. Do what does it for you.'

'Thanks, take care.'

'See ya,' we said, and raced down the stairs. We quickly hailed a cab and piled in. It was time to see Darren.

Conrad slumped in the back, 'Let's hope he's not too rough on me.'

'I think he will be.'

'I'll tell you this,' said Conrad coming over all serious, his forehead doubling its wrinkles. 'If he hits me, you get smacked straight after. Only twice as hard. By me.'

I laughed. Conrad's impression he was a hard nut always amused me. If he'd drunk enough he'd think he could handle someone the size of King Kong.

'You can't hit as hard as Darren,' I said.

'No, but I can give it a fucking good go.'

The cab made its way to the bar and pulled up. Conrad knocked on the glass frontage.

'Well, I'll be buggered,' said Darren as he strode over and opened the door to the Kiss Bar. 'What the fuck are you doing here?'

'I made a big fucking mistake,' Conrad said holding his hands up in surrender. 'I've come to straighten it out with you.'

'You've got some fucking explaining to do, sonny,' he growled, 'let me tell you.'

Conrad half smiled and launched into his pre-prepared apology speech. Darren listened with his arms folded, eyebrows furrowed. He nodded while Conrad talked, sometimes cocking his head to one side.

When he was finished, Darren hit him with a firm right hand. Not full force, just a glancing blow to Conrad's right eye. Enough to bruise it purple but not black.

'That's for even thinking about ripping me off,' he bellowed and then laughed at Conrad's shocked expression. 'My God you're the maddest bastard I ever met.'

Conrad rubbed his temple before laughing. 'You wanker.'

'That's your going away present,' Darren told him. 'He

deserved that, didn't he Josh?'

I agreed.

'Thanks a fuck.'

'Pleasure my old friend.'

'Do I get a drink to numb the pain?'

Darren laughed again. 'One last JD and Coke then. Why not? Hopefully I'll never see you again.'

Conrad chuckled some more. 'That's what I always liked about you Darren. Your ability to make me feel good. Make it a treble.'

We made it to the Body Shop five minutes later. Time to get the passport.

Conrad bounded up the stairs to the studio with uncharacteristic athleticism. I followed. The tattooist was putting the final touches to a full back piece on a young Chinese man. We waited. He hardly acknowledged our presence.

'Triads have tattoos like that,' Conrad said to me in a whisper as he watched the blood ooze from the man's back like juice coming up through orange peel. 'Funny people.'

'Yeah.'

After the man had his back bandaged to prevent his shirt infecting the newly perforated skin, the tattooist ushered him out and locked the outer door. He put up the closed sign and went behind his desk, unlocked the drawer and removed a dog-eared black passport.

Conrad took it from him. 'Very good,' he said, turning it over in his hands. 'Very nice.'

'Okay?' said the tattooist. 'I think you come yesterday.'

'I was busy,' Conrad smiled, pulling his wallet from his pocket and counting out four thousand dollars.

The tattooist watched him carefully. When he was finished he bowed curtly at him. 'Fankyou.'

Conrad removed an extra five hundred dollar note and placed it in the man's hand before leaving. 'You're a life saver, you take care, eh?'

The man bowed again and unlocked the door. 'Good luck,' he smiled, letting Conrad through. 'I fink you need it.'

The cab wound its way through the Hong Kong traffic, eventually pulling up at Kai Tak. I paid the driver while Conrad commandeered a trolley with wheels on it that went forwards and backwards rather than sideways.

I heard my flight announced on the speakers. A last call.

'I've got to shift,' I said. 'That's my flight.'

'You go for it,' he said. 'I've got a couple of hours to kill, so I might hit the bar.'

'Now there's a surprise. When are you going to be in Bangkok?'

'You know me, brother.'

'Yeah, I do. I'll see you whenever. You know where I'll be.'

Conrad gave me a bear hug before I headed off to the check in desk.

'You're the best friend I've got,' he said. 'Don't go changing.'

'You neither,' I said. 'I've got to run.'

'Cool brother. See you in Bangkok,' Conrad called after me again. 'We'll have a party!'

Chapter Twenty Eight - Bangkok. The Present.

I often think about that moment in the airport. The quick goodbye followed by the dash for the plane and the flight back to Bangkok. I never felt more alive. Dr Miller often asks if I can remember being happy. Yes I can. I was happy then. I was definitely happy then.

But after the high comes the low. Once you've climbed the mountain, you have to descend. When I arrived home, I realised I'd left both black bags with Conrad. Stupid. I had no money, and I hadn't been earning.

On Marcus' advice I'd borrowed from Ratty. I got sick. The debt got away from me, as debts with high interest do and before I knew it he was heavily on my case to pay back the loan.

Hong Kong was an enjoyable mistake. I was now in the mess Conrad had been in, an irony that didn't escape me. I owed Ratty close to three thousand and rising. I kept hoping Conrad would show up, but the more time passed the more I began to wonder if he'd got out of Hong Kong okay. Those Chinese guys kept popping into my head, wielding machetes. I tried not to think about what may have happened.

Right now I'm on my way back from the night out with Cho. The tuk tuk I'm in is particularly uncomfortable. Maybe this driver has given it sports suspension, or maybe the suspension's just wrecked. I know I am. I've got the money but I'm tired and I'm half drunk and I want to go to bed and forget all this shit.

Walking wearily towards my door, I realise this won't happen. My heart sinks as I approach. I can hear girls screaming at the top of their voices. I walk into the living room to find Lek swinging an open palm at Pim's cheek. The contact sounds like a brittle branch breaking.

In the stunned silence that follows I get myself between the two of them, my arms out stretched like a boxing referee. Neither girl moves. They're both in shock.

"What's going on?" I say. "You guys are friends. We're all friends."

I look at the empty beer bottles littered round the place. For two little girls they've drunk a huge amount.

Lek points at Pim. "You slip wit her before you slip wit me, yes?"

I look at the floor.

"You slip wit her, yes?" Lek repeats.

I rub a hand over my brow. "It's a long story, Lek."

"But it true, yes?"

"It was before I met you."

"Before you meet me? So? Why you not tell me like this before?"

"Because I thought this would happen? How did this come up?" I ask.

"I solly," says Pim. "We drinking and I tell her. I think she don't mind because it long time ago. And not for love, right. Not for love."

"Exactly. Lek? You've got this all wrong."

"I don think so. I hate you! You lie with me. I hate that. I tell you many time. Don lie. Don lie with me. And you do. You think I stupid or what? Stupid like a child, or what? I hate you. I fucking hate you." Lek launches herself at me and starts pounding my chest, angry fists clenched.

'Lek, I can tell you the whole story," Pim says. "You can trust Josh. He's a good man. Come with me please and I'll tell you everything."

The Body is a Temple

I look down at Lek. I tell her to go and discuss it some more with Pim, and then she'll realise she's being crazy. But Lek doesn't want to go anywhere.

"But Pim can explain everything if you just let her," I coax.

Pim backs me up. Lek appears calmer. She looks at me, then Pim. She apologises for being drunk. She says she's been under a lot of stress recently with the baby and that she's very angry about lots of things. Pim gives her a hug and after a little more discussion they agree to have a coffee together at a nearby restaurant and sort out their differences. I tell Lek I love her and then they're gone.

I flop on the sofa and close my eyes. I tried to do the right thing by keeping my mouth shut and this happens. If I'd have told her, it'd have been wrong too. A lose-lose situation. I screwed up in Hong Kong, now I'm messing up in Thailand. In an attempt to avoid becoming a consumer driven, money chasing nine to fiver with two point four children and a mammoth mortgage, I'm still getting it wrong. Only now my mistakes are affecting people I really care about. Lek and I agreed to grow up, but with the past so close, so insistent and so real, I'm finding it difficult. I suddenly feel a huge weight of shame, like wet concrete falling on my shoulders. I lose myself by staring at the cool white tiled floor and for a second I glimpse again the little boy on the blue Chopper cycling carefree down a London street.

Several hours later, still zoning in on the tiles, I get a call from Lek.

'I stay with Nong tonight,' is all she says, before she hangs up.

I put the phone down. This is not good. In an attempt to cheer myself up, I phone Ratty to tell him I've got the money. He doesn't answer. I phone Pim. She isn't in.

I go to bed with a bottle of vodka. I play some hard rap at full volume on my CD player that vocalises the anger I feel. Half way through the album and the vodka, I pass out.

Nightmares filter through the booze. I feel desperate and hunted. I run down the long narrow, low ceilinged tunnel, the beast right behind me. There is no escape. There is no exit.

When morning finally comes I decide the old enemy routine will peg down the billowing canvas of my troubled mind. I block the problems out. Ratty can have the money when he comes to get it. I'm tired of chasing him up.

I go to the gym and work out, concentrating on the punch bag. I instruct one client, then go swimming in the adjacent outdoor pool. It keeps my mind busy enough that I don't choke with worry. But none of it gives me any pleasure, or any relief.

Pim and I have a special friendship, something Lek doesn't know about, and should never have found out.

When Marcus got me into the whole gigolo deal, he asked Pim to spend a week in a hotel room with me to teach me how to satisfy a woman.

'Imagine a lady like beautiful, clear water,' Pim told me. 'She start cold, but she want to warm. You have make her like that slowly.'

Me and Pim spent the entire time in bed, only taking short breaks to order room service, or shower, or get some air on the balcony.

I'd never realised how little I knew. When it came to giving a girl a kick, knowing where to touch her, how hard and for how long, it turned out what I'd thought was good sex was as exciting as viewing an aunt's stamp collection on a wet Sunday afternoon.

Pim set me straight. She taught me tricks to improve my performance and stamina. She helped with my breathing and my orgasm control. She showed me all the areas on a woman's body where I could extract pleasure and made me an expert at mining it.

By the end of the week, I'd improved so much I had Pim crying with pleasure as I took her through a whole series of orgasms.

The Body is a Temple

The week with Pim was intense and personal. By the end I was convinced I loved her. Again Pim taught me a valuable lesson: good sex is not love.

A customer may become confused, but the prostitute must never.

'Remember that,' she had said. 'Otherwise you get big problem here.'

I was disappointed, but I understood. It took me weeks to get over it, but when I did, it all made perfect sense. It wasn't a rejection at all. It was business. We became friends after that and it was good for both of us. It was reassuring to know someone so well who worked in the same industry.

Now Pim was a good friend, and that was all. We hadn't slept together since.

I return home for lunch to find Lek sitting on the balcony, tranced out.

I move towards her, putting my arms around her. "It's so good to see you. How are you?"

"I go hospital in morning," she says. "Samsook still sick."

Her mood makes the memory of the previous night recede. I tell her it'll take time.

"I don think she make better now," Lek says.

I rub the side of her neck and slide my hand down her back. I offer to make breakfast, but Lek isn't hungry. I tell her she should eat something, but she doesn't reply.

I go inside and put some yoghurt in a bowl with some muesli.

"Eat this," I say taking it out to her. "If you don't eat, you'll feel worse."

Lek takes the spoon and swirls it round the bowl. Tears roll down her cheeks as she takes the first very small mouthful.

Not wanting to, but somehow driven towards it, I ask her about Pim.

Lek frowns. "I drunk," she says. "Jealous."

"So you're not angry any more."

"I no happy, but no angry. I worry Samsook more."

"So we're okay."

"Yes. But don lie, okay?"

"I won't, babe. I love you."

I decide to leave it there. Forcing her into showing me any kind of affection now may make her back track, or side step, like a crab.

"I'm going to have a shower," I say. "Cho gave me the money, by the way. I can pay Ratty."

Lek stares at her muesli, dragging her tea spoon through it in a figure eight.

I go to the bathroom. As the water pours over me I have an overwhelming urge to burst into tears. The pressure of everything unraveling is becoming too strong. I massage my scalp to get over it.

Back in my gym clothes, shorts and tshirt, I wander into the living room and tell Lek I'm heading out, but I'll be back for lunch.

"Wait," Lek says. "I speak with doctor today, babe. They need money for Samsook. To take care her."

She mentions almost to the baht the amount Cho gave me. They need it straight away. Fighting the urge to scream I tell her I'll take care of it. I give her a kiss and head straight for the hospital

In the clean, white reception I hand over the printed bill and the rolls of baht.

"*Kap kun kah*," says the receptionist.

"And thank you too," I reply. And I mean it, despite the difficulties. I look in at Samsook before I go. There is no apparent change.

In the afternoon I have two sessions in the gym. I administer them like a robot, devoid of emotion. My mind is above the clouds. My mind is stratospheric. It's like a rocket orbiting the earth, completely detached.

"Okay that's it for today," I say to my client as he rubs the sweat off his brow. He's well exercised now, looking toned after three months of my guidance. He appears years younger than his forty, having lost some kilos. He's more energetic and his sagging skin has tightened.

Where he was lost, now he is found, I think. Where he is finding himself, I'm losing myself. It has a nice symmetry, at least. I ask him in an off hand way if he can pay his bill today, but he says he doesn't have his wallet with him. I nod, hoping I don't look as close to a breakdown as I feel.

"That's not a problem," I say and go to wash my hands.

Chapter Twenty Nine

Lek is at the hospital when I return and I decide not to join her. I have a client at seven and though I'm tired and don't want to go, I know I have to because we need the money.

I lie on the sun lounger on the balcony, looking up at the white brickwork. The stereo inside plays some house CD. The lyrics are beautiful, breathy and tranquil. The girl sings, 'There is so much to do. There are so many people to forgive.'

I listen to the music and the traffic passing below.

At six I have noodles with a huge amount of chilli to wake me up. Then I have a coffee, followed by a shower. I dress in a cream suit, tailor made by an Indian in West Bangkok, and a tan shirt. At six thirty I leave the flat, catching a taxi to the Hyatt.

The girl I'm meeting is a first timer. For some reason I feel nervous, so I have several beers in the bar while I wait. When she turns up I'm pleasantly surprised. She's forty-ish, but fit. Under the dim lights we talk, but I don't ask too many questions. I let the girls say what they want. It's their night.

She likes it hard and fast, the condom splits. I don't realise till I withdraw and find I've pushed right through it. I rush to the bathroom and rip it off. I stare in the mirror, taking deep breaths whilst washing myself. I return to the bedroom where the girl gives me American dollars for the service and asks if we can meet again. I tell her to call me.

She sits up in bed, her heavy breasts hanging low on her

chest, her nipples large and almost black.

"What?" I say.

"Kiss me," she says.

"You can't touch me now," I say, backing away. "Your time is up."

As I leave I look in the envelope. It contains a hundred dollars. This kind of money is getting me nowhere, not with the amount I'm drinking now. Leaving the hotel I walk to a nearby bar, the night air still hot and close, and order a small bottle of Singh Thip. It's only eighty baht. Just over a pound. I can still afford that.

I sit at a table outside and slug it straight from the bottle. I put my mobile on the table and my wallet. As I drink I idly scroll through the numbers. Finding no-one I want to call I transfer my attention to the myriad business cards in my wallet. Cards I've been given on nights out with some of the other working guys, when I've been drunk enough to describe or offer my services. As I flick through them I charge down more Singh Thip. Half way down the bottle I find a thicker, embossed card of excellent quality. I pick it out and inspect it, running my fingers over its surface, turning it over and over. There's a home address hand written on the back. Oh yeah. Mr Pampoon. I think back. Smart guy, in his forties, buys and sells property. Strange to meet him in Koa San, I thought. But not so strange when I found out he was cruising. I told him I did girls only, but he'd had a few drinks and pushed on. He told me if I ever changed my mind, there'd be good money in it. He said I looked like a movie star. I told him I didn't feel like one.

I look at my watch. It's half ten, still not too late to call. I swig back the rest of the bottle of Singh Thip and go inside for another. When I come back out I enter Mr Pampoon's number into my mobile and put it back on the table. The luminous screen shines up at me like a miniature sun, or moon, then extinguishes. I take a ten baht coin from my pocket. I turn it over in my hand examining its gold centre, its silver edging. I swig a third of the bottle of whisky, the amber liquid scorching the back of my throat.

King's head, I call him. Spire side, I go home.

I spin the coin high into the air, the wind moving round its surfaces make it sound like a cicada. I watch it arc and fall before catching it in my sweaty palm and quickly slapping it on to the back of my left hand. I take a breath and slowly reveal the coin. I look down at the ninth king of Thailand's face. I press the green button on the mobile. The phone rings.

"*Sawat-di krab*," says a Thai voice.

"Mr Pampoon," I reply. 'It's Joshua Stone. I'm free tonight if..."

He cuts in with a place we can meet.

I hang up and drain the bottle, buying another before I leave.

In the morning I call Ratty on his mobile. It rings and there's no answer. I phone Marcus and we arrange to meet for lunch at the Monkey Bar. When I arrive I give him an envelope stuffed with cash: the money from three gym sessions, the girl, and Mr Pampoon. I ask him to give it to Ratty.

The Monkey Bar is quiet today. People are obviously having noodles at work. Marcus and I are drinking whisky. Red Label, not the Thai stuff. Marcus is paying. My hangover is so bad I can hardly think straight. My life is hurtling downward at terrifying speed. I feel like a pilot falling from a damaged plane, pulling the ripcord, and the parachute refusing to open.

Marcus takes the envelope and puts it in his black jacket pocket. He doesn't look like he's slept in a while.

"I'll give it to him," he drawls, stretching his legs out. "I have been meaning to ask, actually. How come you're in such a difficult financial situation at the moment. Was it just the Hong Kong thing?"

"Mostly yeah. Just lending a load to Conrad. My savings. I

actually made money out there. It's just he's got it."

"Loaning to friends is not good," says Marcus. "They always see it as a gift."

"Yeah, I know your stand on it. Personally, I think it's the best thing you can do. If the guy really needs it… Can you just make sure Ratty doesn't come round my place again? I don't need that right now."

"Yeah," says Marcus. "I was thinking about that. You should stay at my place. You can get away from everything. Stay in luxury for a change. We can talk, have a few beers. Go out, maybe. I'll need to do some work, but this need not concern you. What do you think?"

"I think I should be with Lek right now."

Marcus says he thinks she needs her space.

"I'll have to talk to her about it."

Marcus shakes his head. "I hope you don't mind, but I asked her already. She thinks it's a good idea."

This rocks me back a bit, but I accept it. I guess it's a come back to the time I spend with Wow.

"And what do you get out of this deal?" I ask. "I mean I know we're friends, but you haven't invited me round in months. I didn't think you even liked me that much anymore."

"I do have one very good reason. Wow has left me. I could use the company. Someone to talk to. A person who knows us both."

"Fuck me," I say. Shocked and scared.

Marcus laughs.

"Well, I might have to take you up on that offer, Josh. Because I won't be fucking her, will I?"

His comment rocks the very core of me. Details from last night's events rise from the very place I'm already trying to bury them. I sit, rooted to the spot, until the surrounding muted noises become louder and louder, back to their original state. A sudden movement catches my eye, pulling me back from reverie.

It's Marcus getting up from the table, telling me he'll see me tonight, before he strides out into the sunshine. I sit there for a little while longer hoping those feelings, the memory, the numbness that's descended around me like a thick fog, would stay behind once I leave.

I head home on the Kawasaki. I think back to my chat with Conrad in Hong Kong, the one where I asked him if he felt BAD. It was a real question, not a joke, and it turned out he was. He was as bitter, alienated and desperate as any of the ex-pat screw ups, and now, my self esteem plummeting, I am joining the club. As I ride home I can't get Michael Jackson's voice out of my head. It loops round and round singing the final line of that song. Who's BAD?

And I smile without humour.

Chapter Thirty

Marcus' place is five minutes south from mine. The fifteenth floor, Rama I tower block, Ratcha Withi.

From the outside, with its whitewashed walls and modern minimalist style, the building looks similar to mine.

Inside the difference is apparent. Marcus owns the whole of the top two floors. Two apartments on each floor connected by brushed aluminium spiral staircases. Marcus has money inherited from family, and lots of it. He's travelled on it his entire adult life. His dad, who died young, made a pile from manufacturing.

When I arrive, around eight, I park my bike in the basement garage and take the lift to the top all the way. I have to enter a code to gain access to the last two floors. Coming out of the lift, I have a choice of pale oak double doors at the south or north side, shutting the apartments off from the lift wells. I head for the south and hit the buzzer. The door clicks automatically, and I walk in. The sound of a heavy rock album plays out through high quality speakers.

As Marcus said, Lek was happy for me to spend a few days at his place. I asked her when I got in and she reassured me it was a good idea. I hugged her and gave her a kiss. Then I packed a small rucksack, gave her some money for a taxi and left. I suppose Marcus was right. At a time of grief, perhaps you do need to be with your own. The men with the men. The women with the women. The Thais with the Thais; the *falang* with the *falang*. I felt relaxed about Lek staying away from home. Nong was strong and stable. If anyone could comfort Lek, it was her.

I find Marcus preparing dinner in the kitchen. His kitchen is like his clothes. Black, cool and stylish.

"How're you doing?" I ask, sitting on one of the bar stools positioned by a high surface, dividing the kitchen off.

"Cool," he replies, without looking up. He's chopping some chillies on a wooden board, set on a square kitchen table. Behind me is the living room. Four sofas set in a square round a coffee table, a gap, two steps up, then eight chairs round an oval table: the dining area. The space is dim lit with low watt up lighters. The wall to my left is glass. A gateway to the city. The apartment is involved but remote. It reflects Marcus's personality perfectly.

"Need any help?"

"Could do with some advice on women probably," he says.

His mood is different from before. He's sullen now. The effect of Wow leaving has fully permeated his consciousness, leaving him feeling empty and depressed.

Marcus is dressed in black tracksuit bottoms, nothing else. His body is well muscled and defined, even in the dim light. I feel awkward being here. It should be Wow sitting on this stool.

"Do you want something to drink?" he asks.

I do. I feel awkward here. Marcus doesn't want me, he wants Wow.

"Help yourself," he continues. "Fix me a Jack and Coke would you?"

The booze is to my left. Shelves and shelves of it between the kitchen and the window, packed in like books.

I fix two big JD and Cokes, throwing in some ice.

"Cheers," I say, handing one to him. "What are we eating?"

"Spicy beef and pad thai, fucking hot."

I murmur my approval before asking Marcus where he

thinks Wow may have gone.

He throws the strips of beef into the steaming wok. They crackle in the hot sesame oil. "I was hoping," he says, looking up for the first time since my arrival, "that you could tell me."

"I haven't spoken to her. I don't know."

"But you used to speak to her often, right?"

"Yeah. You know that."

"So?" He stirs the beef. Adds the chillies. "Any ideas?"

I decide to play dumb on this one. Like I decided to play dumb about him hitting Wow. "No. No idea. Do you think she'll come back?"

"I hope so, Josh. I can't stand the thought of her with someone else."

I've finished my drink now and am pouring another. The beef is ready. Marcus takes the pad thai from the microwave and lays two plates on bamboo mats, and arranges the ingredients.

"Finish your drink," he says, draining his. "Red wine with this will be better."

At the table, half way through our food, I realise Marcus is very drunk. He doesn't slur his words, but his eyes are double glazed. His spiky mood begins to relax into inebriated sentimentality.

"You know how much I love her," he says. "She knows how much I love her. So..."

He pushes his food away and concentrates on the wine instead. He looks at me for the first time. His eyes seem to have no iris. They are so dark and deep, they seem to go on forever.

"So...?"

I realise this is not the time to remind him of his drunken rages and unreasonable demands.

"She'll come back," I say.

Marcus grabs my wrist as I'm taking the chopsticks to my mouth. Beef and pad thai scatter the surface of the table.

Much later, we're slumped on the sofa, on a third bottle of red and passing a joint back and forth.

"I love her so much," Marcus says again.

"Yeah. But you always do what you want. You do what you want and you always expect Wow to be there for you," I'm now drunk enough to say.

"But I look after her. I gave her a lovely home. I buy her anything she wants... What more can I do?"

"Give her some time. Some space."

We first saw Wow in a club in Pat Pong. Marcus and I, both single, were on a boys drinking night. We hadn't seen her before, but we noticed her as we walked in. You couldn't miss her.

There she was. A tall, nervous looking girl waiting at the bar. Too shy to mingle with the drinkers, or even to talk to the other girls. The disco lights picked out her perfect features. The eyes, nose and mouth... I couldn't stop staring at her. Nor could Marcus.

She looked like a startled foal as he approached, moving her body away from him, angling her hips protectively towards the bar.

'I'm not a mosquito,' he had said in Thai. 'I don't bite.'

The corners of her mouth moved up into a vague smile.

He offered to buy her a drink. She looked terrified, but with some shoving from another girl who said, 'It's your job! You have to. Otherwise you will starve in this town,' she followed Marcus to a secluded table, where she drank her beer. I stayed at the far end of the bar, watching. After a few minutes she appeared more relaxed.

She told Marcus she'd taken cheap local buses down from outside Nakkhon Sawan, not having enough money for the train. She was staying at an aunt's house in Ekamai, on the kitchen floor, with two of her cousins and other relatives.

The house was full to bursting. She got the job the day

after her arrival. She said she hadn't slept with anyone yet. Not in Bangkok or in Chiang Mai. She was a virgin.

Wow's story lacked originality. Marcus and I both knew that, but she was so fresh, we believed her. Her history turned out to be true. Marcus checked it out.

He made up his mind that she would fall in love with him. Over time she did, but it hadn't worked out like he'd hoped. And it hadn't been great for Wow, either. Jealousy and insecurity are terrible, destructive things.

"Do you think she'll come back?" Marcus asks again, stirring the ice cubes in his glass with his finger. "I can't phone her. She's left her mobile at home. I don't know where she is. I need to speak to her again."

"If you believe she'll come back, she will. If you really want it, she will. If you wish for anything hard enough, it will happen."

We fall into silence, brooding on this drunk prophesy.

So Samsook should recover, I think. Lek will forgive me. Sophie will find happiness. Zack will come back to life. Yeah, right.

"You never fucked her did you Josh?" Marcus asks.

The words hang in the air. I don't reply for some time. I don't know what to say. I stare at the coffee table, then at my bare feet resting on it.

"If you think I'd do that to you, you've got me really wrong."

The room goes quiet. Then I ask him if he hits her.

When Marcus doesn't reply I look over to him and realise he's passed out.

I take the joint from his hand, push him over sideways so he sleeps more comfortably and collapse back on the other sofa. I finish the joint, turn off the lights and am soon asleep.

The next morning Marcus slaps me on my chest to wake me.

"Hey," he says looking down at me. "Four double beds in the place and we sleep on the sofa."

I open one eye. "I feel like someone's using my head as a basketball."

"Don't worry. I have the best hangover cure."

I cough and squint. White light enters the room through the gaps in the blinds. I get off the sofa and stretch my arms over my head, my body forming a surfboard. Marcus gives a dummy karate kick to my chest before leading me up one of the spiral staircases to a room next to his bedroom.

"You didn't know I had a sauna here, did you?"

I shake my head. He opens the door to the pine-slatted interior. Heat waves filter out.

Marcus seems in a much better mood this morning. He doesn't appear to remember his last question to me, and I don't feel the need to remind him.

"Wait here," he says. "I'll get you a towel."

He disappears through the bedroom into the en suite bathroom and emerges with two white towels. We drop our trousers by the door, put the towels round our waists and shut ourselves in the interior shed. The sauna hasn't been on long, but it's already stiflingly hot. Marcus continually adds water to the coals, filling the space with steam.

"Marcus I can hardly breathe, man," I say.

"Don't worry. I find it the same. I had these put in." He reaches behind him and produces two masks. "Press the red button when you have it over your head, okay? And breathe. It is perfect, man. Pure oxygen."

I put the mask over my head and hit the button. It feels like plunging into a cool lake on a humid day. I give Marcus the thumbs up, close my eyes, and just breathe.

We stay in the sauna, sweating it out, for half an hour. After I've showered (first warm, then ice cold, then warm again), I feel like I've been drinking nothing but mineral water for the last decade.

"That is amazing Marcus," I say, once again lounging on one of the enormous sofas.

"And for the final stage," Marcus says, handing me a glass of tomato juice and a bowl of Laos salad. "A Bloody Mary and something bloody hot."

"Perfect."

Marcus sits on the sofa opposite me, and lights a cigarette. "I'm sorry for what I said last night."

"I didn't think you'd remember."

"I just remembered in the shower."

"I love Lek,' I say. "You know that. I wouldn't do anything to upset her. And I wouldn't do anything to upset you. We're friends, aren't we?"

Marcus blows smoke at the ceiling. "Of course," he says. "Tell me. Do you still enjoy what you do? You seem different, something's changed."

"No I don't. I've been trying to stop for a while. Getting paid to have sex… I used to think that was the ultimate job. It was, for a while. When we first did it, it was a buzz wasn't it? Now I just want a quiet, normal life with a nice girl."

"Me too," Marcus agrees. And I see his mind drift off to memories of Wow. I don't think he hit her. He couldn't have.

"A man paid me the other night… for some… stuff," I say suddenly. We're friends again. It feels good to get it out. I stare at the floor. "Did you ever do that? When you were working?"

I keep looking at the floor. Marcus sighs. The tension is like that between a pint glass and a beer mat when the mat is wet.

"Once," he said. "The money was huge. It was a mistake."

I feel relieved. I look up. The pint unsticks. "I did it for the money, I can't do it again."

"Me neither. There are many things I cannot do again… and some I can. I'm not an angel after all," he says, laughing.

I laugh too, sip my drink and finally nod. A long silence unfolds around us.

We spend the afternoon playing backgammon, Marcus beating me every time. Somehow, whether he's playing with the white discs or the black, he wins. He always lands on my men before I can get close to home. Marcus likes backgammon. I think it's the slow, inexorable domination he finds so irresistible, picking the pieces off the board one by one. His eyes gleam as he stacks them to his left, little tower blocks of counters, a city of his own making.

When I can no longer handle losing we order in pizza and play Tomb Raider on the PlayStation. Then we arm wrestle. I beat Marcus, four out of four. He doesn't allow me to beat him at arm wrestling as often as he thrashed me at backgammon. This is the dynamic of our friendship.

In the evening I suggest we go out, just to see if we can recreate the kind of fun we used to have. Marcus thinks there's a guitarist playing at a little club not far away.

"We could go there," he says. "Have a couple of drinks after. Get hammered."

"Cool, let's give it a go."

"I'll get dressed. Watch some TV or something?"

Marcus goes upstairs to change. I reach for the remote control. Just as I'm about to sit down the buzzer rings. I walk to the door, thinking it could be Wow.

I open the door. Standing in front of me is a beautiful Thai girl. But it's not Wow. It's Jiab.

"What the...?" She's barging past me already and now in the living room standing in front of Marcus, who's come down the stairs.

"Jiab," he says. "Long time. How are you?"

"I pregnant. It your baby." This girl doesn't waste time getting to the point.

Jiab is dressed in a transparent red dress. She is completely naked beneath it. Dark nipples show through the material and further down the dark triangle of hair. The sight of a woman's almost naked body can confuse a man's mind. She knows this.

Marcus offers her a seat and a drink.

She wants a whisky.

"Josh would you mind?" Marcus says.

I go to the kitchen and fix her a large one. I get Marcus a JD and Coke and carry it back into the living room. "Do you want some space, or... ?"

"No, stay," he says. "We're all friends."

I get another beer and sit on the sofa opposite them.

"So," Marcus says. "You have another baby. This is a very happy time, yes?"

Jiab agrees, gulping her drink. Marcus asks some questions. Is it a boy or a girl? Which would she prefer? All the time he's very calm and considerate.

"And it might be mine?"

"It yours."

"And you want money?"

"Yes."

"So," Marcus gets up and walks over to the window. He looks out over the city. "I don't think the baby is mine, but... "

"It yours."

"After the baby is born, we can do some tests and... if I am the father, we can arrange something."

Jiab's eyes narrow. "I need money now."

Marcus shakes his head. His tone becomes much firmer, less conversational. "I cannot do that."

"Why?"

"Because. We must wait."

Jiab rushes forward and strikes him in the chest. "Why you like this?" she screams. "Why men alway like this? You want fuck, fuck, fuck, but you no care nothing, you no care baby, the lady... "

I move forward and pull Jiab away. Her arms and legs thrash as I lift her up. She screams and shouts and wriggles for some time before exhausting herself.

I put her down. Marcus looks vaguely amused.

"Who gave you the address?" I ask.

"Lek," she laughs. "I tell her I looking for Wow."

"Genius."

"I think you should go now," says Marcus, rearranging his shirt.

Jiab looks at me. Her face is red. Her eyes lit with anger. "You tell him I need money. You tell him."

I raise my eyebrows.

"You fucking *falang*. All the same. Wow have to leave Marcus because he bastard. Lek for sure, she can leave you. You bastard too. I can talking wit her and make her go."

"You can try," I laugh. "I think Lek trusts me."

This seems to enrage Jiab even more and she lunges again at Marcus. This time he defends himself, and with my help we eject her from the apartment.

"I'll have to change the code," Marcus says after she's gone. "Avoid any future visits."

Hours later, after a few calming drinks and another few games of backgammon which I lose, Marcus and I leave for the club. As the cab takes us through the night, and the dim street lights flicker in the side windows, I tell Marcus I can't believe Jiab's cheek.

"She's not so bad. I find her funny. I havn't slept with her in more than a year. The baby isn't mine. She will have other guys to visit."

"So why the big drama?"

Marcus laughs. "Women are all the same."

He keeps laughing until we arrive at the club. It's smoky and crowded and hot, but the American blues guitarist playing tonight is worth the discomfort. He's fat and sits on a stool. His weight looks like it would make it difficult for him to move freely, but his fingers are quick. The sweet sound of the guitar complements his deep, gravelly voice, which sometimes rumbles, sometimes glides over the top.

Some of the Thai girls clap their hands and stamp their feet in time, the music taking hold of them. Marcus and I drink at the bar. He spends the whole night looking at the girls. More for his business perhaps, though I still don't know what this is.

"Do you want another drink?" he asks, tearing his eyes away from the talent.

"Go on then."

After the drinks arrive Marcus continues assessing the girls. It begins to make me feel vaguely sick. Looking round I think I see the girl from The Monkey Bar. I nudge Marcus and he squints into the darkness, but it's not her.

He gulps back his drink. "I never told you did I? My father used to beat me like a dog. He beat me a week before he died. Even though he was very ill."

I don't know what to say, or why this has suddenly come up.

"He beat my mother too, and abused my sister. He was not a nice man. But I dream all the time that he's still alive. And I'd still like to have a relationship with him. I miss him. I think maybe we could have sorted out all the problems."

This is the first time Marcus has ever mentioned his family in terms other than money. I look at him to see what's in his eyes, but he keeps staring into the bottom of his glass as if he'll be able to see the world more clearly through it. I don't know what to say, so I just put my hand out and squeeze his shoulder.

"I should have stopped him," Marcus says. "But I couldn't."

I'd always thought there was something hiding beneath Marcus' confident exterior. His need to be in control stems from a childhood where he was surrounded by chaos.

"Did you ever hit Wow?"

"Yes," he says in a shaky voice, a hand going up to rub his forehead. Now I know why this information was suddenly forthcoming. He's been wanting to make a confession, and he needs to excuse his behaviour. "Just once. I couldn't stop myself. I'll never forgive myself for it. And I don't think she'll

ever forgive me either."
 I sip my drink and look into the darkness.

Chapter Thirty One

Two days after I return from my stay with Marcus, Lek and I visit the hospital and talk to the doctors. The smell of disinfectant catches in the back of my throat, making my eyes water, as it always does.

"We have done everything we can for her," they tell us as we stare down at the tiny form in the cot. Her gaze is still unfocused, her face numb and freakishly lifeless. She looks like a cabbage patch doll.

"Time will tell. The swelling in her brain has diminished. We will have to wait and see what happens. The chances are she will improve some more."

"Will she ever be normal again?" Lek asks.

The doctor shrugs. "With a trauma of this kind it is hard to tell. You should bring her in every week for a check up. There have been many cases where near full recovery has been made, but I wouldn't like to predict anything."

We take Samsook home in a taxi. Lek sits her on her lap, nuzzling and kissing her all the way back. I put my hand behind Lek's back and massage her neck.

"How do you feel?" I ask as we go up in the lift to our flat.

"I feel like a bad mummy," says Lek. "I feel like I can do nothing good. I love my baby. I want the best for my baby and this happen. I pray Buddha all the time, I know I bad girl, but Samsook, she newer hurt anyone."

Her eyes fill with sadness. I kiss her on the cheek.

"I think she'll be okay, and you're not a bad mother. It wasn't your fault. It was mine."

Back in our flat, Lek puts Samsook in the cot in our bedroom while I make us some lunch. We sit out on the balcony and slurp our way through egg noodles, while Samsook sleeps inside. Lek looks pained, her face fixed, struggling to keep her emotions under control.

"I wish I never bring her here that night," she says. "The first time she come here we have big problem. I cannot understand that."

"It's tough," I say, finishing my lunch, the chilli and sugar leaving a buzz on my lips. "You can never tell what's going to happen."

Lek stares into her bowl. "Do you love me still? Even though I bad mummy?"

I smile at her. "You're a lovely mum. You care about Samsook so much. You have to know it wasn't your fault." I hold her hand, giving it a squeeze. "Hey, I tell you what, why don't we go for a ride out into the country this afternoon? We can take some food with us, have a picnic somewhere."

"What about Samsook?"

"We'll take her round to Nong's before we go. She'll be safer there any way. Come on, you could do with some fresh air. It'll help you forget about everything. I'll tell you what, I'll take her round now while you get ready."

"I don know, can you take a taxi? So Samsook safe?"

"Sure."

I give her a kiss and gather Samsook up in the baby harness.

When I get out on the street I wait five minutes for a taxi that never comes and then think, sod it, we need to get moving, and get on the bike. We shouldn't be wasting money on cab fares and it'll be quicker on the Kawasaki. Lek will never know.

Samsook gurgles in concern as I start the engine, but seems

to settle as I move off. I ride the bike the slowest I've ever done, glancing down at Samsook squashed in to my chest in the carrier every other second. Every car that comes too close makes me cringe. Any bike that roars past makes me want to stop and call a taxi or a tuk tuk. I tell myself to be cool. Lek will never know.

When I finally pass Samsook into Nong's warm arms, my heartbeat begins to return to normal.

"Lek will probably visit tomorrow," I say as I leave.

Nong nods and kisses Samsook's soft cheek, two moon faces pressed together.

When I get back to the apartment I find Lek preparing a picnic, carefully wrapping food in newspaper, making sure bottles are sealed. She's dressed in a blue striped sarong and a little white tshirt. She looks about fourteen-years-old. A light wind from the balcony blows her hair over her face, before she tucks it behind her ear. "Samsook okay?" she says.

I nod.

Lek's the one girl I never wanted to hurt. She's the one I wanted to protect from life. Yet life has got to her more than most.

"Where we going, babe?" she asks, now sitting cross legged on the floor of the kitchen, putting the food into her little pink rucksack. She doesn't look up as she asks the question.

"It's a secret," I say, leaning against the archway from the hall to the kitchen, trying to look charming.

"A surprise?"

"Yes," I say, walking over and bending down to kiss her.

"We go on the motorbike, or we take a taxi?"

"We're going on the bike. You'll need to wear some jeans."

"Okay," she says, putting the last parcel in the sack and tying it up. "Can you get some drink?"

"We'll buy something on the way."

Lek heads for the bedroom. "Five minute, okay?"

I know it'll be more like quarter of an hour, so I grab a magazine and head out to the balcony.

Chapter Thirty Two

On the way to Samut Sakhon, winding our way south along the twisty country roads, we stop at a tiny shop, which is really just a dilapidated family home with an awning on the porch. Under it are an assortment of pre-packaged goods, dried fruits, and a little stove for cooking noodles. The awning flaps in the wind like a kite, kicking up dust. Steam rises from the boiling water, the smell of spices fills the air.

Round the side of the house a young man is working in the lean-to garage, tinkering with a 125, fixing the clutch. He wears only tracksuit bottoms, red and ragged. His body is lean and glistens chestnut in the sun.

A few yards back from the road and further up, several men sit drinking whisky. Turns out they're the family, a father with his two sons.

Lek and I approach, asking for ice cream.

The old man, rake thin with leathered skin from working in the sun all his life, calls over. A round woman appears, a scarf tied over her head. She beckons us to a well-hidden freezer and reveals a collection of ice pops. Lek takes a couple of orange ones and offers the woman a few baht. She smiles back at us, her mouth blackened and gap toothed like she cleaned her teeth with charcoal and wire wool. But even with her rugged appearance she's not short on charm.

Taking some more glasses off a nearby table she leads us back to the group of men and sits down with us. "You must drink before you go," she says. "It's my husband's birthday."

The old man smiles, revealing teeth as distressed as his wife's.

I don't ask how old he is. He could be any age over forty-five.

Once we've sat down to drink, they're not keen to let us go. The men are fascinated by Bangkok. They rarely go there, even though they only live twenty minutes away: it's just too expensive for them. They want to know what we do for a living. Lek and I have well rehearsed answers to these questions. I stick to my previous job in Hong Kong: Futures Broker. I like the irony of this. It's all in the past, and for me, there's no future in it. Lek tells them she's a waitress, training to be a secretary. This is true in the broadest sense. She serves drinks where she works, and she is saving to learn how to use a computer. But she does want to work in an office some day, or in tourism.

Our bit of tourism for the day is to be surrounded by the sea air of Samut Sakhon, so we finally drain our glasses and say our goodbyes.

"They are nice people," says Lek as we wander back to the Kawasaki. "They have nothing but they give us whisky."

"That's why I bought them a bottle," I say.

"You buy one for them?"

"Sure. When you went to the loo."

She hugs my arm. "Then you good man, also, I see that the first time."

"Sometimes," I say. "I have my moments."

The drive to Samut takes only another quarter of an hour. The land we travel through is flat with few trees, almost like desert. Riding with my shirt off, the sun feels intense on my back, even with the wind rushing past. Lek, riding pillion, amuses herself by plucking hairs out of the backs of my arms as we shoot along. In return I swerve the bike from side to side, making her yell with fright.

"I no want to die young!" she screams, her voice only just cutting through the wind resistance.

"You're old already," I shout back. "You'll be twenty next year."

"But I no old like you! I newer be old like you."

"Unless I die today. And you carry on living till you're twenty-seven."

"Don say like that!"

"Don't worry. I'm going to live to be a really old, really grumpy old man."

"What grumpy?"

I tell her in Thai.

"You can die then!" she says and I swerve the bike on to the baked grass and we off-road for half a mile until she screams at me to stop.

Samut Sakhon is a busy little port I often visit when I feel the need to escape. The fresh air whipping in from the Gulf of Thailand lifts my heavy soul. I like the rhythm of the place. The large ships anchored off shore like great, floating cities. The smaller boats and sampans, bobbing up the That Chin river in small fleets to deposit their cargos, before flowing back out to sea. I find the constant activity of people going about their daily lives some how calming. It all seems so uncomplicated to the outside observer, so natural, a microcosm of life.

When we arrive we spend a few minutes cruising round, taking in the atmosphere before coming to a stop under a secluded group of palm trees. They're set back from the river, which flows idly out into the twinkling gulf. To our right are the busy markets, the traders and customers haggling vocally over price. To the east, on the west coast of Thailand, I can just make out the golden beaches of Pattaya. I squint up. The sky is vivid, so bright, it's almost white. I lie back, watching the long boats bob along as Lek lays out our picnic, carefully unwrapping the food.

"Just like Christmas," I say to her.

"For you," she says. "No for me. In Thailand we no have Christmas."

"What did you have this year then?"

"Oh yes. That was my first one."

I made Christmas dinner for Marcus and Wow shortly after we moved into our new apartment. I think the girls were confused by the whole celebration but seemed to enjoy it. Why wouldn't they enjoy a party? We enjoyed the King's birthday, a big day in Bangkok.

I smoke a Kron Thip while Lek arranges the provisions. I can't remember feeling more relaxed. It's as though all my troubles are too far away to touch me. Thoughts of Ratty, the worries of Samsook, the endless concern over money, none of them can touch me here.

"Are you happy?" I ask her.

"Today I happy. Today I try worry nothing. You?"

"I'm the same. Come here and give me a kiss."

Lek bends down and her soft, plump lips press against mine. Her kiss sends a shiver down my spine. I feel deeply touched, like she's actually reached inside me. I part her lips with my tongue and she responds. After some gentle petting we have our trousers off and I'm inside her, our modesty covered only by a thin sarong. Lek locks her arms round me tightly as if she never wants to let me go. I come quickly. The feeling is so explosive it makes me wince. Lek clings to me even tighter.

"I love you, *tilak*," she whispers in my ear, her voice like a soft spring breeze. "I love you. *Kum lak koon*."

Afterwards, we eat, lying in each other's arms. Lek makes Laos salad while I break up dried fish and dip it into the soy and chilli sauce. We also have strips of beef and chicken curry kept warm in a thermos. Lek brought some sticky rice to soak everything up and some dried snacks I refuse to eat.

"You must try," Lek cajoles. "It taste very good, babe."

"I'm not eating dried scorpion or whatever that is, I'm full now anyway. Do you want me to get fat?"

"You fat already. Look you tummy!"

"I'm not as fat as you," I say pinching her nose. "Pretty soon I won't be able to get you on the bike, you'll have to run next to me."

"I can buy my own motorbike," Lek says, sticking her tongue out. "I can have fat arse if I want."

"That's true, but there's no rush, is there?"

For this I get cuffed over the head and then we wrestle on the ground. I put a stop to it before anyone gets hurt. This isn't the real reason, though. I stop because I can feel myself getting hard again, but don't have the energy to pull Lek back out of her jeans.

"You know there a temple near here?" Lek says when we've stopped laughing. "You want go when we finish eating?"

"Yeah. That's a good idea."

The temple is small. Just an altar, a statue of the Buddha and four walls surrounding it, pierced with arches. It's beautiful, though. It feels peaceful. Entering from the front, Lek and I leave our shoes on the steps and kneel down, our heads bowed, feet facing away. Lek clutches some incense burning sticks. The smoke drifts over our heads.

Kneeling here I pray for what I always pray for. Good times and laughter, good health and good friends. Lek always prays for the same things too. Luck for her family, and that she will be guided towards being a better person. I can't help but sneak a look at her solemn face as she's praying. She looks so cute when she's serious.

Once we've got our shoes back on we wander down to the water's edge and skim stones.

"Shall we go back now? I think we go now, we can see

Samsook, yes?"

"That's not a bad idea," I say. "I'm sure she'd like to see her mummy."

When we arrive at Nong's her husband is home from work so we all have a shot of Singh Thip. The guy looks exhausted, his face thin and drawn, his dark eyes receding into deep hollows. He looks like he's floating dangerously close to the brink. He needs help, but help costs money he doesn't have.

Samsook has been in her cot all afternoon, so Lek picks her up.

"How is she?" she asks Nong.

"She's very well. Smiling all the time. I think her eyes look better than before. It's funny when Joshua arrives with her, her hair is standing up like a candy floss because of being on the motorbike!"

I wince. I wish she hadn't said that.

"What do you mean?" Lek asks. "Didn't he come in a taxi?"

"Oh." Nong looks down.

Lek looks at me.

"There weren't any. We waited for ten minutes, so I decided to use the bike. We only went at walking speed."

Lek's face darkens. "How can you do like that? What if another car come out and she fall? I think next time accident she die!"

"She's okay isn't she?"

"She okay, yes. But you must not make danger. And you lie to me. I hate that. I hate that."

"Sorry," I say. "I won't do it again."

I turn to Nong's husband who shrugs at me, perhaps happy my life isn't perfect either.

"And don look at him," says Lek. "This is not funny."

That night the atmosphere at home is cool, even on this warm night. In bed I'm denied the pleasure of a cuddle. I have trouble sleeping. I stare up at the grey ceiling wondering what life would be like if I'd never left London. After several hours I decide it would have been essentially the same, all about love and money.

The morning brings little more in the way of warmth. Lek goes straight to Nong's to check on Samsook, leaving me in no doubt as to her mood. I spend the day doing little else but worrying. It's not very productive, but at least it's all consuming.

When she returns home we hardly speak.

I sleep badly again.

The following morning, after she's gone to Nong's once more, I get up late, bursting to go to the loo. When I get to the bathroom and stand over the bowl it feels like I'm pissing acid.

I've caught a dose. I don't know who from for sure, but with the condom ripping incident, I have a good idea. It isn't any fun, and certainly not good for business. I go straight to the hospital.

At the hospital they stick a tiny version of a wire cocktail umbrella in my penis, open it up and pull it out. This makes my eyes water, and my buttocks clench. I can't describe what it does to the rest of me.

For several days I lay up on the balcony, taking the antibiotics, drinking heavily, though I know I shouldn't.

When I'm feeling almost recovered, I have an afternoon session with Dr Miller. I fail to mention the state of my manhood.

"You never told me why you left Hong Kong," he says after a few opening gambits. "Is it a painful subject?"

"Not really," I say, taking another Kron Thip out of the pack. "Should it be? Why did you leave London?"

Dr Miller smiles. "You know we don't talk about me."

"Yeah, I know we don't. But I'm not big on rules," I reply.

I always feel very combative in the chair.

"I'm not going to tell you," he says.

"I knew you wouldn't. And I'm not going to tell you why I left Hong Kong. Fair's fair, yeah?"

Dr Miller smiles again.

"It's your therapy, you can tell me as much or as little as you want. But it may help you to discuss the difficult times in your life. We need something to work with."

"I'll tell you. Eventually. In fact, no. I'll tell you now. I left Hong Kong for the same reason I left London. There you go."

He knows not to push this one. "Do you sometimes wish you never left?"

I think about this. A still of the boy on the blue chopper flags up in my mind, but I know staying in London would not have kept me in this state of bliss.

"I sometimes wish I was back in Hong Kong."

"Why?"

"I have good memories of it."

"But at other times you've said how much you needed to get out of there."

"Yeah. That's true. It wasn't perfect. Nowhere is."

"Do you perhaps think it's not the places that are wrong?"

"What do you mean?"

"I mean you're running from something you can't escape. You will find the same problems wherever you go."

"Because I'm still me, you mean?"

Dr Miller seems pleased I've picked up on his inference. "Exactly. Because you're running from yourself."

"I know this," I say. "It doesn't take a genius to work that out."

"So what are you doing about it?"

"I'm seeing you. I'm trying to address what it is inside that makes me run. And I'm not going anywhere. I'm staying here in Bangkok. Even if it gets really tough. And it is pretty hectic right now."

Dr Miller lets this thought hang in the air.

I fiddle with the lace on my boot.

"Do you feel guilty about running away?" he says.

"I do feel guilty. I feel guilty. Yeah. But not about that so much. About other stuff."

"What other stuff?"

"Loads of things. People I've hurt, let down. Opportunities I've wasted. I'm not the person I want to be."

"Who do you want to be?" Dr Miller asks. The session's almost over.

I tell him I want to be a success. I want to have a job I love. I want to be teetotal, super fit. A non-smoker. I want to have a girlfriend who thinks I'm amazing. I want to think she's amazing, too. I want to be good at everything I do. I never want to fail. I want everyone who meets me to love me. I want to be pure. I want to be uncomplicated. I want to bounce out of bed every day and go, 'This is my life and I love it!' I want what everyone wants, and can't have.

"But I only ever feel good when I'm out of it," I say.

He nods and looks at his watch. "Why is it you have to drink and take drugs?"

"We live in a world where we're so critical of each other, where we're so threatened by what might come out of someone else's mouth, we have to do something. To, you know, protect ourselves from embarrassment and hurt. Who can handle life without blurring the edges a bit?"

"We'll work on this next time," he says.

I put my hands by my sides, nod politely and leave the room. It all comes down to time, I think as I jog down the stairs. Everything is time.

And we never have enough. Or we have way too much.

Chapter Thirty Three

I stop at a riverside bar before going home and have a couple of Singha, watching the red and gold boats chug up and down the brown murk of the Chao Phraya. The sun glints off the chrome on the Kawasaki, branches of palm trees rustle nearby. The smoke from my Kron Thip swirls round my head before crossing the river and dissipating. When I've finished it, I reluctantly head home.

"Lek," I say when I walk in the door, having got my nerve up. "There's something I have to tell you."

Lek is lying on the sofa, the balcony doors open. "What is it?" she asks.

"Where's Samsook?" I ask, suddenly self-conscious.

"She with Nong, right now. What problem babe?"

I tell her I've caught a dose.

"A what?"

"I mean I caught a disease, from a customer."

"Oh no," Lek groans. "I not need this, I think."

"I'm so sorry," I say, though it sounds lame. I move over and give her a hug which she accepts, I think, without too much loathing.

"Do you want a drink?" I ask several hours later after Lek has had an extended bath and long chats on her mobile.

"Yes," she says, coming out of the bedroom dressed in a very sexy Thai silk shirt in deep and sky blue, kind of tie dyed, but a little more complex.

"Yes, I do. I clean myself very big and I hoping I no have problem, so yes, I want drink to forget."

"Do you hate me?"

"I don hate you," says Lek, "I don."

The next night, because I'm wracked with guilt I take Lek to a posh French restaurant in North Bangkok. She's never been to it before, but has wanted to check it out for ages. Why she wants to come here I have no idea but I assume it's been recommended by some guy who's chatted her up at work. It's a subtle kind of revenge. I no longer have a problem with this. It's part of the job. With the money for Ratty set aside, I find enough extra cash. I want Lek to relax, enjoy herself, just like the old days.

We're ushered into the quiet dining area with unusual reverence by a tall, thin guy who I assume is actually French as he welcomes us with a *bonjour*. The red carpet beneath our feet is so thick I feel like I'm wading through it.

Seated at a table near high, curved windows which overlook a small garden at the back of the restaurant, we scan the menu.

Lek orders moules marinieres followed by rare steak. I have garlic prawns and chicken stuffed with a ham, cheese and herb sauce.

People at the other tables hardly speak. The only sounds are the chink of cutlery delicately touching china plates. I look over at Lek and raise an eyebrow. She's sitting straight backed with a look of wonder on her face.

"Is this what you were expecting?" I ask.

Lek grew up in Ekamai, a suburb of North West Bangkok. Her family were poor, her father often out of work. Lek owned her first pair of shoes at the age of eight. Her toys on her birthdays were always handmade. Restaurants were not a part of the family's week. Eating at a market stall was a treat.

She shakes her head. "I think this place happy and friendly with good food. But this, I feel like I can't move like myself.

I feel strange."

"Me too," I say. "Let's eat quickly."

Our food is delicious and the wine helps to dissolve our tension, but by the time I come to pay the bill we're ready to go.

"So," I say as we walk back into the night, feeling instantly free-er. "Are you up for the Hollywood tonight?"

Lek looks at me through hooded eyes. I don't know if she wants to or not. I take her hand and give it a squeeze.

"I think we should have some fun. This has all been too stiff."

Once we've made the decision we're excited to be going dancing again, tickling each other in the taxi on the way there, until Lek tires of it.

"Stop, please," she says, smoothing her ruffled hair. "I not want to look like an animal."

The cab pulls up. I pay and we walk straight into the club through the wide, bright entrance, not having to queue. We make our way through the mass of people to the front of the room where large speakers hang like big black gorillas from the ceiling. There are a troupe of Madonna impersonators running through some of her back catalogue on the high, wide stage. They're dressed in conical black bras and have long blonde hair. Their dance routines are well worked out, their vocals loud and high pitched. The crowd, a classy, well dressed group of Thais, love it, showing their appreciation with loud applause at the end of each song. I am the only *falang* here.

Lek and I hold hands, swaying in time to the music, enjoying the energetic atmosphere. The Madonna troupe finish on 'Lucky Star' and file off the stage.

An MC strides on in a dinner jacket, no tie and asks us if we're having a good night. We all shout back, "*Chai, mac, mac!*"

"Do you want more?" he asks, raising his hands before

offering the microphone towards us.

We all scream, "Yes!"

"I can't hear you," he teases, and so he continues before announcing a very popular Thai rock act who begin their set with a classic building format: on a dark stage, drums lay down a solid beat, the bass and snare hitting our chests like the gorillas above us. Then on bounds a lithe, big haired, girl bass player, nodding to the beat and joining it with an earthy dum, da, dum, dum in a low octave. A single spotlight follows her. Next a guitarist, whose fashion sense seems to have been borrowed from Jimmy Page sidles on to the stage in a silk suit embroidered with dragons. The neck of his Les Paul is only six inches from the ground as he leans into a funky, twinkling riff which perfectly off sets the deep bass. There are more lights now. Red and blue and green. We hear a hiss and smoke pours out of the drum riser.

The singer, tall, sinewy, with an arty, floppy fringe walks on clutching a mike stand like it's a baseball bat. Stripped to his tight black jeans and trainers, he has a strong sexual presence and when he sings the opening line to this first song, he seems to stare into the eyes of every member of the audience.

We are all momentarily mesmerised. Our troubles vanish. Time stops travelling forwards and moves sideways, like a crab.

Lek jumps about, her eyes glinting. "I love this song," she shouts and yanks my arm to get me to dance.

The band has my total attention for the first four songs, all grinding, driving, fist pumping numbers, but half way through the show, during a slow ballad, I have to go pee. I brush my way through the heavy, hot, undulating crowd to the back. In the loo, I use one of the cubicles in case I have to grimace from the pain of my infection, but luckily it doesn't feel too bad tonight, the antibiotics must be working. As I unlock the cubicle door and turn to leave, I find a pair of girl's knickers on the peg. On them is written, I LOVE LEK. I smile, absently ensuring my fly is buttoned.

When I get back out to the cavernous black club I can't find her. I do three circuits of the perimeter of the dance floor, like an anxious bouncer, before spotting her at a table near the bar. She's laughing in a carefree, head back way as she brings her drink to her lips. Next to her sits the gingery blonde haired Belgian, Eric, who stands out in this Thai crowd like a lighthouse on the edge of a dark, swirling sea. He's got his hand on her back and is whispering in her ear. She's giggling. The mental static in my head increases from a burble to a roar. The TV of my mind blows a tube. The vertical hold slips, the screen fades to black, leaving only a flickering line, a millimetre or two thick.

I take three long strides over to the table and flip it on its side sending the drinks looping into the air. The neon lights catching the glasses like mirrors before they bounce and shatter on the wooden floor, the glinting shards indistinguishable from the ice. My heart bulges, the TV in my head explodes. I grab Eric by the back of his shirt and pitch him forward off his stool on to my knee. His jaw crunches against my thigh and he groans. With an open palm I hit him on the back of the head, pitching him to the floor. Lek takes hold of my shoulders, imploring me to stop, but I shrug her off. I kick Eric twice in the ribs, then crouch down next to him. "I thought I told you to leave her alone."

"I'm a paying customer," he manages to say. "I can do what I like."

And suddenly all I can think is the night Lek came in and said, 'I slip with someone else. For money. For Samsook.' I draw back my fist, the bulge of my bicep squashing my forearm and slam it straight into Eric's right eye.

"That what you call a weak punch?" I shout. Eric squints up at me. Lek gapes. "Don't ask me why I did that," I say pointing a finger at her. "I can't fucking believe this."

"But," Lek starts, reaching out for me. I shrug her off and

The Body is a Temple

storm out. I don't stop to look back. I sprint up the street.

Not wanting to spend the night anywhere near Lek, or anyone, I book myself into a cheap guesthouse. I throw myself on the rice paper thin mattress and struggle to find sleep. I fail. I spend most of the night doing press ups, ripping the pillows to shreds and pulling the legs off the bed with my bare hands.

In the morning I get up, pay for the shameful damage, and wander the streets. Now I'm sober and my anger has dissipated I begin to feel remorse. Lek didn't deserve the treatment I gave her last night. It wasn't her fault Eric turned up and started flirting with her. I wander round with a mounting sense of shame. I wish I had my sunglasses, the sun is so bright I have to have my eyes almost closed to see where I'm going. At some of the market stalls in Banglampoo I search for a reasonable pair of sunglasses. Finding none, I instead buy a black baseball cap with the words LOVE IT stenciled above the peak.

As I'm about to get in a tuk tuk to take me back to Sukhumvhit a young Thai boy runs up to me and tugs at my arm. He's seven or eight years old, and the colour of rosewood. I shake his hand off my sleeve and tell him to get lost, but he's very persistent. Perhaps because I'm still guilty from last night, I eventually stop and ask him what he wants. Smiling, he takes hold of my hand and leads me back up the road to where his sister is standing holding a wicker basket. The girl is younger than the brother, I'd say about six, and very shy. She doesn't look at me as I ask her what she has in the basket, she only glances nervously at her brother and holds it up.

I look down to see an undulating mass of fur.

"What is it?" I ask in Thai.

"They're kittens," the boy replies. "Hundred baht for one."

I stare down and realise what I'd thought was one animal is actually four or five tiny cats no bigger than the palm of my hand. "Hundred baht for one?" I say. "I'll give you sixty for two."

The boy looks pleased but tries to hide it. "Hundred," he says, like he's been taught.

"Eighty," I say putting the money in his hand and taking a tortoiseshell and black kitten from the basket. "It's good money for you."

Once the kids have the money they scamper off, chattering excitedly. I look down at the kittens cradled against my chest. "Come on. We've got to go home."

When I arrive back mid morning, I find my apartment, like the room I have just left, is a mess. There are broken plates, knives and forks scattered like builders rubble all over the tiles. The sheets have been torn off the bed. The air smells rotten. Disturbed.

"Lek," I call out, already regretting not coming home. "Lek. What have you done? What happened? I got you a present. Come and see."

There's no answer. I put the kittens on a cushion on the floor and search the flat but she isn't there.

I phone Nong and ask her if she's seen her.

"I see her yesterday morning," she says. "She bring Samsook. She say she coming back today. But I don't see her yet."

"You don't know where she is now?"

She doesn't.

I sort through the rubbish and find Lek's little red address book. I phone Pim and ask her if she's seen Lek.

She hasn't.

"This problem with me again?" Pim asks, sounding wary.

"No."

"I come over. You sound like you need a friend."

I sit on the balcony, swigging from a bottle of cheap supermarket brand vodka which I hope is going to sort out my headache while I wait for her. The kittens are curled up asleep in an old cardboard shoe box I have next to my feet. Occasionally I pluck one out by the soft skin on the back of its neck and hold it in my lap for a while, idly stroking its tiny head. My mind stutters along like a clapped out motorcycle. I'm so lost in my thoughts Pim has to ring the doorbell several times before I get up to answer it.

"Hi," she says as she comes in. "What keep you?"

I let my arm fall to my side and give her a hug. She hands me a newspaper and some fresh fish, saying she knows when she's depressed she doesn't like to go out. Clearly she thinks the news and a decent supper will get me through this. I thank her, putting the fish in the fridge. Pim follows me, getting a beer as the door opens. She looks even smaller than normal in her flip flops.

We go out on to the balcony and stand looking over the city.

"It very crazy today," she says meaning the smog. It's hard to see beyond the next street. "It very hot."

"For me, yes," I say, wiping sweat out of my eyebrows. "For you, no. You're Thai. This is okay."

Pim isn't sweating at all, even though she's wearing jeans and a white shirt. She turns to look into the apartment, resting her back against the railing when she spies the shoe box. She goes over and looks in it before shrieking with delight and hauling the black kitten out. She smothers it in kisses and hugs it under her chin, her fingers dancing over its walnut sized head. After much exclaiming about how beautiful they are she finally sits down with them on her lap and starts asking me questions.

"So what going on with you?" she asks, looking at me. I tell her Lek's gone. "And the cleaner?" Pim jokes. She sits on one of the loungers. "She do like this one time before, yes?"

Lek had disappeared before. A while back I had a client who requested my services up to four times a week. Lek was convinced we were having an affair, and forbade me to see her. I said if we were ever going to save enough money to live a normal life I should take advantage of how much this woman was paying us. Lek said she understood, but she couldn't handle it. One night when I got home from seeing this client she was gone and the apartment was wrecked, damaged by her jealousy.

"We had an argument last night and... this time it was me being jealous of Lek. She has this guy, Eric who... "

"Shit, not him," says Pim, "I know the problems. It the usual thing, yes. He's flirting with her." She looks at me swigging from the bottle. "I get you a glass, some ice," she says and wanders back into the apartment. I ask her where she thinks Lek could be as she pours the drink. She guesses at her parents, or in a hotel. She's not with any of her other friends.

"Her parents don't have a phone, do they?" I say.

Pim shakes her head. "Don worry, Lek can take care herself. She can crazy, but she okay inside. She love you very much. She tell me like this many time. When we talk we sort everything out. We friends again. No more problem for Lek and me."

Pim carries on chatting, but I'm not listening.

"Hey. What you thinking about? Hello."

"That week in the hotel," I say.

"I know then," Pim says. "This no the job for you. You too... shy. Too English. Too *falang*. That why I tell Lek. I think she understand."

I manage a half laugh. I thought I was escaping all my problems by leaving Hong Kong and starting something different.

Pim shakes her head. "You cannot run from your problem. Your problem like a very strong man." She flexes her little biceps, curling her arms in towards her ears. "It run with you. Man like you have to make love with some girl he love. No can do for money. That why you have problem with me." Pim holds my hand. "But everything will okay for you. You have beautiful girlfriend. Her baby will be okay. And then you happy." She gives me a hug before looking at her watch. "I have go now. You take care, okay? Love you big, big Josh. Bye!"

And she skips out the door.

After she's gone I spend some time staring at a photo I find of me and Lek. It's broken, smashed, the glass distorting the picture inside. I brush the shards into the bag and stare at the picture. I remember it well.

Lek and I had been going out for a few months when we decided to go down to Koh Samui.

We spent days roaring round its dusty roads on 125s. The evenings getting wasted in the little bars dotted along Chaweng Beach Road, not far from the hotel.

Marcus joined us after a few weeks, with Wow. It was a great holiday. I just didn't have a thing to worry about. I laughed myself to sleep at night, and woke up with a big grin on my face in the morning, the sun streaming in through the beach hut window.

Down in Samui I realised I'd fallen in love with Lek. She was the first girl I ever said it to and felt like I meant it. She thought I was joking when I first told her. We hadn't been seeing each other that long and she had trouble trusting men. She told me I could only say these things if I meant it from the heart. A couple of nights later I told her again. This time she accepted it, but she was still nervous.

'I love you too,' she had said. 'But... '

'But what?'

'But I don know if I can trust you. You very hansom man. Maybe you get bored with me and find another girl. More beautiful.'

I cupped her cheek in my hand.

'There is no-one more beautiful,' I said. 'Everyone knows that.'

I put the photo down on the coffee table. I wish I hadn't lost my temper last night. Lek wouldn't do anything to upset me. It was just that prick Eric trying to wind me up.

As I go to sleep that night I put my brain on a loop. Please come home. Please come home. Please come home.

Chapter Thirty Four

The next morning I wake feeling better. Lek wouldn't stay away for long, she never did. She'd come home soon. We'd have the chat about trust. There'd be some soul searching and some tears, and then we'd make up. It was almost worth falling out in the first place.

I lie in bed for some time, looking forward to this get together, hoping it will come soon. Eventually I haul myself up and get in the shower. I turn the tap, the strong jets surge out, beating down on my head. After a long time under the water, I turn the tap to off, wipe the condensation from the mirror and shave, standing there naked. I gel my hair, apply moisturiser and finally aftershave. I stare at myself. The minutes tick by.

Back in the bedroom I sling on a pair of tracksuit bottoms and put some music on. As I start to tidy up, the door buzzer goes. Thank you God. I cross the cool tiles to the door and gently pull it open.

"Babe," I say, looking at the floor, contrite. "I'm really sorry..."

There's a moment of confused silence. I'm aware the presence in front of me is way too tall. I look up. A guy smiles and throws his arms wide.

"Don't 'babe' me darling," he roars as he gives me a bear hug, lifting me up and spinning me round. He carries me into the apartment. "Fuck! And you said my place was a dump.

Look at yours!"

I push him away. "God, it's you. I thought you were Lek."

"Hey, I hope I'm a bit bigger than her aren't I?" Conrad laughs. "More manly. She's not a ladyboy is she?"

"Fuck off. What happened to your hair?" I say staring at the crew cut.

"I had it chopped. That haircut I gave myself in Hong Kong wasn't the best, was it?"

"You're a few things, man, but none of them is a hairdresser. You're definitely not a hairdresser."

"My mother would be so disappointed."

I stand back and look at him. It's taken some time to recognise Conrad with the new haircut and it's taken another beat to get over the disappointment of him not being Lek. But now I realise how pleased I am to see him.

"I don't believe it," I say. "It's like a miracle. You turning up at a place where you said you'd be."

"Well, not quite, brother. It has been known, on occasion. But I do have something that is fucking miraculous… " He takes off his rucksack and throws it on the sofa. "… and I'll show you later. How're things with you?"

I don't even know where to begin. There's so much to tell.

"Let me sit down with a beer," he says. "I can see I need to catch up."

We sit out on the balcony with bottles of Singha. I tell Conrad everything. The financial crisis. Eric. Ratty. Lek. Samsook. The lot. When I've finished he apologises for the whole Hong Kong thing and not turning up sooner.

"Man, I was desperate then," he says. "Losing it, you know. And then the Philippines thing took longer than expected. I met these cool people and… they inspired me to paint again. Miniatures this time, happy stuff… " He trails off looking embarrassed, before pulling himself together. "So what do you want to do now? Go sort Eric out. Twist his little arms off?"

"I want to know what your miracle is," I say, hoping it's what I think it is.

Conrad picks up his rucksack. I notice his missing finger, but don't comment.

"All it is," he says, opening a bottom panel in the rucksack, "is this." He pulls out baggies full of what looks like tin foil.

"Open one," I say.

He slits a bag open with his penknife and unwraps the foil, revealing wads of Hong Kong dollars.

"Your share, plus some more I managed to make. About seven grand."

I look at all the money. The money is good. I grab Conrad and kiss him full on the lips. "I knew you'd come through for me, man, I knew it."

"I'm not so bad, am I?" Conrad pushes me away, wiping a hand over his mouth in distaste. "So, the question remains. What next? You want to take this money round to Ratty. Pay your debt. Get him off your case?"

I'm happy to sit tight. If Ratty shows up, I can give him the cash. There's no point in running all over town looking for him. Besides I have to hang around for Lek. Conrad reckons this sounds sensible. He suggests popping out for a few beers while I stay put. I tell him to get some cat food, some wire mesh and some self tapping screws. He looks confused. I tell him where the hardware store is.

"Think about it on the way," I say.

While he's gone everything that's been happening slowly starts to sink in. I can't believe I've managed to cope with the pressure without a decent friend to talk things through with. Now Conrad's here I can at least discuss my worries. That should help. I can make a joke out of the bad stuff and we can laugh, if I can remember how.

When Conrad gets back I've dug out some photos. Me and Lek. Me and Cho. Marcus, Wow, the whole gang. Conrad flips through them, making jokey comments about the people in the background before he suddenly remembers something and fumbles for his wallet.

"Meant to give this to you in Hong Kong," he says.

He hands me a picture of Zack and me. He says he found it in his stuff when he left. The shot was taken on a night out in London. I think I was about eighteen, Zack twenty-seven. His hair is peroxide blonde. He'd just got back from a sailing trip in the Caribbean. We're both laughing at the camera, he's digging me in the chest with a bunched fist. I think we're outside a pub in Camden. I look at the photo for a while, before putting it on the coffee table.

Conrad, seeing I'm groping back to the past, holds up a picture of Lek and says how gorgeous she is. The picture shows her in a straw sunhat, a tight tshirt and a red and white sarong. She's sticking her tongue out cheekily, holding an ice cream. Her feet are ankle deep in the turquoise sea off Lamai Beach.

"This is what I'm here for," he says. "To do what you've done. Settle down with a nice chick and raise kids."

"Had enough of the wild life?"

"Hey. I'm thirty-six. It's time. I'm ready."

"In that case you should practice your D.I.Y. I've got just the job for you."

Together we unwind the wire mesh and stretch it round the base of the balcony.

"I thought if I hold it," I say, "you could just drill the screws on the railings top and bottom, and that should keep them from falling off, shouldn't it?"

"Keep what from falling off. Your marbles?"

I go into the bedroom and come out with the shoebox. I didn't want the kittens lying in the hot sun all afternoon. I thought they might get dehydrated. I hand it to Conrad and he shrieks in surprise, then starts baby talking to them. While he goes all goo-ey with the kittens, I rummage around under my bed, eventually finding the drill and extension lead I used to put the mirrors and pictures up. Back in the living room I take the shoe box from Conrad and hand him the drill. I take the kittens back to the bedroom and shut them in.

It takes five minutes to rig up the foot high safety net, carefully fixed to the metal struts top and bottom. When it's done I feel a sense of relief. The last thing we need, with all the other tragedy, is a little animal slipping off the balcony.

"Good job," I say to Conrad, going to the fridge to get a couple of beers. On the way I catch sight of the photo of Zack again, lying on the work surface. He would have been thirty-six now. He's been in my head a lot since that ambulance ride to the hospital. It felt so similar, so painfully the same.

"I can't believe it's six years since I was here," Conrad says once we're settled on the balcony. "Thank fuck I wrote your address down when you came to Hong Kong. Man, it's cool up here. I could happily spend the rest of the day here with my best buddy."

He runs a hand over his hair. His tan is deep. He looks well, much better than the last time I saw him. He tells me he lived the beach life in Mindoro and stayed off the booze for a while, took his oral agents properly. Ate fruit for breakfast, went swimming mid morning and spent the rest of the day lying in the sun, before getting an early night.

He tells me about the diving he did in Mindoro and shows me some new ink work he's had done on his back. A chameleon that runs the length of his spine. I tell him what's been up in Bangkok, briefly outlining the kind of life I lead. We stroke the kittens and have a few more drinks. While we chat I keep looking round the flat. Eventually I can no longer look at the state of the living room. "You wouldn't help me clear this shit up, would you?"

We move back into the apartment and start re-stacking shelves and picking up bits of broken glass, joking about how Conrad used to actually enjoy living in this kind of chaos.

Going into the kitchen to get a coffee, I knock against some magazines on the work surface. I catch them before they fall, but a small sheet of paper zig-zags to the floor. I bend down to pick it up. Turning it over I see a message.

'I have Lek.'

That's all it says. I read it again.

I have Lek. I have Lek.

I say it out loud to get it to sink in.

I look at the hand writing. It's a childlike scrawl, like Ratty's. Fuck. The heartbeat accelerates. I immediately dial his number. His phone is switched off.

"What the hell's going on, Ratty?" I say to his voicemail. "Where's Lek?"

I put the phone down and try to get my brain to work.

"What's up, man?" says Conrad, coming from the bathroom. "You look like you've just been told you're girlfriend's been sleeping with your best mate."

I hand him the note. I feel my mind starting to fragment with panic. I need to talk to someone who might know something. I collapse on the sofa, then pick up the phone and call Pim.

"You've got to come right over," I'm breathing heavily now. "Can you come over?"

Hearing the rising panic in my voice, Pim tells me to stay calm, she'll be right over. I put the phone down.

Conrad gives me a hug. "Be cool, brother," he says.

It seems like years before Pim arrives. In that time I lose the ability to think at all and simply pace up and down the tiles in the living room, covering miles in minutes. Conrad does his best to reason me out of my panic but he doesn't succeed.

When Pim comes in she looks as composed as ever. She looks at the note, then at me. I tell her my suspicions. She asks me why I haven't phoned Marcus. I tell her I don't trust him any more. He may suspect I encouraged Wow to leave for Belgium, and I've suddenly worked out what his profession is. He's a pimp. I've been trying to ignore it for months now, but I can't kid myself any longer. Marcus is a pimp, a liar, he's screwed up beyond belief, and I can't trust him.

Pim gets the phone. "Don be stupid," she says. "I think better phone him." She holds the phone tightly against her ear.

Conrad gives me a cigarette. "Calm down, brother," he says. "It'll work out. Come and get some air."

We go out to the balcony.

"Marcus," Pim says after a pause. She's standing inside, near the sliding windows. "I with Josh. You know we think Ratty take Lek. What happen?"

I stare up at the cloudless sky, then swig from a bottle of Singh Thip, hoping the amphetamines will wake me up.

Conrad takes the bottle off me and takes a hit, handing it back. "Don't worry," he says. "Worry is the biggest waste of time, man."

Pim puts the phone down and comes out to join us. She says Marcus is coming over and that we should stop drinking.

"I don't know if that's good or bad," I say, putting the bottle to my lips. "How long will he be?"

"Not long."

She looks at me. Conrad looks at me. Marcus arrives half an hour later. He's dressed all in black as normal, looking relaxed. He scans the drinks, pained to see there's no JD.

He fixes himself a Singh Thip and Coke with a sigh and comes and sits with me and Pim and Conrad on the balcony. The beeping, rumbling traffic does its thing below.

"So you think Ratty has taken Lek?" he says, lighting a Marlboro.

"I got back here yesterday and she was gone," I say stiffly, handing him the note.

"It's possible," Marcus agrees. "That fucking idiot. That addict." He shakes his head, his dark hair brushing his shoulders. I wonder if he gave Ratty the money.

"So what are we going to do?" says Conrad.

"Who are you?" Marcus asks.

"A friend," Conrad says, squaring up.

"Josh thinks you help Ratty," Pim cuts in.

Marcus looks at me and tells me not to be so fucking stupid. "Why would I want to do that?"

I don't want to mention Wow. Or Jiab. Or the reasons why he would do any number of things. The reasons why anyone with problems would do anything that might distract them from their pain. I keep quiet.

"The drink is sending you crazy," he says to me.

"But Ratty has Lek."

"Don't worry. He hasn't got the balls to do anything to her."

"He might not have the balls," I say, "but he's so mad on speed, he could do something by mistake."

Marcus looks at me with unusual intensity, his eyes much darker than normal. We've been friends through a lot of ups and downs yet I've never seen him give me this look and something about it worries me.

"I will get some people to find Ratty and we can straighten this whole thing out," he says.

"Can you get Lek?" I ask, confused now if he's my friend or enemy. "Will you call me later?"

"I will call as soon as I have found Ratty. While I'm away, don't do anything, okay? Get your friend to look after you," he says looking at Conrad.

"I'm not going anywhere, buddy boy," Conrad replies, clearly put out by Marcus' presence. "Josh has been a mate of mine for years."

Marcus gives a mock salute and is gone.

"I don't trust him a fucking inch. No way. He's bad news. He looks like a funeral director. And we don't want it to be your funeral," Conrad says.

Pim stays for a while after Marcus has left. We watch the sun turn red and drop beneath the level of the taller apartment buildings, the fading light reflecting orange off some of the windows. It feels good to have her and Conrad with me, my own surrogate family. I tell Pim, Wow left Marcus. She knew about the Belgian guy, but she didn't know she'd finally gone.

"Why did she go?" she asks.

"I said if she wasn't happy she should change her life," I say. "She wasn't happy, so she did."

"It don matter what you say, everyone have to make their own life. Wow, anybody."

She takes the kittens out of the box one last time and gives them a stroke before announcing she has to get back to work. She gives me and Conrad a kiss, tells me to call her if I need to and skips out of the apartment.

Conrad looks at me. "She's cool," he says. "Marcus, I'm definitely not sure about."

"Well he's not as good looking is he?"

"Not by a country fucking mile. Stop drinking the whisky, Josh. I'll get you a beer."

I hang on to the whisky, not letting Conrad pull it away from me.

He gives me his new intense, 'I've grown up' look. "Josh," he says. "You're digging yourself the same hole I dug myself in Hong Kong. If you want to bury yourself, use mine, save yourself the trouble of finishing yours."

I look at him blankly.

"Or do what I did, with your help, and stop digging and drag yourself out."

I let go of the bottle. He has a point. I don't want to end up in the mess Conrad did.

We sit on the balcony smoking, listening to dance music. I watch the kittens curled contentedly in their box, their tiny bellies moving in and out. Occasionally they stir, but soon collapse back to sleep.

I pad into the kitchen on bare feet and open one of the cans of cat food. I put a few spoonfuls on a saucer and take it out to the balcony. Then, worried that they won't be able to eat it, I return to the kitchen to get a saucer of milk. Conrad suggests I give them some water as well, in case the milk is too rich, so I do that too.

I sit back down, stretching my legs out and stifling a yawn. Conrad talks while I worry. He's doing his best to keep me upbeat, but it's not working. At eight I can't stand the tension anymore. I phone Marcus. His phone rings forever but isn't answered. I phone Cho, but again no answer.

Bad thoughts filter through my head like poisonous gas.

What if Marcus has found out I suggested Wow go to Belgium? He isn't the type to sit back and take it. He'll see that as a huge betrayal. He'll want revenge. His pride won't allow him to let it slip. If he took Lek that'd even the score. If he got Ratty to take Lek, that'd be even better. He wouldn't have to get directly involved. He could just laugh from the sideline and pretend he wasn't involved. Deny, deny, deny.

It all made sense. Marcus' lack of sleep had finally sent him mad. He'd got Ratty working directly for him. Marcus hadn't phoned. He wasn't going to phone.

"Fuck!" I shout, jumping up. "Fuck, fuck, fuck."

I tell Conrad my thoughts.

"I don't know all the details," he says. "But I wouldn't trust the guy. Is he German?"

I dial a number and put the phone back to my ear. "Please pick up, please pick up, please pick the fuck up… Adrian!"

He immediately catches the desperation in my voice and invites me over to the restaurant.

I'm flying down the stairs now, Conrad behind me. No time for the lift, keys jangling in my hand. It takes us ten minutes on the Kawasaki. I'm hunched over the speedo like a racer, weaving my way through the traffic, front suspension working hard with all the braking, Conrad riding pillion screaming, not to slow down, to keep going, loving the journey. I swerve the bike into the curb early, doing a ten metre skid, leaving a smouldering rubber exclamation mark on the grey road. Conrad just about manages to hang on. A group of Thai lads sitting on an outdoor table applaud as we rush in. They're clearly passing a joint round. All of them stripped to the waist, showing off sleeves of tattoos. Not one of them can be over twenty.

"You crazy *falang*!" one shouts. "You all crazy!"

"Not as mad as you boys," says Conrad high fiving one of them. "You kids are certifiable. I'm just happy you don't have passports."

"You want passport?" one asks, standing up.

Conrad waves him away. "I've done all that shit already. Save it for someone else. I'm a good boy now."

We find Adrian in the kitchen, a hazy mirage through the steam.

"Josh," he says. "Conrad. Good to see you. We didn't think you'd ever make it."

"Me too, brother," says Conrad giving him a hug. He looks round. "Beats Hong Kong, hey?"

"Better to have a good meal in your own restaurant than pay for it in some overpriced place in Lan Kwai Fong. And you don't have to tip."

Adrian, Conrad and I used to hang out in Hong Kong. Hence the photo on my bathroom mirror. On those nights I had to keep Conrad on his best behaviour. He wasn't used to dealing with people in suits. When two worlds collide it can be difficult, but Adrian liked him. He appreciated the wild streak, so long as he didn't get covered in beer, and none of our clients thought he worked for our company.

"Right," Adrian says turning to me, all his army training seeming to come out in that one word. "What's the situation?"

"We need to find Ratty and I don't know his address," I say in a rush, "the only person who will is Cho and he's not answering his mobile, which means he's out on the piss. We need to track him down."

"He could be anywhere, couldn't he?"

"I know all the places he drinks. Most likely, he'll be on Koa San. It won't take long to find him. But it'll be quicker with your help."

"And then what?"

"Then we'll go round to Ratty's and get Lek and... "

Adrian shakes his head. "Hold on cowboy," he says. "If you want my help, you're going to have to do this my way, okay? First, let's find Cho and get the address. We'll take it from there."

He quickly ducks round the corner and calls Jane, who comes running from the kitchen, looking tanned and radiant.

"You can come with me and Conrad," Adrian says.

"Where are we going?" Jane asks, looking at Conrad longer than necessary. Conrad's eyes flicker as well.

"For a game of hide and seek. Josh, you lead the way, I'll follow in the jeep."

We take it easy, heading out to Koa San. I constantly look in my mirrors to check Adrian's keeping up. I intend to search all the bars in Banglampoo before Cho's house. The chances of him being there are virtually nil. I've learned this over time.

When we arrive, we park up at the serene temple end, a place I used to visit often, to gather my disjointed thoughts. Conrad and Jane jump out of the Jeep, they both seem thrilled about something. I'm not that interested right now. I have other concerns on my mind. I show them all a picture of Cho. Adrian starts looking where we park. I go to the other end and work my way up. Conrad checks out the little bars round the market a couple of streets over with Jane.

My first stop is the Suzi pub. By Koa San standards this is smart, it even has a pool table. I ask the girl at the bar if she's seen Cho. She'll know who I'm talking about. Everyone knows Cho. He's like the George Best of Banglampoo,

The Body is a Temple

without the footballing skills.

The girl bumps her hips forward against the bar in a languid movement and runs a hand over her neck. A v neck top accentuates her cleavage. She says Cho was in the previous night, but hasn't been in since. I make her promise to tell him to phone me if he turns up. I jot down my number and hand it to her. She smiles flirtatiously, perhaps thinking this is an indirect invitation for her to call me. I turn and make my way up the road, blisters of sweat springing up on my forehead. I'm convinced it's hotter on Koa San than anywhere else in Bangkok. Maybe it's the street stalls suffocating the place, crowding out any chance of a cooling breeze.

I check out four more bars, all of them populated by colourful travellers and drunk Thais, then walk to The Buddy Beer. I spot Adrian sitting at one of the tables with Conrad and Jane, still in animated conversation. As I join them five beers arrive. I sink into a comfy low chair.

"I'm so sorry about your girlfriend," Jane says with real emotion in her eyes, breaking off from Conrad. "That's so terrible."

"The important thing is not to panic," says Adrian. "If you panic, you can't think straight. Josh. We've found your guy."

"Where is he?"

"He's gone for a piss," says Conrad. "He's coming back."

Relief washes over me. I was wondering why we had five beers. I thought maybe two were for Conrad. We drink and chat. Jane is very sympathetic and also optimistic. I know she wants to talk to Conrad but she puts her energies into cheering me up. About five minutes pass and Cho still hasn't shown up. I decide I'd better check out what's happening. I walk to the small toilet at the side, but he's not there. As I begin to feel the panic rising, I hear laughter from the restaurant, coming through the narrow door. A laugh that's very familiar, high pitched and worn. I slide my way round the network of tables and through the door.

The back restaurant is not busy. There are almost more waitresses than customers. The girls look very young, they can't be more than fourteen or fifteen. They seem to be getting younger all the time.

The laugh I heard is Cho's. He's sitting with a group of giggling large busted Australian girls, who keep leaning into him and rubbing his short hair and saying how cute he is. Coming out of the toilet he'd been lured back to the restaurant by these voluptuous flirts. I pull him through to the bar with promise of more Singh Thip.

I guide him to our table by the shoulders and introduce him, a vague sense of relief washing over me. At least we've achieved phase one.

"Hi, guys," he says as he sits heavily in one of the low chairs. "How's it going?"

Conrad gives him a warm shake of the hand, Adrian slaps him on the shoulder. Jane smiles politely, her eyebrows raising almost imperceptibly.

"Man," says Cho. "You're beautiful, where are you from?"

Jane gives a shy laugh, her eyes looking down at the table.

Cho's drunk, but not completely out of it. His eyes are alive, not yet dulled by the drink.

"Cho knows this area like the back of his hand," I say. He's lived here all his life, apart from a few years in America. Bangkok is his hometown. You need anything, Cho's your man.

"Hey, shall we have a drink?" he asks.

Conrad laughs, warming to him. I order a small bottle of Singh Thip, then, while the waitress pours his drink, I ask Cho if he knows where Ratty lives.

"Sure, man," he says. "I never go there, but I know where he lives. I try not to see him too much. We used to drink, you know, but he got into drugs and I don't like that shit. We used to drink, man, we were drinking partners. Drinking buddies. Used to drink in here, The Buddy Beer. Good name for a pub.

The Body is a Temple

You drink with your buddies in The Buddy Beer, beer and buddies, man. That's cool. That's alright." Cho laughs out loud. "Yeah, drink with your buddies in The Buddy Beer."

I'm starting to think he's more drunk than I thought.

"Could you take us round there?" I ask. "Could you take us round to his house. I think he might have Lek."

"She's lovely, man. He take her? Why?"

We haven't got time for this.

"I'll tell you on the way," I say. "Come on. Bring the bottle. We need to do this quickly."

Cho shakes his head. "He would never have done that shit before. He's changed, man. He used to be a friend of mine."

"We're going," I say to Cho, helping him up.

"Right now?"

"Yes."

"Have you got your bike? Can I ride your bike?"

"You can hardly walk," I say. I suggest we take Adrian's car, and I'll pick up the bike later. Cho flings an arm over my shoulder and one over Conrad's as we head up the road.

In the Jeep, I sit in the back with Conrad. Cho is between us. Jane rides in the front with Adrian. Cho seems keen to slump on my shoulder. Setting him upright, I ask him where we're going.

"Straight, man," he says, squinting through the windscreen.

"I wish you were," Conrad laughs. "But you're twisted as a car wreck."

Cho seems oblivious to the comment and continues with his directions. We set off, moving slowly while Cho makes up his mind which way we should turn. Conrad and I hold him forward so he can see out of the windscreen better. He looks like a ventriloquist's dummy.

"Can we have some music?" Cho asks after a few minutes.

I ask Jane to put it on quietly so we can still hear what Cho's saying. She fiddles with the knobs for a while, displaying a cute technophobia, before music fills the cab.

We get entertained with half a Thai rock tune I don't recognise followed by some rapid speaking, then a Van Halen song comes on. Cho explodes. "Oh man," he says. "This is a song. Eddie, man. He can play. He can play!"

Cho starts air guitaring it next to me, almost gouging my eye out. I push him away, asking him to cool it. Cho can be good fun on a drinking session, but in a serious situation, he's turning out to be a nightmare.

With Cho distracted by his frantic head banging, we make slow progress. Sometimes I'm convinced we're going round in circles but eventually Cho orders Adrian to stop.

"Here it is, man. This place Ratcha Withi. The King of Thailand's monument over there," says Cho pointing. "King number eight, I think. Or seven."

"And where is Ratty's house?"

"It's up there," says Cho, pointing now up the narrow street. I follow his hand.

"The one with the red door? It looks like a hut."

"Yeah, it's small, man. He doesn't care, you know. He never there."

We walk up the road. There's grass growing through the shattered tarmac and litter round the houses. We pass a tramp sipping from a bottle in a shady doorway. Cho gives him a couple of baht, takes a swig from his bottle and shares a joke with him.

"You never know when you might end up on the street, man," he says, putting his arm over my shoulder. "You never know when your life can change."

Conrad winks at me.

At the red door, Cho stops. "You want me to go in and see if he's there? You might freak him out, man. You're a *falang* and everything. They don't get many in this neighbourhood."

I grab Adrian's forearm and signal Conrad. "We'll wait up the street. You look out for any signs of anyone else staying there."

Cho nods and knocks on the door. He waits but there's no answer. He walks round the back. We hear him shout, "Ratty! *Sawat-di krab*."

"Do you reckon this is his house?" Adrian asks.

"There's no guarantee with this guy," says Conrad. "You pay your money, you take your chances."

Cho reappears after a couple of minutes. He hasn't found a thing.

"You want to take a look? There's nothing there."

We follow him to the back door and into the kitchen. Empty cans litter the floor. We move into the living room. An old leather sofa watches over the space. White tiles stretch themselves across the floor, their edges not quite lining up. The walls are yellowed from cigarette smoke. Empty bottles sit on the air conditioning unit set in the window. There are newspapers strewn on the floor, more cans.

"What a dump," says Adrian. "Even the army mess wasn't this much of a, you know… mess."

"Not even my place was this much of a dive," says Conrad.

I raise an eyebrow at him, thinking he and Ratty would have made pretty good flat mates.

"Ratty," says Cho again. Still nothing. We make our way to the stairs, Cho having checked the fridge for beer on the way. There is none. The fridge is unplugged.

"Ratty!"

The stairs are wooden, flaky with dry rot. They creak under our weight. The banister wobbles as we grip it.

Upstairs there are two bedrooms and a bathroom. We check them all. They closely resemble the squalor of downstairs. Empty cans of Heineken squat on the floor. Only one bedroom has a bed. It's a single, made from low grade pine. There's a mattress on it, the depth and colour of cheap oak veneer, one dirty sheet and no pillow. Next to the bed is a pile of dirty clothes.

"And this," says Conrad in the tone of an estate agent, "is

the master bedroom. A beautifully appointed boudoir. If you want the bed, however, it will be extra to the asking price..."

"Of ten baht," Adrian finishes.

"What do you reckon?" I say, interrupting their attempts to lighten the mood.

"There's no evidence to suggest he's been back here recently. Certainly no evidence of a woman's touch is there Jane?"

Jane shakes her head.

"So he hasn't been here with Lek?"

"I don't think so. You'd be surprised at how much of a trail a woman can leave."

We go downstairs and back out into the bright white of the street.

"I think," says Cho, squinting against the sunlight, "if Ratty want to make sure she not get away, he take her somewhere else. A friend's house, something like that."

"Any ideas? Does he have any mates you can think of, where he might be staying?" I look up at the red sun, then back at Cho.

"I tell you what, man. Why don't you come back later? He may show up, you know?"

I look at Adrian. His grey hairs picked out by the sun. I guess Cho doesn't know any of Ratty's friends, or Ratty doesn't have any.

"I think that's our best plan," Adrian says.

I tell him I'm going to wait for Ratty here. They can go if they want.

Adrian refuses to let me stay. "You'll only arouse suspicion hanging around all day. Far better to come back after nightfall."

I argue that we could waste valuable time. Adrian counters if we stay the afternoon Ratty might be tipped off to our presence and not return. Whatever reason I come up with he has an answer. Eventually I agree to his plan.

"But as soon as it's dark we come back, right?"

Adrian says, "Of course."

I phone Marcus again. His phone simply rings. It rings. It's that simple.

Chapter Thirty Five

Conrad and I spend the afternoon at Adrian's restaurant chatting with Jane. Or rather they chat while I worry about Lek. I vaguely register this story: the night Conrad arrived in the Philippines was the night Jane was leaving. They were both celebrating. They'd only said a few words to each other, but they seemed to have made some connection. She was as big on diving as he was, and having a small tattoo – a daisy chain round her ankle – had admired Conrad's more extensive work.

Jane's catalyst to pack up and leave Christchurch, she told us, had been getting fired from her job. She was working in a popular restaurant while training to be a vet and working part-time at an animal shelter for homeless or abused pets. Often there was plenty of food left over from the restaurant at the end of the night. She used to take it to the derelicts a few streets away on a plate with knives and forks. She was doing a good thing for those disadvantaged people, but the management found out and reprimanded her. Company policy stated all food should be disposed of in the correct manner. It wouldn't do business any good for customers to see down and outs eating the same food as they did for free, by the side of the road.

Jane was originally put on a warning by the restaurant but she told them to stuff it. I couldn't quite see her saying it in that way – she was the mildest person I think I've ever met –

but she definitely had her principles.

"It was ridiculous," she said. "Good food going to waste and people going hungry. I thought I needed to get away, you know. See another culture."

I'm distracted listening to Jane and Conrad talk, but I don't want to go home. It'll feel lonely and depressing. We sit at one of the tables out the back. I stare down at the grass, trying not to think too much about what's happening. I have some ideas, but I suppress them. I remember Adrian saying Ratty wouldn't harm Lek. It wasn't worth his while. I take some comfort from this, keeping it in my mind while the hours grind slowly by, the sun drifts down.

Conrad and I play a few games of Jenga. My hand shakes as I move the wooden pieces, collapsing the tower. Conrad silently rebuilds the structure before we continue. Eventually Jane takes over, though she's not much better than I am. She and Conrad laugh and joke as the building repeatedly crashes.

As the light fades, Adrian comes out, checking on us. He tells us he managed to get hold of his friend Jonah. I think I have a vague recollection of meeting someone with this name. He was in the army too. Adrian wants him to come along, so we're ready if Ratty puts up a struggle. I thank him and he heads back into the restaurant.

I pick up a copy of the *Bangkok Post* and flick through it, a candle shedding light on its pages. Acrid smoke from the mosquito coils making my eyes water. The BP is much like any newspaper. It chronicles death, rape, disease, bad news. What's so wrong with good news, I ask myself. Why can't we have some of that? I put the paper down and study my hands.

"What are you thinking?" Conrad asks.

"I'm trying not to. I am anti-thought right now. Thinking… it messes you up."

"But to think you're anti-thought puts you in a Catch 22, doesn't it?"

"Probably. Ask my therapist."

"You have a therapist?"

This slipped out by mistake. I ignore Conrad's question. Jane gives me a sympathetic look.

"I just want you to know," Conrad says. "I just want to say I'm here if you need to talk. You've always been there for me. And I won't forget that, man. I mean, I haven't forgotten it. You really have a therapist?"

"Drop it."

Conrad brushes his knuckles over his shaved hair. "Okay. Cool, you know."

As I'm folding the paper, I suddenly remember I was supposed to take Jane to Wat Po. I apologise for forgetting all about it.

"Don't worry! Christ, I think there's other stuff going on for you now," she gives my hand a squeeze. "You must be worried sick."

"It's not the best," I admit.

Jane tells me a friend of hers disappeared in Bali for four days. She was so scared something terrible had happened to her, but when she finally turned up, she was fine. She'd met a guy at the club they were at and was just spending time with him.

"The worst hardly ever happens," she says. "I think even Adrian was speaking to his wife yesterday. They might get back together."

I'm intrigued to find Adrian, the emotionally closed ex army guy, has been opening his heart to this beautiful young New Zealander. And then again perhaps it's not so strange. She has the most gorgeous, empathic eyes I've ever seen. As I lean in to question her further, Adrian comes out and tells us it's time to head off. She stands up to give him a hug. I see Conrad eyeing her figure.

"Be careful won't you?" she says.

"I've been to war," says Adrian. "This won't be a problem."

"You know what they say about accidents and short journeys," says Jane. "It's when you feel most safe you're in most danger." She then hugs Conrad and me in turn.

"Thanks," says Adrian, leading the way out and striding ahead of us, then shaking his head. "Women know how to worry, don't they?"

"I think she's gorgeous," says Conrad and blows her a kiss, before we go inside and make our way through the diners. "She is hot," he whispers, as we weave our way through the tables.

"Can we try and focus on my problems?"

"Yeah, right sorry. You can understand why I'm distracted. It's not that I'm forgetting your problems, I'm just trying to help you chill out."

We stride away from the restaurant, up the road, away from the lights of the restaurant, and get into the jeep. Conrad in the back, me and Adrian in the front.

Adrian notices the look on my face. "How are you feeling?"

"I've got to the point where it can't get any worse. Whatever happens tonight can't score higher on the shit scale than the other stuff that's happened this week. I've kind of arrived at the door which says, 'Enter if you have nothing to lose' and I'm happy to turn the handle to see what's inside, you know. But I'm nervous. I am nervous."

"A few nerves are good," says Adrian. "It'll keep you on your toes."

When we arrive at Ratty's place, Adrian quietly organises us. The atmosphere is eerie. The area looks even more in need of paint and humanity than before. It's dark. Faces are glimpsed in half light. The street lamps are dim and far off. Voices seem very loud. The sound of feet moving on the flaking tarmac amplified by the uncomfortable silence of the Bangkok suburb. A dog wails at the stars. Not enough energy to bark, and not enough moon to bark at.

Adrian has told us not to smoke, or do anything that would draw attention to our presence. If we're going to wait in ambush at Ratty's, we have to do it his way.

He sorted it all very quickly on arrival. We hardly had time to talk.

I'm behind a tree not far from the side door. Adrian is standing inside Ratty's living room, waiting with Conrad.

The sound of a misfiring engine rumbles over the air waves. I crouch a little further down the wall, heart pounding. Tensed.

Inside, through the window, I can see Adrian waiting, swinging the broom handle experimentally. It's not what he would have ordered, but under the circumstances, it's not bad.

Conrad is opposite with a floorboard.

I hear the pick-up come to a halt. A man gets out, his footsteps rushed and uneven as they hit the ground. He hurries towards the door, yanking it open. I hear a loud crack followed by a dull thud before the door clatters shut behind him and I rush forward to the front door.

I hear scrabbling and screaming as I approach. As ordered I roll an old oil drum towards the door, to prevent escape.

"Get him!" Adrian shouts as we hear more struggling.

Ratty's quick out the door, running like a wild pig. The combination of speed and adrenalin making him fast beyond his physical capabilities.

But I'm ready. The oil drum is in his path. The door springs open and we come face to face. For a second the drum blocks him. Long enough to let Adrian get behind him, his enormous forearms gripping Ratty's twiglet neck.

His legs lash out, trying to grip the ground, but Adrian lifts him clear. He has a shocked look on his face. Mouth open. Eyebrows raised. The lack of air in his lungs has frozen his expression. He has no energy to change it. A lonely, muted croaking noise comes from his throat.

Adrian digs his knuckle into a pressure point at the back of

Ratty's neck. Soon he stops struggling and goes limp.

Upstairs in Ratty's house amid the beer cans, the man is laid out like a corpse. Me and Conrad watch as Adrian applies some pressure.

It's not something they taught in the army. It's something they were taught how to deal with, if ever they were caught by the enemy. Like walking on coals, you had to put your mind somewhere else. In a cool relaxed place where nothing could hurt you.

Ratty clearly doesn't know this. All he knows is he doesn't want to feel pain.

Tied to his own shabby bed with strips of ripped sheet, his head lolling from side to side, he whimpers like an injured dog.

Adrian hasn't done much yet. Just roughly cut off half Ratty's dreadlocks with a blunt kitchen knife. Some pulling and yanking. That's all. It hasn't involved any real pain. A man's spirit can be broken in many ways.

"All you have to do," he says whilst butchering the great thick tendrils, "is tell us where you've put Lek. Tell us where she is and we'll leave you in peace."

I repeat this in Thai, in case Ratty's so scared and confused he can no longer understand the small amount of English he knows.

Ratty hears what's being said, though its message takes time to register through the pain. Not of having his hair chopped, not from the anxiety his body's experiencing but probably from the heavy speed withdrawal.

"Tell me," Adrian coaxes, "or I'm going to forget the haircut and move on to something more serious."

"I tell you already," Ratty says. "I… Lek. I don know."

"We don't believe you," says Adrian.

"It true!"

"What do you think, Josh? Adrian says.

I shake my head.

"Hold his hand," he says to me, flicking the wheel on his Zippo. A broad yellow flame shooting upwards. "I'm going to have to be more persuasive."

Ratty's eyes bulge. The flame licks the flesh on his forearm. The little hairs spitting as they sizzle. He smells like a pork barbeque.

"I tell you," he says. "For real."

Adrian holds the flame steady until the smell of burning flesh fills the room. He stops for a second.

"You sure?" he asks.

"I sure," Ratty grimaces. "I sure! I want money. No Thai girl. Thai girl I can have, no problem."

Adrian flicks the wheel again.

"I sure!" Ratty screams. "Believe me. Please! I sure! I don't know where is she."

Adrian removes the flame. "I think he's telling the truth. He would have talked now."

"Do it again," I say. Ratty is not the man I had come to fear. He is different from the thug that broke into my flat the night Samsook went to hospital. Nerves from earlier have now all but disappeared.

Adrian replaces the lighter.

"I don know, I don know!" Ratty shouts, over and over.

Adrian removes the lighter. "It's enough," he says. "He doesn't know."

"So what are we supposed to do now?"

Ratty squints up at me, but his gaze is unfocused. I look over at Conrad. He looks uneasy.

"We should go," Adrian says.

"What about him?"

"He'll be fine. He's hardly singed."

"Conrad?"

"I'm with Adrian. Come on."

I give Ratty one last look, his eyes fluttering, and we leave.

"Sorry," I say. I can hardly believe what we've just done

to this man, and the remorse is instant. I walk out of the hut. How much further can one man sink?

Chapter Thirty Six

In the Jeep, bumping and swerving back east, Adrian does his best to cheer me up.

"I'm sorry it didn't work out with Ratty, but he doesn't know where she is. You can see that can't you? He's not involved."

"If you say so. The question is who has got her?"

Adrian rubs a hand round the back of his neck, one bulging arm controlling the steering wheel. The car smells of stale nicotine and damp. "That's the Mastermind winning question."

"The other one is," says Conrad. "What do we do now?"

Adrian looks at the luminous dials of his diving watch. "It's two fifteen in the morning. We can't do anything now. I suggest we all sleep on it and meet in the morning."

"I can't leave Lek another night," I say. "We don't know what could be happening to her. We have to do something."

"Kidnappers never do anything without warning. Wherever Lek is, she will be asleep. You should be too," Adrian says. "There's no point. I suggest you and Conrad go home and wait by the phone. Now we know it's not Ratty you might get a call. If you do, get in touch. Immediately."

"And if I don't get a call?"

"Like I said. We'll meet tomorrow.".

"Conrad?"

"Sleep is probably best, brother."

"How are we going to get back?"

"I'll take your bike from Adrian's," says Conrad. "You're too screwed up to drive."

"Good," says Adrian. "Let's all go and get some sleep."

Back at my place, still wound up, Conrad and I have a few calming whiskies. I was convinced Ratty had Lek; now we know he doesn't I'm thrown into confusion. It's scary. If Ratty doesn't have her, it must be Marcus and he has much more money and power in Bangkok to do what he pleases. Though I'm tired beyond belief I want to keep drinking. The only thing that'll keep the nightmares at bay is booze.

Sitting in the living room with the lights dimmed low, the stereo playing quietly, I sink into the drunk zone, slouched on the sofa. The edge of reality has been shaved off, left discounted on the floor. I'm dimly aware of Conrad telling me how fantastic Jane is. He's trying to keep the conversation light to distract me, but I don't really hear him. He hands me a six inch square painting he did in the Philippines. It's of a sunrise. It's beautiful. Yellow, vibrant orange, red. I thank him, but I can't lift my heavy mood.

"Tell me, Conrad," I say suddenly. "Tell me everything's going to be okay."

"Don't worry, brother," he says. "I told you about that."

"She's everything to me," I blurt. I really am drunk. "I mean our friendship is great, Conrad. And it's great you showed up. But Lek, man. Is everything. I breathe with her. My heart beats in time with hers. She's perfect. She is my life. She is… IT."

"I know, man."

"I've lost a brother I loved. I thought I'd lost you. I can't lose Lek." I'm getting carried away, but the emotion needs to bubble to the surface. I finally have someone to talk to who can understand and I'm making the most of the opportunity.

"So tell me. Tell me we'll find her."

"We'll do what ever it takes." He gets up and re-fills my glass. "Adrian is army trained. He's a blood hound. He'll find her."

I kick my drink back and slide the empty glass over the coffee table.

"If she doesn't come back," I whisper, "I think… shit... I don't know."

I get up on weak legs and stagger out to the balcony, my chest hitting the railing hard. My head sags down and I see lights below. They look close, but small. Conrad pulls me back by my shoulders and hugs me.

"I know it's tough," he says, "but let's not get carried away."

In the warmth of his chest I cry. Wracking, heartrending sobs that I think will never end. With my eyes screwed shut, I see the boy on the blue chopper wobble and crash to the ground. Childhood innocence has long gone. It's time to be an adult.

"Let it go, man," Conrad says. "Let it all go."

He leads me inside and lays me on the sofa. I close my eyes and fall into a troubled sleep.

Morning comes and I'm still on the sofa in the living room. I have a headache. I get up, drink a glass of water, check my mobile, the answer phone, the area near the door for letters, then go to bed. When I wake, the phone is ringing. In a daze I stagger out to answer it.

"Hello."

Nothing.

"Hello."

"Try the Nikko Chan," a muffled voice says. The line goes dead. I slump on the sofa, the phone in my hand, dead.

"Who was that?" Conrad says, coming into the living room.

I write Nikko Chan on a scrap of paper.

"I have no idea. No idea."

Conrad picks up the piece of paper. "What's Nikko Chan?"

"A big hotel not far from here."

"And what's its significance?"

I stare at the floor. Thinking.

"Shit. I'm sure I've heard of it."

Conrad sits silent. Willing me to pull something from the blackness.

"I think we should go round to Adrian's," I say finally. "I may think of it on the way."

"Okay, brother," says Conrad, standing there in union jack boxers. "I'll just jump in the shower and we'll get there."

I look at my watch. It's already half eleven. I don't remember crashing out. I don't know what time it was. Time seems to go incredibly slowly, then quickly, then slowly again. I'm finding it hard to get my bearings.

Conrad comes out of the shower, his hair wet, a towel round his waist. "Come on," he says, pushing me towards the bathroom. "You'll feel better after you have a shower."

In the bathroom I strip and stand under the jets of water. It feels comforting. It feels separate from the world. Unreal. Towelling myself dry I catch a glimpse of my reflection in the steamed mirror. Even with its flattering soft focus I look like shit. My eyes are glowing red, like they've been photographed with a cheap camera. My skin is pallid under the tan, my cheeks hollow. I know I need to lay off the booze, but I can't, with all the worry, I just can't.

I go to my bedroom and dress awkwardly, with stiff, hungover limbs. I wear clean blue jeans, a new white tshirt and biker boots. I hope the freshness of the clothes will cheer me up. To complete the 'I'm in control' firewall I go heavy on the aftershave and deodorant.

While I'm looking for my shades, Conrad pops in, comments on the melting hot day and starts chatting about something. I don't hear him. I'm too busy trying to think who that phone call could have been from. "We should go. Are you ready to go?"

Conrad's ready.

On the ride over to Adrian's I almost crash the bike. It isn't my fault. A tuk tuk pulls right out in front of me at a crossroads. I have to jam on the brakes and swerve to miss him. Plumes of acrid smoke billow out from under the tyres. Conrad's weight thrusts against my back as I tense my arms to hold him. I don't have the strength. I end up with my chest on the speedo, Conrad almost firing over me like a heavy torpedo.

"You wanker!" he screams as I pull us out of the swerve and shove my weight back into the saddle, correcting Conrad's position.

"I didn't do anything," I shout.

"I was talking to the tuk tuk driver. You did fine. Maybe we should slow down a bit, though, huh?"

In my eagerness to get to Adrian's my hand's been heavy on the throttle. I ease off, the growling engine reducing to a low whine. We get to the restaurant without any further problems.

Soon after we arrive time seems to speed up again. Or the decision making process slows down. Either way, I get edgy. I pace around the back garden, scuffing the scorched grass. Conrad tries to keep me calm with banter and jokes until Jane arrives and he gets distracted talking to her, his hands moving like a raver's, he's so animated. Eventually Adrian decides on a plan and calls Pim. All I have to do is wait for the people to show up without exploding.

I'm irritated he's taken control of the situation, but I don't have a lot of choice. I haven't got a clue what to do in this situation. I swig beer while the others sit and chat. The sunlight is bright today, but it doesn't lighten my mood. A gentle, almost imperceptible breeze licks lazily against the stone sidewalls. Soft Thai music comes from the restaurant stereo.

"What time is it?" I ask after I've made it round the garden three more times.

"One o'clock. Slightly before, even."

"Pim should be here by now. Shall we go without her?"

Adrian tells me to calm down and have something to eat, indicating the bowls of rice and curries on the bamboo table. I keep wishing we'd gone straight there and my temperature rises.

Suddenly I stand up and say, "Actually, what the fuck do you know about anything, anyway, Adrian? You can't even stay married five minutes without cocking it up."

The second the words come out of my mouth I regret saying them. I start apologising, but Adrian grabs my arm, leads me through the restaurant and out on to the street. His eyes glitter with anger. He grips my arm tighter as I try to pull away.

"There's something you should know right now," he says. "Lisa went back to Hong Kong because she was missing her boyfriend, alright? She's been having an affair for the last two years, with some American guy who works for The Hong Kong and Shanghai Bank. She's flown back there to be with him and it's unlikely she'll be returning. I didn't want to tell you, because I know how much you like her. But life isn't perfect, Josh, as you know. Sometimes, you have to just take it on the chin. Now get yourself together."

My eyes widen in momentary disbelief, then my shoulders drop, and I feel full of remorse. I tell Adrian I didn't mean a word of what I just said.

"I know this is a difficult time," Adrian says, "but we need to stay in control, okay?"

He leads me back through the restaurant to the garden. Jane and Conrad look up at me from the table. I take a deep breath and sit down.

"Sorry about all that," I mutter and light a cigarette.

Pim arrives about a second before the pressure's built up

inside me again to the point where I'm about to storm out and do it on my own. Pim holds my hand and tells me not to worry.

I roll my eyes. Less of the advice. I'm impatient to leave. "Sorry, some things can't wait."

"Right, we need someone to cause a distraction. Pim can do it much better than any of us. You come too. But you do exactly as you're told."

Pim rolls her eyes. "Yes, sir, master."

Conrad smirks. We leave.

Chapter Thirty Seven

As we approach the entrance of Nikko Chan, Adrian asks again if everyone's ready and that we know what we're doing. We mumble our agreement.

"Just remember the important person in all this is Lek. Don't worry too much about Marcus, or whoever else is in there. Just make sure we get her out," I say, swivelling in the front seat of the cab to turn and face them.

I rearrange myself in the front seat and stare out the side window. I look ahead but don't see. My mind is exploring every possible permutation of what I might find in the Nikko Chan. I'm scared, but I'm trying to act in control.

The taxi pulls up outside the hotel. The mid afternoon sunlight reflects off the reception canopy. It looks space age, harsh and intolerant, not welcoming like it should. But we're not coming here on holiday, we're not on the look out for the friendly rep.

We get out, squinting at the darkness of the reception area. A few guests wander out into the day, chattering excitedly. My heart rate picks up.

Adrian pays the driver, putting a few extra baht into his grubby hand.

"Right," he says, pulling us away from the main entrance and surveying the building. "Is everyone clear what they're doing?"

We all nod solemnly.

"My guess is head for the suite, so straight to the lift and it'll be the top floor. Everyone got that?"

"Cool," Conrad agrees. He looks nervous too.

"Okay. Let's go. Pim, you first. We'll be watching."

Pim clears her throat, runs a hand through her hair and walks into reception, the revolving door spinning behind her. Only one person occupies the space behind the vast check in desk. The afternoon lull before more guests arrive in the evening requires only a skeleton staff. The others will be showing visitors their rooms. We've timed it well.

"Do you have a double room available next month?" she asks the young man. He seems tired and bored.

"When for?" His voice is flat, disinterested.

"The 25th to the 30th. It's for my parents. They're coming from Sukothai to do some shopping, and see me and my sister."

The boy is flicking through the booking calendar. "The 25th..."

Pim glances back towards the glass doors. We stare back at her. She beckons us.

The young man looks up, his fringe falling over his eyes. "We have rooms available until the 29th. The 30th is all booked out."

Pim asks if she can put in a cancellation for that day. He sighs, explaining he will need to get a form for her to fill in, glances round the reception area to make sure there is no-one approaching. "Wait here."

He wanders into the office behind the enormous desk. The swing door closes behind him.

Pim wheels round but we're in the door already. We reach the lift and hit the button. The indicator on the wall moves down agonisingly slowly.

The swing door to the office comes open. Pim lets out a wail and turns from us, clutching her hand. The check in boy is bemused, but doesn't say anything.

The Body is a Temple

"Ee aa-ah. I've got cramp in my hand," says Pim, moving further down the desk in mock agony. "Can you massage it for me?"

I watch her as the lift doors open.

"Aaaiee-ah," she groans.

He takes her hand and roughly kneads it.

In the lift, Adrian looks relieved, his stern face relaxing.

"I wanted to make sure we didn't get seen," he says. "If any crime is committed, it has to be like we were never here. I don't fancy getting involved with the Thai police. We all know about the Bangkok Hilton."

"He definitely didn't see us," I say, offering a glimmer of hope.

We fall back into silence. The lift moves slowly up, creaking slightly.

"Everybody clear what they're doing?"

"We're getting Lek."

"You're getting Lek," Adrian corrects. "Me and Conrad are handling whatever else may be up here."

"I still think I need a knife or something," I say.

"I'm the only one with a weapon, Josh, because I'm the only one who knows how to use them."

"I'd feel safe if I had something."

"Well, we wouldn't. You have a weapon you don't know how to use, it's more likely to get taken off you than anything. Don't worry, I can do it better than you could yourself. I'll look out for you man."

"What if they have guns?"

"I find it highly unlikely, but I'll go in first and you wait."

"What about you?"

"I know these kind of situations," Adrian smiles. "I'm good at dodging trouble, you probably aren't."

"I won't argue with that, brother," says Conrad.

The lift reaches the top floor. We exit and turn left,

following signs to the main suite. The top floor has a subtle smell of air freshener. The chambermaid has been earlier in the day.

"Good luck guys," Adrian says, almost under his breath.

We approach the room, the chandeliers casting moody shadows over our faces. There is to be no talking now. Nothing to raise alarm behind that big heavy door.

Adrian knocks twice.

Silence.

He knocks again.

Still silence.

He knocks once more, louder this time.

We all strain to hear the slightest sound. Nothing.

"There's only one other option. And we'll have to be quick."

Before we have time to process the information, he raises a big army boot and slams it into the door. The door shudders and groans, but doesn't open.

"Shit," Adrian mutters, backing up quickly.

He repeats the process. Second time the door splinters and buckles and slams open so hard it bounces and nearly slams shut again.

But Adrian is quick. With muscles tensed and bulging he forces his way in. Me and Conrad follow right behind.

The main bedroom is still as a dead dog. Eerily quiet, and ice cold from the air conditioning.

Adrian scans the room. "I'll check the bathroom, Josh, you wait here. Conrad, you go back out and wait down two flights of stairs. If someone comes bolting towards you, make sure you stop them, okay?"

Conrad and I look at each other.

"This is fucking mad," he whispers. "I feel like I'm in a film."

"Get out there," I say.

"Sure, brother," he says, leaving the room.

Adrian enters the bathroom then returns, his face set, as if struggling through harsh weather.
"What?" I ask.
"Come and see, I don't get it."
We follow him slowly to the bathroom and peer in, there's a tall figure stretched out on the floor with something on his head and a gag in his mouth. I bend forward to look more closely. The figure's either unconscious or in a deep sleep. I move a step closer. The thing covering his face and head is a pair of boxer shorts. There's something written on them.

I pause to think. Adrian brushes past me.

Chapter Thirty Eight

"Get some cold water on him," he says. "Maybe this guy knows what's going on here."

I unhook the shower head from its wall mount and spray it in the man's face. His head lolls from side to side, trying to escape the water, before his neck finally stiffens and his eyes open. He kicks out.

I turn off the spray and pull the boxer shorts half way off the head. It's Marcus. He looks up at me, his eyes glazed. A muffled sound comes from under his gag.

Adrian reaches down and unties it. "You talk to him," he says to me. "We'll listen."

I slap Marcus twice to get his attention. "Where's Lek? Where is she?"

Marcus closes his eyes and his head starts to bow.

I grab him by the ears and pull his head up. I stare straight at him. "Where is Lek?"

Marcus groans. He covers his face with his hands, mumbling he doesn't know. I move his hands away. His eyes look glazed.

"Do you remember what happened?"

His eyes look mad. Insane, twirling wheels. "Some guys," he says. "I was partying with some guys and… and then I was here and… and then… "

I grab his face in my hands and pull the boxer shorts the rest of the way off his forehead. The message on them reads: MONEY IS EVERYTHING. LOVE IS NOTHING. I turn them over. On the other side is written an address in Kanchanaburi.

I show it to Adrian.

"Kanchanaburi? That's two hours from here."

"Not on the Kawasaki," I say, pushing past Adrian and heading for the door.

"Wait," he calls after me. "Josh, don't go on your own."

But with the sound of my heart thumping in my head I'm in the corridor and now sprinting towards the back stairs, legs driving me forward, brain buzzing with fear and I don't hear what anyone else is calling after me.

On the second flight of stairs a figure leaps out at me, bending low to rugby tackle me round the middle. I should have called out. Conrad and I fall heavily to the floor, we roll down four or five steps before coming to a stop against a whitewashed wall.

"Conrad," I shout as I pull him up. "Let's get the fuck out of here."

"What happened?" he says as I pass him.

I drag him down the stairs, telling him I'll explain on the way.

Outside we find Pim hunched in the back of a tuk tuk, the engine revving, about to leave. She makes the driver stop while we get in.

"I have to go," she says. "It look strange me standing outside with nothing to do."

Conrad and I jump in, explaining we need to go back to Sukhumvit to get my bike. I tell the driver the address and we lurch off, soon accelerating to a screaming speed. We rattle along. The sound of the three wheeler rises above the other traffic noise like a giant, angry bee.

"Where's Lek?" Pim asks.

I tell her what we've found.

"Oh no," she says. "So Marcus never have her."

I tell the driver to hurry. The white stripes on the road rush past in a continual blur. The alternate black of the road and white of the lines eventually become grey. The tuk tuk's wheels bounce over the potholes, so deep they jar my back. The road's busy but we make good progress, particularly as the driver burns the lights.

"Take the girl wherever she wants to go," I say, handing over the fare as we skid to a stop outside my apartment building.

I turn to Conrad and tell him to wait for me while I go inside.

I give Pim a quick kiss on the cheek, ignoring her shocked expression and sprint up the steps three at a time. I burst in the door, lunge for the bike key and run and jump back down the stairs, my thick boots clattering on the thin metal skids.

When I get back outside Pim is still there in the tuk tuk. Conrad is standing next to her.

"What are you doing?" I say.

"I can help," she says. "She my friend too. I know her more long time than you."

"Okay, meet Adrian back at the hotel. Tell them where we've gone."

I thrust the underwear with the address on in her hands. This is not the job she wanted. She opens her mouth to complain, but I butt in, "Please Pim. We have to go."

"Okay," she says reluctantly. "But we come later okay?"

"Whatever you do, be careful," I say.

I throw my leg over the bike and hit the starter button. Conrad gets on the back.

We pull away, overtaking the tuk tuk.

"See you," Conrad shouts at Pim. "Thanks."

Pim waves at us. I accelerate hard, telling Conrad to hang on tight. My anxiety to find Lek leaves no room for fear.

The ride up to Kanchanaburi blurs my eyes. The cold wind rips through my tshirt. I'm pleased Conrad has come along. His fat stomach bulging into my back at least keeps me half warm. His chin digging into my shoulders is strangely comforting.

As I drive I try to make sense of the last few days. I was convinced Marcus was pulling the strings. To find him tied up in the Nikko Chan came as a shock. Marcus was in the clear and Ratty was out of it. I was stumped, but determined.

I twist the throttle even tighter on the Kawasaki. The more I think it through the less clear the situation becomes. The glass of my mind becomes frosted, then opaque, then terribly blurred, like turning the focus on a microscope the wrong way. The truth is receding. I have no idea what will confront us in Kanchanaburi.

We make it there in good time. My arms are shaking from hanging on so tight. My face feels raw from the cold wind, like the skin has been peeled off.

Slowing so the noise of the engine winds down from a bark to a whimper, Conrad asks me if I know what I'm doing. Where we are.

"Yeah," I say. "Me and Lek have been here a few times to get out of Bangkok. I think I know the address we've got. It's one of the huts down by the river. We'll have to park the bike up here and walk down."

I turn the bike off the main road and park it outside one of the little restaurants, under a wilting palm tree. The sun has set now, leaving very little light. Most of it comes from the loops of bulbs, strung like shining spider silk on poles across the river. The candles on the floating restaurants further downriver add an additional flicker. There's been a power cut. We look down the steep slope at the roof of the huts crowding over the murky water. I can hear the hum of mosquitoes, the lapping of water on the shore, some distant Thai chattering. I look at Conrad, his face set serious in the half light.

"It's further along," I say, nudging his shoulder. "Down there."

We walk along the shingle path, our shoes scrunching as we go. A light wind blows through the palm trees, making a sound like breaking rice crackers.

"What are we doing when we get there?" Conrad asks.

I've thought about this on the journey up. I want Conrad to wait up near the path while I go down and check out what's going on.

"If I'm not back in ten minutes, or if you hear anything strange, get help."

"Wait, what if I follow you down, but at a distance. So I can see what's going on. Then I can either dive in, or get help."

"That could be better, but don't get too close."

I walk forward, treading as lightly as possible, though every twig under foot seems to break with deafening clarity. When we reach a set of shabby steps that descend to a group of huts near the water's edge, I give Conrad a grateful look. I'm so glad he's here with me.

I take the first step down while Conrad waits for me to get a way ahead. As I descend, my heartbeat picks up. With each step my throat becomes tighter.

Everything will be alright, I say to myself. This is not a film, it's life. Very bad things don't happen in real life. They happen in the news, in papers, on the screen and most of all to other people. They don't happen in my life. Not anymore.

I reach the door. On it is brushed the number six in heavily diluted white paint, so it looks almost like a snail trail. I rub my hand across my forehead. Mosquitoes buzz round my ankles. A fish breaks the surface of the water, making a sound like a mug of water being thrown in. I raise my hand, pause for a second, then bring it down on the ply board. Once. Twice. I can see Conrad to my right, hanging back, at the top of the steps. He gives me a thumbs up.

My breathing stops. I hear movement inside, someone walking towards me, and then the door opens. I stare straight ahead into the gloom. My eyes slowly become accustomed. Now is the time.

The rest of my life starts or finishes here.

Chapter Thirty Nine

I can breathe again. As my pupils dilate I make out a small figure. It approaches slowly, as if in a trance. I recognise the walk.

"Lek," I say, throwing my arms round her, hugging her close to me, kissing her on the cheek. "You're okay. Thank God you're okay."

I pull back to look at her. She looks very tired. Her eyes are dark half moons, but she seems okay. There are no scratches or bruises on her.

"How are you, babe?" I ask, kneading her shoulders. "What are you doing here?"

"I okay," she says. "I… "

I give her another hug, squeezing the breath out of her. Relief flooding me. She ran away, that's all. We fell out, and she needed some space.

"Let's get you home," I say. "Come on. Let's go. I can't believe you disappeared up here. We didn't argue that bad. I'm sorry."

"I… "

"You what?"

"Josh."

"Come on. We can talk on the way." I know the situation isn't this simple but something in me says if we can just leave right now, this will be the end.

"No. Look."

Moving away to study her, I see another figure further back, just becoming visible in the candlelight. My heart stops. My worst fears rush towards me. And as in a film, the background recedes at speed. Of course Lek's disappearance wasn't so simple, but I thought I could will it to be.

"Innit sweet?" the voice says.

My mind stops. Then scrolls back through the verbal tones it knows.

I've heard this voice before. But not since Hong Kong. I didn't think I'd hear it again. It takes a while to sink in. I feel my body deflate.

The stocky figure moves closer. Nick puts his hands on his hips and sneers. He's still wearing the same cut off combats and boots he wore in Conrad's flat, but the tshirt is different.

"What's going on?" I say feebly. "Why have you got Lek here?"

"Made sense, didn't it? We couldn't find any money at yours, so we took her."

"We?"

"Me and Boris."

My mind pulses. I think back to Nick leaving Conrad's flat that afternoon. Boris. His deal. Half the drugs.

"I remember," I say.

"So he weren't too happy when you nicked it all back."

So this was what it was all about. I thought it had been Marcus or Ratty after me. It wasn't. It was about the stolen E's.

Nick steps forward, pulling a gun from a pocket in his cut off combats. The gun he had that afternoon on Lantau. "You owe us.".

"No. You left us a grand and a half short."

"You fucking nicked from me," he says, his hand tightening on the gun's grip.

As I half put my hands up, the door opens behind me and someone else walks in. I keep looking at Nick.

"Ah. You are here sooner than expected," the man says, putting bottles of beer on the table.

I recognise the voice.

"Cheers, mate," says Nick.

I turn to look at him. The well built body. The blonde hair. Eric. "Fuck," I can't help saying. "You're Boris?"

He nods, opening two large bottles of Singha. He gives one to Nick and one to me. "Sure," he says.

I ask if I can sit. My head's in a spin.

"Of course," Eric nods. Ultra cool. His eye is still black from where I hit him. "Put your girlfriend on your knee."

I sit on a bamboo chair and pull Lek towards me, though she stays standing.

So these guys were friends in Hong Kong, business partners. They'd come to reclaim what was theirs. And Nick had come to see his girlfriend.

Now I remember the photo in his flat. The attractive girl. The guidebook. The hotel Nikko Chan, one of the most expensive in North East Bangkok. That's where he'd been staying, the place we found Marcus.

I look at Eric again. He gestures to Nick who gives him the gun.

"I was in the Belgian army for three years," he says leveling it at my head. "I know how to fire. Can you give me the girl, please?" Nick smiles, clearly loving his work.

"Wait," I say feeling very nervous now, clutching Lek tighter. "What's going on here?"

"Pay day," says Nick. "The ten grand you owe us. Fair trade, innit, for someone you love?" He wiggles his tongue at Lek.

Eric moves forward, his arm swinging round so the gun is now several feet from Lek's forehead. "Do you want me to fire or are you going to give her to me?" he asks.

I release her. Eric yanks Lek's arm, pulling her forward. I see her hands are held with cable ties. He passes her back to Nick who kisses her cheek. I pretend I haven't seen, not wanting to give him the satisfaction of knowing he's got to me.

"We want the money," he says. "Or we come to some other arrangement."

I look over at Lek. She looks scared. I just want to get her out of here. I tell Nick I have some money. The stuff Conrad brought from the Philippines. Thank God I hid it in four separate parcels. I direct him to one of them.

Nick considers this. After a quick frisk and a few more questions, he seems satisfied. He dangles my keys in front of me. "These for the bike and the flat, yeah?" he says. They are. Nick grins again. "Look after him, alright?" he says to Eric. "I'll be back tomorrow with the cash." Nick picks up a denim jacket and walks Lek out the door. Then, as he's about to leave, he turns. "Hang on," he says. "I'm forgetting myself here."

He strides across the room and hits me with a punishing right, followed by a left jab to the stomach.

"Dunno how I forgot that," he says. "You fucker. See you."

I bend in pain, but keep quiet so I can listen to what's going on. I strain but all I can hear is Eric laughing.

"Not so tough now, are you," he says, cracking his foot into my shin. "Your punch is maybe stronger, but you are not tough."

I grasp my leg but conquer the will to groan.

"I'm going for a piss," he says. "Don't do anything stupid, weak boy."

I hunch against the thin wooden door, listening. I want to know what's going on out there. I strain at the cable ties now around my wrists. I listen so hard I find myself holding my breath again. I hear nothing but Eric's piss splattering the leaves outside, like gravel landing on wet concrete, the wind and the pain zinging on my jaw and in my gut. Then I hear some faint female voice talking in Thai. I try to get my heart to slow so I can hear more clearly. I squint down at the floor to concentrate. A pause. Then sound. The Kawasaki's engine being kicked into life, its wheel skidding as it moves off. The engine note rising, and then dipping as the gears are changed up. Next a bang, a gun shot, I think. My heartbeat surges. I hear wheels skidding on the shingle, then another sound. A louder, throatier engine, possibly that of a four wheel drive. I hear brakes locking, tyres skidding. A yell, followed by a metallic crash. Two vehicles meshing, combining, followed by a thud.

I panic. That thud. Lek, I think. That thud. That sickening sound. And where the fuck is Conrad?

Eric charges back in from where he's been pissing looking confused and anxious. He bolts for the front door, opens it, and immediately staggers back, screaming.

"Josh?" Adrian says, following him in, fingers in a horizontal 'v', having jabbed Eric in the eyes. He grabs him at the back of the neck and does something with his thumbs. Soon Eric is limp in his arms and sliding to the floor.

Pulling a hunting knife from his pocket, Adrian cuts me free. "You shouldn't have gone off on your own," he says. "We didn't know how to get here."

"But you're here now. Is everyone okay?"

"No."

I feel the deep panic in me rise.

Adrian turns and leaves the hut with me following. We sprint up the slippery steps to road level. I keep following Adrian. My heart's hammering. We jog thirty metres towards the twin beam of headlights, one of which is angled wrong, like a wandering eye. Adrian's Jeep.

Lying close to it is Conrad, legs crossed. Crouching next to him is Lek, holding a bloody shirt to his chest.

I give her a hug. "What happened?" I ask, looking down, trying to get my breath.

"I on the bike with Nick," Lek says. "Conrad coming

behind and take me, boom! off back." She stops.

Adrian continues. "We were coming up in the Jeep, and Conrad shot out of the bushes and grabbed Lek off the back, covering her on the ground. Nick had a gun in his hand. He swiveled himself on the bike to turn and shoot..."

Adrian's voice seems far off now as I try to picture the scene.

He shot Conrad. Then he crashed into Adrian's Jeep. Nick crashed into the bonnet and came off. He ran into the trees. Lek has called for an ambulance.

I look down at Conrad. His eyes are half closed. "Hey, buddy," I say.

"What?" he mumbles.

"Thanks for everything."

He manages a half smile. "No problem," he whispers. "But... next time you want to come up here, count me out. This is no holiday."

Lek looks at me with tears in her eyes. The strain of the last few days is catching up with her. I rub the back of her neck. She looks beautiful in the moonlight.

"I love you," I say and kiss her cheek.

Chapter Forty

Standing in the kitchen, the city pulsing round me, I prepare breakfast, frying some eggs, slicing some beef and chopping chillies.

Still I'm thinking about getting out. I'm always trying. Like a salmon swimming upstream: Thrusting forward. Falling. Jumping up. Crashing back down.

Never quite making it.

Dr Miller says I should accept who I am. I should accept my situation. I don't know about you, but I can't do that. I can't give up like that.

And so the little pink stereo plays a Thai pop station. Sukhumvhit Road picks up the rhythm of the Bangkok beat. Steam rises from the cooking noodles. The sun's yellow fingers reach down to the balcony, spread into the room, and spread like butter on Conrad's miniature painting. The quality of light makes me smile. This is a new beginning.

Conrad lies on a lounger, his arms folded on his chest. The sunglasses I put on him last night, slightly crooked now where he must have moved in his sleep, shield him from the harshest of the sun's rays.

I look over at him. The wound where Nick shot him in the chest is healed now. It looks like a patch of glue the size of a ten baht coin, dried hard.

The ambulance arrived at the scene soon after me and Adrian. I was full of all the dread that visits to hospitals fill me with. Zack. Samsook. It felt like my insides were being sucked out of me. Like all that loneliness would return. I feared the worst, but Conrad pulled through. He even had the energy to crack a few jokes that night. A week later, he was happily resting in my spare room.

The day after the incident I tracked Ratty down. I went with Cho. We had a chat. He hadn't been involved with Nick, or Eric or Marcus. He had his own reasons for being desperate for the cash. Reasons clear in his eyes and jumpy attitude. We called a truce. He had his money now.

So we were in the clear. Me, Lek, little Samsook, who the dedicated doctors now thought would make a full recovery, and Conrad. Apart from one thing. After paying Ratty and the hospital, we had no money.

We have no money.

"Good morning, babe," Lek says in her best English accent. Her hair is still a mess from her night's sleep. She's been almost herself again since the whole kidnapping business. It was all pretty painless. She'd been drugged and couldn't remember much. Her time in Kanchanaburi was dreamlike. They didn't do anything bad to her. Or not that she could remember.

I've thought about Eric many times since the incident. I've gone over the times we met. In The Peppermint. Outside my apartment that night. In The Hollywood. He took pleasure in scaring me. He enjoyed it. He had no interest in Lek. And the time in The Peppermint, he'd told me what would happen.

'I'm going to get you,' he had said. 'With Nick too.' I just hadn't heard him right.

So they'd got us.

But it hadn't done Eric much good. The next morning in Kanchanaburi, he was found lying face down in the river. Nick had somehow managed to escape the woods that night. Then he'd worked his way back round to the huts without being noticed. When he got there, he'd dragged the still unconscious Eric into the river and left him to drown. Conrad wasn't surprised. Nick would have hated to see me escape. He would have had to blame someone.

"He wanted that money," he said. "He was always about money. Nothing else, man. He wasn't like the rest of us. He seemed laughable, in a way, didn't he? But he was a bad guy. A proper bad guy."

I nodded. And I understood. There were those who regretted their actions, and those who didn't. That was the divide.

"Thank God the police got him," I said. "I can't think of anything better for him than to rot in a Thai jail. I never liked him. And my first impressions are usually good."

I stare at the boiling water, lost in thought, one of the little kittens purring and figure eight-ing round my ankles.

"Good morning, babe," Lek says again, noticing I'm distracted.

I pull myself back. She picks the other kitten off the floor and cuddles it under her chin. Its little pink tongue darts out and licks her throat.

"Good morning, darling," I say giving her a kiss. "Sleep well?"

"No as good him," she says pointing at Conrad. "You want I wake him?"

"No I will," I say. "Can you look after the noodles?"

"Sure."

I get a beer from the fridge and go out to the balcony. I look down at him. So much of him reminds me of Zack. The energy. The impulsiveness. I'm pleased he's in Bangkok now.

Marcus and I have resolved our differences, too. He couldn't believe I thought he was out to get me. He was totally loyal. And he wasn't a pimp, he was setting up a fashion model agency, keeping it quiet until he made a success of it. I apologised for misjudging him. He told me to forget it.

One good thing, though. I don't feel so alone anymore. I feel like I have people round me I can rely on. That's good.

The memories of my childhood have receded into the distance, like they should. And a sense of adulthood is flowing towards me, through the cross current of teenage guilt.

I look down at Conrad again, lean forward and lie the beer on his stomach. He wakes with a jolt. I like to give him these moments of *déjà vu*.

"Oh fuck," he says. "Don't do that to me, man. I'm too old for that kind of shit."

I smile and ask how he's doing.

"Great," he says, sitting up. "You know what? Last night, I had this great idea. I was lying here and it hit me."

"What. You're going to marry Jane?"

They've been behaving like a couple of love sick teenagers for the last few weeks. There's something very unsettling about Conrad holding hands with her and giggling in her ear, but I am happy for them.

"No. Well. No. A money idea. It would make us a fortune."

"Oh no," I say as he cracks open his beer. "No way."

"You're going to love this," he laughs, looking inside, calling Lek to get me a beer.

As she moves to the fridge, there's a savage knock at the door.

Conrad and I look at each other. Lek turns, her hand still on the stainless steel handle.

"Fuck," I breathe. Panic rising. I turn to Conrad and a worried, knowing look crosses his face. Now isn't the time to ask why. "Lek. Come here. Now!"

A loud crash, followed by another, and the door splinters as she runs towards me, the dead bolt still in place, the door ruined round it.

I grab Lek's hand and help her over the balcony after Conrad. I waste no time flipping myself over the railings. I smile as we descend. Ratty taught me something. I've learned something. I haven't got out. I'm not the person I want to be… yet.

LUKE BITMEAD BURSARY

The award was set up shortly after Luke's death in 2006 by his family to support and encourage the work of fledgling novel writers. The top prize is a publishing contract with Legend Press, as well as a cash bursary.

We are delighted to be working with Luke's family to ensure that Luke's name and memory lives on – not only through his work, but through this wonderful memorial bursary too. For those of you lucky enough to have met Luke you will know that he was hugely compassionate and would love the idea of another struggling talented writer being supported on the arduous road to securing their first publishing deal.

We will ensure that, as with all our authors, we give the winner of the bursary as much support as we can, and offer them the most effective creative platform from which to showcase their talent. We can't wait to start reading and judging the submissions.

We are pleased to be continuing this brilliant bursary for a fourth year, and hope to follow in the success of our previous winners Andrew Blackman (*On the Holloway Road*, February 2009), Ruth Dugdall (*The Woman Before Me*, August 2010) Sophie Duffy (*The Generation Game*, August 2011) and J.R. Crook (*Sleeping Patterns*, July 2012).

For more information on the bursary, visit:
www.legendpress.co.uk

On the Holloway Road by **Andrew Blackman**

Unmotivated and dormant, Jack is drawn into the rampant whirlwind of Neil Blake, who he meets one windy night on the Holloway Road. Inspired by Jack Kerouac's famous road novel, the two young men climb aboard Jack's Figaro and embark on a similar search for freedom and meaning in modern-day Britain.

Pulled along in Neil's careering path, taking them from the pubs of London's Holloway Road to the fringes of the Outer Hebrides, Jack begins to ask questions of himself, his friend and what there is in life to grasp. Spiting speed cameras and CCTV, motorway riots and island detours, will their path lead to new meaning or ultimate destruction?

Shortlisted for the Dundee International Book Prize

The Woman Before Me by **Ruth Dugdall**

They came for me, just like I knew they would. Luke had been dead for just three days.

Rose Wilks' life is shattered when her newborn baby Joel is admitted to intensive care. Emma Hatcher has all that Rose lacks. Beauty. A loving husband. A healthy son. Until tragedy strikes and Rose is the only suspect.

Now, having spent nearly five years behind bars, Rose is just weeks away from freedom. Her probation officer Cate must decide whether Rose is remorseful for Luke's death, or whether she remains a threat to society. As Cate is drawn in, she begins to doubt her own judgement.

Where is the line between love and obsession, can justice be served and, if so… by what means?

Winner of the CWA Debut Dagger

The Generation Game by **Sophie Duffy**

Philippa Smith is in her forties and has a beautiful newborn baby girl. She also has no husband, and nowhere to turn. So she turns to the only place she knows: the beginning.

Retracing her life, she confronts the daily obstacles that shaped her very existence. From the tragic events of her childhood abandonment, to the astonishing accomplishments of those close to her, Phillipa learns of the sacrifices others chose to make, and the outcome of buried secrets.

Philippa discovers a celebration of life, love, and the golden era of television. A reflection of everyday people, in not so everyday situations.

Winner of the Yeovil Literary Prize

Sleeping Patterns by **J.R. Crook**

In a run-down student residence in South London, Annelie Strandli, a beautiful but confused designer, who is disorientated after leaving her native Finland, finds herself gravitating towards Berry Walker, an insomniac and aspiring writer.

Berry is often introspective and withdrawn, but in his writings Annelie sees the chance to glimpse him as he truly is. With the help of the narrator, she conspires to discover parts of a secret story that is concealed within his desk. As Annelie gradually puts the pieces together, she finds herself questioning not only her relationship to Berry, but ultimately the dividing line between fiction and memory.

Sleeping Patterns is a novel of intricate layers, hidden within each a tale of love, uncertain meanings, and the relationship between writer and reader.

Also by Luke Bitmead:

White Summer (Legend Press 2006)
Heading South (Legend Press 2007)

White Summer

White Summer is a fast-paced and vibrant comedy that offers a hilarious insight into infatuation, sex, hangovers, dead-end jobs and making ill-advised decisions that come back to hurt. A perfect summer read, this is a story for those who have lived but won't learn.

Guy Chamberlain finds his life so dull, it makes his head throb. However, when the heart-stoppingly attractive Daisy walks in, Guy finds himself on a tour of coffee-shops, parks and banks – anything to see her again.

This begins a hilarious roller coaster that he finds himself unable to stop. The persistent 'Kathy' has him pencilled in for marriage, his laddish best mate starts dating his sensitive sister, his mother's health takes a turn for the worse and a sexy workmate has revenge on her mind. Eventually, at a New Year's Eve party the rollercoaster ride is finally turned upside down.

'Great stuff. Wonderfully witty and sexy.'
   DEBORAH WRIGHT, BESTSELLING AUTHOR

'Reading *White Summer* is like a breath of fresh air.'
   ROUNDTABLE REVIEW

'*White Summer* is a page-turner, punctuated with humorous incidents that will ring true to all men and women.'
   BBC RADIO OXFORD

'A sparkling debut from an author with an eye for details and wit.'
   ESSENCE MAGAZINE

Heading South
co-written by Catherine Richards

Cassie:
Why am I so lacking in confidence? I mean my legs aren't that fat, my hair isn't that out-of-control, I'm not hideously ugly or terribly reconstructed by cosmetic surgery. How perfect this quiet country living would be with just a tiny bit less babysitting and a smidgen more sex.

Nick:
I don't know what made me ask her out. Well I do actually: she's jaw-droppingly fit. Listen to me; I sound like a dirty old man. I suppose that's what several months of celibacy does for you. Or perhaps it's all this fresh country air. Though do you know what made me ask her out, even more than the flirty eyes and curvy bum? It's this nagging feeling that I've seen her before somewhere...

When was life and love ever straightforward? A hilarious comedy also featuring vindictive exes, posh admirers, births, deaths, three dogs, two cats, a pheasant, pony and mallard.

'Written from the viewpoints of Cassie and Nick, this is a great romantic comedy that will appeal to both sexes.'
CLOSER MAGAZINE

'A sparkling romantic comedy which tells both sides of the story – both girls & guys will love it!'
DEBORAH WRIGHT, BESTSELLING AUTHOR

'A light-hearted, funny...insightful novel about the minefield that is the dating game.'
ROUNDTABLE REVIEW

Come and visit us at

www.legendpress.co.uk

www.twitter.com/legend_press